ALSO BY NINA LEVINE

NITRO'S TORMENT

SYDNEY STORM MC | BOOK 2

USA TODAY BESTSELLING AUTHOR

NINA LEVINE

This is a work of fiction. Names, characters, places, and incidents are a product of the author's imagination. Locales and public names are sometimes used for atmospheric purposes. Any resemblance to actual people, living or dead, or to businesses, companies, events, institutions, or locales is completely coincidental.

Editing by Hot Tree Editing
Cover Design ©2016 by Romantic Book Affair Designs
Cover Photography: Xie4t
Cover Model: Alex

To those of us still searching for home

to love

gentle self-care

opening ourselves up

trusting

so much trusting

believing in someone

that they will hold our heart in their palm

and cherish it

cherish us

to finding our home

that place where our souls can breathe

where our hearts can smile

to finding the person who can give us that

love & home

Chapter One

Nitro

"The Hammer's Coming Down" by Nickelback

Scanning the busy casino floor, my gaze locked onto the guy I'd come here for. *You're mine, fucker.* I stalked in his direction, pushing people out of the way. Being Saturday night, a crowd was in residence. That would only help my mission. Less chance of anyone involving themself in what was going down.

About ten steps from my goal, a leggy blonde ran into me. I stopped and attempted to move swiftly around her. However, she had other ideas.

Turning to face me, the glare on her face said it all, but she insisted on wasting my time with her words. With an arch of her brows, she said, "Do you give a shit that I just twisted my ankle in these heels because you weren't watching where you were walking?"

My eyes held hers. "You wanna back that up and get your facts straight?"

"My facts *are* straight, asshole. You're the one who was barrelling through here, not me."

My gaze flicked quickly to the guy I was after. Still at the table, thank fuck. Eyeing her again, I barked, "I don't give a fuck who was doing what. You need to move out of my way." If the casino wasn't so damn packed, I wouldn't even bother to argue with her, I'd just continue on my way. As it was, I couldn't move either side of her.

"Does that usually work for you?"

I raked my fingers through my hair, keeping an eye on my target. "Yeah, it does." I drew my attention back to her and lowered my face. "Now, get the fuck out of my way before I physically move you myself."

Her nostrils flared. "Men like you don't scare me. Just so you know." With that, she stepped aside and I strode away from her without a second glance.

A few minutes later, I stared into the eyes of the man I believed was able to give me the information my club had been after for weeks. "You need to stand and leave with me now."

Hatred bled from him as he glared at me. "I don't need to fucking do anything."

"You do. Because if you don't, that tight cunt waiting for you at home won't be breathing when you get there."

He scowled. "You're full of shit."

I clenched my jaw and shoved my face closer to his. "You wanna fucking test that theory? I can phone my boys waiting outside your place if you want. Have them send over a photo."

He shoved his chair back. "This isn't going down how you think it is, Nitro."

I pushed him. "Start fucking walking and shut your mouth. The only way this is going down is how I say."

Neither of us would be leaving until I knew who was responsible for all the pain dealt to some of our club's family members over the last few months.

* * *

"Today's not your day, motherfucker." I grunted the words out as I reached for his throat. Gripping him hard, I squeezed until he could no longer suck air down into his lungs. "You

2

wanna fuck with my family, you're gonna deal with me. And I don't give second chances."

Clawing at my fingers, he attempted to struggle out of my hold, but it was a fruitless battle. Pathetic sounds came from his throat, the kind of noises that only fuelled my bloodlust. Those sounds rolled through the back alley we were in, lingering in the same way the putrid smells out there did. Thunder cracked overhead and lightning cut through the black sky. It was only a matter of time before rain fell, but I didn't care if we spent the rest of the night getting drenched; I would get what I came for.

I ripped my hand from his throat to fist my fingers in his hair. Yanking his head back, I roared, "Give me the fucking name!"

His lips curled up in a snarl. "Go to hell. I don't rat on my club."

Anger blurred my vision as I spun him around and shoved him headfirst into the brick wall in front of us. His scream of agony as he smashed into the bricks and crumpled to the ground rushed through my veins like a hit of cocaine. This was the kind of high I craved and I clenched my fists, ready to keep going. My boots thudded on the bitumen as I moved to stand over him. Blood covered his face, pouring from the deep gash I'd inflicted on his forehead.

Wrenching him up by his shirt, I backed him against the wall, slamming his body hard. "By the time I'm finished with you, you'll rat on anyone I fucking want you to."

Drawing long, ragged breaths, he shook his head and opened his mouth to speak, but I cut him off with a punch to his cheek. Blood flew through the air as his head snapped to the side from the impact.

I knew his type, so I knew he honestly thought he wouldn't rat on his club. But it was only a matter of time before he would be in a world of pain and begging me to stop. After that, it wouldn't take long to drag the information I needed from him.

Pulling my knife from its sheath attached to my belt, I dragged the tip of it across the base of his throat, pressing hard enough to draw a few drops of blood. The determination in his eyes wavered. "It's been a long day, asshole, and I don't feel like shooting the shit with you for hours. Let's hurry this the fuck along."

"I'm not a fucking snitch," he snarled.

"Tonight you are. Or else you're dead."

His lips pressed together, a signal that he needed further encouragement. I ran the knife down his chest to his crotch. "But first we'll start with your dick. Ever seen one cut off?"

He flinched and I knew I had him. Even if I had to cut into his skin some more, he'd sing before he'd lose his dick or his life.

When he didn't respond, I took hold of his shirt and ripped it open. Buttons rained down onto the ground before his shirt joined them.

My eyes met his. "Changed my mind. First we'll start with this." I squeezed one of his nipples, and swiftly sliced it off.

"Motherfucker!" His scream of pain echoed around us as his body jerked.

I blocked his attempt to fight back by smashing him against the brick wall again. "Yeah, I am. You ready to lose the other one?" As the words left my mouth, I grabbed his other nipple, ready to make good on my threat. Patience was not one of my virtues.

He gritted his teeth through heavy breaths. "Fuck you!"

Blood streamed down his chest and stomach when I slashed his other nipple off. I hardly processed his string of expletives; I was completely focused on my next move.

4

Gripping the waistband of his jeans, I tore the button off and zip down. I then yanked them and his briefs down. He stood in front of me, naked with his pants around his ankles, anger and fear rolling off him in equal parts.

And then he really started fighting for his life.

Bring it the fuck on.

His punch clocked my cheek as I straightened from lowering his pants. I'd expected it and retaliated by dropping my head and ramming it into his chest while wrapping my arms around his torso. Using all my strength, I swung him around and barrelled him to the ground. He landed so hard I was concerned I'd knocked him out, which was not my intention. But, his body writhed under mine telling me he was still in this fight.

Legs and arms kicked and clawed at me in his attempt to escape. I had to have fifty pounds on him, though, so he was no match.

Pressing my lower body down on his, restraining his legs, I took hold of his wrists and pinned him to the ground, pushing my chest up off his. "You wanna fight? I can guarantee that you won't win."

"I'll fucking die before I'll tell you anything," he spat.

I stared down at him, wondering just how long I'd have to draw this shit out. As much as I could inflict pain all night long, I was aware the cops had increased their nightly sweeps of the city in the last week, so I needed to move this along.

I moved his hands above his head so I could pin both of them to the ground with one of mine rather than both, and then reached into my pocket for my phone.

Pulling Devil's number up, I dialled him. "Get me that photo of his bitch. And draw some fucking blood for it."

"On it." The line went dead and he left to take care of my request.

5

I met the asshole's eyes again. "You might be willing to die, but let's see if you're ready to let us chop your old lady up."

His hard eyes held mine, probably calculating his options. They then narrowed and he said, "You're full of shit. You do that or kill me, my club only escalates this further, and *your* club is down so many members you wouldn't be able to win that battle."

His club, the Silver Hell MC, had spent the last three months exacting revenge on ours for King, our president, killing one of their members. King had killed him because he'd hurt King's sister. But their revenge had involved far more than simply going after King or our members. They'd also gone after our families, hurting them any way they could. The truce they'd called for last week wasn't one we were interested in.

I hissed. "What you're failing to realise here is that King declared war today. You thought we'd accept your truce? No fucking way. You've no idea who he's called in, but I'll tell you now that our numbers have been more than replenished. And one other thing... you should have known that no one fucks with King and gets away with it."

I let go of his hands and slid myself down his body so I could grab his dick. I then scored my blade along the length of it. Not deep, just enough for blood to pool.

"Fuck!" he roared, trying unsuccessfully to fight me. "King doesn't give a shit about you. He's built that club full of members who do his dirty work, and it's all for his own gain. When are you going to wake up and see that?"

I cut into his dick again. His body jerked underneath me while he continued to battle me for control. "When are *you* going to wake the fuck up and see that King gets his hands dirtier than any of us could ever dream of? And what he's built is an army of soldiers, willing to fight to the fucking end."

6

My phone buzzed with a text and I smiled when I saw the photo Devil had sent.

Blood and tits all wrapped up in extreme terror. This guy didn't need to know we'd never make good on our threat to harm his woman. He also didn't need to know the amount of blood in the photo was exaggerated by Devil smearing a small cut worth of blood over her skin.

The end justifies the means.

I leaned forward, pushed my hand against his chest to keep him down and shoved the phone in his face. "You ready to lose that?"

His chest heaved with heavy breath after heavy breath. Finally, he broke. "Room 1242." Regret and fury spewed out of his mouth along with his tip-off.

"What the fuck is that?"

"That's the room he's staying in tonight."

"Where?"

"Here."

Fuck, so close.

I stared at him and saw the moment he realised where this was heading. Sitting calmly atop of him, I moved my knife from his dick, ready to rid his club of another member.

He thrashed under me, trying like hell to buck me off.

It was that fight I loved the most.

That last ditch attempt to cling to life while I took his last breath.

Chapter Two

Tatum

"When I Go" by Keaton Simons

Numbers.

My days drifted past in a sea of numbers.

14004.

My bank balance.

6.

The number of meals I should eat a day.

3.

The number of people in my life who looked out for me.

5.

The number of flights I took to visit my mother while she was dying last year.

4.

The number of men I'd slept with over the past twelve months.

90000.

The amount of cash it took to crash my life to the ground.

8.

The number of years I lived a lie.

My days drifted past in a sea of numbers while I numbed my pain by disconnecting from life as much as I could.

As the guy I'd been watching in the casino all night slipped me his room key and said, "Room 1242," I knew I'd be using that key.

I might have given up on a lot, but I never gave up on revenge.

Especially when it involved the opportunity to seek vengeance against the man I thought murdered my brother.

* * *

His greedy eyes trailed a path over my body after he let me into his room. I felt nothing but disgust and had to work hard not to vomit.

You can do this.

For Chris.

I flinched when his palm roughly connected with my breast.

"You came here to fuck me, right?" He watched me, waiting for my answer, his hand squeezing my nipple through my clothes.

Swallowing down my nerves, I nodded.

Fuck, Tatum, get your shit together. It's not like you don't deal with these kinds of men every damn day.

He kept his hand on my breast while his other one gripped my hip and pulled me hard against his body.

Against his erection.

He ground his dick against me as his gaze dropped to my neck. "Those are some tattoos you're rocking. Who's your guy?"

No way was I giving him my girl's name.

"Dane Shepherd," I lied.

His brows pulled together. "Haven't heard of him."

I reached my hand around his neck. "Are we gonna fuck or are we gonna stand here and talk shit all night?"

Heat flashed in his eyes and his fingers dug into my waist. "You've got a fucking mouth on you, bitch. How about you get on your knees and show me what it's capable of."

9

No way was my mouth going anywhere his nasty dick. "I've got a better idea. How about I give you a show you'll never forget? And *then* I'll suck your dick."

"I don't need a show. I just need you to blow me and then get your tits out before I fuck you."

I tilted my head and hit him with a sexy smile. "Everyone needs a Billy-Jones-worthy show."

He whistled low and his expression quickly turned from disinterested to intrigued. "You're one of Billy's girls?"

I nodded. "I do things for Billy that none of his other girls do." Not a lie. Just a little creative storytelling.

He took a step back, dropping his eyes to my body. "Okay, but you better make this worth my while. I've got shit to do after I get my dick wet."

It was time to give the performance of my life.

It was time to dance with the devil himself.

I placed my palm against his chest and nudged him backwards. "Sit on the edge of the bed."

His brow raised at my order, but he did as I said. Once he settled there, I raised my arms over my head and linked my fingers before slowly gyrating my hips. I'd worn a tight black strapless dress that hit me midthigh with the express purpose of distracting him. It appeared to be working. His eyes were all over me; he didn't seem to know where to look first.

"Fuck, I need to see those tits," he muttered as he unzipped his pants to free his cock. Pumping himself, he groaned. "Show me."

I shook my head and continued working my hips while I rotated on the spot so he could catch a glimpse of my ass as well. "All in good time. We don't give up the goods that fast. If you know *Billy's*, you know that."

10

"Bitch, I give no fucks what you usually do, I want those tits out and in my fucking mouth right now."

I stared at him, weighing up my options. I knew he was a man without a conscience, who would kill you just as soon as he'd show you an ounce of compassion, so I had to tread carefully. But I'd watched him for long enough to also know he had a thing for blondes and tits. I just had to play my cards right.

"I'll show you mine if you show me yours."

That was clearly not something he'd expected. The flash of confusion in his eyes passed quickly though. "What the fuck?"

I cupped my breasts. "I have a thing for chests, so these bad boys come out when your shirt comes off."

His shirt hit the floor a moment later and he stared at me expectantly.

My gaze fixed on the tattoo on his chest. The proof I needed to know he was the man I believed him to be.

"Tits. Out," he roared, startling me.

I shrunk a little at his angry tone, but recovered fast. Pulling my dress down, I exposed my naked breasts.

He sucked in a breath. "Fucking perfect."

I ran my hands over my breasts as I continued to dance for him. Every second sickened me. When I finished with him, I would spend hours washing his grime off me.

The end justifies the means, Tatum.

It did.

Every single minute of every single day of the last nine months had been spent working towards that end. I wouldn't back the fuck down after all that. And I certainly wouldn't lose my chance to settle the score.

He slapped my hands out of the way and yanked me to him. His movements caught me off guard, and before I knew it, he had his hands on my ass and his mouth all over my breasts.

Fuck.

I froze.

Our eyes locked and he must have seen something there that made him question this. Gripping my hair, he pulled my head back. "I wanna know who the fuck you are. But first, I want my dick in that ass of yours."

Ice slid through my veins at the cold emptiness laced through his words. My mind raced with possible scenarios of how I would get myself out of the shit I was in. Before I managed to settle on a plan, he stood, picked me up and threw me on the bed face first.

I scrambled to flip myself onto my back, but he was faster than I gave him credit for. His strong arm scooped me around the waist while he reached under my dress to rip my panties off.

The sound of them tearing filled my ears, right before the sound of his groan. "Fuck, this ass is something else." He rubbed my ass cheeks before slipping his hand between my legs to reach for my pussy. "I'm fucking you everywhere tonight so get ready, because this isn't gonna be pretty for you. You're dry as a fucking desert."

I squeezed my eyes shut while he shoved his finger in my pussy. My body shook with dread, but no fucking way was I going down without a fight. I'd anticipated this could get messy, and I'd come prepared.

Waiting for that moment where his attention would be on himself for at least a split second, I focused on getting my breathing under control.

You can do this.

You can't let him get away with the shit he's done.

He finished fingering me, and his hold around my waist loosened. I knew that was my moment, so as fast as I could, I thrust my body forward, away from him. As soon as I was out of

12

his hold, I flipped over and reached for the knife I'd secured around my ankle in my boots. Gripping it hard, I lunged at him, aiming the knife at his chest.

I almost succeeded.

Again, he was too fast, his reflexes finely honed for battle. He grasped my wrist and twisted my arm. "Fucking bitch," he snarled as he forced the knife from my hand. "You'll pay for this."

My heart crashed into my chest. "I've already paid for it, asshole. There's nothing more you can do to me that will make it any worse."

His fist smashed into my cheek, delivering pain that slowed me down. I ended up almost falling off the bed. My head and upper body dangled off the side while the rest of my body lay sprawled sideways across the mattress. I tried like hell to force myself onto the floor; however, he had other ideas.

The bed dipped as he planted himself either side of me. A second later, he grabbed a handful of my hair and wrenched my head back, twisting it to the side so he could see my cheek. His heavy body covered mine, almost suffocating me, and he punched me hard in the face again. So hard I saw black.

I gasped for air as the pain consumed me.

I'm going to die.

I'm going to die at the hands of a filthy biker.

It was a good day to die.

As much as I'd gone there to kill him, I'd always known there was a good chance he'd kill me instead.

I was okay with that.

Because the truth was, I'd died nine months ago.

The day he'd taken the one person I cared about the most in the world was the day I gave up wanting to live.

And now he would take my life, too.

Chapter Three

Nitro

"Hell's Bells" by AC/DC

The smell of sex hit my nostrils.

And blood.

I smelt it, too.

Then a voice came screeching at me. "Huge fucking mistake!" And a fist flew at my face.

I presumed he referred to the fact I'd barged into his hotel room and interrupted the filthy shit going on. I hadn't had a good chance to see what he was doing, but I'd taken in a blonde lying facedown across the bed. She didn't look conscious so I figured he'd been fucking her without her knowledge.

Not something I ever fucking condoned.

He'd pay for that, too.

Adrenaline spiked through me as every muscle prepared for battle. I grabbed his fist, clamping my fingers tightly around his wrist. With great force, I pulled him towards me with one hand while I pointed my gun in the direction of his dick.

It was a beautiful and almost-too-easy meeting of karma and victory when I pulled the trigger and shot his dick to shit.

Truth be told, the blonde had helped me. She'd provided the distraction I needed to take him by surprise. I'd moved fast once I got through the door, because I'd expected him to react swiftly. He hadn't, and so there we were—him on his knees clutching where his cock used to hang, and me staring down at him.

"Doesn't look like a mistake to me," I muttered. Crouching, I held the gun to his head. "What I'm trying to figure out now is whether to make this quick so I can get out of here, or whether to deliver a slow death that would give me the kind of satisfaction I'm craving right about now."

His empty eyes stared at me. He made no move to fight me. Simply knelt there in his agony, drawing ragged breaths and grunting through the pain.

When he said nothing, I continued, "I think I'll do it fast. But only because I'm more than ready to feed the news of your death to Dragon." *Silver Hell's president.*

His lips curled. "Kill me, motherfucker. Dragon's got more men ready to take my place."

"Not once we're done with him tonight. When we refuse a truce, we don't just sit back and wait for your next move." Dragon would wish he'd never started this with us by morning.

My phone rang. I stood to answer the call and the asshole decided to give his life one last shot by punching my crotch.

"What?" I barked into the phone as I fired the gun, ignoring the pain radiating from my balls.

"You done?" King demanded. "We need you back here."

I looked down at the lifeless body on the floor. "It's done. I'm on my way now."

He terminated the call without another word and I shoved the phone in my back pocket. Glancing at the blonde on the bed, I wavered between the decision to check her pulse or get the fuck out of there. In the end, it was the moan she expelled that drove me towards her.

Making my way to the side of the bed where her head hung, I swung her body so she lay the length of the bed with her head on the pillow. She was regaining consciousness, and as I moved her, she cried out in agony. The noise splintered through the room, shards of her torment fracturing the stillness around us.

He'd done a fucking number on her. Blood messed up her face and stuck in her long hair. It was the swelling, though, that gave me pause. She'd be black and blue from this beating.

As my gaze moved from her face down her body, I realised this was the blonde I'd had an altercation with earlier. Her face was unrecognisable, but the tattoos covering her neck clearly identified her. I'd recognise them anywhere. They painted her neck, flowed down to her breasts and extended out to her shoulders to meet the tattoos on both arms. They were the kind of tattoos I'd like to study. Whoever did them was clearly talented and believed in quality.

She swallowed and tried to move. The pain appeared excruciating, because her face contorted and she cried out again. She squinted at me through her swollen eyes. "Fuck," she rasped. Her breathing picked up and she swallowed madly, probably trying to lubricate her dry throat.

When her body jerked on the bed, I figured she was attempting to leave, but there was no way she'd be walking out of there anytime soon.

"Where's—" she started, but I cut her off.

"He's dead."

My phone rang again.

Renee.

I answered it. "I'm in the middle of something. Can this wait?"

The blonde cried out again as she sat up.

"Who's that?" Renee asked.

I watched the blonde wiggle her way to the edge of the bed, wincing with each movement. "No one. I'll call you back in a minute."

16

"She sounds like she's in pain."

Renee had a fucking sixth sense. "She is."

"You don't sound like you care."

"That's because I don't."

Silence for a beat. "I hate that, Nitro. You should care. And you should help her."

I raked my fingers through my hair. "I'm hanging up now, Renee."

"Call me back."

Shoving my phone back in my pocket, I eyed the blonde. Her tits spilled out of the dress that sat scrunched around her middle. She wore no panties either; her bare pussy was on full display. Blood had dried on her neck and chest. That was in addition to the blood on her face and in her hair.

I'd bet my last dollar she had broken ribs. I'd also bet he'd raped her. I'd noticed cum on her ass and on the back of her dress when I moved her body. She was a fucking mess and I doubted she'd be able to leave without assistance, which presented me with a dilemma. If I left her there, the hotel staff would find her with a dead body. No way was I leaving a witness at the scene of my crime.

I had two options: kill her or take her with me.

By far, the easiest option was to kill her. It was the choice I was leaning towards. The last thing the club needed was to deal with this.

As I made the choice I had to make, she craned her neck so she could look at the dead body of the man who'd assaulted her. She then looked back at me and said, "Thank you." Her voice was scratchy and she had trouble getting the words out, but her gratitude rang out clear as day.

I stilled.

People didn't thank me for shit.

17

Well, except for Renee.

"Who was he to you?" I asked.

She exhaled a long breath. "He murdered my brother."

My fingers squeezed the gun in my hand.

Itching to shoot.

Her eyes dropped to the gun. "Are you gonna hurry this up?"

You should care.

You should help her.

Fucking Renee.

My chest tightened.

"Fuck," I muttered as I holstered my gun. "Can you stand?"

"Why?"

"Because you're coming with me."

She stared at me, wasting my time. "I'm not going anywhere with you."

"Yeah, you are. Now stand the fuck up." When she didn't do as I said, I barked, "Stand up or else I'm gonna pull you up and that shit's gonna hurt way worse than if you do it yourself."

Eyes that bled hate stared up at me. "Fuck you." She may have been sitting on that bed in a world of pain, but her body straightened with determination. "Just kill me."

I stepped forward and placed my hands under her arms. Keeping hold of her resentful gaze, I pulled her up. She managed to stand and I was surprised when not one sound of agony came from her.

"It's not your night to die. Fix your dress," I ordered.

She glared at me, but did what I said. I had a feeling that if she wasn't battered, she'd be fighting me every step of the way. Either that, or taking the gun off me and blowing her own brains out.

After she repositioned the dress, I shrugged my leather jacket off and said, "Put your arms out. You'll need to wear this out of here to cover as much of you as we can. I don't need security looking at us any more than they already will."

Once we had the jacket on, I guided her into the bathroom and cleaned her face and hair up as best I could. I also cleaned the cum off her dress. She gritted her teeth through the pain, again not uttering a sound through the process.

"Right, I'm going to put my arm around you and you're not going to pull out of my hold. Keep your head down and don't make eye contact with anyone. Your face is a fucking mess; I don't need anyone getting a look at that."

She didn't respond, just continued watching me like she wanted to jam a sharp object in my chest.

I gripped her bicep, squeezing just hard enough to draw a cry of pain. "You make a fucking scene and that beating he gave you will seem like a walk in the park. You got that?"

Drawing herself close to me, she spewed her anger in a violent surge of words. "What I've got is that you're no better than he was. How men like you sleep at night eludes me. Forcing women to do shit they don't want to is one of the lowest acts a man can do."

My whole body tensed and my nostrils flared as I took a deep breath. "Don't fucking say that shit to me again. You know jack about me."

With that, I yanked her out of the bathroom, and flung the hotel door open. Shoving her into the hallway, I draped my arm around her shoulders and led her to the elevator.

Every sense alert, I was ready to take on anyone who got in our way. I'd shoot my way out of this fucking casino if I had to.

Chapter Four

Tatum

"Ghost" by Massive

There were moments in your life that brought you to your knees. Moments that punched the absolute fuck out of you.

I was having one of those moments.

I thought life had already handed me my heart on a platter. Bleeding and bruised. Turned out life wasn't done with me yet. Bleeding and bruised wasn't enough.

"Stop dragging your feet," the big guy muttered as he dragged me through the foyer of the casino. His arm tightened around my shoulders as he picked up his pace. The front door was in view and I practically smelt his desire to make it through that door.

I could hardly match his pace a moment ago; I wasn't sure how he expected me to match his new speed. My whole body ached, and I was convinced my ribs were broken. The pain was excruciating and breathing only made it worse. On top of the pain in my body, my head throbbed, slowing me down further. I didn't want to walk and I sure as hell didn't want to think, but this asshole was giving me no choice. If I wanted to make it through the night, I'd have to do both.

I attempted to walk faster, but my efforts only caused me to stumble. As I went down, his strong arms clutched me, holding me up.

The new surge of pain through my body killed like a motherfucker and I couldn't hold my agony in. I cried out, stifling it as much as I could, but the sound was enough to draw the attention of casino security.

Suspicious eyes narrowed on me before swiftly looking at the big guy. Clearly the security guard didn't like what he saw. He stopped us as we tried to exit the building.

"Ma'am, are you okay?"

The arm around me gripped my shoulder harder and I contained my wince. Nodding, I said, "Yes."

The guard stared at my face before glancing at my body. "No, I don't think you are. Is this man hurting you?"

My life flashed before my eyes for the second time that day. Was I really ready to die? Because that would surely happen if I didn't do as the big guy had ordered. I knew that for a fact. He'd go down in a blaze of glory before he'd concede defeat, and I'd get caught in the crossfire.

So, I pushed every thought out of my mind and focused completely on convincing the guard he was wrong. Pulling my shoulders back, I turned my body towards the big guy's and wrapped my arms around his waist. Looking at the guard, I said, "He's my boyfriend; there's no way he'd ever hurt me. The bruises you see on me are from another asshole who assaulted me earlier tonight if you must know. Now, if you'd please let us past, I'd like to go home and forget this day ever happened." The body my arms were wrapped around stiffened.

The guard stared at me. Shocked. "Umm...." He cleared his throat, not seeming to know what to say.

The big guy took his opportunity. "Thanks for your concern, man, but I've got this. I just wanna get her home, okay?" He may have tacked a question on the end of that statement, but his tone made his stance clear—he wasn't actually asking for permission.

The guard nodded as he took a step back. "Sure."

"Thank you," I murmured as I was whisked past him, although I wasn't sure what I was thanking him for. For all I knew, I may have just made one of the worst decisions of my life.

* * *

The ride on his bike was unbearable. Trying to cling to someone on the back of a moving bike while every muscle and bone ached was like playing Russian roulette. There were moments my mind drifted to thoughts of letting go. I imagined flying off the bike, falling to my death.

Finally.

No more pain.

No more heartache.

And then I imagined not dying. It'd be just my luck to survive that and end up in a wheelchair. My fighting instincts kicked in at that thought. I'd rather take my chances with the biker and try to find my way out of this mess than give up without a fight.

We rode for what felt like forever. I breathed a sigh of relief when he slowed the bike and pulled into a back street. However, when I realised he'd taken me to his clubhouse, apprehension knotted in my stomach.

Time to suit up, Tatum.

The property appeared to be under heavy guard. A high fence surrounded it, with a gate manned by two men. They stopped us and after a few words with the biker, let us through. After that, two more men stopped us halfway down the long driveway before allowing us to pass. I wondered if this was normal procedure and figured it well could be. From everything I knew of the Sydney underbelly, you couldn't trust many in this city.

He parked the bike, killed the engine and ordered me off. "Keep your mouth shut in here unless you're spoken to."

The lighting that illuminated the outside of the clubhouse cast a bright glow on him, revealing his hard, cold eyes to me. I'd avoided taking a good look at him in the hotel room after the assault, but in that light, I saw him vividly. His height and muscular build was almost intimidating as he towered over me. I was only five three, where he had to be over six feet by a few inches. It took a lot to intimidate me, though, and while he came close, perhaps the fact he didn't kill me made the difference. He'd hesitated for some reason, which told me he had some humanity left inside.

I nodded at what he said. While I wanted to tell him where to go, I had to be smarter. I had to shut up, stay calm and dig deep to silence my natural inclination to resist. Not to mention, I needed to suppress the agony screaming through my body until I was alone and could deal with it.

He walked me inside and I gave all my attention to cataloguing the building, taking note of doors, windows and possible escape routes. I'd expected more bikers to be inside, but I only saw five. That seemed strange for a Friday night. One would have thought the clubhouse bar would be hopping over the weekend.

The biker's warm breath on my cheek startled me as he dragged me down a hallway. "If you think there's a way out of here, think again, Vegas."

I ignored him, unwilling to accept defeat. I also ignored the name he gave me. It was better he called me that than ask me what my name was.

We reached the room at the end of the hallway and he shoved me through the doorway after waiting a moment for someone inside to grant access.

Darkness filled the room, the only light coming from a lamp in the corner. Squinting my eyes, I made out a large wooden desk with a computer and paperwork on it, a filing cabinet, a worn couch along one wall and a few seats scattered around the desk.

I almost jumped out of my skin when a deep voice barked, "Who the fuck is she, Nitro?"

Nitro.

"She's a witness." He let me go and I placed my hand over my arm where he'd held me. As if I could soothe the pain.

A man emerged from the shadows and my breathing faltered as he came into sight. It could have been the jagged scar that ran down one side of his face, or his massive build, or the way his body language told me to be wary that did it, but it wasn't.

It was his eyes.

While Nitro's eyes were cold and hard, this man's glittered with crazy. I'd lived with crazy most of my life. And I knew to watch it with vigilance and always expect the unexpected.

He moved so he occupied the space directly in front of me. Staring down at me, he said, "She's a complication we don't need. Why is she here?" His nostrils flared before he turned to face Nitro. "Why the fuck is she still breathing?"

Every muscle in Nitro's body appeared taut as he watched the other man. "She wanted him dead as much as we did, King."

"No one wanted him dead as much as we did."

"Trust me, she did."

24

They stared at each other, both seemingly unwilling to bend. "You need to deal with her before I do," King said. When he said *deal with her*, I was under no illusion as to what he meant. I filed through my options, and was about to interrupt their conversation when Nitro spoke again.

"He raped her."

King's body tensed and his gaze flicked to me so he could scrutinize my appearance. As his eyes held mine, he said, "She's a liability." Then, looking back at Nitro, he said, "One you need to take care of."

I swallowed hard. King's order sent a chill through me. I knew men like him and when they decided something, they didn't back down. If I had any chance of surviving, I needed to find a way to get through to him. "I'm not a liability," I said, holding my head high and my body tall.

King's eyes snapped back to mine. "I don't give a fuck what you think. To my club, you are a fucking liability."

Taking a moment to get my breathing under control, I reminded myself it was the Storm MC I was dealing with. Nitro hadn't been wearing his colours so I hadn't known earlier, but the clubhouse announced this fact. These bikers weren't known for their compassion or their leniency, but maybe I had a shot in hell. I would have died at that asshole's hands earlier, but Nitro saved me. Then he gave me a second chance when he brought me here rather than shooting me. Maybe luck would come in threes.

Suit up, Tatum.

Suit the fuck up.

I stepped forward.

Closer to him.

"I work for Billy Jones. He would not want me dead."

King stilled. "You're one of his girls?"

"Yes." *Kind of.*

His eyes narrowed at me. "How long have you worked for him?"

"Six years."

That number was a winner for me. Everyone in Sydney knew that if a girl worked for Billy for longer than a year she was gold. He went through his girls like he went through his women. *Fast.*

"Fuck," Nitro muttered.

It was also common knowledge that Billy would kill for his golden girls.

King glared at me like he wanted to wrap his hands around my throat and squeeze the life out of me. "What's your name?"

My name was the last thing I wanted to give him, but I'd have to if I had any hope of escaping them. "Tatum Lee."

He turned away from me. "I don't have time to deal with this at the moment, Nitro. Get her out of here and watch her until I can verify this."

With that, King stalked out of the office, leaving Nitro and me alone. Raking his fingers through his hair, he said, "I see you changed your mind about living."

"I decided I didn't want to die at the hands of a filthy biker."

He scowled. "But you'd be happy to go back to Billy fucking Jones?"

I returned his scowl. "He treats me better than you have."

Tension punched through the air between us and if I thought I'd seen Nitro angry before, something I said made his mood far worse. Dipping his face to mine, he snarled, "Get your ass out that door and to my bike. And don't say another fucking word about Billy Jones to me."

"It would be my absolute pleasure to not say another fucking word to you, full stop," I snapped, before spinning on my heel and marching out of the clubhouse.

I decided then that I could deal with a lot of things, but bikers weren't one of them.

Chapter Five

Nitro

"Pretty Vegas" by INXS

Tatum Lee was a pain in my ass.

We'd arrived at my house an hour earlier and after she had a shower, I'd given her a shirt to wear and set her up in my bedroom because it was the only room with a bed. If she'd been anyone but a woman who meant something to Billy Jones, I'd have tied her to a fucking chair and left her alone. As much as I loathed Billy, he was one of Storm's loyal allies and since we'd declared war on Silver Hell, we needed to keep every ally on side. Pissing him off was not a good move.

"You're not sleeping next to me in this bed," she said as I entered the room and lifted my shirt over my head.

"I'm not sleeping, Vegas. And I'm doing that in the bed next to you."

Raising her handcuffed hands in the air and jerking her chin at her feet that I'd tied together, she said, "You've detained me. I can't go anywhere. I hardly think you need to be so damn close to me."

Sitting on the edge of the bed, I reached to remove my boots. "You and I would get along a hell of a lot better if you stopped thinking."

She muttered something under her breath that I didn't catch. Not that I cared to hear it. The less talking we did, the better.

Once my boots were off, I settled on the bed, my back to the bedhead, legs crossed at the ankles. Eyeing her, I ran my gaze over her body. Ignoring the bruises and swelling, I remembered how she'd looked when we first met on the casino floor. Besides the fact she had curves in all the right places, muscles that only accentuated those curves, long blonde hair that was exactly my type, and a beautiful face a man would never forget, Tatum Lee had skin that was inked to perfection. She had quotes tattooed on her legs that I wondered about. What had she been through in her life to permanently ink them into her skin?

"What?" she demanded.

I met her gaze and we watched each other cautiously for a few moments. Getting into a conversation may not have been on my list of priorities, but she seemed to be dragging me there.

"I'm wondering what the hell possessed you to put yourself in that situation tonight? Because I'm guessing that you being in that hotel room wasn't random. Not if you knew that guy murdered your brother."

Her mouth curled up in anger. "And I'm guessing that you'd do the same thing if someone murdered your family."

"Yeah, but I'm capable of not getting myself raped or killed."

"He beat me, and he got his dick out, but he didn't fuck me with it."

I leaned in close to her. "He might not have, but he sure as fuck would have if I hadn't shown up. And a word of warning— you may not play with those kinds of men often, Vegas, but they don't hesitate to kill you if you piss them off."

She pushed her face near mine. "Why didn't *you* kill me? And why the hell do you keep calling me Vegas?"

Fuck, her fight caused my dick to harden. Waiting with a hard-on while King decided what we were doing with her was the last fucking thing I needed, so I moved off the bed. "Go to sleep," I ordered as I left the bedroom.

After I grabbed a beer out of the fridge I headed to the couch in the lounge room. As far away from Tatum Lee as I could manage. The desire to fuck her wasn't one I needed to fuel by being near her. She'd complicated shit enough already.

* * *

"Nitro!"

I jerked awake at the sound of Renee's voice to find her standing in front of me, a worried look on her face. Sitting forward, I rubbed my eyes. "What time is it?"

"You never called me back."

I ignored the accusation in her voice. Pushing off the couch, I said, "What's the time, Renee?" The dark night clung to the windows still. I guessed it to be about three or four in the morning.

"It's just after five. Mum's not good. I needed you and you weren't there for me." Her accusatory tone disappeared and all that remained was her broken spirit.

Fuck.

"What happened?"

"Nothing happened. But she's not coping, and she's getting worse." She paused for a moment, her face crumpling before the tears fell. "I don't know what to do anymore."

I wrapped my arms around her and pulled her close while she sobbed. Forcing down the fury that tried to punch its way out of me, I said, "You're not alone, kiddo. I had some shit to do last night, but I'm here for you." Those motherfuckers would pay for what they'd done to my family.

30

She clung to me for a while before letting me go and saying, "You need to make her see that psych again. She did better when she saw him."

I raked my fingers through my hair. Easier said than done. "Yeah, she did."

"I don't care if you have to freaking kidnap her to get her there, just make that shit happen. Okay?"

I raised my brows. "Condoning crimes now, are we?" Renee should have been born into a family of lawyers or fucking cops with the beliefs she held about crime.

She ignored my question. It was a long-running difference of opinion between us that we'd probably never resolve. "She's your sister. You need to fix her, because I've tried and I failed."

"Jesus, Renee, you're seventeen and she's your mother. It's not your job to fix her and you sure as fuck haven't failed her."

More tears slid down her face as she stood staring at me, pleading with her eyes for me to make this all better. If only life were that fucking simple. I didn't want to break her even more than she already was, though, so I pulled her close again and said, "I'm going to sort this out, kiddo. You just need to focus on school and your shit, and let me get your mother better."

She hugged me like she never wanted to let go, but Tatum chose that moment to interrupt us. "Nitro! I need to use the bathroom."

Renee's arms dropped from around me as she took a step back. Frowning, she said, "Who is that?"

"A friend."

Spinning around, she headed towards my bedroom. "A friend who can't walk to the bathroom?" Her intelligence and instincts were out of this world, and she liked to challenge me.

"Renee," I called out. "Stop walking."

She didn't.

"Renee!" I barked.

My niece was as fucking stubborn as I was. She took after me more than her mother, probably because I'd practically raised her. At times like this, that came back to bite me in the ass.

Spinning back around, she stalked my way. "Is that the woman from earlier who was in pain? The one you didn't care about?" she demanded. "What's going on here?"

I grabbed her hand. "You need to go home. This doesn't concern you and I don't want you tied up in it."

"Nitro!" Tatum yelled out again.

Ignoring Tatum again, I continued to hold Renee in place. "Go home. I'll come by later and see Lynny."

She huffed out a long breath. "Fine, but only because I really don't want to know what's going on. Just promise me you won't hurt her."

I took a moment to answer her. Finally, nodding, I agreed. "I won't."

I fucking hoped I could keep that promise. There weren't many people I cared enough about to want to honour my agreements with anymore. Renee was one of those people. Hell, she was the one at the top of the list.

Chapter Six

Tatum

"Beaten Dog" by Massive

Every muscle in my body ached. That filthy biker had given me the beating of my life last night. I'd copped bruises at the hands of men before, but not like that.

Easing myself to a sitting position, I squinted when the sunlight streaming through the window hit my eyes. Rain had fallen in Sydney all week and the news had forecast more, so the sun surprised me.

Welcome to your bright, shiny future.

"Fuck!" I screamed out as I wiggled some more to straighten. The pain that shot through my entire body was enough to knock the wind out of me, but I wouldn't let it. My momentary lapse last night when I'd practically begged Nitro to kill me would never happen again. I refused to allow another human to push me to that edge once more.

I swung my legs off the bed so I was sitting on the edge. Nitro had tied my ankles together with rope, but I was going to attempt to shuffle out of the room. I'd been lying awake for what had to be at least an hour and I hadn't heard him in that time. He also hadn't come when I just screamed out. Maybe he was asleep. Or, while I highly doubted it, perhaps he had left the house. Either way, I had to take any opportunity to escape that presented itself.

When I stood a moment later, I held my breath as another round of agony took hold. Squeezing my eyes shut, I counted to ten and then back to zero, centring myself.

They will not break you.

You will get through this.

"You going somewhere?" Nitro's voice boomed from the doorway, jolting me.

My eyes flicked open. "Yes, out of this damn room. It'd make my day if you untied my feet."

Amusement crossed his face momentarily. Then the hard set of his jaw that I knew so well, even after only meeting him the night before, settled back in place. "It'd make my fucking week if you did as I said and stayed put on the bed."

"I wasn't put on this earth to make your week."

He crossed his arms over his chest, drawing my attention to his body. That was a bad move. The man had everything going for him physically that would usually turn me on. Muscles that declared strength, and tattoos all over that told a story were my downfall when it came to men, and Nitro had plenty of all those. He also had thick dark hair and a beard, two more preferences of mine.

Concentrate, Tatum.

You're his fucking prisoner for God's sake.

"That mouth get you into trouble a lot, Vegas?"

"It keeps the people out of my life who shouldn't be in it."

He nodded slowly, arms still crossed. "Yeah, I imagine it does." Dropping his arms, he strode to me, his face darkening. "King's just arrived and I suggest you keep it shut around him. He doesn't have as much tolerance as I do."

I squared my shoulders and started to speak, but King appeared in the doorway, interrupting us.

His eyes came straight to me. "Seems you were telling the truth, Tatum. Billy is desperate to get you back."

"Thank fuck," I muttered, earning a scowl off Nitro.

I returned his scowl before shifting my attention back to King. Holding up my hands that were still handcuffed, I said, "Awesome. You can remove these now."

"Not until you tell me what you saw in that hotel last night," King said as he moved towards me.

Staring at him, I mentally acknowledged the crazy glint still in his eyes. Knowing what he was after, I said, "Nothing. I wasn't even in that room."

"Where were you?"

"At the blackjack table all night."

"Did you win?"

"Five hundred bucks."

"Who did you leave with?"

"No one."

Nitro moved out of the way, allowing King to invade my personal space. He didn't say anything for a few moments, but his body language and eyes were a menacing presence. I knew what he was doing; it wasn't like I'd never dealt with a man like King before. Finally, he said, "Good."

"Can I go now?"

Something caused him to snap. His hand wrapped around my throat and he squeezed hard until I almost choked. His fingers dug in, blocking my ability to breathe and causing me pain. When he had me gasping for air, he leaned close and hissed, "I'm not a fan of your smartass mouth, Tatum. Nitro's gonna take you home and you're gonna show him around your house so he knows every inch of it. By the time he leaves, he'll know every point of entry. And if you so much as look at me the wrong fucking way, I'll send him over to do what I wanted to do in the first place." He applied a little more pressure, until just as I thought I would pass out, he let go. "Do we have an understanding?"

I gasped for air, sucking in huge wheezing breaths while staring at King with hate. When my breathing finally stabilised, I snarled, "We have an understanding, but you do that shit to me again and you won't just have Billy to deal with. You think I'm a fucking stripper? I'm not." I held up my hands. "Now fucking undo these and take me home."

Fucking bikers.

King's body tensed and he clenched his fists by his side. He wouldn't hit me, though. Billy would have been out of his mind looking for me last night; he would have made it crystal clear to King to let me go. And King had to know that Billy didn't like it when those close to him were hurt. Everyone in Sydney knew that.

"Get her out of my sight, Nitro," he spat before stalking out of the room.

I watched him leave, more than happy to see the back of him. When I turned to face Nitro again, I found him watching me with an expression I couldn't put my finger on.

"What?" I snapped.

Whatever he'd been thinking was replaced with his standard anger at me. Reaching for my hands, he ignored my question and muttered, "Thank fuck this is over."

Fuck yes.

I felt exactly the same.

* * *

Walking into my kitchen, I took a deep breath and closed my eyes. It was good to be home, but most of the tension in my body remained. Until Nitro left it wouldn't shift.

His hand curved over my shoulder causing my survival instincts to ratchet up another notch. "Time to show me around, Vegas."

I turned, shrugging out of his grip even though the movement killed like a bitch, and glared at him. "Don't touch me again." Jerking my chin, I added, "Show yourself around. I have calls to make."

Without waiting for his reply, I grabbed my phone out of my bag. Swiping to see how many calls I'd missed, I squinted through swollen eyes and discovered sixteen missed calls from Billy. "Fuck," I muttered. He really was desperate to get me back.

Nitro watched me for a few moments. He didn't utter another word and he didn't move, but still he managed to knot me with more unease. I had no idea what he was thinking or what he was likely to do. I guessed that was exactly how he liked things to be. It was something I understood, because it was how I operated in my life, too. Being an open book hadn't worked out for me. All it had left me with was betrayal, divorce and no fucking job, so I kept a tight lid on shit these days.

When he finally left the kitchen, I placed my hands on the counter and spent a few minutes taking some deep breaths. God knew, I needed them, even if each one was pure torture. In the space of twelve hours, my life had taken another detour, not one I relished. Having the President of the fucking Storm MC threaten me wasn't something to take lightly. As much as I had Billy and some others in my corner, this town was renowned for turning people against each other.

Maybe it was time to get out. Besides my cousin, Monroe, I didn't have anyone left who I cared for enough to stick around. Leaving this city was something I'd thought a lot about since Randall had screwed me over, and now that Chris's death had been avenged, maybe it was finally time to disappear.

"Three bedrooms, one bathroom, one toilet, a kitchen, lounge room, dining room, and laundry all with bars on every window," Nitro said, entering the kitchen again. "Nine rooms locked up tight, along with security cameras on each entry and throughout the house, triple deadlocks on the front and back doors, Crimsafe doors and windows, a gun, and two knives stashed in the house... you don't fuck around with security, do you?"

I met his gaze, determined not to flinch away from him again. "There're some assholes in this town, so no, I don't fuck around with it."

He moved closer to me, only stopping when our bodies almost touched. "Getting in your home might prove harder than usual for me, but take heed of King's threat. He knows where you live and he knows who you work for." He dipped his face to mine. "We can find you if we want to. Keep your mouth shut and don't ever mention the Storm MC, and shit will be good between us."

His eyes bored into mine while his order settled between us.

Placing my hand on his chest, I pushed him away. "If I never see or hear about you or your club again, it'll make me the happiest woman on this planet."

His nostrils flared and he made a growling noise deep in his chest. "We have a deal then." With that, he swept one last menacing glance over me before turning and exiting my kitchen.

The sound of the front door closing a moment later, and his bike roaring to life kicked me into gear. Ten minutes later, I had every door and window locked tight. Watching from the front window in my lounge room, I scanned the street making sure no one was out there. You could never be too careful. Not in the line of work I was in.

Once I was sure of my safety, I collapsed onto the couch. My heart beat faster as I remembered the events of the previous night.

The biker.

His hands on me.

His fingers inside me.

The beating he gave me while he got off.

His cum on my ass.

Disgust prickled my skin while the memories came at me relentlessly. I wrapped my arms around my body, needing to feel like I was capable of consoling myself. There was no one else there to hug me; I had to look after myself.

I'd been stupid to go to that hotel room. I knew that, but nothing would have kept me from it. That man murdered my brother. My twin. The one person who loved me to the moon and back, no questions asked.

I shivered as the cold winter air blanketed me. Trying to block the memories, I closed my eyes.

I was so tired.

And my body hurt like a bitch.

I had to be strong; I always was. But in that moment, I clung to the tiny amount of strength I had left. It would be so easy to surrender to the pain, the grief and the exhaustion.

Tears wet my cheeks and for once, I allowed them to.

I didn't hold them back and I didn't deny the sadness swallowing me.

But I only gave myself that moment to feel it. And once I'd let the memories, thoughts and emotions roll through me, I wiped those tears away and sat up straight. Dwelling in the shit of life wasn't productive. Either you checked out or you checked in, and I chose the latter. Which meant I had places to be and people to see.

This life isn't for the weak, Tatum.

You made your bed and now you need to lie in it.

Time to get to work.

Chapter Seven

Nitro

"Bring Down The City" by Massive

"You made it clear to her not to open her mouth?" King asked when I arrived at the clubhouse later that morning. I'd found him at the bar and had pulled up a seat next to him to discuss Tatum.

"Yeah. She's not gonna talk, King." I didn't know what Tatum was messed up with, but I'd wager a bet she was almost as deep in shit as we were. Working for Billy guaranteed it. She'd be dead the minute she so much as parted her lips, and it wouldn't be us pulling the trigger.

He nodded as he swept his gaze around the clubhouse bar. The boys had started arriving for Church, and I knew King was keeping track of everyone because he made a point to always know who was in the clubhouse at all times. "Lotta shit going down, so I need you to stay on top of her. First sign of trouble, you deal with it." Turning his attention back to me, he said, "I just got word that Silver Hell paid a visit to Eric Bones early this morning."

"And?" We'd expected that.

"They trashed one of his clubs and roughed him and some of his girls up. I need you and Devil to check in on him after Church, and make sure he's still on board. Max and Calvin have signalled their support, and Kick's checking in with Stu. Bones, though, is the one I'm unsure of."

"Will do." We had some of the most powerful men in Sydney behind us and I'd make sure Bones didn't forget where his support was best put.

King's attention shifted to Brittany behind the bar. She placed two drinks in front of us. "Rum is the best way to start a day, don't you think?"

King didn't hesitate. He drained his glass in two gulps. "Today, it's the only way." He nodded at mine. "Drink up, brother, we've got Church to get through."

I watched as he left, and then threw back some rum. Gritting my teeth as it went down, I eyed Brittany. She watched me with a concerned look. "What?"

"King's on edge. I've never seen him like that before," she said.

I drank the rest of the rum and stood. Handing her the glass, I said, "King's always on edge. He usually just hides it better."

She leaned across the bar. "Shit's getting a little too real around here, Nitro. I'm not sure I can hang around much longer."

I narrowed my eyes at her. "Why?"

She ran her fingers through her hair. "Someone slashed my tyres yesterday. That's three things now that they've done to try to scare me, and it's working. I know you said the club would keep me safe, but I'm worried." Her voice wobbled as she looked at me with wide eyes full of fear.

I stared at her. She had no grit and we didn't need any weak links. People like Brittany only put everyone else at risk. "We'll find someone to replace you."

She frowned. "I didn't mean I wanted out completely. Maybe I could just take some time off while you guys sort it out."

"No."

Her lips flattened. "So just like that you'll replace me? After everything I've done for the club, you'll just send me on my way without a backwards glance?"

"Everything you've done for the club? You poured beers and ran the bar, which you were paid for."

"I did way more than just make drinks and you know it," she snapped.

"What the fuck else did you do, Brittany? Suck some dick and try to fuck your way onto the back of a bike? That was your choice."

Her face scrunched up in anger. "You're an asshole, you know that? I can't believe I thought that underneath it all, you had some good inside of you."

My body tensed, my own anger surfacing. I should have known better than to fuck someone who was so close to my daily life. "I can have someone here to replace you in an hour. You want me to make that call?"

She flinched. And then, straightening her shoulders, she said, "No, I'll finish out this week and then I'll leave."

I rested my hand on the bar and leaned towards her. "No, you'll finish up today. We'll pay you for the week, but you won't step foot inside this clubhouse after today."

As I walked away from her, I eyed Kick entering the building. When he reached me, I said, "We need to replace Brittany. Today. You got anyone?"

He nodded, always a yes man. "I can find someone."

"And organise for Jacko to pay Brittany for the week."

"What's going on? Jacko's gonna ask why, so I need to know what to tell him." He was right. Our treasurer never paid bills without verifying them first.

43

"She's weak, Kick, and she'll burn us if anyone gets to her. I'm not willing to take a chance on that. The stakes are too fucking high and we've all paid a price. I won't pay again."

He nodded. "Consider it done."

I'd never make this mistake again. Brittany had fucked other club members besides me, but it had been clear in her eyes just then that she wanted more from me. Sex would never be about something more for me. Not when trust was a necessary part of that equation. I trusted a handful of people in life and I wasn't looking to add to that small group.

* * *

King's lip curled up as he snarled at our newest patched member during Church, "Are you with us or not, Slider? Because if you're not, you need to get up and walk out of here now."

Slider threw him a filthy look. "I'm with you, but—"

King slammed his fist down on the heavy wooden table as anger flared in his eyes. "There's no room for buts. We all agreed upon our course of action before last night, and I for one am fucking committed to it. Silver Hell *will* be decimated. Now, are you fucking with us or not?"

Slider clenched his jaw before giving King one firm nod. "I'm with you."

King shoved his fingers through his hair and blew out a harsh breath. "Right, now that's settled, this is where we stand at last count. Seven of their club members were taken out last night, including their VP and Sergeant-at-Arms"—he glanced at me— "and the motherfucker who has been fucking with our families."

Conversation broke out at that news; it was what everyone had been waiting to hear. We'd all had family members suffer at the hands of Silver Hell.

"And their strip club?" Skull asked, breaking through the noise of everyone talking.

King nodded. "Hyde and Devil were successful there. It's out of action for a while."

Hyde's face lit up. "Watching it burn to the ground was the highlight of my week."

King continued, "Next up is to hit them hard where it will hurt the most after the loss of that club. Bronze and his boys will raid their other clubs and find drugs, which should close them down. They'll be in a world of financial hurt after that, but we need to be ready for the unexpected. Dragon will come after us with everything he has, so I want you to keep your ears to the ground and bring me anything you hear." He lifted his chin at me, indicating that as Sergeant-at-Arms, it was my turn to take over.

Shifting so I could rest my arms on the table, I said, "Our plan hasn't changed. I've given each of you the information you need to carry out the next step. You need something, you come to me." I turned to Kick. "How did you go with that security footage from the casino?" I'd texted him the previous night asking him to take care of wiping all traces of me from the casino.

"All done," he said.

"Thanks, brother."

As I sat back, King asked, "Any questions before we get to work?" When none were forthcoming, he ended the meeting and everyone filed out.

Although the first round of attacks had gone to plan, the mood was anything but celebratory—we had a long way to go before that.

Chapter Eight

Tatum

"Sucker For Pain" by Lil Wayne, Wiz Khalifa, Imagine Dragons

Billy took one look at me when I entered his office the afternoon after Nitro dropped me at home and swore. "Those motherfuckers will pay for this!"

I held up my hand as I took the seat across from him at his desk. "Storm didn't do this to me, Billy. It was the Silver Hell biker they killed who did it."

He ran his eyes over my body, taking in the bruises that had settled into place on my arms and face. The ones on my back and legs were covered by my clothes. They were nastier and I was glad he couldn't see them. Meeting my gaze, he said, "Fuck, Tatum, did you go to the hospital? Is anything broken?"

I shook my head. "Maybe a rib or two, but other than that it just looks bad. Nothing some painkillers and time won't fix."

He threw his pen down and leaned back in his chair. "You're always so damn practical. It's what I fucking love about you, but this time I'm taking charge and calling the doctor in to check on you." At my scowl, he held up his hand and shook his head. "Don't argue with me. I'll have him here within the hour. In the meantime, you can start figuring out a way to get Posey off some drug charges brought against her last night. Fucking dumb bitch."

I pursed my lips. "Don't talk about the girls like that, Billy. They pay your fucking bills."

"They also give me more headaches than I care for. Sort it out, Tatum, because otherwise she's gone. I don't need her problems on top of all the other shit we're trying to deal with."

I stood. "Is she here?"

He nodded. "Yes. And once you've fixed that, I need you to work out the scheduling issues they're having before we go over the licencing for the new club." Reaching for his phone, he added, "I'll text you when the doc arrives."

His concern meant something. It wasn't often Billy Jones cared about someone enough to call a doctor for them. But gushing displays of emotion and thanks weren't something either of us was good at or known for, so I simply nodded. "Thanks, Billy."

As I turned to leave, he called out, "Six years, Tatum."

I frowned as I glanced back at him. "Six years, what?"

Moving to where I stood, he came close and ran his finger down my cheek, so lightly I could hardly feel it. "It's been six years since you smashed your car into mine. Six years since that day you told me to go fuck myself when I accused you of driving like an idiot."

I had no idea where he was heading with this. "And what, Billy? You're not going all fucking sentimental on me, are you?"

The hard glint in his eyes that he was known for remained when he spoke again, as did the hard tone he usually took, and yet there was something undeniably caring in his words. "I was fucking worried about you last night. Don't do that shit again."

I stared at him for a beat. "So long as no one else murders someone I love, we're good."

"Jesus, Tatum." He waved me away. "Go. Take care of business and try to stay out of fucking trouble."

* * *

48

I found Posey in the dressing room. Her eyes came straight to mine and I nodded at the regret I saw there. Taking a seat next to her, I said, "You fucked up."

She fidgeted in her lap, but she didn't shift her gaze. "Yeah," she agreed on a long exhale of breath.

"I'm presuming it was Dwayne's." At her nod, I asked, "Why?"

Hands still fidgeting, she mumbled, "He threatened to kick me out if I didn't score for him. The cops picked me up before I got home with it."

I stared at her for a long moment. Posey was one of our best strippers, always in demand as well as one of the easiest girls we worked with. Nothing was ever too much of an ask for her and she never caused problems for the other girls or the customers. But she had a personal life from hell that caused her no end of issues, which then became my issues. "Fuck, Posey, we've talked about this before. Dwayne is a dick and you need to get your shit together where he's concerned. If a guy loves you, he's not going to threaten to kick you out all the time just to get what he wants from you."

She nodded like she understood and agreed, but I knew she didn't. Posey was too damaged to understand her own worth. I doubted her ability to stand up to Dwayne, but that never stopped me from trying to get through to her. "I know, Tatum, but you don't understand how hard it is for me. He's all I've got. I don't have any family or friends to rely on, and I know you said you'd help, but—"

I stood and paced in front of her, angry at her woe-is-fucking-me attitude. "That's bullshit you keep telling yourself, Posey, and I'm not interested in hearing it anymore." I jabbed my chest. "*I* have one family member left in my life. Besides her,

I have Billy and that's it, so don't give me that sob story, because you're not the only person in the world who doesn't have a tonne of people in their corner. You rely on yourself in this world, and if you can't, you find a way to get through until you can."

Her eyes widened as she took in everything I said. Swallowing hard, she whispered, "I don't know how."

"Do you want to try?"

She blinked as she stared up at me. "I think so."

I shook my head. "Not good enough. It's either a yes or a no answer. Do you want to leave Dwayne and sort your life out?"

I expected her eyes to dart away from mine, but she surprised me when she held my gaze. "Yes." Her voice may have still had a trace of uncertainty in it, but it didn't waver like I thought it would.

Nodding, I said, "Okay then. What time does Dwayne finish work?"

"Five this afternoon."

"I want you to go home and pack a bag, just the essentials. Then I want you to come back here so I can take you to my cousin's place and get you settled. I'll organise for one of our guys to go back with you in a day or so to get whatever else you want, but for now just pack some clothes and toiletries."

She frowned. "I'm working tonight so maybe I should just stay here until after my shift."

"No, Dwayne will come looking for you. I'm going to get one of the other girls to fill your shift tonight. I want to give you some time away from him, somewhere he won't find you."

"Thank you," she said softly.

"Yeah. Promise me you won't fuck this up, Posey."

She lost her cool then, and tears fell down her cheeks. Wiping at the tears madly, she said, "I'm gonna go to jail, aren't I? For those drugs."

I reached out and moved a stray piece of her hair out of her eyes. Shaking my head, I said, "No, I'll get you a good behaviour bond."

Staring at me in disbelief, she said, "But the cop told me they'd lock me away for this."

I crouched in front of her. "Babe, why do you think Billy keeps me around? It's sure as hell not to dazzle customers with my exceptionally bright smile. You concentrate on that and I'll do what I do."

My phone buzzed with a text.

Billy: Get your ass back here. Doc is on his way.

Standing, I looked down at Posey. "I gotta go. Text me when you get back."

As I headed to Billy's office, I sent a text to Duvall, my contact in the public prosecution's office.

Me: Lunch is on me today.
Duvall: No.
Me: You still owe me, Duvall.
Duvall: You're never gonna let that go, are you?
Me: No, those days are long gone.
Duvall: Fuck.
Me: Twelve at the usual place.
Duvall: Screw you, Tatum.
Me: See you then.

Duvall, of all people, should have known the devil always came collecting once you'd made a deal.

* * *

The busy lunch crowd hum filled my ears as I took a seat in the café Duvall and I used to meet at for lunch almost every day for two years straight.

How times change.

His eyes met mine, concerned, before he took another look at my bruises. "What the hell happened to you?"

"Let's just say I had a difference of opinion with someone. I look like I lost, but I actually won in the end, so can we not talk about this anymore."

The concern lingered in his expression, but he frowned. Duvall knew that when I didn't want to have a conversation it was fruitless to pursue it. "Our friendship is slowly disintegrating, Tatum. I try like hell to be there for you, but you freeze me out and only call when you want something. I'm almost done."

I ran my gaze over him. Times might have changed, but Duvall hadn't. He still wore his blond hair cut close to his head, and he still wore the same dark suit he'd always worn. And he still refused to acknowledge or care that nearly every set of eyes in the café was on us, judging us, just like they always were whenever we met.

"I'm a bitch, but I'm a bitch you can't hate, Duvall. Too much has happened between us for that. And as much as you might believe our friendship is dying, it's simply not true." I leaned forward. "Even after all this time, you haven't told me you want to meet somewhere else, away from prying eyes. Why is that?"

"Because I don't give a shit what anyone thinks of the fact I am still your friend. But I will tell you that just because I don't care about the opinions of others, I *do* care that you're using me."

"I'm not using you. I'm calling in what I'm owed."

His shoulders tensed and he scowled. Raking his fingers through his hair, he muttered, "Jesus Christ, is that fucking deal ever going to stop haunting me?"

"The old me would have said yes, but the new me can't. You know that."

"I liked the old you much better."

"Yeah, well you should forget her because she's never coming back. Now we both have to deal with Billy and whatever he throws our way."

"You have a choice when it comes to Billy, but I don't seem to have that luxury."

I stared at him. "You think I had a choice when he was the only one offering me a job in this fucking city?"

"You always had a choice, Tatum, you just made the wrong one. And you still are. You're smarter than this life you've chosen."

A shiver of annoyance ran through me. He had no idea why I'd made the choices I did. "You know what, Duvall? Billy might be a criminal and involved in some dirty shit, but for the first time in my life, I feel accepted, which is a hell of a lot more than I can say for when I worked on the other side of the law."

He raised his brows. "*Involved* in some dirty shit? That's a fucking understatement. The man runs one of the dirtiest operations in this state. Hell, he *is* the definition of dirty. You've changed completely since you left the law—tattoos, gambling, drinking… if that's what feeling accepted does for you, I'd hate to see what not feeling accepted would look like."

I shifted forward in my seat. "I haven't changed. I simply stopped trying so hard to be something I wasn't."

"No, Tatum, you let yourself be swallowed by the filth and the grime. You took so many wrong turns that you just don't know the right way anymore. Saying yes to the devil too many times will do that to a person."

He wasn't wrong, but I also believed the devil had a way of showing a person who they really were underneath all the layers of pretence society encouraged. "I just let my demons out to play, Duvall."

His eyes turned cold before he averted his gaze, looking at something over my shoulder. He was silent for a moment except for a few angry breaths. Then he turned his attention back to me and leaned his arms on the table. "Whatever it is you need from me today, you've got, but if you still want a friendship with me, this is the last time. And for the record, I would have loved you, demons and all. You didn't have to hide them or pretend they didn't exist."

Heaviness settled deep in my chest at his declaration. I wanted to reach out and touch him, maybe hold his hand, but I didn't. I couldn't. Duvall wanted something from me I didn't have to give. Not anymore. Instead, I pulled a slip of paper out of my bag and slid it across the table to him. "I need these charges to either go away or for her to be given a good behaviour bond only."

He took the paper, his eyes never leaving mine. Searching for something. What, I wasn't sure. He'd never find it, though. Duvall was always looking for the good in people, the redeemable. I didn't have much of either anymore.

As I walked away from him a few minutes later, I said, "For the record, you could never have loved my demons, Duvall. If you got a good look at them, you'd run as fast as you could. And I wouldn't blame you."

* * *

"Holy fuck, Tatum. Who the hell did that to you?" My cousin, Monroe, stared at me in shock, her heavily made-up eyes glued to the bruises visible on my arms, neck and face.

I grabbed her by the arm as I moved past the front counter of her tattoo parlour where she stood. Pulling her with me, I said, "You need to make me a coffee."

Her brows arched. "Shit." She knew that meant I had something to tell her that she probably wouldn't like. Glancing at Fox, the only staff member there that day, she said, "I'll be out the back for a bit. Yell if you need me."

He looked up from the tattoo he was working on, showing me those beautiful blue eyes of his that I could get lost in for hours, and smiled as he nodded. Fox and I had a history of the kind of sex you had when you were lonely or just needed to work the tension out of your body. He was the perfect guy for that, being that he ran from relationships as much as I did.

When I had Monroe alone in her staff kitchen, I closed the door and took a moment to collect my thoughts. "He's dead."

She stilled and her breathing slowed. Her long eyelashes did a slow sweep of her skin as she closed her eyes briefly. She then exhaled the kind of breath that felt like it had been trapped inside for years. I knew, because I'd exhaled that same breath. "Good."

I leaned against the counter, placing my hands on it either side of me. "*He* did this to me."

She lowered her gaze to take in the bruises again. "Babe, how are you even opening that eye? It's so fucking swollen. And how

55

the hell did you go from him beating you to you killing him? Have you got some Lara Croft moves I don't know about? Why the hell were you alone with him? And did you go to the doctor? I can take you if you haven't."

I smiled. Monroe was my person, and she always wrapped me in love. She never failed to find a way to sprinkle some light over my darkness. "Billy called a doctor this morning. Nothing broken and nothing they can do for me. I'll heal in time." I lowered my voice, although I wasn't sure why. It wasn't like speaking softly would change anything about what I was going to tell her. "I found him at the casino and went back to his room with him. I would have killed him if things hadn't turned to shit. A Storm biker saved me. He killed him." We never had secrets and I knew she would keep this information to herself.

Her eyes widened. She knew this was bad news. Monroe had been around the block a few times with me; she understood how this city worked. "Fuck, the fucking irony. You replace one nightmare with another, and they both involve bloody bikers." She frowned. "He left you there?"

I shook my head. "No, he took me with him. I know you don't love Billy, but I'm only breathing today because of my association with him."

She scrubbed a hand over her face. "Jesus, Tatum." Pointing a finger at me, she said, "You have to get out of Sydney now. *Right fucking now!*"

She'd been telling me this for months and I'd been ignoring her, needing to see retribution for Chris's death. What she didn't grasp was that now it was too late. "I can't. Storm have people everywhere, Monroe. You don't escape them. And they have ways of using family to get what they want. I won't put you in it like that."

"Fucking put me in it! I don't care. I just want this to all stop for you." Moving closer to me, she said, "Your life went to shit when Randall screwed you over and I just want to see you smile again."

I took her hand. "I'm safe so long as I don't talk. And I have no plans to do that. I just would have preferred not to get myself on their radar."

She processed that and then said, "Do you want to stay with me?"

I tried not to smile. "So you can keep me safe?"

Her smile matched mine. "Smartass. I could, you know. You might be Lara Croft reincarnated, but I've got skills."

Letting go of her hand, I said, "I know. I've seen you take guys on. You've injured many balls in your life."

"They all deserved it." She sighed. "I'm sick of men, Tatum. Why can't we find the good ones? They have to exist somewhere out there."

"What's your definition of good, though? Maybe you're expecting something that just isn't realistic." I was glad to change the course of the conversation from Storm to her issues with men. Talking about bikers was the last thing I wanted to be doing. And Monroe and I were so close that I knew she'd changed the subject on purpose.

"At this point, I'd settle for a few things—honesty being at the top of the list."

"A-fucking-men. What else?"

"God, I just want someone who knows when to take charge and when to back the fuck off and give me some space. I'm sick and tired of men who want to try to control me, or at the other end of the spectrum, men who don't have any balls to go with their dick. And a guy who picks up after himself would be fucking awesome. Oh, and a piercing or two. Before I die, I need to be fucked with a pierced dick."

I couldn't help it, I laughed. "Good luck on finding a man who picks up after himself. I'm sure the rest should be manageable. And if push comes to shove, surely you could just sleep with a guy who gets his dick pierced here."

She rolled her eyes. "I've told you, I don't sleep with customers."

I shrugged. "You could make an exception for that. It's not like you'd have to see him again."

"Babe, I'm not you. I actually want a relationship and hate one-night stands."

"I don't love one-night stands."

"True, but you also don't want a guy to get too close." She paused for a moment. "Not every guy is Randall."

I sucked in a breath at the mention of him again. "Can we not say his name again today? It's been a bad enough day as it is."

She flicked her long red hair and frowned. "Whose name? I have no idea who you are talking about."

"Yeah, me either." I pushed a stray hair out of my eyes. "I need to ask you a favour."

She smiled. "Anything, you know that."

"One of my girls needs a place to stay while I help her leave the guy she's living with. He's an ass and I'm concerned what he might do once she leaves, so I want to find her a place he would never find her."

"Of course. And if he does come around, remember, I've got skills. I could take him on," she said with a grin.

I laughed. "You could. Thank you, I owe you one."

My phone sounded with a text.

Duvall: All sorted.

Me: My demons thank you.

He didn't reply, so I looked back up at Monroe when she asked, "Who's that?"

"Duvall. I think he's done with me."

"No, he's not. That man has it bad for you."

"Not anymore, but that's a good thing. I don't want to drag him into my shit."

She narrowed her eyes at me. "Did you ever consider dating him when you two got close?"

Memories of Duvall being there for me after my marriage exploded filled my mind. I allowed myself a moment to dwell in them, because while that was one of the hardest times of my life, he'd made me feel hope. But hope wasn't always productive. How could it be when the dark had already consumed you? When you couldn't remember what light looked like anymore.

My shoulders sagged as I answered her honestly. "I thought about being with him. I thought about how different he'd be to what I'd always known in a partner, and I wanted that. But I don't know the first thing about giving that kind of love back, Monroe. I'd ruin Duvall if I gave myself to him, because dark will always kill light."

"Or maybe light would mix some new shinier colours," she said softly.

I loved her for being a dreamer. As much as I'd given up on in life, I still held onto some of my tattered dreams. Monroe was the one person who helped me remember to breathe life into those dreams occasionally.

As I left Monroe's, a text buzzed through.

Duvall: You're wrong. I could never run from your demons.

59

Chapter Nine

Nitro

"The Red" by Chevelle

After Church, I headed over to my sister's house, not sure if I'd find her there or at the bank where she worked. She lived a block from me, having moved out of my place a few years ago.

I found her sleeping on her couch, a bottle of cheap wine still in her hands. Swiping it out of her grip, I crouched next to her. "Lynny, wake up." Finding her in this state was becoming a common occurrence. Marilyn had never been a drinker, but lately she'd started, and I hated watching her sink further into a depressed state.

She stirred as I nudged her.

"You took the day off work?" I asked.

Nodding, she sat up slowly. "Yeah." She grimaced in pain and placed her hand against her forehead. "God, why did you wake me?"

"You feel like hell?"

"Don't give me grief, Nitro. I needed to take the edge off."

I stood. "I get it, but fuck, you're not even trying."

Anger filled her features and she stood, too. "I *have* been trying."

"No," I snapped. "You *were* trying. Now, you've given up, and I'll be fucked if I'm gonna let you fucking give up. Not after everything we've been through already."

I watched as the anger seeped out of her, hating every second of that, because I didn't want her to lose that feeling. You could run on anger, and I needed Lynny to fucking run. "I'm tired of trying. That man...." Her voice drifted off and tears streamed down her face. "He wrecked me, Nitro." Staring at me through those tears, she uttered the words I'd feared for years, "I don't want to try anymore. I'm done."

Fuck.

I wrapped my hands around her biceps and held on tight. "That man is dead. He can't hurt you anymore. And you are *not* fucking done."

"You don't get it. I don't want to go on."

I let her go and she dropped back down to the couch. Raking my fingers through my hair, I paced the small room, my mind turning over possibilities for dealing with this situation. Eventually, I pulled out my phone and called her doctor.

She sat motionless and watched as I made an appointment for her. After I ended the call, I yanked her up and said, "Get dressed, your appointment is in forty minutes."

"He can't help me."

Red blurred my vision and my muscles tensed. Anger punched through me, and while I knew I wasn't so much enraged by her, but by the asshole who did this, I couldn't contain it while around her. One look at my sister and all I could think about was him. And I couldn't stop myself from spewing words laced with the anger that consumed me. "Yes, he can, and he will. And you will let him. I'm not taking no for an answer, Marilyn. You got that?"

She shrunk away from me as I bellowed my order. When I'd finished, she slapped my face. "Fuck you! You're supposed to be on *my* side. You're not supposed to treat me like shit."

61

I forced out a harsh breath and scrubbed my face. This was not going down how it should have. And yet, I kept going, fuelled by a desperate need to save my sister. Yanking her to her bedroom, I ripped open her closet. "Choose something to wear, put it on and meet me in the lounge room within five minutes." I turned to leave the room without waiting for her reply. As I left, I barked, "*This* is me being on your side, Lynny. Fucking deal with it."

* * *

"Thank you."

Eyeing Renee, I nodded. "She fought us all the way, but in the end she agreed to go voluntarily."

I'd just returned from the hospital where Marilyn had been admitted. Her doctor held the same concerns I did, so he'd pushed for her to agree to treatment.

"Should I pack a bag for her and take it to the hospital?"

"Yeah." I checked my watch. "I'll come back in about two hours to take you. I've just got some club stuff to do."

"Okay."

"And you'll stay with me while she's there." At her frown, I added, "Don't argue with me, Renee. I've got some serious shit going on with the club at the moment and I don't need to be worrying about you out there on your own."

Her frown morphed into a scowl. "I swear, you'd think you were my father with the way you carry on."

A text from Hyde distracted me.

Hyde: Where are you? Got a problem with Sutherland.
Me: At Marilyn's.
Hyde: Get ready to leave. We'll swing by.

"I've gotta go," I said to Renee. "A problem's just come up, so I may be longer than two hours. I'll text you to let you know."

"I'll be a good girl and move into your place while you're gone."

"Fucking amazing," I muttered. "A female who listens to me."

"Don't go getting too excited. It won't happen too often."

I shoved my phone in my pocket. "I'm under no illusions."

She grinned. "That's what I love about you."

"What?"

"You might be unpredictable out there in the world, but here with us, you're predictable in all the right ways. You're always here for me and Mum."

I held her gaze. "Always, kiddo."

She didn't know the half of it.

Thank fuck.

* * *

I stared up at the building in front of me before turning to face Hyde. "What's going on? Why the fuck am I standing in front of Billy Jones's strip club?"

"Sutherland has cut us off," Hyde said.

King stepped up onto the footpath. "Dragon got to him."

Jesus.

Sutherland was our gun supplier. We'd discussed the possibility of this happening if we pursued Silver Hell, but I hadn't thought it likely.

"We need ammo, and we need a fuckload of it," Hyde said.

"We stocked up, Hyde. We have time to sort this out," I said. Billy would supply us if need be, but he was the last person I wanted to call on.

"I don't want to take that risk," King said. "I want a plan brought into play today, and Billy is our best option."

"He's also our most expensive option," I pointed out. "I can make some calls, King, work out something else that won't bleed us like Billy will."

"We can do that, too, but I'm not ending this day without knowing this is sorted for now," King said before striding into the club.

Hyde agreed. "I'm with King on this one, Nitro."

Against my better judgement, I followed them. Billy and I didn't have the best history, so fuck knew what would take place when we were in the same room.

A brunette with not much on besides a black dress that barely covered her tits and ass greeted us. Glancing between the three of us, she pasted a hesitant smile on her face. "I'm sorry, but we don't open for another couple of hours."

"We're not here for the show, we're here for Billy," King said.

Smile still in place, she said, "He's not here at the moment, sorry."

King's nostrils flared and he stepped closer to her. "That might be what you tell everyone else, but it's not what you tell me. Let him know that King's here to see him."

She blinked as she faltered on her words. "Honestly, he's not here at the moment."

King's voice darkened with menace. "I don't believe you. Take me to his office." He paused for a moment before barking, "Now!"

Fear chased her smile away and she jumped in fright. She opened her mouth to speak, but no words came out.

"Gentlemen," a commanding female voice sounded from behind us. A voice I knew. "I don't appreciate you intimidating my girls."

Turning, I found Tatum standing with her arms crossed over her chest, a hard glare in place. Black jeans painted her long legs and a leather biker jacket covered her tits. Stilettos gave her height, and her eyes met mine with little effort. "Vegas," I murmured, taken aback. This woman standing in front of me was not at all like the woman I rescued the previous night. Sure, her eye was swollen and her face and neck were bruised from the beating she suffered, but she stood tall and fucking fierce. And as she shifted her gaze between the three of us, she didn't back down.

King moved towards her, snarling. "Tatum Lee, we meet again."

She squared her shoulders. "So it would seem, King."

"Where's Billy?"

"He's stepped out for a couple of hours to deal with a family matter. Can I help you with something?"

King stared at her like she'd lost her mind. "I highly fucking doubt that. I didn't come here for a lap dance."

She uncrossed her arms. "And you wouldn't get one off me even if you did."

He gripped her arm and I caught the wince of pain that escaped her lips. Pulling her to him, he said, "I'm not a fan of your smart mouth, Tatum. Now call your fucking boss and set me up a meeting."

She didn't fight him, didn't even attempt to wiggle out of his hold. Instead, she simply stood there and said, "The last time I saw you, I told you never to touch me again, so take your fucking hands off me and then I'll see what I can do for you."

He continued to hold her for another few moments before eventually shoving her out of his grasp.

With eyes that roared her hatred of him, she held his gaze while pulling out her phone. When Billy answered her call, she turned and walked away from us to talk with him.

I tracked her ass as she moved away. Tatum had an ass made for sin and legs that begged a man to spread them. I imagined cutting those clothes off her and sinking my dick deep inside her. That cunt of hers would—

"Nitro!"

Fuck.

I snapped out of my thoughts to find King staring at me. "What?"

"Bronze texted. The raids on Silver Hell clubs will go down tonight." Bronze had been on our payroll for years and never let us down. If the New South Wales police force knew they had a dirty cop as high in their ranks as he was, they'd probably kill him before they'd admit it to the public. Just over a year ago the state flushed out what they thought to be all their dirty cops, along with the handful of dirty lawyers they had in the DPP. Since then they had heavily promoted their clean force. For Bronze to have survived that, I knew there had to be more amongst their ranks.

"So we need to sort our supply issue out today," Hyde added.

"Yeah, I'm getting that, Hyde," I muttered, my eyes still on Tatum.

She ended her call and came back to us. Eyeing King, she said, "Billy will be back in two hours. He'll see you then."

66

With one last glare at her, he turned and stalked out of the club to his bike. She watched him for a beat and then looked at me. "Your president is an ass."

Hyde scowled at her and left, but I closed the distance between us and said, "You'd do well to keep your thoughts to yourself, Vegas." Unable to stop myself, I dropped my gaze to her chest. The little I could see of her tits was hardly enough, but I took what I could and then looked back up at her.

She lifted a brow. "If you knew me, Nitro, you'd know I never keep my thoughts to myself. And right now, I'm thinking *you'd* do well to keep your eyes off my tits."

"I only take orders from one person in this world and I'm not looking at him."

"So maybe you should turn your ass around and leave so that you *are* looking at him."

I reached out to touch her, wanting to run my finger over those lips that were giving me attitude, but she wrapped her hand around my wrist faster than I saw coming, halting my progress.

"You'd also do well never to touch me without my permission," she said calmly before dropping my arm and turning to leave.

Fuck, she was feisty. I wasn't a fan of attitude off a woman, but I couldn't deny my dick was hard as hell. I wondered what kind of man Tatum Lee usually fucked, because it sure as hell wouldn't be a man like me. I'd have to fuck that feisty out of her and I doubted she'd surrender easily, if at all.

* * *

I sat on my bike in the clubhouse car park later that night, watching as Brittany left. Thunder cracked overhead as another

67

storm threatened. It'd been a long fucking day and my mind ticked over with thoughts of stopping by a club I frequented to find a woman to lose myself in for the night.

"Nitro."

Turning, I found Kick approaching, a look of concern etched on his face.

"What's up?"

"Silver Hell got to that casino surveillance before we did. They're looking for the blonde who was with you."

"Fuck."

"Yeah, I figured that wasn't good news since she's tied up with Billy."

I scrubbed a hand over my face. It definitely wasn't good news. Not after we'd managed to get Billy to agree to supply us with guns and ammo. If Silver Hell found Tatum, they'd kill her, and Billy would blame us as much as them.

"I'll take care of it," I said.

He nodded. "One other thing, I found someone to replace Brittany. Recommended by Nash, so I'm hoping that means she's not gonna cause any problems." Nash was a member of the Brisbane Storm chapter so I figured he wouldn't recommend someone he didn't trust.

Lightning streaked through the sky as I sped out of the car park. So much for finding some pussy for the night. Instead, I'd be finding Tatum Lee.

Chapter Ten

Tatum

"I See Fire" by Ed Sheeran

I stumbled as I tried to avoid the cracks in the path as I walked the short distance between my front gate and my front door. I wasn't sure if it was because of the heels I wore or the rum I'd consumed, but I leaned heavily towards the rum. Unfortunately when I decided to drown my feelings with alcohol, I did a bang-up job of it. My feelings were successfully numbed for the night. The only problem with that was they would all return tomorrow. Missing my brother was something that would never go away.

As I pushed open my front door, a figure emerged from the shadows on my veranda and a deep voice I'd heard too many times that day, spoke into my ear, "You've been drinking, Vegas. Not the best move when people are after you. You're lucky it's me here tonight and not someone else."

As I attempted to process what he said, he placed a hand on the small of my back and guided both of us inside.

Fuck.

He was right; I should have known better. I should have done everything to maintain my vigilance, but the painful memories had assaulted me and rum had been my only escape.

And now Nitro was inside my fucking house.

He directed me down my hallway to the kitchen before my mind finally kicked into gear. As it did, I forced my elbow back into his gut and picked up my pace to move ahead of him.

"Fuck," he swore as I stepped out of his hold.

Turning to face him, I reached into my handbag for the pocketknife I kept there. Flicking it open, I held it between us defensively. "Don't take another fucking step."

Surprise flared in his eyes and he stopped moving. "Go fucking figure," he murmured.

"Go figure what?" I snapped.

He watched me silently for a few moments before stepping forward. His damn reflexes were faster than mine and he swiftly took the knife from me. His hard eyes met mine. "You've got a thing for knives, Vegas?"

I slammed my hands against his chest. "Why the fuck do you keep calling me Vegas?"

A vein pulsed in his temple and he clenched his jaw. "Because you're pretty on the outside but dark and dirty"—he pressed a finger to my chest—"in here."

My breaths lay trapped in my throat as heat flamed my cheeks. I stared at him while self-loathing filled me. He had no idea how right he was. "Fuck you," I spat, taking a step back, almost stumbling again.

With a clenched jaw and flared nostrils, he lunged forward, catching me around the waist. He then backed me up against the wall, pressing his body hard against mine. Our breaths came hard and fast as we glared at each other. "I recognise fucked-up when I see it, Tatum. It's like looking in a fucking mirror."

I wiggled my arms up between our bodies so I could try to force some space between us, even if it was only a tiny amount of distance. The pain this all caused was almost too much, but no way would I show him that. Instead, I focused on breathing through it, hoping it would subside quickly. "I am nothing like you."

He nodded. "Yeah, you are. I've done my research."

I swallowed hard, taking in what he'd said while trying to force my shame away. It didn't matter how many times I told myself I'd moved past my self-disgust, it was a lie; it still consumed me.

When I didn't speak, he continued, "I don't know what drives a lawyer to forget which side of the law she's on, but I'm guessing it was something she's not proud of. And then, after her profession kicks her out, to go to work for the dirty criminals of this city, getting them out of shit any way she can, that says a fuck-of-a-lot about a person. So don't tell me you're not fucked-up because not only do I recognise it, I've read all about it, too."

I pushed against him, but he was too heavy and strong for me, and didn't budge. I wanted to scream at him and kick him and beat against his chest, but I knew it wouldn't get me anywhere. Nitro had me trapped. In the end, I simply said, "What do you want?"

He kept me caged against the wall. "Silver Hell know you were in that room when I killed their man. They're looking for you."

Of course they were.

Fucking brilliant.

"So you've come to save me? Like a white fucking knight?"

Anger growled out of him. "That fucking attitude of yours will get you killed one day, but today is not that day. I'm only here because you mean something to Billy and at the moment he means something to Storm. The minute that changes, you're on your fucking own." He stepped away from me, but kept his hard

71

eyes on mine. "Now, pack some shit, because you're coming with me."

He had to be kidding. "So you can tie me up again and chain me to your fucking bed?"

His boots thudded as he closed the distance between us again. Taking hold of my arm, he yanked me with him while he stalked into my bedroom. I did my best to ignore the pain his grip caused, but it was too intense and a cry fell from my mouth. He scowled at me, as if he wanted me to contain it. "Pack your bag or I'll pack it for you."

He left me then and I sat on my bed, desperate to gather my thoughts. The alcohol hindered my ability to think straight, as did the pain racking my body.

Fuck.

A knock on my front door caused my head to snap up. I groaned when I heard Duvall call out, "Tatum." And when I heard Nitro's boots cut a path to the door, I practically ran in that direction. The last thing I needed was Duvall going up against Nitro.

I arrived just in time to see Duvall's eyes flare with distaste as he took in Nitro. "Who the hell are you?" he asked. He knew the kind of people I worked with, which meant he also understood the risk I took with my personal safety. I guessed he was concerned for me, and that was something I needed to alter if I had any hope of him leaving.

Staring at my friend, willing him to go, I said, "What's up?"

Jerking his chin at Nitro, he said, "*This* is how you're spending your nights now?"

"Careful," Nitro warned in a deep voice. "The next words out of your mouth better not insult either her or me." It surprised me that he'd even care about me being insulted, but I didn't have time to dissect that.

72

Duvall stepped closer and by the angry expression on his face, I knew he was about to disregard that warning, so I cut him off.

"Yes, this is how I'm spending my nights," I said, knowing he'd back down if he believed I was seeing Nitro. He might have wanted to start something with me, but Duvall never cut in on another man's territory.

He pursed his lips. "Really? You're a biker whore now?"

Nitro growled again, anger spilling out of him. When he took a step forward, my instincts took over and I flung an arm out in front of him, covering his chest and halting his progress. His eyes came to mine, a hard glint in them. I returned that look, now willing *him* to not turn this into something more.

I glanced at Duvall as I angled my body towards Nitro and placed my arms around him. "Yes, really. Did you come here to tell me something?" I hated treating him like this but felt it was the only way.

Nitro's body tensed and he didn't reciprocate my gesture. I couldn't see his face, but I could imagine he'd fixed a filthy look on Duvall.

Taking a step back, Duvall said, "No, nothing that can't wait. I'd hate to interrupt you two." With that, he muttered something else under his breath and strode down my path towards his car.

As soon as he was out of sight, I dropped my arms and returned to my bedroom, resigned to the fact I had to go with Nitro. The front door slamming caused me to jump, and a moment later, Nitro filled the doorway to my bedroom. "You ready?"

"No, I'm not ready. I'd barely started thinking about packing when I had to come and stop my friend from trying to take you on."

He crossed his arms over his chest. "You call him a friend?" The way he said it was as if it was the last thing he'd call Duvall.

"Yes." I didn't encourage any further discussion about it, because I had no desire to hear his thoughts.

He had other ideas. "So you're okay with a friend treating you like shit?"

I grabbed an overnight bag from my closet and started packing it. "He didn't treat me like shit."

He cocked a brow. "You really believe that, Vegas?"

I stopped throwing clothes in the bag. "You don't know anything about my friendship with him or why he said the things he did to me."

"That may be the case, but I still don't believe a friend would insult you the way he did. I sure as fuck wouldn't put up with that."

"I'm not interested in what you think. I just want to get through whatever I have to in order to forget I ever met you and your biker friends. Do you think we can do that?"

He dropped his arms. "It'd be my fucking pleasure."

I took a few deep breaths after he left and then finished packing my bag.

One day at a time. That was all I had to do. If I could get through the shit Randall put me through, and the crap I went through at the hands of the legal world, I could survive a biker.

Chapter Eleven

Nitro

"Me, Myself and I" by G-Eazy, Bebe Rexha

Renee stared at me as Tatum and I entered the house. I never brought women home. Ignoring her puzzled expression, I directed Tatum to my bedroom.

She stopped as soon as she realised where I was taking her. "I am *not* sleeping in your bed."

"It's either that or the floor. Take your pick."

She left me to make her way to the couch. Dropping her bag on the floor, she took a seat and stared at the television that Renee was watching.

Renee's eyes widened as she glanced between Tatum and me. "Hi, I'm Renee, Nitro's niece," she said, giving Tatum a smile.

I couldn't see Tatum's face, but I could hear the tightness in her voice when she replied. "Tatum, and I'm Nitro's prisoner."

Renee's smile disappeared. "A prisoner wouldn't come willingly and I'm pretty sure that's what I just saw." Even when she was frustrated or mad with me, that kid was on my side.

"Trust me, if I had a choice I wouldn't be here," Tatum muttered.

"And if you weren't here, you'd be out there dead," I said.

She swivelled in her seat to look at me, as much irritation on her face as I felt. "I could have gone to Billy's. He'd keep me alive."

"When I want someone kept alive, I trust no one to do that job except myself. You'll stay with me until the threat passes."

Bewilderment filled her as she left her seat. Grimacing, she clutched her ribs and said, "That is never gonna happen. That threat could take forever to pass."

"During which time you'll be with me," I barked.

"So what, you're gonna take me with you everywhere you go? And what about my job? I've got shit to do."

"That's what phones are for, Tatum. And yeah, you'll be with me. Where I go, you fucking go." Jesus, she had a way of riling me up that usually only Renee or Marilyn managed to do. I didn't often give a fuck what most women said or did. And I sure as hell didn't spend time arguing with them over it.

She stood fuming at me but didn't utter another word. Eventually, she sat and resumed staring at the television with her arms crossed over her chest.

Renee stole one last glance at the both of us before leaning back in her seat and saying, "Well, this should be fun."

* * *

I yawned as I made coffee the next morning. It had been a long night and I'd only managed about three hours of sleep on and off. Lifting the mug to my mouth, I eyed Tatum as she entered the kitchen. My gaze dropped to the singlet she wore. It was long and covered her ass, but her legs were bare and I couldn't take my eyes off them or the tattoos inked into her skin.

"I need coffee. Your floor is hard as hell," she grumbled.

I leaned against the counter. "All floors are hard as hell. I offered you a bed."

She moved next to me to make her coffee. "Sleeping next to you is the last thing I will ever do."

Her scent wafted in the air and I froze as a long-forgotten memory surfaced. Visions of a smiling woman and three children laughing at the beach filled my mind.

My mother.

The scent Tatum wore was the same one my mother had worn.

I shoved the memories away. Nothing good came from them. I glanced down at Tatum. "Aren't you cold?" I snapped. "It's the middle of fucking winter and you're wearing a singlet."

She looked up at me. "My, aren't you a cuddly teddy in the morning? And since when do you care about my warmth or comfort?"

I drank the rest of my coffee and pushed off from the counter to place my mug in the sink. "Put some clothes on. We're leaving in half an hour."

"I won't be ready in half an hour, Nitro."

I turned back to face her. "Yeah, you will be."

As I left the kitchen, she called after me, "I don't know what kinds of women you've been associating with, but this one does not get ready in half a fucking hour."

Renee passed me in the hallway, already dressed for school. She was an early riser and had probably already completed an hour of study. "You know, I think I kinda like Tatum," she said with a smile.

Ignoring her, I walked outside and sucked some air into my lungs. Between Tatum's attitude, Renee's smartass comments, my sister's mental breakdown, Storm's problems and memories of my mother, this week was going off with a fucking bang.

My phone rang then, and one look at the caller ID told me the week was only just getting started with me.

My brother.

* * *

"I need somewhere to stay," Dustin said ten minutes later when he arrived at my house.

I pushed my fingers through my hair as I listened to my brother. "What happened to the place I found you three weeks ago?" I'd found him a share house and helped him move in, hoping he'd settle there okay. It seemed he hadn't.

His lips flattened in a hard line. "The woman who ran it kicked me out."

"Fuck, what did you do?"

"I didn't do anything. I just tried to kiss her."

Jesus, Dustin would be the fucking death of me.

I slammed my hand down on my table. "I've told you, Dustin, you can't go around kissing women you aren't involved with."

He jumped and his eyes widened. I tried never to lose my temper with him, so my outburst must have confused him. "I don't."

Blowing out a long breath, I said, "Yeah, you do. Problem is, they don't know you like I do, so they don't know you'd never force yourself on them." Dustin was a simple guy looking for love, who had no clue how to attract a woman. Most women didn't give him the time of day so he tried harder than most men had to. Unfortunately, his efforts were mostly misguided and ended up in these kinds of outcomes—him inappropriately touching women, them crying foul and me cleaning up his shit.

"Can I stay here until I find somewhere?" The hopeful look on his face caused my guilt to surface. If it weren't for me, he wouldn't be in this mess in the first place.

I nodded. "Yeah."

A grin broke out on his face and he threw his arms around me. "Thank you, Nitro." *As if I'd caused some miracle to happen.*

The bathroom door opened across the hall from where we stood and a gust of perfume blanketed us. Our attention was drawn to Tatum who exited the room and announced, "I'm good to go. Quickest fucking time I've ever gotten ready, which means you"—she pointed at me—"owe me coffee."

"Wow," Dustin exclaimed while staring at Tatum. She'd dressed in skin-tight jeans again, this time with knee-high boots that had a killer heel. The jeans showed off her legs and ass while the black fitted long-sleeved top she wore could stop traffic. And although bruises and some swelling still painted her face, her beauty couldn't be mistaken.

"Put your tongue back in your mouth," I said, not taking my eyes off her for one second. I didn't need to look at him to know he was drooling. Any straight male would be.

Tatum shifted her gaze to Dustin and did something I hadn't seen yet—she smiled. When she moved to where he stood and extended her hand in greeting, my breathing slowed and my chest expanded. All the tension I'd felt a moment ago vanished and I watched in fascination as she spoke to him.

"Hi, I'm Tatum. I'm guessing you're Nitro's brother." Her smile filled her face while she waited for his reply.

He shook her hand and I knew his shyness had kicked in by the way his body shrunk a little and his eyes turned down. "How can you tell? We don't look anything alike." Even his voice had softened and turned hesitant. Disbelieving. He had a point; no one ever assumed we were brothers.

"Oh, I can tell. You have the same nose and even though your eyes have more sparkle in them, they're the same beautiful brown that his eyes are." I was fairly certain she'd never thought

79

of my eye colour as beautiful, but I appreciated her referring to his as that. God knew, Dustin could do with the confidence boost.

I watched as my brother, for the first time in his life, visibly drew his body up and puffed his shoulders back. Returning her smile, he said, "I'm Dustin."

"It's great to meet you, Dustin." Facing me, she lifted her brows and said, "You're gonna need some more linen and maybe a mattress or two if we're all gonna be staying here."

I fought the smile tugging at my lips. Grabbing my keys off the table, I muttered, "Smartass."

She shrugged. "Just stating facts. I don't wanna sleep on that floor again."

I held her gaze. "And I told you how to avoid that."

She pursed her lips but didn't say anything else on the subject.

"Can I come, too?" Dustin asked.

I shook my head. "No, you stay here. There's ice cream in the freezer and noodles in the cupboard." His two favourites.

His face lit up. "And Netflix."

Tatum smiled. "Netflix is the best."

He turned his grin to her and nodded. "It really is."

Renee joined us. "Are we still on for this afternoon?"

I frowned. "What's this afternoon?"

"You were going to take me out driving so I could clock up some more hours."

"Sure. Five?"

She nodded and then headed into the kitchen.

I eyed Tatum and jerked my chin towards the front door. "Let's go, Vegas."

The smile she'd given Dustin disappeared. "Joy," she said sarcastically before traipsing out to my garage.

80

I ignored her sarcasm and instead focused on her ass. Not a bad trade-off at all.

Chapter Twelve

Tatum

"We've Gotta Get Out Of This Place" by The Angels

Rain beat down on the roof of Nitro's ute as he drove us to a destination unknown to me. This weather was depressing as hell. I'd never been a fan of rain that lasted longer than a day. Looking out the window, I saw puddles of mud everywhere, which only further depressed me. Mud meant dirt and water that found its way into your shoes and onto your clothes if you accidentally stepped too hard in it or if a car sloshed it at you. Mud was messy. I hated messy.

"Where are we going?" I demanded, turning to face him.

Those brown eyes of his met mine, and a shiver struck me at what I saw there. "Thanks for what you said to Dustin back there." The words pretty much choked themselves out of him. I doubted Nitro was a man known for giving thanks.

I nodded as his emotions washed over me. This was a whole other side to Nitro. "How old is Dustin?"

"Thirty-four."

"That's younger than you?"

He glanced at me again but didn't reply straight away. I wasn't sure if he would, but then he did. "Yeah, two years."

"I've worked with a lot of guys like Dustin, guys who get themselves into trouble because people confuse their intentions in all sorts of situations. Just because they don't process shit as fast as the rest of us doesn't make them any less of a person." I'd overheard his conversation with Dustin about women misunderstanding his behaviour and had heard Nitro's worry for his brother. His concern showed a new side to him that I'd been surprised to discover.

"You took on their cases?"

"Yes."

"How did they afford you?"

I angled my body so I leant against the window, facing his direction. "Some had family that paid, but a lot I took on for free or cheap. Billy brought a lot of them to me for help."

He frowned. "Billy?" The name dripped from his mouth in distaste.

"Yes, Billy. A lot of people think he's the scum of the earth—"

"That's because he *is* the scum of the earth."

"Not always, Nitro. Sometimes the man surprises you."

Silence settled between us for a few minutes while we each turned over our thoughts. I ended up breaking it when I said, "So, you have a brother and a sister. Is she younger than you, too?"

His grip on the steering wheel tightened as he nodded. "Marilyn's five years younger than me."

"And your parents? They're still alive?" I wasn't sure what fuelled me to keep talking, but that sliver of emotion I'd seen from him had gotten to me. It made me want to figure out why he was the way he was. It was the lawyer in me—always digging, searching, wondering what made people tick so I could figure out their next likely move.

His knuckles whitened as he squeezed the wheel even harder. "I'm not here to talk about my family," he snapped.

It figured. I was actually surprised he'd given me what he had. But still, I wanted more. Shifting in my seat, I said, "You didn't tell me where we're going."

"To the clubhouse."

My phone rang.

Billy.

"Tatum, where the fuck are you?" he demanded when I answered his call.

"And good morning to you, too, Master."

"This isn't the time for your smart mouth. I'm standing outside your house and you're not here. And I fucking need you."

"I'm not there because I was kidnapped by a biker last night and I'm with him." I ignored Nitro's grunt next to me.

"What the fuck?"

I sighed. "I'm okay. But apparently Silver Hell want me dead because of my involvement in their member's death the other night and Storm want to keep me alive. They sent one of their guys to look after me until this all blows over. The only catch is I have to stay with him."

"Jesus, the shit you get yourself into. How the hell am I supposed to get stuff done without you?"

"I can work from anywhere, Billy. What do you need?"

"I could protect you, you realise. You don't need to do what Storm say."

"I don't think they're gonna let me go."

He was silent for a moment. "We'll see. But until then, I need you to work on Graham's defence. They formally charged him last night." Graham was one of Billy's security guys who'd managed to get himself into some trouble over a fight between club patrons. He'd punched one of the guys a few times too many and the cops had been brought into it.

84

"Shit. Okay, can you email whatever you have and I'll work on that today. Is Jensen taking the case?" *One of the lawyers Billy used.*

"Yeah."

"Good. I like working with him."

"I'll send the file when I get back to the office. And Tatum, I'm getting you out of there." He hung up before I could respond.

Dammit.

This was going to get messy.

Turning my face to the window, I counted to ten slowly and took a few deep breaths while focusing my thoughts.

"You still do law work even though you were disbarred?"

Looking back at Nitro, I said, "I don't practice law anymore, but I advise the lawyers that Billy hires."

"As in, they're puppets doing whatever you tell them to?"

"That's one way to put it."

He stopped at a red light and stared at me. "You must be good."

"I am. I dig for the shit that can't be found easily, and put in the hours most don't want to. And I figure out how to make whatever I find work for us."

"You win every case for him?"

I nodded. "I haven't lost a case in years."

You're so full of shit, Tatum. You even believe your own lies. Lying to win doesn't really count as winning.

My stomach knotted with guilt and self-hate.

Not wanting to talk anymore, I said, "Your niece seems like a good kid."

"She is," he said before we fell into silence again. Exactly the path I'd hoped the conversation would take.

It was the truth about Renee. After Nitro took me back to his house last night, they'd discussed some family stuff they had going on. I'd deduced her mother was in hospital due to her current mental health, and it appeared that Renee was perhaps more able to care for herself than her mother was. It also seemed to me that she got away with a bit where Nitro was concerned. She'd given him hell for a few things and he'd let her. That had both surprised me and impressed me. It was another side to Nitro I wouldn't have expected.

And then he'd grunted at me about my sleeping choice and gone to bed after I reiterated that I would not be sleeping there with him. Renee had set me up with a pillow and blankets. She'd also apologised that there was only one couch and she had taken it.

I stared at the rain streaming down the front windscreen of the car and thought about Nitro. He was turning out to be a contradiction, but then, I should never have doubted that. If there was one thing I'd learnt in my line of work, people always were. Especially the troubled ones.

We reached our destination and, after making his way through the two security checkpoints, he pulled the car into a car park that was miles from the front door of the clubhouse. The reason being, that there were a lot of bikes there that morning.

I met Nitro at the front of the ute. "You having a meeting here today?" I asked, glancing at all the bikes as we walked towards the clubhouse.

"You could say that." He jerked his chin at a biker who we passed on the way. "Slider."

The guy nodded in response. "Nitro."

"You boys are big on conversation."

He stared down at me and ignored my sarcasm. "We get the job done."

Another sarcastic comment died as it left my mouth when a loud bang sounded from behind us. Shock rippled through me as confusion set in, and Nitro's arm came around my shoulders right before he pushed me to the ground.

My ears rang with the sound of an explosion and the vibrations of it slammed into me. A scream tore from my mouth, but I couldn't hear it and I couldn't feel it. Numbness set in as I tried like hell to process what was happening.

Nitro's body covered mine, his strong arms sheltering me from the terror of what was happening.

I was suffocating.

Couldn't breathe.

My chest is going to explode.

And then—"Vegas, you breathing?" Nitro's heavy body moved off mine and he pulled me up.

I stared into his concerned eyes, surprised to see worry there. It was all I could focus on. Even the pain ricocheting through me didn't register. *Why is he bothering to check on me?*

"Tatum!" he barked, shaking me. "You good?"

Men ran past us.

Yelling.

Bodies colliding.

Confusion.

Anger.

And all the while, Nitro stayed with me, making sure I was all right.

I blinked. Nodding, I croaked, "Yeah, I'm good."

His chest heaved with a heavy breath. "Go inside and wait for me."

He let me go, and when I didn't move, he yelled, "Now!"

87

My attention drifted beyond him and I took in the car that had exploded. As the realisation settled in my bones that we'd been that close to danger, I turned and ran towards the clubhouse.

What the fuck had I gotten myself into?

Chapter Thirteen

Nitro

"Live And Let Die" by Guns N' Roses

King barked orders like he was running World War III. It felt like he was. The bomb in Slider's car had killed him and injured three more members who had been entering the grounds on their bikes. They'd been lucky to escape death.

A hand landed on my shoulder and I turned to find Hyde behind me. "You and I are gonna round up some boys and go take a look at Silver Hell's clubhouse. I have a feeling they're not gonna be there, and wanna confirm it before we set new plans in play."

"We also need to sort out what we're gonna do with our families, Hyde. Our resources will be spread thin now, too thin to allocate a watch over everyone." Ever since we'd realised Silver Hell's agenda to harm club members' families, we'd stationed men to watch over them. We needed those men back after this and I'd be fucked if I was gonna leave Renee and Dustin out there on their own with this kind of threat hanging over us. I wanted them at the clubhouse, safe.

"Yeah. You round up the boys while I discuss that with King," he agreed and left me to go talk with King.

* * *

Two hours later, Hyde, Devil, Kick and I entered our clubhouse after verifying that Silver Hell were nowhere to be found. We'd checked their clubhouse, as well as the bars and clubs we knew they frequented. After that, we called around to see if anyone knew where they were, and were met with silence. Either no one knew or they weren't talking.

Chaos had broken out while we were gone. We returned to find the clubhouse packed with men, women and kids. The noise was deafening, the tension visible.

Pushing our way through to the office, the four of us relayed what we'd discovered to King.

"This had to be Silver Hell," he said.

Hyde nodded. "Seems that way."

King's face hardened. "I want them flushed out, and I don't care how we do it. Visit all their strip clubs, all their friends, anyone and everyone, and find out where they are."

His phone sounded with a call and he dismissed us as he pressed it to his ear.

I was halfway down the hallway outside of his office when he called me back. "You look like you wanna kill me," I said when I stood in front of him again.

"That blonde is proving to be a fucking headache, Nitro."

"Why?"

He held his phone up. "That was Billy. He's outside and wants her to leave with him. Says he'll reconsider our new agreement for him to supply weapons and ammo if we don't allow her to leave."

"I'll take care of it."

"Make sure you take care of it so that it never causes me another headache."

I lifted my chin at him signalling I would and then stalked out of his office to find Tatum.

I found her sitting in the clubhouse bar talking to a woman behind the bar who I'd never met. "Vegas," I barked, cutting in on their conversation.

Her head whipped around and I was met with a glare. "I'm in the middle of a conversation."

Ignoring that, I said, "I need you to come with me."

She remained silent for a good few moments. I figured she was weighing her options, but there were none to be had and she figured that out fast. Sliding off her stool, she said goodbye to the woman and followed me out of the bar.

I led her outside to the front gate where Billy waited. The expression on his face was pure rage. "What the fuck, Nitro? I'm not good enough to enter your fucking clubhouse?"

Before I could answer, Tatum cut in. "What are you doing here, Billy? I told you I couldn't leave."

His eyes darted between the two of us before settling on her. "And I told you I could protect you. You don't need to stay with him." The contempt was clear in his voice. Billy and I had a hard history.

I spoke up. "She's not going anywhere, Billy. Silver Hell has her on their radar. They get to her, you'll come after us, and that's not something we need."

He stepped closer to me. "I don't think you understand that if you *don't* allow her to come, I'm pulling our deal."

I held my ground. "No, you're not."

His lip curled up. "Get King here. I'm sick of talking to an idiot who doesn't know what's good for his club."

Fury punched through me, and not just for this conversation, but for the shit he'd put Marilyn through in the past. Gripping his shirt, I snarled, "King's busy. You'll deal with me—"

"I'm not leaving," Tatum cut in.

We both faced her.

91

"What the fuck?" Billy snapped.

She pushed her shoulders back. "I said, I'm not leaving."

"Jesus, Tatum," he muttered, and I sensed the kind of irritation that sounded like it was common between them. "Why do you always have to argue with me over shit?"

"Why do you always have to try to control me?"

He scrubbed his hand over his face, pissed off. "You stay with him, I can't guarantee your safety."

"I'm not asking you to, Billy. I'm asking you to trust that I know what I'm doing."

"I do trust you. I'm just wondering why the hell you're choosing a biker you've just met over me who you've known for years?"

"I have my reasons." Tatum projected an image of strength but somewhere in those words I heard that waver. And like Billy, I had to wonder why she willingly chose Storm over him.

Stepping away from him, I said, "I'll be by tomorrow to pick up our supplies."

His eyes bored into mine, full of hatred and venom. "I'm not sure I want to supply you anymore."

I didn't have a chance to reply before Tatum went to battle. "Billy, whatever you've got going on with Storm has nothing to do with me. They saved me from that asshole and now they're looking out for me again. If I really wanted to leave, there's not a damn thing Nitro could do to keep me. It's my choice to stay. Don't base your business decisions on this."

Billy's hate-filled expression didn't alter as he took a step back, but he listened to everything she said. "Send someone else tomorrow, Nitro. I don't ever want to see you again."

As he strode away from us, Tatum said, "What the hell happened between you two?"

"A lotta shit a long time ago," I muttered before stalking back inside the clubhouse.

Shit I'd never forget. And if I was the kind of man who forgave, I'd never forgive it either.

* * *

After I dealt with Billy, I searched for Renee and Dustin in the clubhouse. I'd called them earlier to let them know it wasn't safe to stay at the house. They'd both promised to be at the clubhouse by the time I returned. However, I couldn't find either of them anywhere. Instead, I found Tatum.

"Vegas, you seen Renee or Dustin?"

She glanced up at me from the table she sat at in the bar. "No, should they be here?"

"Yeah. It's not safe for them to be out there on their own." I pulled out my phone and sent both a text.

"Do you want me to go get them? Like, if you have other stuff to do, I could take your ute and find them."

I paused as her words settled over me. It was an offer I wasn't used to people making. In my world, help didn't often come from those outside my family or the club. And I didn't much trust anyone else. But whichever way I looked at it, I couldn't see what Tatum would be angling for by making the offer.

When I didn't reply, she pursed her lips and said, "Or not. If you don't want my help, that's fine, too."

I pulled out the seat across from her and sat down. Tension rolled across my shoulders as unease punched its way through my body. "Why did you choose to stay here rather than go with Billy?"

"You were hardly going to let me go."

93

"Billy went into bat for you. I would've thought you'd have let him try harder."

"I'm not dumb, Nitro, I could see a problem ahead for you if I hadn't chosen to stay. Billy would never have let it go."

"Since when do you care about my problems?"

Her eyes searched mine as silence hung between us. She sat back in her seat and crossed her arms. "I wouldn't exactly say I care about your problems. I just didn't want any part of Billy losing his shit with you."

I turned that over in my mind. Something still didn't gel for me. "I'd imagine you see Billy lose his shit often."

"I do."

I leaned forward. "So why did you care about that happening between us?"

"Why do you care why I care?"

"My job is to keep you safe. I don't need any surprises catching me off guard, so I want to know the shit running through your mind."

"Bullshit. What's running through my mind has nothing do with your ability to keep me safe."

I slid my chair closer to her, taking note of the way her whole body tensed. "Maybe I just wanna know why you chose to stay here with me."

Her breathing slowed a fraction and she remained silent for a beat. She lowered her voice when she finally answered my question. "You've saved my life twice now. Both times you didn't have to. I don't know why I chose to stay with you, but if someone helps me when they get nothing out of it, it means something to me."

Not the answer I expected.

Not by a long shot.

I stood and reached for her phone. After I sent myself a text so I had her number, I said, "I'll text you when I'm ready. You can come with me to find them. It'll give you a break from the noise here. Turning to leave, I paused and added, "I did get something out of it, Vegas. I kept Billy on side."

Her voice filtered through the crowd as I walked away. "Not the first time."

Chapter Fourteen

Tatum

"Voodoo Child" by Rogue Traders

The silence in Nitro's ute was bliss. After a morning of being cooped up in the clubhouse with rowdy bikers and their family members, I craved the peace and quiet. Nitro had taken forty minutes or so to text after he left me in the bar, and I hadn't hesitated to meet him out the front when the message came through.

"You waiting on a call?" he asked after about fifteen minutes of us keeping to ourselves.

I looked up from my phone that I held in my hands. "Yeah, from my cousin. One of my girls is staying with her at the moment and I just want to make sure she's doing okay. Her boyfriend is an ass and it wouldn't surprise me if he's gotten in her head and convinced her to go home."

"Does she usually take this long to return your calls?"

"No." And that had me worried.

He nodded but didn't say anything further. We drove the rest of the way to his house in silence, but instead of my mind being focused on Monroe for that time, my thoughts were completely fixated on Nitro. I wondered what had happened to him in life that made him so closed off? I'd met a lot of men who didn't do much talking, but none quite as detached as Nitro. As much as I didn't want it to be the case, the man fascinated me. Because while he appeared to be a moody asshole, I'd become convinced there was a lot more to him under all that. It was probably buried deeper than most people would be willing to search, but I wasn't most people.

He pulled his ute into the driveway of his house and jumped out. I followed him inside as fast as I could in an effort to escape the rain. Nitro's home was as cold as he was and I shivered as I entered it. Following him down the hallway, it struck me again how bare his home was. Each room had the absolute necessities in it; actually, some rooms didn't even have that. Two out of the three bedrooms were completely empty of furniture, the lounge room had only a couch and television, and besides those rooms, there was only a kitchen, dining room, bathroom and laundry.

"How long have you lived here?" The words were out before I could stop them.

Nitro didn't slow down to answer me; he simply called over his shoulder, "Fifteen years."

"*Fifteen years?*"

He finished searching the bedrooms and turned to face me. Frowning, he replied, "Yes, fifteen years."

"Why don't you have any furniture if you've lived here that long?"

Staring at me like I'd asked the world's most redundant question, he said, "I gave it to my sister when she and Renee moved out."

"They've just moved out?"

"No, they got their own place a few years ago." He continued his search of the house while I followed blindly behind him, unable to let go of my need to understand him.

"And you still haven't replaced the furniture?"

He stopped abruptly and gave me his attention again. "Why the twenty questions, Vegas?"

I held his gaze. "I'm trying to figure out why you don't have any furniture."

"No, you're trying to figure out *me*. You're a lawyer, it's what you do. But I'm telling you now, there's nothing to figure out. I'm a man who has no interest in furniture or decorating or any of that bullshit, so quit with all the questions."

I stepped closer, leaving very little space between us. "I don't believe that, Nitro."

"Believe what?"

"That there's nothing to figure out. I think there's a lot you keep hidden."

His nostrils flared and when he spoke again, his voice held a dangerous tone. "Last night you wanted nothing to do with me. I'm not sure what the fuck happened between then and now, but let's go back to the way we were."

My lips spread out in a grim smile. "That's the thing about life... We can't often go back to the way things were."

"Yeah, well, *we* can, and we will." His words fell out in a harsh directive before he pushed past me and stalked to the front door. When he reached it, he called out, "Wait here while I go check for Dustin at Marilyn's house. Lock the door after I leave." With that, he left, the front door banging after him.

I strode to the door and locked it.

God, he could be a prick. A moody, stubborn prick who I would avoid if I knew what was good for me.

It seemed I never quite learnt my lessons very well in life.

* * *

He'd been gone for about ten minutes when two men snuck into his front yard, balaclavas in place, and guns in their hands. I'd been keeping watch from the front window of his lounge room when they appeared.

98

They were almost to his front door when one of their phones rang. The guy with the phone paused to answer it while the other one waited behind him. A short conversation ensued before the guy with the phone slipped it back into his pocket and said something to his mate. They then continued their trek towards the front door.

My fingers curled around the gun I'd found stashed in Nitro's cupboard when I searched it just after he left me alone. I hadn't been able to resist snooping, but had been disappointed when all I'd found was the gun. As well as owning very little furniture, he didn't keep many personal belongings.

I watched as Nitro entered the yard, picked up his pace and advanced on the two guys fast. A few moments later, he punched the guy at the back in the head, causing him to stumble forward. With the element of surprise, he managed to wrap his arm around his neck and knock the gun out of his hand.

The guy struggled, trying to shift Nitro's arms. As he fought, his friend turned around to help him, but Nitro pointed his gun in his direction. "Stay where you are or you'll stop breathing," he barked.

The guy ignored Nitro's threat and immediately lunged at him. Nitro fired, but the guy had ducked low enough when he'd lunged to avoid the bullet. When he landed, it was with enough force to knock all three of them to the ground. A fight then broke out, and I feared that Nitro was at a disadvantage being on his own against two.

Exiting the house, I made my way to where they fought. Nitro's eyes briefly met mine as he knocked one guy flat on his back before turning to deal with the other guy who was right behind him. I didn't miss the scowl in his glance, but chose to ignore it. Pointing the gun I held at the guy Nitro had just knocked down, I said, "Don't move, asshole."

He stared up at me, his eyes holding a clear challenge. "Or what, blondie?" As he said the words, he moved to stand.

Without hesitating, I shifted the gun so it aimed at his leg, and I pulled the trigger. "Or I'll fucking shoot."

"Motherfucking bitch!" he roared, his agony spilling out all over the place.

The gunshot slowed him, but it didn't stop him completely. Figuring from the way he moved that I must have only grazed him with the bullet, I took aim again. That time, the bullet did what I wanted it to—it slowed him right down, planting him on the ground, clutching at his bullet wound. A string of expletives and threats spewed from his mouth, but my attention had already shifted to Nitro.

"You got a spare bullet there, Vegas?" He had the other guy on his knees facing me. Nitro had his arm around his neck in a vice grip, and the guy struggled for breath while trying to claw his way out of the choking hold.

I nodded. "Where do you want it?"

"In his leg."

As I took aim and shot, a black van screeched into Nitro's driveway and two Storm bikers jumped out. Everything happened in a blur after that. Nitro and the two bikers quickly moved the two men into the back of the van and then the vehicle and all the men were gone, leaving me staring at Nitro in surprise.

"Where did they come from?" I asked as he guided me inside his house.

"I saw their bikes on my way back here from Marilyn's and called King for backup."

I jumped as he slammed the door closed behind us. Staring at him, I processed the anger written across his face. Anger that seemed to be directed at me rather than at what just happened. "What?" I demanded, tensing for an argument.

"I gave you one directive when I left the house—stay inside." His eyes flashed with as much fury as his body seemed filled with.

"You needed help so—"

"No, I didn't. What I needed was to know you were inside away from those assholes."

"I seem to recall that you asked me to put a bullet in one of those guys *after* I already did the same thing to the other guy. How is that *not* needing my help?" God, he was so damn infuriating.

"While I appreciated that, I would have preferred for your safety to not have been compromised."

"My safety wasn't compromised so I don't know why you're carrying on about it."

He blew out a long breath and raked his fingers through his hair. "I'm carrying on about it because I don't want this kind of shit to happen again."

We faced off, both glaring at each other in silence for a few moments. I was annoyed as fuck at his inability to admit my help was appreciated, but the lawyer in me took the time to think through what he'd said and why.

Finally, the tension in my shoulders eased and I said, "You were worried about me."

He blinked and his breathing slowed. It took him a beat to reply, and when he did, it came out a little snappish. "Of course I was. The last thing I need is Billy coming down on me because you got hurt."

I shook my head. "No," I said quietly, "you were worried about me and it had nothing to do with Billy."

His face clouded over and he clenched his jaw. "Tatum, we don't have time to stand around arguing over this. You need to get our ass outside and in my ute so we can find Dustin and Renee and then get back to the clubhouse." He barked his orders like he was used to them being carried out.

Stepping closer to him, I said, "I'm not sure why you can't just admit you were worried about me, Nitro. It's okay to care about someone's safety." With that, I pushed past him so I could head out to his damn ute. Bloody men and their inability to admit when they cared about someone.

Chapter Fifteen

Nitro

"Kick Start My Heart" by Alannah Myles

I'd had enough of Tatum Lee and her argumentative ways. The woman seemed intent on pushing as many of my buttons as possible. Every time I thought we were getting somewhere and that she would just do as I said, she managed to get under my skin, again.

And yet, she fucking impressed the hell out of me. When she'd put a bullet in the Silver Hell member without flinching, and then done it again, I'd watched in awe. I wanted to wring her neck for not staying inside while at the same time, I wanted to rip her fucking clothes off and see just what she was made of.

I wanted to know if she fucked the way she seemed to live— full of passion and fierce energy. And that shit right there sent alarm bells ringing all over the damn place because wanting to know that about a woman wasn't something that ever interested me.

I turned to her, my hands squeezing tightly around the steering wheel as I thought about her naked body wrapped around mine. "What's your cousin's address?"

She'd been silently watching the streets pass by as I drove. At my question, she faced me, a frown set across those gorgeous lips of hers. "Why?"

"So you can check on her."

"What about Dustin?" Renee had texted just after we'd left my place to say she was at the clubhouse, so Dustin was the only one we still needed to find.

"I'm pretty sure I know where he is. The fact Silver Hell sent two members to my house just now tells me they didn't send anyone earlier, so I'd say he's safe and we have time to look in on your cousin."

"I thought you were in a hurry to get back to the clubhouse."

I gripped the steering wheel even tighter. "Fuck, Tatum, do you ever stop questioning shit?" I glanced at her as I asked this and caught the flattening of her lips as she stared at me.

A moment passed, and then she rattled off an address before adding, "Thank you."

I gave a quick nod and steered the car in the direction of her cousin's place.

Fifteen minutes later, we pulled up outside a tattoo parlour. I cut the engine and turned to her again. "She works here?"

Reaching for the door handle, she shook her head. "No, she owns it."

As I followed her inside, I wondered who I was about to meet. If her cousin was anything like Tatum, I'd have my hands full.

* * *

"Monroe, meet Nitro, the pain-in-my-ass biker who likes to boss me around," Tatum said, gesturing towards me before adding, "Nitro, meet Monroe Lee, my cousin."

Monroe eyed me warily before asking Tatum, "This is the biker who saved you?"

Tatum nodded.

The wary glint in Monroe's eyes didn't leave, and resentment crept into her voice as she said to me, "Why can't you leave her alone? She's done nothing to you or your club."

Before I could reply, Tatum held her hand up. "It's okay, Roe, he's actually trying to keep me alive. Silver Hell found out I was there the other night." Her eyes met mine. "But he does like to issue orders left, right and centre, which is annoying as hell."

Her cousin didn't back down and I saw Tatum's feistiness in her. They looked nothing alike—Monroe had voluptuous curves and huge tits whereas Tatum's curves were much smaller, and Monroe had flaming red hair in contrast to Tatum's blonde— but their inner fight seemed the same.

Monroe squared her shoulders and challenged me. "So you'll keep her alive and then let her out of your sights?"

"I don't make promises to anyone."

"Figures," she muttered, her glare not letting up. I had to respect a woman who stood her ground.

"Why haven't you been returning my calls and texts this morning?" Tatum asked, diverting her cousin's attention. "I've been worried about you."

Something passed between the two women and Monroe's eyes softened. "I'm sorry, I forgot to charge my mobile and I paid the shop's phone bill late, so they suspended my service."

Tatum let out a long breath and her body visibly relaxed a little. "Thank God."

Monroe touched her on the arm. "Posey's okay. She's out the back with Fox, giving him a haircut."

Tatum frowned. "Huh?"

"Yeah, who knew your girl was a hairdresser as well as a stripper? We've been quiet this morning and got to chatting, and when he found this out, he asked her to cut his hair." Her gaze

105

zeroed in on Tatum's face. "How are you? That eye still looks nasty."

"I'm sore, but I'm okay."

"That eye's gonna take a little while to heal and so are her ribs," I said.

Monroe's attention swung swiftly back to me. "If it wasn't for bloody bikers, she wouldn't be in this mess," she snapped.

I stepped forward and got in her face. "Careful," I warned. "Far as I can see, Tatum got herself into that mess."

Monroe's eyes flashed with venom and she shoved her face closer to mine, which intrigued me. These Lee women seemed to have no fear. "Because a *biker* murdered her brother!"

Tatum slid between us, her back to me, and forced Monroe away. "Let it go, Roe. Nitro hated that man as much as I did."

"I don't get it, Tatum. Yesterday you wanted nothing to do with Storm and now you're defending *him*."

"A lot can happen in a day. I'll fill you in later, okay?"

Monroe sent one last glare my way before agreeing to what Tatum had asked. It was obvious to us all, though, that the last thing she wanted to do was let it go.

"Tatum," a petite blonde woman said as she entered the parlour from a back room. She walked with hesitation, her eyes not meeting mine. "Did Dwayne go by the club last night?"

"I haven't heard anything to say he did," Tatum replied. "How are you doing?"

Before she could answer, a guy joined us. Tattoos covered almost every inch of skin I could see, and I figured the familiarity between him and Monroe that he worked with her.

Leaning casually against the front counter of the parlour where we stood, he frowned at Tatum. "Who the fuck gave you those bruises, T?"

I folded my arms across my chest and clenched my jaw. This guy may have been familiar with Monroe, but there was something intimate about the way he spoke to and looked at Tatum. *Something that irritated the fuck out of me.*

"No one important, Fox, and he won't ever do it again," Tatum said. The fact she seemed closed off to discussing it with him caused the tension in my shoulders to ease a little.

"Yeah, well if he does come back, you call me, okay? I'll take care of him for you, babe."

"He won't be back," I grunted, unfolding my arms. "And I've got Tatum under control."

Her gaze swung to meet mine and she raised her brows. "You've got me under *control?*"

"I've got the situation under control." I didn't let her gaze go.

"Yeah, that's better," she said, irritation still clear in her tone.

We stood watching each other for a few moments, a new tension settling between us. It was as if everyone else in the room faded away leaving only the two of us. Again, I found myself facing an inner battle of being both frustrated with her and turned on, all at the same time. This was an unfamiliar feeling and it unsettled me. I usually kept sex separate to every other part of my life. The women I fucked weren't women I associated with, and I never formed a relationship with any of them. Brittany was the exception to that and my association with her hadn't turned out well.

Monroe's voice cut through my awareness. "No one controls Tatum, Nitro."

Without taking my eyes off Tatum, I said, "I'm getting that impression."

Fox pushed off from the counter. As he moved past Tatum, he placed his hand on her stomach and slid it across her body as he said, "I've missed you, T. You should call me."

She gave him a smile, and although it seemed vacant and didn't reach her eyes, I couldn't help balling my fists at my side.

Fuck.

My stomach churned with annoyance, which in itself also pissed me off. What did I care if he was fucking Tatum? She was nothing to me. Nothing but a woman I had to keep alive for my club.

And yet I couldn't deny that the sight of his hand on her stomach sent a wave of fury through me. I didn't want his hand anywhere on her body.

Chapter Sixteen

Tatum

"Break On Me" by Keith Urban

I eyed King warily. The man scared me, and it wasn't often I said that about anyone. Nitro and I had arrived back at the clubhouse hours earlier after finding Dustin and since then, Nitro had been busy with club stuff. I spent the afternoon catching up on work in the bar as well as chatting with Renee. King had wandered through the bar a few times, directing a glare my way each time. There was something about him that I wasn't quite sure of. What I did know for certain, though, was that King was a man to be kept at arm's length. The sooner I escaped his radar, the better.

"He's okay," Renee said, dragging my attention back to her.

"Who? King?"

She nodded. "Yeah." At my frown, she continued, "I know he comes across as freaking scary, but he's helped our family a lot over the years. Don't get me wrong, I wouldn't cross him, but I definitely know he's loyal to those who are loyal to him."

I looked back over at King who stood near the entrance to the bar. He was deep in conversation with one of the club members, a nearly bald guy who glanced at me a few times while they talked.

Turning back to Renee, I said, "All I know is that for those he has no loyalty to, he's unpredictable and can be an asshole. And word on the street is that he's a man to avoid, so it'd be fair to say I'm not impressed by him."

She smiled. "I like that about you, Tatum."

"What?"

"That you say it like it is. And that you don't let Nitro get away with shit." At my surprise, she added, "He might be my uncle and I might love him to death, but he can be a jerk. He's way too bossy and I like that you challenge him."

I laughed. "You're smart for a teen, you know that?"

She stared at me in mock offence. "Are you saying teens aren't smart?"

As she spoke, my attention shifted from her to the bald club member King had been talking to. He made his way to us and rested his hands on the backs of our chairs. "Tatum, you got a minute?"

Looking up at him, I asked, "Who are you?"

"Devil."

I liked that he asked me rather than bossed me into giving him a minute. "Sure," I said, standing and following him out of the bar to a kitchen.

I was surprised to find Nitro there, his head down while he scrolled on his phone. When Devil and I entered, he looked up but didn't say anything before going back to what he was doing on his phone.

He'd pretty much ignored me since we left Monroe's. He ran so hot and cold with me, but since he'd spoken to Fox, he'd been like ice. I hadn't asked him yet, but I wondered if he knew Fox somehow, because irritation had rolled off him while in Fox's presence.

"What's up?" I asked Devil, ignoring Nitro.

"Got a question for you about Billy. How likely is he to renege on a deal?"

110

"Your gun deal with him, you mean?"

"Yeah."

"Usually I'd say that if you don't piss him off, you'll have no worries. The fact he's pissed off at Nitro doesn't help you."

Nitro's head snapped up. "In other words, you're telling us he's unreliable."

"No, what I'm telling you is that *you* shouldn't be involved in the deal at all."

He scowled. "That's not practical. We don't make deals with assholes who dictate which member they will and won't work with."

"There's always a first time for everything, Nitro."

"No," he said, his voice rising, "there's not. Not for me."

"God, are you always this frustrating?" His refusal to bend did my head in. As far as I could see, this was a no-brainer. All they had to do was get another club member to take over this deal.

He shoved his chair back and stood, his chest puffing out as he pushed his shoulders back. "I'm trying to get shit done for my club, and all we need to know is one simple thing, Tatum—will your asshole boss go back on the deal we made with him?"

I stepped closer to him. I had no idea what caused him to get so worked up this fast, but I was just as worked up now. "I don't like you referring to him as an asshole all the time. And I've answered your damn question. You stay out of it and there won't be any problems." With that, I stalked out of the kitchen back to the bar. Trying to have a rational conversation with Nitro was ridiculously hard, and it was safer for me to leave than to keep arguing with the man.

Pulling up a stool at the bar, I ordered a drink. If I had any luck, it'd put all the irritation out of my mind for a few hours.

* * *

111

"Tatum, I think you've had enough for tonight," Renee said at around ten that night.

I blasted a smile her way and raised my glass. "I'm only getting started." With that, I emptied my glass and placed it on the bar for a refill.

The chick behind the bar had kept the drinks coming all night and she didn't let me down. Swiping the glass, she said, "The same?"

I nodded before glancing back at Renee who frowned at me.

"I'm going to bed," she said. "Don't drink too much more. You really have had enough."

"You're a sweet kid, Renee. Nitro's lucky to have you in his life."

Watching her walk away, I couldn't help but think about my brother. Chris used to look after me in the same way Renee appeared to care for Nitro. I missed him so much it physically hurt. Monroe loved me hard, but it would never be the same as a twin's love. That kind of love came from a place I couldn't even begin to describe. Without having to think, we just knew how the other was feeling; we knew when the other needed us; we felt pain and hurt and all the emotions of each other on a bone-deep level. Knowing I'd never have that again had almost killed me. I'd wanted to die when Chris died.

"Tatum."

I squeezed my eyes shut as Nitro's voice washed over me. When I opened them again, I found him sitting on the stool next to me. "I'm not in the mood," I said, weariness kicking in. I really wasn't. The last thing I wanted to do was go another round with him.

"Not in the mood for what?"

I drank some of the rum that had been placed in front of me before saying, "For your bullshit."

He didn't respond straight away, but I did note the vein that pulsed in his temple. I drank some more rum and waited for him to speak. Finally, he said, "Renee told me you've been drinking all night."

Frustration with him consumed me and I swivelled on my stool to fully face him. Ignoring the pain that shot through me as I did that, I snapped, "Am I not allowed to drink while being held hostage?"

That vein ticked again.

"You can drink as much as you want."

"So why are you here then?"

He stared at me in silence for a long moment. Then, raking his fingers through his hair, he said, "If you've got something to say, say it. I'm not a mind reader."

I drained my glass of rum and leaned closer to him, wobbling on the stool from all the alcohol I'd consumed. "Billy has always had my back and was one of the people who dragged me from hell after my brother was murdered. You might not get on with him, but I do, and I refuse to talk to you about him anymore, so if you've come here to ask me more about him, you can leave now." The words rushed out and I was almost breathless by the time I got them all out. I gripped my empty glass hard as I acknowledged the tension I felt in his presence. I'd never had this kind of feeling around a man before. It was putting me off my game, causing my mind to short circuit.

He curled his hand around my wrist. "Anyone ever tell you how fucking sexy you are when you get all passionate about something?"

My gaze dropped to his hand. His touch fucked with my ability to concentrate even more than his presence already had.

My lower belly was in a state of what-the-fuck-are-you-doing? My skin was in a state of "holy fucking hell let him touch every part of you" and my vagina had pulled out the fucking welcome mat.

"Vegas," he growled, and my eyes immediately shot back up to meet his.

"I don't know why you insist on calling me that," I muttered. Nicknames were for people you liked. I didn't want him calling me that. We had no relationship other than the one where he made sure I survived and then we never saw each other again. I could ignore my desire for him if we could just get to the part where we went our separate ways.

"And I don't know why you always argue about shit."

"Because you make me!" I blurted it out and instantly regretted the outburst. It was so unlike me, and that right there was what Nitro did to me—he made me forget who I was now and what I needed to do to get through my days. He caused my mask to fall.

"How the hell do I make you argue with me?"

I snatched my arm from his hold and moved off the stool. Picking up my bag, I said, "I don't know, you just do."

He slid off his stool. "Where are you going?"

"To bed."

"Yeah, where?"

It was then I remembered where I was and the fact I had no clue where I would sleep that night. As that realisation hit, I did something I never did. I burst into tears.

"Fuck," I spluttered, madly wiping the tears from my face. *Why the hell am I crying? I never fucking cry.*

The harder I tried to stop crying, the harder I sobbed. It was all too much. The fact I was almost raped; Nitro and King dictating what I had to do; another club after me; a fucking

114

bomb… it all overwhelmed me. And although I was damn good at not acknowledging when I felt like life was too hard, I struggled with that this time.

Nitro stared at me, his body stiffening as a look of complete bewilderment settled on his face. In amongst all the thoughts flying at me, I wondered if he'd ever seen a woman cry before because it sure as hell looked like he had no idea how to handle me.

And then he did something that took me by complete surprise. He moved close, put his arms around me and enveloped me in a hug. It was an awkward hug, but one nonetheless.

I rested my head against his chest. I was tired. So damn tired. Closing my eyes, I cried my exhaustion out. Nitro's arms remained around me, like a reassuring blanket keeping me warm when all I felt was freezing cold.

I didn't move when I stopped crying. I didn't want to. And Nitro didn't force me to. Instead, he said, "Come, I'll show you where you can sleep." With one arm still around my shoulder and my body pulled into his, he led me out of the bar. It didn't escape my attention that while he held me firm, he did his best not to hurt my injuries.

His room was small. It contained a double bed, wardrobe, and chair, as well as a tiny bathroom. Totally like his house—minimal furniture, no personal items to be seen. Renee slept on the bed, and there was an inflatable double mattress on the floor.

Letting me go, he jerked his chin at the bed. "You sleep next to Renee."

I looked up at him. "Where's Dustin sleeping?"

"He's in another room."

115

I nodded. "Okay." Moving to the empty side of the bed, I removed my boots and jeans before sliding under the sheets.

Nitro watched me and once I was settled, he left the room. It didn't take long for sleep to claim me. The long day full of drama and the alcohol I'd consumed made sure of that.

* * *

"Mum!"

Where was she?

I ran to her bedroom to find her.

She wasn't there.

I searched the whole house.

She was nowhere.

Tears fell down my cheeks as my body crumpled against the wall.

My heart raced in my chest.

She was always home. She never left us alone after school.

Chris entered the room, and I knew from his face and the way his shoulders hunched over a little that he didn't have anything good to tell me.

"Mum's gone," he said, waving a piece of paper in the air, his eyes sad. "And she's never coming back."

My dream slammed into my consciousness and I sat up straight in bed, pain from my ribs spreading through my body like ripples across water. Sweat coated my forehead. My hair stuck to my neck in a clammy mess. Tears wet my cheeks.

"Oh, God." I dry-heaved as I shoved the blankets off and stumbled into the bathroom. This dream always made me feel sick, and the alcohol in my system only made it worse.

Leaning over the toilet, I vomited.

More pain ricocheted through me.

I vomited again.

Another round of pain gripped my body. I thought for sure my ribs would snap from the violent shudders as I threw up.

Please make this stop.

Please.

I swayed as another wave of nausea assaulted me.

Squeezing my eyes shut, I reached out and placed my hand on the wall to hold myself up. My head swam with dizziness and I struggled to draw breath in.

Just as I thought I would pass out, strong arms circled me from behind, taking care to avoid my ribs as best they could. Warm breath hit my ear as a deep voice said, "Vegas. I've got you."

Always saving me.

I leaned my head back, against his chest, and took a deep breath. Nausea rolled through me again and I retched one last time. Nitro held me and pulled my long hair back as I vomited. I wasn't sure why, because it was already coated in puke.

When I finished, he slid one arm across my chest and held me tight. His body leaned away from mine as if he was reaching for something. A moment later, he flicked the tap on before then placing a wet washcloth to my forehead.

"You need to vomit any more?" he asked.

I shook my head slowly. "No, I'm done."

His arm dropped from my chest and he turned me to face him. Handing me the washer, he said, "Here, clean your face. I'll get you a towel so you can have a shower."

He was right—I needed a shower. But I wasn't sure I had the energy to give myself one. I took the washer, though, and nodded. "Thanks." It barely came out as a whisper, but he heard and returned my nod before leaving to find a towel.

The coolness was a welcome relief against my warm skin. I held it over my face the entire time Nitro was gone. Truth be

117

told, I didn't want to move it away. I liked the dark shield it gave me from the world.

I didn't want to deal with the world that night. All my emotions had been stirred up in the last forty-eight hours, and I'd gone from being numb to feeling like I wanted to come out of my skin. My soul was alive with feelings and I didn't know what to do with them. My usual response was to bury them deep, but that didn't seem possible.

"Here."

With another deep breath, I removed the washer from my face and looked up at Nitro who stood watching me with a serious expression tinged with concern.

I placed the washer on the vanity and took the towel he offered.

When I didn't speak, he asked, "You need anything else?"

"No, I'm good. Thank you."

He hesitated for a beat, as if he was unsure whether he was still needed. It seemed so out of character for him. Well, for the man I knew so far. Something told me there was a whole other Nitro hidden under the gruff asshole exterior he presented to the world. Certainly not a Mother freaking Theresa, but I'd seen enough to know he had the ability to care for people.

Once he decided I was okay on my own, he left the bathroom, closing the door quietly behind him.

I sagged against the vanity.

Fuck.

I took a minute to centre myself before pushing off from the vanity and slowly removing my clothes. It fucking killed to move because of the agony my ribs were giving me, but I eventually stepped into the shower and let the warm water soothe my aching body.

118

I cleaned myself and washed the vomit from my hair. Nitro's toothpaste was in the shower so I also cleaned my teeth. I couldn't recall the last time I'd been that sick. Usually alcohol didn't cause me that kind of hell. Which told me it also had to do with my messed-up mind.

When I finished, I dried myself off and wrapped the towel around me. I had clean clothes in my bag that we'd picked up from Nitro's house earlier that day, so I opened the bathroom door to go in search of them.

Nitro sat on the seat waiting for me. Darkness surrounded him except for a small amount of light shining in from outside, just enough to see. Enough to make out the uncertainty etched on his face. He stood as soon as I entered the room. His gaze dropped to take in the towel I wore and he immediately reached for my bag and placed it on the chair.

"Thanks," I murmured and unzipped it.

He remained silent while I dug around in the bag for something to wear. The stillness in the room unnerved me more than I already was. I suddenly found myself in a state I hadn't found myself for years.

I need shelter.

Someone to tell me it was going to be okay.

That I'd get through this Silver Hell nightmare.

I needed to borrow someone's strength to make it through the night. Because for the first time in a long time, I felt so alone in the world.

Swallowing down my desperate urge to beg Nitro to be that person for me for one night, I concentrated on dressing.

He stood close, watching, waiting. When I was done, I glanced up at him. "Sorry to wake you."

He frowned and opened his mouth to say something but quickly snapped it shut. "You good now?" His voice was gruff.

No.

"Yeah." My voice cracked and I tried to cough it away. When tears pricked my eyes, I quickly turned away from him and muttered, "Night."

I took a step away, my body slicing through the heaviness that clung to the air around us.

A single tear slid down my cheek.

I took another step, holding my breath, willing the tears away.

God, what the hell is wrong with me?

Nitro's hand clamped around my wrist. "You were crying in your sleep." His voice was still gruff and it sounded like he was uncertain about pursuing this conversation.

I stilled and slowly turned back to look at him. As I did that, an avalanche of tears fell. I didn't even try to hide them. Instead, I stared up at him in all my vulnerability. The effort it took to hide myself was too great to keep up.

My hand turned as I did, and I curled my fingers around his wrist. Holding tight, I said, "Can I sleep next to you tonight?"

I wasn't sure what I expected from him, but it wasn't what he gave me. His eyes held mine, never wavering. His uncertainty vanished and he nodded. Letting me go, he stepped back to let me past.

Sometimes the person you least expected was the person there for you in the dark of night. *In the middle of your nightmare.*

Nitro gave me what I needed that night. He let me settle on my side next to him and when I reached for his arms, he spooned me, wrapping me in his embrace.

He lent me his strength.

And for the first time in longer than I could remember, I slept like a baby.

120

Chapter Seventeen

Nitro

"Knockin' On Heaven's Door" by Guns N' Roses

Something shifted between Tatum and I during the night. Our bodies were tangled when I woke up, my dick hard as hell and the desire to fuck her stronger than I'd ever known with any other woman. Aware that her ribs still gave her hell, I attempted to untangle us slowly. One of her legs was draped over my body, as was an arm. Half her body was actually on me and her face was buried in my chest. As I moved, she stirred. A moment later, her eyes met mine.

The way her body moved when she woke meant she pretty much ended up completely on top of me, her tits pressing into my chest and her pussy sliding over my morning wood. Which meant my dick screamed its need loud and clear for both of us to notice.

She'd worn only panties and a T-shirt to bed and the shirt had ridden up. My hand landed on the bare skin of her waist when she shifted. The control it took not to slide it down into her panties was immense.

"Morning," she said with a sleepy smile as she planted her hands on the mattress either side of my body and pushed herself up so she straddled me.

"Fuck," I groaned. "You trying to kill me here, Vegas?" Glancing down the length of my body, I took in her pussy and legs either side of me. My dick was fucking straining in his effort to get inside her. And to be hit with that smile first thing in the morning—if a man wasn't already awake, that smile would wake him up.

"I'm pretty sure you're invincible, Nitro."

I raked my fingers through my hair and took a deep breath. "And I'm pretty fucking sure any man who had you sitting on top of him when he woke up couldn't withstand you." Jesus, Tatum was the only woman I'd ever known who'd managed to make me want to flirt with her. I could have spent hours in that bed trying to get in her pants.

She grinned and it struck me that she'd had a complete turnaround in mood from the middle of the night. "You're so much nicer first thing in the morning." With that, she moved off me and stood.

"No, I'm nicer any time a woman shoves her tits in my face. It's got nothing to do with the morning."

She glanced down at me. "I didn't shove my tits in your face. If they came anywhere near you it was accidental."

I sat up and tracked her ass as she walked into the bathroom. The door closing behind her caused me to groan. I wanted more of that sexy banter with her. And fuck if that thought didn't come out of the fucking blue.

My phone rang while she was in the bathroom.

King.

I answered it, "What's up, King?"

"Need you to go for a run today, brother."

"Where to?"

"We got a tip-off about where Silver Hell are hiding out. I want you to take some of the boys out there to check on it."

"I'll be ready in ten."

We ended the call and I waited for Tatum to finish in the bathroom so I could take a shower. When she exited, I said,

122

"I've gotta head out to check on something. Can you do me a favour?"

"Depends what that favour is," she said, her tone a little flirty. Fuck Silver Hell and them getting in the way of me staying in this room.

"Can you check on Renee and Dustin for me this morning? Make sure they're okay." Renee was already out of bed and had left the room. She loved to watch the sunrise every morning.

Her eyes softened. "Sure."

"Thanks." I took the few steps to the bathroom, but before I entered, I turned back to her. "You good, Tatum?"

Surprise flickered across her face, as if she hadn't expected me to ask. "Yeah," she said, but I heard the hesitation in her voice. "Thank you for last night."

I nodded and slipped into the bathroom.

I wasn't sure what had happened during the night, but I couldn't deny the pull I felt to her. From everything I'd seen so far, Tatum was fearless, but in the middle of the night, her nightmares had come to life. I told her she'd been crying in her sleep, but what I didn't tell her was that she'd also been thrashing around in the bed.

I'd wanted to wake her up and drag her into my arms.

I'd wanted to take her bad dreams from her.

When she'd asked if she could sleep next to me, I hadn't hesitated to say yes. Because if there was something I knew well, it was the nightmares that claimed your sleep and fucked with your head. I couldn't stop mine, but maybe I could help ease hers if only for a night or two.

* * *

123

"Where did this tip-off come from?" I asked Kick as we stared at the empty block of land we'd been told Silver Hell were staying at.

"I'm not sure, but I guess it was to lessen the number of members at the clubhouse."

"Yeah, my guess, too." I'd called King to advise him to be alert.

King had sent us, along with four other members, to check the site out. Our orders were that if we found anything we were to call it in and sit tight, keeping an eye on them, rather than to take them on. King had more members ready to send if we found anyone. The site was just out of Gosford and had taken us a little over an hour to get to. I was pissed off at the time we'd wasted.

"Right, let's round the boys up and head back," Kick said, his expression revealing he was as annoyed as me.

Five minutes later we pulled back out onto the highway and straight into a shit-storm of bullets. We'd discussed the possibility of that happening and had been vigilant, but our enemy had hidden well. Before my brain caught up to the fact that bikers were roaring onto the highway from behind trees, one of our members copped a fatal bullet and his bike careened off the road, crashing into a tree. There was no time to think about that, though, because eight Silver Hell members were gunning for us. If I wanted to keep breathing, I needed to think fast.

Thank fuck we brought a van with us. King always insisted on it whenever we went on a run. He liked to ensure we always had extra weapons if we needed them. Blow was driving it, and when I made the signal for him to pull up, he screeched to a halt. I was the closest to him and quickly circled back and pulled in behind. The back doors opened and he threw me a rifle.

124

Kick and Devil had taken point, which gave me some breathing space. Silver Hell members fanned out across the highway about fifteen to twenty metres in front of us. I stepped out from behind the van, took aim at the closest member and squeezed the trigger. His attention had been on Kick, so he never saw the bullet coming.

As a Silver Hell member fired at me in retaliation, I ducked behind the van for shelter. Blow took over from his point at the front of the van, as was our practiced plan. I waited a few moments before sticking my head around the side to see what was happening. Kick was stationed on the ground behind his bike, narrowly avoiding bullets, as were two of our other members. Devil ran my way.

I moved back behind the van and reached inside for another rifle. Devil rounded the back of the van, and over the sound of gunfire, I yelled, "Anyone else taken a hit?"

He shook his head as he took the rifle from me. "No."

We stepped out from behind the van together, rifles ready. I whistled loud, alerting our members to get down. They immediately ducked and we opened fire. Blow also fired from in front of the van while Kick and the boys continued shooting from their positions.

Devil and I had the best aim of any Storm member and soon half the Silver Hell members were down. As the gun battle waged on, I knew there was only one way this fight would be won. And so did they.

Kick made the first move, running from his bike towards Silver Hell. Devil and I covered him while also moving forward. Our other members followed suit and soon the battle plan changed. Knives and fists replaced guns as our weapons of choice and we engaged in a furious fight to the end.

The lonely stretch of highway was a silent battleground, but we filled that silence with the sounds of shattered bone and tortured grunts.

My face was a blood-coated sticky mess by the time we'd managed to shrink our enemy to two. Blow had been knocked unconscious, but not before he took out a Silver Hell member. Kick dragged him to the van before re-joining us. With Silver Hell losing so many members, I thought we had a good chance at making it out without losing any more of our men, but I was proven wrong.

"Kick!" Devil shouted, drawing my attention because of the horror-filled tone he used.

Time passed in slow motion as I watched Kick take a bullet to the chest. He didn't go down straight away, but as soon as he did, my fighter instincts took over.

Without processing the consequences, I charged at the guy who shot Kick. Grunting low and deep, my body slammed into his and pushed him backwards. I didn't stop moving until he was on his ass, at which point I bent over him and punched him hard in the face. I punched him straight on, so fucking hard that his skull hit the road with a loud thud.

Running on autopilot, I delivered bone-crushing punch after punch to his face. My hands were coated in blood and he'd stopped moving, but I continued slamming my fist into his face.

It felt good.

Satisfying.

My brain filtered out the sounds around me. My only focus was killing this motherfucker.

"Nitro! Fucking put a bullet in him and be done, brother," Devil yelled out.

With one last punch, I straightened, wiping the sweat from my forehead, really only succeeding in replacing it with blood

126

from my hand. As I did this, another gun sounded and I whipped around just in time to see Jerry, another of our members, go down. Bullet after bullet riddled his body and I knew he had no chance of surviving that.

"Motherfucker!" Devil cried out. Aiming his gun, he shot the guy who killed Jerry. At the same time, I pulled my gun out and fired at him, too. I then turned and pumped bullets into the asshole who shot Kick, ensuring he would never take another breath.

As I surveyed the scene in front of me, my breaths came hard and fast. Devil and I were the last men standing. Blow was unconscious in the van. Jerry and Kick lay dead on the road, and Cruise, our first member to take a bullet that day, was dead on the side of the road.

"Fuck!" I roared, meeting Devil's eyes. "Fucking hell." I could hardly catch my breath as adrenaline and anger raced through my veins.

Devil's eyes were wild. Murderous. Clenching his jaw, he thundered, "They will fucking pay for this. I don't care if it takes me the rest of my life, they will regret this day."

We stood in the middle of the highway with bikes and bloody bodies strewn around us with the smell of death and destruction in our nostrils, and I vowed to go to hell with him. We would burn in the depths of hell to exact our revenge.

A grunt filled the silence around us as we promised retribution. My head whipped around to see who made the noise. It was Kick. His leg twitched as he gasped for air. Jesus, he was still breathing.

Devil and I moved fast, getting Kick into the van. I drove while Devil did what he could to keep Kick alive. On the way, I called King so he could organise a clean-up crew and the collection of our bikes. And I sent prayer after fucking prayer out that Kick survived this. Not that I believed in the power of prayer, but at that point I figured we needed as much help as we could get. I wasn't sure Kick would make it.

Chapter Eighteen

Tatum

"Falling For You" by Lady Antebellum

The day passed slowly. Or maybe that was because my mind kept drifting to Nitro, and that then caused the ache between my legs to intensify, which in turn made me wonder when he'd be back. This all, of course, led to time dragging while I waited. Not even my work managed to consume me like it usually did.

"Fuck," I muttered. *Who am I today?* I never spent my time thinking about a man in this way anymore. I couldn't deny, though, that most of my time had been spent on him that day.

Nitro had been there for me last night. When I'd been an emotional mess, he'd looked after me in ways a man never had before. Not even Chris had been there for me like Nitro had. Who would have thought a man who appeared so closed off from people would be the one there in the middle of the night?

When I'd woken that morning, I'd felt like shit. My head hurt—from both a mild hangover and from crying during the night. I'd expected Nitro to be all awkward with me, so the first thing I did was smile at him, trying to stop any possible awkwardness. Either that smile worked really well or Nitro was so horny that his dick was doing all the thinking.

He'd flirted with me, which was the last thing I'd expected from him. For a guy who wore moody like a uniform, he sure knew how to have some sexy fun with a chick. It was absolutely what I'd needed that morning. The only problem being that he'd stirred a whole lot of desire in me that I'd been trying to avoid thinking about since I'd met him. Being attracted to his looks was one thing, but this was something else altogether. I was beginning to see Nitro in a new light and I couldn't deny I liked these new sides to him.

"You waiting for your man?"

I glanced up to find the dark-haired woman behind the bar watching me expectantly. She was the one who'd kept my drinks coming the night before. I shook my head. "No, I'm not with any of the bikers."

Frowning, she cocked her head. "What about that guy you were with last night, just before you left?"

"Nope. I'm stuck here with him, but he's not mine."

Still frowning, she said, "Huh, coulda fooled me. The way he hung off every word you said and the way you guys argued... I would have sworn you two were together."

My belly fluttered. I placed my hand on it as if to tell it to settle the hell down. "You misread him. Nitro doesn't hang off any words I say. Although, if I were to tell him I wanted sex, he'd probably hang off those words."

She laughed but her expression soon turned serious. "I know what I saw and trust me when I tell you that I don't generally misread people. I have a kind of sixth sense about people."

I paused for a moment. "Are you a psychic or something?" She did have that look about her with her long wild hair, crystal jewellery, earth-mother waif figure and flowing dress.

She hit me with a brilliant smile that turned her pretty face into magnificent beauty. "I wouldn't say that, but I do sense things." She held out her hand. "I'm Kree by the way."

I shook her hand. "Tatum. Nice to meet you." And I actually meant it. I didn't bother with most people anymore, but Kree had an energy that drew me in.

"You want a rum?"

"God, no." Memories of being sick during the night ran through my mind. "But I would love an orange juice."

She frowned. "It sounds like that rum last night didn't treat you well."

"Let's just say I won't be having any more for a long time."

As she poured me a juice, a blood-curdling scream filled the bar and I turned to see who it came from.

King had a petite woman in his arms just outside the doorway and I could vaguely make out her head buried in his neck. Loud sobs came from her. And then she lifted her face to his and screamed, "No! He can't die!"

King said something to her that I couldn't hear, and she once again placed her head on him and sobbed. He held her for a few minutes. I was fairly certain he would have held her for longer except for the fact a screeching noise outside distracted him and he left her to go out there.

The woman leant against the wall near the bar entrance and I watched as her body slid down it to the floor. Shudders racked her body. The pain she felt was palpable. So much so, it pierced my heart. Feeling my way through that pain, I slid off the bar stool and made my way to her.

Joining her on the floor, I pulled her into my embrace. Running my hand over her hair, I tried to soothe her and take some of that pain from her. But I knew—*God, how I knew*—people couldn't carry your load; they could only wipe your tears and wait your time out with you.

I'd only been sitting with her for a few minutes when King stormed back inside. He halted when he saw me, surprise in his eyes. A beat of silence passed between us and then he nodded, as if he was pleased with what he saw.

"Can you take her to Nitro's room?"

131

I put two and two together and knew why he wanted her taken away. Nodding, I said, "Yeah."

"Thanks," he said gruffly. It was the first sign of emotion other than anger or frustration that I'd seen from him.

He turned and exited the clubhouse, and I somehow managed to get the woman to a standing position. Her arms clung to me and her head remained down while she cried.

I placed my hand under her chin and tilted her face to look at me. "I'm going to take you somewhere quiet now. You good to walk?"

Eyes that held her distress stared back at me. She didn't speak but she did nod, so I held her close and led the way to Nitro's room. I laid her down on his bed and settled myself next to her, sitting with my back to his headboard with my arms wrapped around her.

We sat like that for a long time. I wasn't sure how long it had been when she sat up and said, "I-I need to go." She stumbled over her words and gulped back a sob. "Need to know if he—" Her hand flew to her mouth as her face crumpled. "Oh, God."

Her long hair had fallen across her face so I tucked it behind her ear. "King will come to you when he has news. He knows where you are."

She blinked a couple of times as she processed what I said. As she did that, her vacant stare seemed to shift and her awareness altered so that she actually saw me. "Who are you?"

"I'm Tatum. You?" I didn't bother giving her any further details because I figured she was in no frame of mind to even want them. She surprised me, though.

"I'm Evie, Kick's wife. Are you with one of the guys or a family member?"

"Neither."

Her forehead crinkled. "Huh?"

132

"It's a long story."

She grimaced. "I have time."

Yeah, I guessed she did and maybe I could help her pass it. I leaned my head back against the headboard and exhaled. "I'm here because Nitro's under orders to keep me alive. Silver Hell want me dead, and Storm want me alive because of my ties to a guy they're in business with."

"Why do they want you dead?"

"One of their guys murdered my brother. I was involved in his death recently and they found out." The words came out clinically as I stared straight ahead and concentrated on keeping my mind as blank as the wall I was looking at. *Concentrated on keeping my sadness at bay.*

She reached for my hand and held it. The gesture took me by surprise. Touch was something I'd denied myself for a long time. Well, except for sex, but that didn't count anymore because that was purely physical. There were no emotions tied to it. Evie's gesture was bound with emotions and I sucked in a sharp breath. Monroe was my person. My *only* fucking person. No one else was allowed to breach my walls. And yet, in the space of a few days it felt like my damn walls were being scaled all over the place.

I ripped my hand out of hers at the same time the door flung open. Nitro entered in a gust of caged energy, his eyes wild, his face covered in blood, his clothes torn and dirty. He came to a sudden stop when his eyes landed on us.

"Fuck," he muttered, his chest rising and falling with hard thuds.

Evie bolted forward in the bed, scrambling in her haste to get to him. "Is Kick—" The words tore from her, cutting off abruptly as if she didn't know which word to use next.

My soul twisted with an ache I'd never rid myself of at the pain I heard in her voice. That kind of agony would always touch me regardless of my efforts to maintain immunity.

Nitro faltered and his eyes came to mine. Searching. Needing. *Unsure*. He shoved his fingers through his hair as he shifted his gaze back to Evie. "He's with the doc."

I left the bed. Looking up at Nitro, I said, "Evie will be the first to know when there's news, right?" I wanted him to reassure her of that and hoped he would.

He didn't let me down. "Yeah."

Evie, however, seemed anything but convinced. "No... I need to see him now." She was confused. Disbelieving. Before either of us could stop her, she ran from the room.

"Christ!" Nitro turned to go after her, but I grabbed hold of his wrist to stop him.

"Let her go. She needs to see for herself."

He frowned. "There's nothing to see. The doctor is still working on him."

I nodded. "Yes, and she needs to see and hear that from King."

He moved past me to the bed, sitting on the end of it. His shoulders hunched and he lowered his chin to his chest. He remained silent until I closed the door behind me. Looking up, he said, "Thanks for looking out for Evie."

I sat next to him. I wasn't sure why except that for the first time since I'd met him, he seemed like he needed someone. Even if it was just to sit with him. I stole a glance at his face. It was hard to find skin under all the dried blood. "I take it the other guy lost."

He held my gaze for a long time before answering me. God, how I wondered what thoughts ran through Nitro's mind. It felt like he either ran from them or got lost in them, but I wasn't convinced he was often comfortable with them. *Something we had in common.* "That depends on your definition of winning."

I didn't need him to spell it out for me. And I didn't push him for more. Instead, I walked into the bathroom. Locating a clean washer in the drawer, I wet it and walked back out to him. Standing in between his legs, I began the task of cleaning up his face.

This was something I knew well. My brother had often turned up on my doorstep in this state. Caring for him had always been my responsibility. How could it not be when his journey in life had been dictated by my own?

Nitro hissed when I accidentally pressed too hard on his cheek. His hand landed on mine and he halted my progress. "I can do this myself."

I pulled my hand away from his face. "Yeah, you can, but I'm doing it, so just let me."

"Always arguing with me," he murmured, allowing me to go on.

I worked in silence and when I'd cleaned the blood from his face, I said, "I'm going to get some ice for your face. Wait here."

I hurried down to the bar because I figured he had work to get back to and no time to waste. Kree loaded me up with ice and a towel to wrap it in. When I arrived back in his room, he was in the shower. He didn't take longer than a few minutes and when he exited the bathroom wearing only a towel around his waist, I sucked in a breath at the magnificence of his body.

Nitro was a powerhouse of hard muscle that went hand-in-hand with his fearless warrior instincts. Standing before me, almost naked, his masculinity caught me off guard and a rush of desire hit me. My thoughts stalled and I momentarily forgot what I was doing. All I could focus on was the throbbing need

135

deep in my core. A new hum filled my entire being, unlike anything I'd ever felt before.

Damn.

Shit.

No.

"You got ice?" His deep voice snapped me from my hypnosis.

"Ah… yeah," I mumbled, shoving the towel with the ice in it at him, almost dropping it as I did so.

He frowned, his eyes searching mine. "You good, Vegas?"

Fuck, no, I wasn't.

I was fucked.

Completely.

I nodded, swallowing hard. "I'm good."

I was so far from good.

I wanted something I didn't want to want.

I wanted him.

How the hell did my world turn in such a short space of time? What the fuck triggered that? Because whatever it was, I needed to un-trigger it.

He took the ice from me and turned to head back into the bathroom, grabbing clothes on the way. I was helpless to do anything but watch him walk away. My eyes stayed glued to the powerful muscles that built his back. And that ass. *God, that ass.* Even covered in a towel it was hard not to stare at.

I was so engrossed in his back and ass that he caught me off guard again when he dropped the towel and dressed without closing the bathroom door.

Fuck it, I was out. I yanked the bedroom door open and left as fast as I could. I needed to find a quiet corner and gather my thoughts. I needed to wipe everything that had just happened from my memory. Somehow, though, I suspected Nitro was not a man to ever be wiped from a woman's memory.

Chapter Nineteen

Nitro

"The Way It Goes" by Keaton Simons

"You're fucking kidding me!" I stared at King in shock, waiting for his reply. It was nearly midnight and I was exhausted after the shit we'd been through, but what he'd just told us had sure as fuck drawn my attention.

Weariness lined King's face; he was feeling it as much as anyone, maybe more so. "I'm not," he said. Although he didn't give me the answer I wanted, I heard the misgiving in his voice. "Bronze is under pressure to clean this mess up and he doesn't think he can keep us out of it much longer if we continue the way we have been. He wants us to lay low for a while and let the dust settle. That shit Silver Hell pulled today didn't help."

"So," Devil cut in, "any idea how long we have to back off for?"

"Not to mention, how the fuck does he expect us to not retaliate when Silver Hell come at us again?" Hyde said, a scowl on his face. "Because sure as shit they're going to."

King held his hand up signalling he wanted the floor. "The list of potential charges he rattled off is enough for me to pay attention. I'm going to call a truce—"

The room erupted in chaos as he made his announcement. None of us wanted a truce; we wanted to bury the motherfuckers.

"Enough!" King roared, slamming his hand down on the table in front of him. "Let me fucking finish!" When he had everyone's attention again, his eyes glittered with the crazy he was known for and he continued, "The truce won't be forever. And we'll use the time to make plans. No one kills a Storm member and gets away with it. I fucking promise you that."

With that, he stood and ended the meeting before leaving the room. I knew he was heading back to see the doctor about Kick. I also knew he wouldn't sleep until he knew Kick was going to pull through. That was King—loyal to his men until the very end.

* * *

Tatum's eyes met mine as soon as I entered the bar after I left the meeting. She looked away almost as fast as she looked at me.

I pulled up a stool next to her at the bar a moment later and jerked my chin at the woman Kick had found to replace Brittany. Kree Stone. From what I'd heard, she'd kept the bar running with no problems the last couple of days.

"What can I get you?" she asked as she drew close. I didn't miss the frown she sent Tatum's way before giving her attention to me.

I ordered a beer and once she left us, I said to Tatum, "Something bothering you, Vegas?"

She'd left me without a word earlier. That was after she made it clear she wanted to clean up my face. Fucking confusing. I had no clue what was on her mind and I had no interest in dealing with female issues that night, but I also didn't need shit interfering with club business. If there was a problem, I wanted to know about it for that reason only.

138

She faced me. "I'm just trying to get through this, Nitro, and right now I don't feel like talking."

I swallowed some beer. "That makes two of us, but I need to know if you've changed your mind about staying here."

The confusion she looked at me with matched my own. "Why would I have done that?"

"Because there's a lot of shit happening around here. And you seemed to be taking it okay until you walked out on me this afternoon. You've gone from wanting to clean my face to not wanting to look at me or talk to me. I don't know what the fuck happened, and I don't really care except if whatever it was causes you to call Billy and screw up the shit we've got going on."

She pushed off her stool and picked up her phone. "I'm not going to screw anything up. And fuck you. Just when I start thinking you've got something here"—she jabbed at my chest— "you prove me wrong." With one last filthy glare, she stalked away from me. If I thought I was confused before, I was at a fucking loss after that outburst.

I threw back some more beer. "Fucking women," I muttered as I raked my fingers through my hair.

"I see you fucked that up."

Jerking my head up, I found Kree watching me. "Fucked what up?" I demanded.

"You were an asshole to her just now."

I gripped the beer bottle tighter. "Most women would tell you that's my specialty, but I don't see how I fucked anything up because there was nothing *to* fuck up."

Her mouth spread out into a small smile as she shook her head. "Clueless too, I see." She rested her elbows on the bar. "I'll give you a tip—when you want to sleep with a woman, you

139

should never tell them you don't care about something that's on their mind. It makes their vagina snap closed."

My shoulders tensed. "Let me give *you* a tip, Kree. Stay the fuck out of my business if you want to keep this job. And for the record, I might have wanted to fuck Tatum, but pussy is easy to come by. And when it comes without fucking baggage it's even better."

"That's where you're wrong. Sure, travelling without baggage seems easier, but when all is said and done, it's what's in the baggage that makes the trip sweeter."

I drank the rest of my beer and shoved the empty bottle her way before sliding off the stool. Without another word, I stalked out of the bar. I didn't need another woman getting in my face that night. Tatum was enough of a fucking handful to be dealing with.

* * *

The next morning, I woke before sunrise after only a few hours sleep. Renee was fast asleep but Tatum was nowhere to be seen. I dressed and went in search of her.

She sat outside, wrapped in a blanket, on the wooden bench I often sat at myself when I was seeking solitude. The first rays of light cracked through the sky as I stepped through the front door of the clubhouse, illuminating her face as she stared out into nothing. She turned to me as I approached, the hard set of her jaw from last night gone.

"It's cold. You should get something warmer on," she said, surprising me. *Always surprising me.* I'd expected another tongue-lashing, not more care from her.

140

She was right, it was cold, but my jeans and long-sleeved T-shirt were enough for me. I didn't tend to feel the cold too much.

I sat next to her. "You sleep okay?"

She stared at me for a long moment before sighing. "Do you really care?"

I scrubbed my hand over my face. "Fuck, Tatum, I'm not a complete bastard. I know you think I am, but—"

Her hand moved over my arm and her fingers curled around my wrist. "I don't think you are, but you sure make it hard for people to think otherwise."

My gaze was glued to her hand wrapped around my wrist. Her touch heated my skin like no other woman's ever had before. The desire to fuck her took hostage of my mind. And on top of that, there was something else. Something I'd never experienced before. A desire to take her into my arms and just be with her. The idea of simply holding her, even if I wasn't inside her, took hold like a needy fucking child.

Jesus, I was losing my shit. Even my breathing was under siege. Breaths forced their way from me in choppy waves. I stood, forcing her to let me go. "I'm hoping to get you home today or tomorrow. We should have things settled soon so it'll be safe for you to be home." I said, leaving the rest of our conversation unspoken.

She blinked. It was her only reaction to my swift change of direction. Thankfully, she moved right along with me. "How's Kick?"

I gripped the back of my neck, massaging the kinks out. "I'm about to check on him. Doc was hopeful he'd pull through the night, but it was touch and go for a bit there."

"So you guys have a doctor on call who comes here rather than you going to him?"

141

I nodded. "Yeah, it's better that way."

"I bet," she muttered, her words full of acid.

I wasn't a fucking mind reader so I had no understanding of why she switched her inner bitch on all of a sudden. My irritation at whatever the hell was happening between us flared into anger. "*You bet?* You have no fucking clue who we are or what we stand for, so don't come here and throw your opinions at me."

Her eyes widened and she stood in such a hurry and came at me with such force that she nearly knocked me over. I didn't see her hand coming until it was too late. She slapped my face and spat out, "That was for all the asshole things you've said to me! And maybe you'll recall that I didn't choose to come here. And as far as me giving you my opinions… get the fuck used to it, because I keep my mouth closed for no one."

As she strode back inside, I tried to push the realisation away that I'd checked on Tatum before Kick. I really was losing my shit.

* * *

"Kick's doing better," King said to me later that afternoon. "Doc's hopeful."

We stood out the back of the clubhouse, the cold wind whipping around us. Winter this year had been a bitch with unusually high winds and heavy rain, and that day hadn't been any different.

I shoved my hands into my pockets. "Evie's doing okay? The baby?"

He nodded. "Yeah, I had the doc check her out, too, and she's fine."

"Good."

"I'm meeting with Dragon tonight."

"And?" I understood the need to call a temporary truce, but I didn't like it. That was why King would always make a better president than me. I would have led Storm right into hell because of my need to seek revenge. There would have been no coming back if I was in charge.

"I'll take Hyde and some of the boys with me while you and Devil watch over things here. I'll call you once it's done." He stopped for a beat, his eyes boring into mine. "If that call never comes, you need to see this through."

Fuck.

"That's not a scenario we ever wanna see around here, King. Take me and leave Hyde. He can see shit through if needed, but you never want to leave that up to me."

Determination lit his eyes as he shook his head. "No," he said with force. "Hyde's not in the right place mentally to do it at the moment. You are."

I sucked in a breath. "I don't know what's going on with Hyde, but I'm telling you, honest as fuck, that I'd take everyone down with me if I had to lead the club out of this shit. There would be no club left."

The determination in his eyes glittered and morphed to crazy. "I'm counting on it, Nitro. If this goes south today, I want you to deliver a level of pain they've never known." His face twisted with hate. "I want you to rip their fucking hearts from their bodies and burn their club to the ground."

* * *

I sat at a table in the corner of the clubhouse bar alone that night, waiting for King's call. The mood in the bar was sombre. We all knew what hinged on the meeting with Silver Hell,

143

although no one besides Devil knew of King's orders for what was to go down if he was unsuccessful. That shit had fucked with my mind since he'd issued the directive. I was a soldier, not a fucking leader. I'd been indoctrinated in the art of war from a young age and had always known my place as a soldier. I served. I carried out orders. I got shit done. What I didn't do was command, so that call from King needed to come.

Tatum entered the bar with Evie and took a table on the other side of the room. My presence remained unknown so I was able to observe her freely. She'd stayed out of my way all day. In fact, I hadn't seen her since she'd slapped me that morning. That didn't mean she was far from my mind. On the contrary, she'd fucking filled it nearly all day.

I couldn't get the night she'd slept in my arms out of my head. Or pretty much anything since that night. Tatum was broken and I found myself wondering who did that to her. I knew a lot about her, yet I knew nothing important. Someone somewhere had shattered her, and she'd built walls of steel around her heart. Her mood altered so often I struggled to keep up. The fact I tried to keep up pissed me off.

"Nitro, you need to come and sort Dustin out."

Renee stared down at me. She'd had a hard few days at the clubhouse, hating the confinement. Most of her time had been spent in my room working on school assignments. Standing, I said, "What's he done?"

A tired sigh escaped her lips. "What do you think he's done? The usual."

"Jesus," I muttered.

"It's okay, he hasn't taken it too far yet, but I can tell the woman has had enough of him. I came to you before it got out of hand." Thank fuck. The last thing I needed to be dealing with was another of Dustin's screw-ups.

144

I followed Renee, stealing one last glance at Tatum. Up closer, I could see that her lips were pressed together in a smile that didn't reach her eyes. She watched Evie talk, but I wasn't convinced she heard her.

I caught her attention as we moved past her. Our gazes locked. She didn't smile, but she did sit up straight in her seat and turn her head to track my movements. She bit her bottom lip and her chest rose as she took a deep breath.

My phone rang at that moment. I held her eyes while I answered it, distracted as fuck. "Yeah?"

"Nitro."

King.

I snapped to attention, letting Tatum out of my sight. "You're done?"

A pause. And then, "It's done."

I let out the breath I'd been holding for hours.

Thank fuck.

145

Chapter Twenty

Tatum

"To Be Loved" by Curtis Stigers

Three Weeks Later

"You look like shit," Monroe said as she poured me a drink. Sliding it across the kitchen counter, she added, "Is Billy working you too hard?"

"It has been busy, but nothing more than usual." I drank some of the rum and Coke she gave me. Friday afternoon drinks had been a thing for us for a year, ever since the day I was disbarred. We usually frequented a pub near her work, but for the last three weeks we'd chosen to have drinks at my house instead.

Her eyes narrowed at me. "So what gives then?"

It wasn't a question I hadn't asked myself. What the fuck *was* wrong with me? I leaned my elbows on the table and rested my chin in my hands. "I honestly don't know, Roe. I thought I'd feel better after that Silver Hell biker was dead, but I don't. I feel worse. Or, maybe not worse, just something different, but still bad. Ugh, I can't even describe how I feel." Tears pricked at my eyes and I sighed. Pointing at my eyes, I muttered, "And look! I fucking cry for no reason these days. Ridiculous." I shoved my drink away. "*And* I don't want rum. I want Milo."

The room turned silent while we stared at each other, me through tears, Monroe through surprised eyes. And then she did what Monroe does—she moved into action and tried to fix me.

She picked up the glass of rum and emptied the liquid into the sink. Then, she pulled the fridge open and grabbed out the milk. Next, she reached into the pantry for the tin of Milo I always had on hand and made me the drink I craved.

Placing the mug of Milo in front of me, she said, "Drink that and let's work this shit out because no fucking way can I have Friday drinks in your house anymore. And I certainly can't do fucking Milo on a Friday afternoon. *Milo!*"

My mouth curled into the first smile I'd smiled all week. Placing both hands around the mug, I drank my drink and waited for her to continue.

"Right, let's count all the ways you're fucked." She held up one finger. "Firstly, you were raped and beaten up by an asshole biker. And I know you say it wasn't rape, but it doesn't matter if he didn't fuck you with his dick, it was rape. That's gotta screw you up and I'm pretty sure you haven't even attempted to emotionally deal with that." She held up a second finger. "Next, your brother was murdered nine months ago and as much as you thought that his murderer getting what he deserved would make you feel better, that was never gonna be the case. The only thing that would make it all better is if Chris had never been killed in the first place." She held up another finger. "Third, you've spent the last three weeks watching your back because although Nitro told you that you were safe, who the hell knows what these fucking bikers are capable of? I know you hate admitting defeat, but, babe, you are scared. And I don't blame you, but you need to talk about this shit and stop bottling it up. That's what's bringing you down—you won't ask for help and at this point, you need all the help you can get."

I nodded slowly. "You're right. You always are." Tears slid down my face. "But I don't know the first thing about asking for help, Roe."

Her face softened and she reached for my hand. "Oh, babe. I'm always here for you. I do think, though, that you should consider therapy."

My whole body tensed at that suggestion. Dredging up my past was the last thing I wanted to do.

When I didn't agree with her, Monroe leaned forward across the counter and said softly, "Let's not forget your mother's death, the end of your marriage and your disbarment. I know those things aren't as recent, but they're all things I don't think you've finished working through. You get up every day and put on your boss-ass-bitch pants, and you take care of everybody else's problems, but you never take care of yourself, Tatum. I want you to love yourself first and I'm fairly fucking sure you're gonna need a professional to guide you through that process."

I exhaled, long and hard. And I made a snap decision. Monroe was right. I was sick of feeling like shit. It was time to reclaim my life. And I was going to need a fucking shrink to even begin to wade through the crap in my heart.

I raised my mug of Milo at her. "Cheers, Roe."

She raised her glass and said, "Cheers to a psych? Or cheers to something else?"

I laughed and drained my mug. "Cheers to a psych and no more fucking Friday afternoon drinks at my house."

* * *

Billy glanced up at me as I entered his office three days later. He did a double take and put his pen down as he frowned and shoved his chair back to stand. "Jesus fucking Christ, Tatum. What the hell happened to you?"

I collapsed into the chair across from him. Leaning my elbows on my knees, I looked at him through puffy, blurry eyes

148

that had done more crying in two hours than they'd done in years. "I hired a shrink. She made me talk."

His body sagged in what looked like relief and he sat back down. "Thank fuck."

I smiled. "You *do* care."

He scowled. "Of course I fucking care. I put a guy on you after King sent you home and you had me worried for a minute there that he hasn't been doing his job."

I sat up straight and frowned. "Wait. You have someone watching me?"

"Did you think I wouldn't?"

"I don't know. I guess I just never thought about it."

He sighed. "When are you going to figure out how important you are to me? And I'm not just talking about the shit you do for me here. It fucking killed me when you chose Storm over me. I needed to know you were safe and with you locked up in their clubhouse, I had no idea. I won't allow that to happen again."

"I don't care what anyone says, you're a good guy, Billy Jones."

"Yeah, well don't spread that around. I have a reputation to uphold and it's easier to get what I want if people think I'm a bastard."

Moments like this were so rare with Billy. Hell, moments like this were rare in my life full stop. My heart expanded to take it all in. For once, I didn't push the warmth away. I let it all in and fuck if it didn't feel good.

Tears threatened again, so I swiftly changed the subject. "Posey's back tonight."

"Good. Almost four weeks without her and they're screaming for her. Has her asshole-ex finally decided to leave her alone?"

"Yeah. He's actually moved to Melbourne." I gave him a smile. "Thank you to whoever you got to help with that decision."

"I should have done that sooner. Any news on those drug charges?"

I stood. "Duvall got them dropped completely. They wouldn't have stuck in court."

He grew pensive for a moment. "It seems Duvall is a worthwhile ally."

"Whatever you're thinking, stop. Duvall has done his time with you, Billy. I won't be asking him to help us ever again."

He raised his brows. "And it seems your heart isn't completely buried."

I crossed my arms over my chest. "You're confusing the hell out of me today."

"Why?"

"When I came to work for you, you told me this was no place for emotions and that I should never get involved with anyone we worked with. Now it seems like you want me to open myself up."

His eyes flashed dark. "To me, Tatum. I want you to open up to *me*. Don't mistake my words for something they're not." He dismissed me with a wave of his hand. "Go work your magic with the girls. I'm sick of hearing them bitch about each other. Sort them out for me."

It was no wonder Billy had the reputation he did. He was a contradiction. One minute you felt the sun with him, the next, clouds. I understood that roller coaster because I lived it, too. And I'd always have his back regardless.

150

Chapter Twenty-One

Nitro

"Cold Hard Bitch" by Jet

"I don't want to," Marilyn said as we pulled up outside my house.

"I know, but even your doctor agreed this is for the best," I said, opening the car door and exiting.

I made it around to her side and took in the foul expression on her face. She shoved the door open, her mood in full swing. "So you and my doctor are going to run my life now, are you?" With that, she stalked inside, leaving me to contemplate the intelligence of my decision to have her stay with me for a while. Yet, there wasn't even a choice as far as I was concerned. I'd go to the ends of the fucking earth to make sure my family were okay.

I grabbed her bag out of the boot and followed her in, ready for whatever she threw at me. As soon as the front door closed, she swung around, glare still in place. "Is everyone staying at the moment?"

Dustin dropped the TV remote and moved off the couch. "The mattress is mine. The floor is too hard for my back. Even Tatum said the floor was too hard."

Marilyn frowned. "Who is Tatum? And just for the record, I'm not sleeping on the damn floor, Nitro. I'll go home to my bed before that ever happens."

A smile lit Dustin's face as he proceeded to fill Marilyn in on Tatum. I blocked his voice out and took Marilyn's bag into my room. He hadn't shut up about Tatum for weeks and I'd heard enough. My dick had fucking heard enough, because every time her name fell from his mouth, it shot straight to my cock. I needed a goddam break.

They were arguing about sleeping arrangements again by the time I made it back out to the living room. Raising my voice, I barked, "Marilyn can take my bed and I'll take the fucking floor. Okay?"

Both heads whipped around in surprise. "No need to yell," Dustin said, hurt flashing in his eyes. He didn't cope well with anger.

I raked my fingers through my hair, agitated as hell and unsure why. "Yeah, well you two need to let up. We all have to stay here for a bit and I'll lose my shit if you keep arguing."

Marilyn withdrew after that, burying her head in a book on the couch. Reading was her preferred way of blocking out the world and her doctor had warned me she was spending nearly every waking hour with her nose in a book. As far as I was concerned, better that than drowning herself in a bottle of cheap wine. The main thing I cared about was that she kept up with her bi-weekly therapy sessions, and I would make sure that happened.

Dustin stared at Marilyn for a beat. He'd always struggled with our sister's tendency to spiral into dark places. His mind couldn't seem to wrap itself around anything but light and happy. They may have fought a lot, but Dustin would do anything to put a smile on Marilyn's face.

Finally, he turned and headed out the back door. I knew I'd find him in the shed if I needed him. He'd be working on one of my bikes. I always had at least two out there I was working on.

It was the one thing we did together. The one thing that eased both of our demons.

My phone rang, dragging me from the problems at home.

Hyde.

"What's up, brother?"

"Need you to meet Billy today to collect our next shipment."

"I thought you were doing it with Devil." I was the last person Billy would want to see. Not that I gave a fuck, but I was all for keeping peace at the moment.

He blew out a harsh breath. "Got some family shit to deal with that I can't get out of. And King's busy. I could send another one of the guy's with Devil, but he wants you to do it with him. He would have taken Kick, but no way would King let that happen." He was right. Although Kick was itching to get back to work, he hadn't recovered enough to do this.

I swiped my keys off the table. "I'm in. What time?"

He gave me the info and then said, "Thanks, brother. I owe you one."

It struck me how odd the conversation was after we ended the call. Hyde never told anyone he owed them.

* * *

Devil and I arrived at the drop-off point dead on time. We'd attempted to be early, but traffic had dictated otherwise. We backed the van into the driveway as were our instructions and sat with it idling while we waited for the signal to reverse into the garage.

Billy used a house in Alexandria for this. The street was narrow with high fences all the way down it. Trees and flowers everywhere gave an impression of a friendly neighbourhood, but

153

I always wondered what people did behind closed doors. Most people I knew had shit to hide.

Two bangs on the back of the van signalled it was time to reverse. Devil eased the van backwards and the automatic garage door closed at the same time as bright lights illuminated the space. I jumped out and took in the length of the garage. It wasn't your standard suburban fit out. By my estimation, another two vans could fit there.

Heels clicking across the cement floor and the jangle of bangles drew my attention. I looked around to find Tatum walking our way. Jesus, could she get any sexier? I adjusted my pants as my gaze travelled the length of her. She wore the tightest fucking jeans known to man and a white tank top with a skull and wing design on it that sat perfectly across her tits and revealed her toned arms inked with those tattoos I could spend hours investigating. I'd checked out her ink briefly when she'd been holed up at the clubhouse, and the designs were so intricate and full of such detail that I knew the more you looked, the more you'd find. I wanted to know what she'd chosen to mark her skin with for life.

"Tatum," I greeted her, planting my feet wide and crossing my arms over my chest.

If she was surprised to see me, she hid it well. Instead, she nodded and said, "Nitro." And then shifting her attention to my left, she said, "Devil."

"Billy's not joining us today?" Devil enquired.

Shaking her head, Tatum said, "No, he's been called away and asked me to take care of this delivery." She motioned for one of the men who flanked her to open the boxes on the wood pallet in front of us.

Devil and I inspected the shipment and once we were satisfied with it handed payment to Tatum. After we loaded the

154

guns into the van, Devil lifted his chin at her. "Good doing business with you, Tatum. It's a sweet change from seeing Billy's ugly mug." With a wink, he headed to the passenger side and waited in the van for me.

Tatum's eyes met mine. It'd been three weeks since I dropped her at her home and told her to stay safe. It hadn't been three weeks since I'd seen her, though. Dustin might not have stopped talking about her, but I hadn't stopped watching her. Not every day, but a couple of times a week at least. I needed to make sure she was okay. That Silver Hell hadn't broken our truce. That was what I'd told myself to begin with, anyway. I wasn't so sure anymore.

"You good?" I asked.

She nodded. No smile, though. "Yeah."

The pull to her was intense. I'd felt it every time I watched her. Pure animal need pulsed through my veins when I caught a glimpse of her and it did my head in. The fact I had never experienced that with another woman told me she was dangerous. So I checked on her, but that was all I did.

Devil banged on the side of the van, reminding me to stop fucking around. Tatum took a step back. Her expression still blank, her thoughts a mystery. No more words were exchanged and a minute later, I exited the garage.

"Billy should send Tatum to do every delivery," Devil said. "A woman who knows how to execute a transaction with no emotions and no problems. She might just be my perfect fucking woman."

My gut twisted at the thought of Devil pursuing Tatum and I gripped the steering wheel hard.

When he continued to describe the ways she was perfect, I scowled. "Can we talk about something fucking useful?"

155

He raised a brow and smirked. "I see the blonde has you wound tight, brother. You tap that?"

My irritation only grew. "No, I didn't fucking tap that."

His smirk disappeared. "I'm thinking you need to. Because I've gotta tell you, you've been a bundle of fucking joy to be around since we called the truce. I'm not blind, Nitro. I saw the way you were with her and any fucker could see your dick was straining to get in her pants. So take care of business and get your shit together because we need your fucking attention on the club right now, not on some chick."

I smashed my hand down on the steering wheel. "*Fuck.*"

Fuck it all to hell.

He was right.

Chapter Twenty-Two

Tatum

"Kill The Lights" by Luke Bryan

I held the glass to my mouth, eyeing the blackjack dealer over the rim. Adrenaline spiked in my veins and my heart beat faster as I contemplated winning this hand. I'd been counting the cards and by my calculation I would win this hand. Throwing some rum back, I indicated to him that I would stand. I then drummed my fingers on the table as each player finished their hand. Holding my breath, I watched in anticipation as the dealer completed his, a thrill shooting straight through me when he busted.

Fuck yes.

"You look like you can afford to buy me a drink, Vegas."

Nitro's deep voice and warm breath on my bare shoulder startled me and I jumped. "Fuck," I muttered, swinging my head around to face him. Amused eyes watched me with intent, affecting me in the way only he could.

I gathered my chips and slid off the stool. Looking up at him, I said, "How do you do that?"

"Do what?"

"Your face is so damn serious but it's like your eyes are laughing at me."

Those beautiful eyes of his flashed with amusement again. "Fairly sure you bring that out in me," he murmured. I had no idea what he meant but didn't ask him to elaborate. At that point, I just wanted to cash my chips in and get another drink. Alone.

"Are you here looking for another biker to send to hell?" Memories of the night we met at this casino filled my mind. It was just over three weeks ago and yet it felt like I'd known Nitro a hell of a lot longer.

"Smartass," he muttered, but he wasn't scowling at me. He actually appeared to be in a great mood. Well, as much as I assumed Nitro could experience a great mood.

When he didn't give me anything else, I said, "Okay, well, I'll let you get on with whatever it is you're doing."

As I took a step away from him, his fingers snapped around my wrist and he stopped me. "What I'm doing here is you, Vegas." His voice took on a husky tone, the kind of tone that hit a woman right in the belly and caused her brain to stop working.

I stilled and my breathing slowed. "Me?" It was a dumb question because he'd made his reason clear, but I needed the extra time to collect my thoughts.

He nodded, his eyes boring into mine.

When I didn't speak, he moved his mouth to my ear. "Let me buy you a drink."

I stared at him in confusion. Nitro asking me to *let* him do something seemed way out of character. Narrowing my eyes, I said, "What do you want?" He had to be after something more than just sex.

"I thought I made that clear."

"I thought so, too, until you asked me to let you buy me a drink. Now I figure it must be about more than just sex." I pointed a finger at him. "I swear to God, Nitro, if Storm want something out of me, they—"

He dropped his mouth to mine and silenced me with a kiss. And Jesus Christ, not just any kiss, this one cracked my soul wide open with its intensity. When Nitro kissed, he fucking claimed you. He used his mouth to say all the things he didn't say with his words.

His hands slid along the sides of my face so he could push his fingers into my hair. Taking hold of me, he bent me to his will. His body pressed against mine while he deepened the kiss. Tongues collided and breath was stolen. My senses were consumed completely by this man who bewildered me with his complexity. One minute I hated him, the next I wanted to know every damn thing about him. I wanted to slap him, kiss him, yell at him, comfort him, understand him, tell him to fuck off. But in that moment all I wanted to do was kiss him forever.

When he ended the kiss, he said, "Why the fuck do you always have to argue with me? When I say I want something, I want it. I don't play games and I don't do shit in order to get something else out of it." The honesty blaring from his eyes grew deeper if that was even possible. "I want to fuck you, simple as that."

Breathless, I pressed harder against him. "In that case, I don't want a drink. I just want your cock."

* * *

The last time I saw Nitro was two days prior when he collected guns from me. He'd asked if I was good. That was it. He'd certainly not given me any indication that he wanted to sleep with me. So I'd maintained my distance even though I hadn't stopped thinking about him for three long weeks.

Standing in my hallway, watching him pull his shirt off before reaching for my waist and yanking me to him, I wondered how I'd missed his desire. It was clear as day in his eyes and it was sure as hell blaring from his body. After we arrived back at my place, he'd hardly let me out of his hold. His hands or his mouth were all over me, often all at once. It had taken him a good half hour to move us to the point of him removing his shirt because he hadn't wanted to let my mouth go.

I placed my hands on his chest. "Things would move along a lot faster if you took my clothes off."

He dipped his face and teased my mouth with his teeth, biting my lower lip before kissing me. "You in a hurry, Vegas?"

Fuck no, I wanted to drag this out for as many hours as possible. But I was eager for that cock of his. Trailing my fingers over his broad chest, I said, "We've got all night as far as I'm concerned, but the sooner we're naked, the better."

He grinned, surprising the hell out of me. I hadn't seen a grin on Nitro's face yet. I liked it. "You make a fucking good point."

Stepping back, he assessed my body, as if he was contemplating something. Whatever it was passed quickly and then his hands went to my thighs. I wore a short red dress and his touch on my bare skin was electric. My eyes fluttered closed and I sucked in a breath when he slid his hands up my legs under my dress. Truth be told, I damn well stopped breathing for a moment.

"You like that?" His voice flooded my body with goosebumps.

Moving my hands from his chest to his waist to balance myself, I managed to say, "Don't stop."

"Wasn't planning on it."

His hands continued their exploration, pushing my dress up to expose my panties. I watched as his eyes zeroed in on them. Nitro might have been a man who held his thoughts and emotions close to his chest, but he sure as hell wasn't a man who hid his need. I loved the effect I had on him—the way his nostrils flared as his breathing laboured, and the way he licked his lips while his gaze lingered on my breasts. Seeing it only caused my own need to blaze brighter.

He dropped to his knees and skimmed his fingers over my panties before slipping them under the fabric. His touch was exquisite and totally not what I expected from him. Nitro vibrated with a ferocious intensity—rage and violence rolled into one—that I thought sex with him would be a frenzy of rough moves and hard thrusts from the get-go. But he proved his unpredictability again.

I threaded my fingers through his hair, gripping tightly when he ran a finger along my entrance. A moan escaped my lips and a shudder ran through me. I glanced down as he bent his face to press his mouth to my panties. The powerful muscles in his back flexed sending another jolt of desire to every nerve ending of mine. There was something about the strength and fearlessness he possessed that spoke to me. Made me feel safe. Nitro seemed invincible and that was something I connected with on a deep level. I needed that armour surrounding me in life because I'd had mine stripped from me.

His mouth explored me through the thin material of my panties before he decided he didn't want that barrier anymore. Strong fingers hooked over the top of them and a moment later they lay on the floor while Nitro's mouth kissed my most sensitive place.

I swayed a little as he grasped my ass and ran his tongue around my clit. He then proceeded to alternate that with pushing his tongue inside me. Pleasure rushed at me and I had to focus hard on standing because his tongue was so damn talented my legs grew weak.

When a growl rumbled from him, vibrating through my pussy, I moaned loud and came. Hard as fuck. Nitro sure did know how to make a woman orgasm. And he also knew how to

161

keep me guessing about what would come next. Before I'd come down from that high, he was on his feet and had me over his shoulder while he carried me to my bedroom.

"Fuck," I muttered, caught off guard, but loving it nonetheless.

His hand connected with my bare ass, slapping me. "I hope you're ready, Vegas."

My legs squeezed together. I was more than ready. Touching his back, because hell, I could hardly stop myself from touching those muscles, I said, "Bring it. For the love of God, fucking bring it."

We reached the bedroom and without slowing, he dropped me onto the bed and removed his boots and clothes. He moved so damn fast I had trouble keeping up. I warred with myself between begging him to slow down so I could take in all those divine muscles, and speeding it along to get to the good part.

Next minute, he was on top of me, taking my dress off. When it lay in a heap on the floor, he rested his arms either side of me on the bed, caging me in. His gaze traced my face before moving down my neck to my breasts. He ran his tongue between them, his eyes back on mine. "You taste so damn good. I want to lick every fucking inch of you."

"You wouldn't hear any complaints from me if you did."

He licked me again and I trailed a finger along my skin following the line his tongue took. Still holding my gaze, he said, "You like touching yourself?"

I smiled and nodded. "I've had a lot of practice at it."

That grin appeared on his face again, causing me to smile harder. Fuck, I loved it when he blessed me with that. "Show me."

"To be clear, I prefer not to do it on my own."

I cupped one of my breasts and jerked my chin down at it, letting him know he should join in. His grin died, replaced with a smouldering look that sent heat to my core. Dipping his face, he sucked the breast I held into his mouth. Swirling his tongue around my nipple, he found my gaze again and held it.

My fingers massaged my breast, moving closer to his mouth. When they almost met, he flicked his tongue out to lick them. He shifted on the bed so he could take hold of my hand and suck each finger into his mouth, one by one. Slowly. It was sexy as hell and I could have watched him do it for hours.

"You surprise me, Nitro."

He stopped what he was doing and placed both hands back on the bed. Shifting so his face came to mine, he sucked on my bottom lip and said, "How?"

I ran my hand through his hair before sliding it down his neck and back. "I thought you'd be more demanding, rougher."

Heat flashed in his eyes and he ground his cock against me. "Careful what you ask for," he rasped.

My fingernails dug into his back. "You think I can't handle rough?"

More heat flashed. Darker. Edgier. He shifted again, pulling me up effortlessly so that he knelt with me straddling him. With one hand around the back of my neck, grasping me tightly, and the other cupping my ass, he said, "I didn't want to give you rough if you weren't ready for it."

I blinked.

"The rape?" It was barely a whisper, but he heard and nodded.

"Yeah."

We stared at each other. The light in the room suddenly became too bright for me. I needed it off. I didn't want him to see me. It was as if my soul was on display and he could see every inch of it.

Every crack.

Every wound.

Every flaw.

I pulled away, trying to scramble out of his hold, but he tightened his grip and held me in place. "Vegas," he said with a shake of his head, his voice low. "Don't."

I wrapped my hands around his biceps. "Let me go, Nitro," I demanded.

His nostrils flared. "I will if that's what you really want. But one minute you're telling me you can handle rough, the next you're shutting down on me. I wanna know what gives. Was it because I brought up the rape?"

My heart beat so fucking fast I thought it would beat out of my chest. It wasn't the damn rape, but I didn't want to admit the truth to him. Fuck, I'd sound like an idiot if I admitted his thoughtfulness had gotten to me. I didn't know what to do with kindness anymore. It confused me. Made me question shit because who the hell dealt in it anymore? And it made me feel more vulnerable than I could deal with. I didn't want him to see all the things wrong with me.

I took a deep breath and tried to get my heart to slow down. Relaxing my body in his hold, I said, "I'm good. I just had a moment there. Sorry."

I expected him to relax, too, and get back to where we were, but he didn't. Again, catching me by surprise. He let me go and moved off the bed. Raking his fingers through his hair, he said, "Don't fucking say sorry for something that wasn't your fault, Tatum. Don't ever do that." His voice had so much emotion and force behind it that I wondered where it came from. It felt deep, like he'd lived it himself. Whatever *it* was.

164

I sucked in another deep breath, thinking about what he said. All the while, he stood in silence watching me. Waiting. Finally, I darted off the bed so I could turn the light off. Relief hit me instantly. Such an odd feeling. I never had an issue having the light on during sex, so I didn't know where this was coming from.

I made my way back to where Nitro stood. Light filtered in from the hallway, but I had just enough darkness to feel comfortable. And I had enough light to make out the confusion on his face. All credit to him, though, he didn't question my choice. He simply stood and waited for me to speak.

"Thank you," I said softly, forcing myself to talk about something that made me want to curl into a ball and disappear.

"For what?" Still so gruff and demanding.

I wrapped my arms around me. Around my nakedness. As if covering that up would cover *me* up. "Fuck," I muttered, stumbling over my feelings. *Why was he forcing me to do this?* He continued watching me intently, still waiting. "Oh, for fuck's sake, for caring enough to take it into account." I threw my words out there like they were a throwaway emotion when they were so far from that.

Nitro's nostrils flared again and annoyance flashed across his face. But he dealt with whatever had pissed him off and regained control. Clenching his jaw, he said, "I want to kill that motherfucker over and over for what he did to you." He reached out and smoothed a flyaway strand of my hair back behind my ear. His gesture startled me with its intimacy and gentleness. Especially when he appeared anything but gentle.

I curled my hand around his wrist hanging by his side. "I want that, too, but more for what he did to my brother," I whispered.

It was true—while the rape had been awful, it hadn't fucked me up as much as Chris's murder. And the fact Nitro was the

165

one who saved me meant I only viewed him as a protector, not as a man who might threaten me.

We stood in silence for a few more moments. Soaking in everything that had taken place. I'd expected none of it. And although I hadn't shared with him how he made me feel exposed and vulnerable, I'd opened up more to him than to anyone in my life, besides Monroe.

He took a step away from me and I let his wrist go. When he reached for his jeans, I halted him. Finding his eyes, I said, "Stay."

"I don't think—"

I shook my head. I didn't want sex. That wasn't what this was about. "Just hold me. Please."

His breaths slowed for a beat. He didn't respond straight away and I thought he would say no. But then he nodded. "Okay."

As I closed my eyes a little while later, with Nitro's arms wrapping me in safety, I let out a breath I'd been holding for three weeks. A breath I hadn't realised was trapped.

Chapter Twenty-Three

Nitro

"Pour Some Sugar On Me" by Def Leppard

Tatum was a furious sleeper. Both nights I'd slept with her in my arms, she'd tossed and turned like she was fighting demons. She'd also cried. Both nights. And had mumbled stuff about someone called Randall. I got the impression he was one of the demons she wanted to kill.

I woke before her and watched as she lay peacefully next to me. She'd finally stopped thrashing at around four and had been sleeping quietly for three hours. I wondered if she survived on that small amount of sleep each night and knew deep in my gut that she did. Tatum's nightmares had her in their grips. The way she lived her life told that part of her story.

Unable to stop myself, I traced her lips. Kissing that mouth was high on my priority list, but I wanted her awake for that. She snuggled against me, a smile flitting across her face. She flung her arm across my chest and buried her face into my side. Fuck, she was softer like this and my dick hardened more than it already was. I was attracted to her fierce side, but this softness called to the part of me that wanted to take care of those in my life. The part of me that never wanted anyone to hurt the way my life had.

Selfishly, I ran my hand over her bare ass and spread her legs so that one of them hooked over mine. I wanted to touch her every-fucking-where but wouldn't until she signalled that was what she also wanted. The restraint this took caused me physical pain. When she mumbled something and lifted her head, relief flooded me.

"Nitro," she murmured and I got a kick out of the smile in her voice.

Smoothing her hair, I said, "Morning, Vegas."

She smiled and shifted some more, pressing her body harder against mine as she did so. "I thought you'd be gone by now."

I frowned. "Why?"

"Most do." Her words fell out absently while she trailed her fingers over my chest.

I had no right to feel what I did over that statement, but I couldn't help myself. I didn't like that she slept with other men, but she wasn't mine and never would be so I let that go. "I'm not most."

Her smile grew and her fingers skated along my jaw before reaching for my lips. Lifting herself up, she straddled me and bent to place a kiss on my mouth. "That, you are not." She stared down at me thoughtfully. "You're a fucking contradiction, is what you are. I never know what I'm going to get with you."

I cupped her ass. "You ready to finish what we started last night?"

Her eyes flared with heat and she drove my dick wild when she bit her lip. "Yeah." She slid her body down mine so she lay on top of me. "And Nitro?"

I dug my fingers into her ass cheeks, eager as fuck to get inside her. God, how I fucking needed to be there. "Yeah?"

Her eyes held mine. "I'm ready as hell for your kind of rough."

I was done.

At the edge.

Nothing would hold me back after that invitation.

I pushed up, my arm tight around her, and flipped us. Once she was under me, I gripped her legs roughly and spread them wide. Positioning my mouth at her pussy, I took what I'd been thinking about half the damn night, and I took it the way I'd wanted to the last time I'd sampled her.

It was a frenzy of need and urgency as my tongue worked her pussy. I held nothing back, giving her a glimpse of what fucking me would be like.

My rhythm was jagged.

The pleasure I delivered, bruising.

Sex was how I dealt with life. I brought all my confusion, hurt, and rage with me and for the hours I was with a woman, handed them to her. Most never came back for seconds. I was too much for them.

Tatum's fingers dug into my scalp as she gripped my hair so hard I thought she'd pull it out. I hissed at the sensation it evoked in me. I fucking loved the pain. "Fuck, Nitro...," she panted. "More... give me more."

I growled into her and squeezed her ass, pulling her up off the bed with me as I moved to a kneeling position. Her head remained on the bed, her back arched up and she wrapped her legs around my neck while I feasted on her.

Sucking and licking, I lost myself in her.

Her taste.

Her scent.

The sounds she made.

It all collided, exploding like a brilliant storm in my mind.

When I finally lifted my face from her, I took in her arms flung across the bed. Her eyes squeezed closed. Her breaths coming hard and fast. She'd totally surrendered to the ecstasy.

169

I dropped her on the bed and quickly moved off it to find a condom. She complained as her ass hit the mattress. "Why did you stop?"

Rummaging in my wallet, I located what I was after. Eyeing her, I said, "Tell me, Vegas, do you fuck as hard as you fight?"

She shifted onto her elbows and met my gaze. "Do you fuck as brutally as you do?"

My breathing grew ragged as we watched each other. Pointing at the end of the bed, I said, "Come here and suck my dick. I need to see your lips around it."

She did as I said, no arguments. Fucking first time for everything. She threw her legs over the edge of the bed and our eyes locked as she took me into her mouth.

Fuck me.

My eyes rolled back and I groaned as she ran her tongue over me and sucked me hard. Fisting her hair, I held her face against me, my instincts to fuck her mouth taking over.

I wanted to shove my dick down her throat.

I wanted to go deep.

I fucking wanted her to swallow my cum.

Her hands moved to my ass and she kept them there while I rocked into her. The urge to thrust grew more insistent, until it got to the point where I wanted to feel her cunt wrapped around me instead of her lips.

Pulling out, I stepped back and quickly slid the condom in place. I then jerked my chin towards the bed and growled, "I want you on your back."

She moved fast and a moment later, I was positioned over her with my dick against her pussy. So fucking wet. I bent my face and ran my tongue over her throat, giving her some teeth at the same time. I bit her, not too hard, but with enough pressure

170

that her back arched up off the bed. When she moaned, I pushed my dick inside her a short way before pulling back out.

"Tell me how much you want me to fuck you, Vegas," I ordered as I licked a path down between her breasts.

"So fucking bad." Her legs came around me, hooking together at my back.

When her fingernails clawed my shoulders, I grunted and dropped my mouth to her breast. Biting with more pressure than before, I marked her skin. The need to leave a mark behind overwhelmed me like never before during sex.

"Fuck," she cursed, but it was clear from her tone how much she liked that.

Unable to hold back any longer, I slammed my dick into her. Neither slow nor gentle, I fucked her how we both needed it.

Raw and animalistic, I thrust into her over and over. It was erotic and filthy all at once. We each clung to the other, our grips needy and hard, while our bodies came together to get our fill.

By the time we came, I'd fucked her cunt so furiously I wasn't sure how she'd stand that day. She'd scratched and bitten me to the point where I wouldn't be able to take my shirt off without someone thinking I'd been attacked. It was downright fucking dirty and I'd never had sex so good.

I collapsed on top of her and she hugged her arms and legs tighter around my body. Dropping my face to nuzzle between her shoulder and neck, I caught my breath, inhaling her scent.

"Jesus, Nitro, you know how to fuck," she said, still breathless. Her head was buried against my shoulder and I felt her warm breath on my skin.

Pushing up off her, I rested my hands on the bed either side of her. My gut squeezed at the sight of her wild, thoroughly-fucked expression. "What are your plans tonight?"

Her tongue swiped over her bottom lip before she sucked it into her mouth and bit it. She hesitated but only for a beat. "I'm free."

I moved off the bed. Reaching for my jeans, I said, "I'll come over."

"I'll be home after eight."

As I headed into her bathroom to deal with the condom, I stretched my neck from side-to-side. Fucking Tatum had worked the kinks out of my shoulders and neck. An awesome side benefit.

I disposed of the condom and put my jeans on. I'd head home for a shower and check on everyone there before going to the clubhouse. Exiting the bathroom, I ran into Tatum.

Dropping my gaze, I took in the exercise gear she held. "You going to the gym or something?"

"Gonna have a shower and then go for a run."

I lifted a brow. "After that?"

"Yeah." At my frown, she added, "I get the best run in after sex. You should try it sometime."

"I'll give it a miss."

As she entered the bathroom, she called over her shoulder, "Lock the door on your way out, Nitro. I'll see you later."

And then the bathroom door closed behind her. And I realised that sex with Tatum might be something I pursued. A woman who fucked like she did and then didn't hang around afterwards was a woman I needed in my life.

Chapter Twenty-Four

Tatum

"Habit of You" by Keith Urban

"You saw the shrink again today?" Monroe asked as she filed paperwork in her tiny office at the back of the tattoo parlour. "Didn't you just see her?"

I sat at her desk and watched her work. She was anal about filing and keeping on top of admin. A bit like she was anal about keeping her house clean. "I saw her on Monday." Three days ago. "We agreed I'd see her twice a week to begin with."

She stopped and glanced at me. "How did it go today, babe?" The concern in her voice could not be mistaken.

I wrapped my arms around myself as a shiver ran through me. "It sucked. I've cried more this week than ever. And now I'm exhausted, which sucks, too, because I've got a sure thing for tonight and I'm gonna need all the energy I can muster."

Her eyes widened. "Okay, sister, let's run through all that. What did you talk about with her today?"

"Mum. Dad. Chris. We're still going over shit from decades ago. I'm ready to move on, you know?"

"Yeah, but you need to get all that shit out. Your mum fucked you up big time."

I hugged myself harder. "That's the goddam truth. And yet, I can't bring myself to hate her. It would be a hell of a lot easier if I could just do that."

"What's your shrink got to say about that?"

I sighed. "At this point she's just doing a lot of listening. She seems to just want me to talk. Oh, and sleep and watch my diet and practice self-fucking-care." Irritation pricked my skin. Therapy hadn't turned out to be anything like I imagined it would be. I was ready for answers and solutions, but all my therapist seemed to be about was everything but telling me *how* to fix myself. I wasn't sure therapy was actually for me.

Monroe laughed. "Tatum, I know you're a big believer in taking action and fixing problems in a logical, efficient manner, but emotions can't be dealt with like that. You can't just follow a generic step-by-step plan and magically fix yourself. This is going to take time and consistent effort. You're going to have to be gentle on yourself." She paused for a moment. "*And* you're going to have to get on the self-care bandwagon, babe."

"God," I muttered. "You sound exactly like her. I think you missed your calling in life."

She left the filing cabinet to come sit at the desk. Her eyes lit up as she said, "Now, tell me about this sure thing. And don't leave anything out. But first, does he have a pierced dick?"

I couldn't help it, I laughed. It broke some of the tension in my body and I unwrapped my arms from around me and relaxed back into the chair. "I love you, Roe."

She groaned. "You kill me, girl. Tell me!"

"No, there is no pierced cock for me."

"Ugh, why don't all men pierce their bloody dicks? I think it could bring about world peace. Like, seriously. Could you imagine all the satisfied, happy women wandering the earth after having sex with big, fat, pierced dicks? World peace, I tell ya."

I shook my head in laughter. My cousin and her crazy sex shit. "We really need to find you a man with a piercing, don't we?"

"Yes. But first, you need to tell me where you found this guy and all about him. Is he a lawyer? No, wait, let me guess. You met him at the therapist's office. He's a doctor!"

I cringed. She would hate what I was about to tell her. "It's Nitro."

She sat up straight and stared at me with shock. "A fucking biker, Tatum? Are you on drugs?"

I held up my hand in defence. "Roe, it's only sex. It's not like I'm putting his fucking ring on my finger and traipsing through the kitchen barefoot."

She blew out a long breath. "Okay, you've got a point. Sorry. I forgot for a moment it's you we're talking about. You of the one-night stands and zero commitment. So long as you stick to that, though. Don't go letting him boss you around."

"No bossing around, I promise."

"So, the sex is good?"

"Out-of-this-fucking-world good."

She narrowed her eyes at me and if I knew my cousin at all, I'd bet money she was about to grill me for every little detail. "Like, on a scale of one-to-ten, he'd be a what?"

I leaned forward and grinned at her. "An eleven," I whispered.

She whistled low. "Fuck me, Tatum. How do you always get the good lays and I always get the flops?"

I kept grinning. "You always go for the good boys. Maybe it's time for you to find a bad one and let him rock your world."

She waved her hand in front of her. "Pfft, you can keep the bad boys to yourself, babe. I haven't got time for their shit."

As we laughed and joked, neither of us acknowledged the fact that I had been the one to marry the good boy all those years ago. The truth was that good guys weren't always what they told

175

you. At least with a bad boy you knew upfront what you were dealing with.

* * *

I drained my glass of rum and refilled it straight away. My third one for the night. I'd needed something to take the edge off and I couldn't wait for Nitro to arrive for that to happen. So, alcohol it was.

It had been a rough day. Both at work and with my head. My damn emotions had put me through the wringer. Seeing the therapist stirred too much shit up that I'd rather forget. I'd forgotten it for so long that it was surprising me as we dug for it. And not in a good way.

I jumped at the sound of someone banging on my front door. *Nitro.*

I placed my glass down and walked the short distance to the door. Opening it, I found him standing with his forearms resting on the door jamb.

"Vegas," he murmured as his eyes slowly travelled my body. Nitro's attention on me like that was addictive. I'd only just begun sampling it, but I wanted more.

He dropped his arms, stepped inside and scooped me around the waist as he kicked the door shut. His mouth landed on mine and he kissed me for a long time. When he ended the kiss, he said, "You got any of that rum left?"

I pulled my thoughts together after that kiss and nodded. "Yeah."

He followed me into the kitchen and I poured him a drink, noticing the exhaustion that lined his face. I knew Storm and Silver Hell had called a truce, so I wondered why he looked so worn out.

176

I added some ice and then passed him the glass as he asked, "What's running through that head of yours?"

"You look tired. Exhausted, actually."

"Got a lot going on." Such a man of few words.

"You know what I can't figure out?"

"What?"

"Why King gave in so easily after everything that fucking club did to yours."

He clenched his jaw and threw half his rum down his throat. "He had his reasons."

"Fuck, do you ever say more than a few words at a time, Nitro?"

He closed the distance between us, the vein in his temple pulsing. "I don't want to waste time with words tonight. I didn't come here to fucking talk."

It was true. My pussy clenched at his words, but at the same time something odd happened. I wanted him to fuck me—no denying that—but a tiny part of me wanted to have this conversation. Wanted to know his thoughts. I pushed all that aside, though, because I didn't want to deal with those feelings. I just wanted him to wipe my mind of everything for a few hours.

He looked at me like he wanted to eat me. Then, he reached for the glass of rum he'd placed on the counter and pulled a cube of ice from it. A second later, he skimmed it across my collarbone and down to my breasts. The fingers of his free hand curled over the edge of my tank and he pulled it down a little so he could run the ice over my breast.

His mouth met the ice and he licked the melting liquid over my skin. Backing me against the kitchen counter, he let my tank go so he could reach under it and caress my stomach, then my waist and up to my breasts. His hand covered me perfectly when

177

he slid it into my bra, and I arched into him as he rubbed my nipple between his fingers.

The ice melted while he massaged my boob, right before his mouth latched onto my nipple. I gripped his biceps and moaned as his teeth nipped at me and his fingers worked their magic. The way he started sex all slow and intimate turned me on so damn much. I knew what was coming, and I wanted it, but *this*, this I could take for fucking hours.

He lifted his head and met my gaze. His eyes were glazed, full of need, the kind that made me want him sooner, *faster*. Fuck, I was needy for him. Grinding against me, he rasped, "These tight pants you wear get me hot as fuck, but I gotta tell you, it's a lot fucking easier to get to you when you wear a dress."

I slid my arms over his shoulder and around his neck so my fingers were in his hair. Gripping him hard, I said, "I'm sure you'll find a way to get them off fast."

His eyes darkened and he dropped his head. Sucking in a few harsh breaths, he looked back up at me. Pained. "You test me, Tatum."

I had no idea what he meant. "How?"

He took hold of my waist, his fingers digging into me. "You make me want things," he bit out, his voice a dark warning.

My heart banged against my chest. Red flags would be flying all over the place for most women at that moment, but not for me. My whole body lit up at what I'd heard in his voice. I leaned closer to him. "Tell me."

He hissed and swore. "Fuck." But I knew I had him when he spun me around, slid his arm around my waist and pushed his erection against my ass. "You sure about that?"

I gripped the kitchen counter, breathless. I hadn't been more sure of anything in a long time. "Yes."

He took a moment and then he produced a pocketknife, pressing the tip of it to my chest. Not hard, but with enough pressure to send my pulse racing. "You ever played with knives, Vegas?"

I stared at the blade against my skin. It both excited the hell out of me and scared the ever-loving shit out of me. "No," I panted out, lightheaded at the thought of what he wanted to do with the knife.

He ran the tip of the blade across my skin, not drawing blood, just lightly pressing against me. His breathing grew ragged and his body dominated me in a way it hadn't yet. Nitro wanted this bad. Even though I couldn't see him, I sensed how turned on he was.

Placing the knife on the counter, he turned me so I faced him, and wrapped his hand around the back of my neck. My scalp burned from the grip he held me with and my breathing slowed at the fierce energy vibrating off him. "I never fuck a woman in any way she doesn't want. Let's just get that out of the way." He licked a line from the base of my throat up to my mouth. He then consumed me with a kiss that he poured all his need into. When he finally let my mouth go, he said, "I want to cut those pants off you. I want to slice your underwear in half. And I want to run that blade all over your skin, but I won't do any of that if you don't want me to." His eyes bored into mine, waiting for my answer.

My heart stuttered. My whole body tensed. What he asked was too much. The danger thrilled me, but my common sense kicked in and prevented me from saying yes to all of that. He might have saved my life a couple of times, but no way in hell did I trust a man I'd just met with a knife anywhere near me.

"I can't. No." I shook my head as the words fell out of my mouth.

179

His jaw clenched and he nodded his understanding. Reaching around me, he swiped the knife off the counter and shoved it away. He then moved his hands to the button on my pants. Undoing it, he met my gaze. "It would have been faster my way, but we'll play this your way."

I exhaled, thankful for that. His signal that he was good with my refusal. Which was a good thing because I wanted sex with Nitro. After he fucked me that morning, I'd gone for an hour-long run and my head had felt so clear afterwards. He'd fucked some of the knots out of my body and some clarity into my mind. And I needed all the help with that.

Chapter Twenty-Five

Nitro

"Animals" by Maroon 5

I leant forward in the ute and watched as Dragon loaded case after case into the back of his van. "Fucking hell," I muttered as I turned to see what Hyde made of this.

His dark expression matched mine. "Yeah, that about covers it."

"He's planning something." Those cases were full of guns, and from our surveillance, we knew he'd had a delivery of guns the week prior also.

Hyde pulled out his phone and dialled King. Leaving it on speaker, he said, "They've got something planned."

I waited for King's outburst. He'd been on edge for weeks and his moods revealed how tense he was. However, instead of a tirade, we got silence. And then—"Keep on him. I'll arrange more men so we can put eyes on him 24/7." We'd been spreading our guys thin watching a few different Silver Hell members, but keeping someone on Dragon full-time hadn't been necessary because he hadn't been involved in anything but sitting in their clubhouse issuing orders. Devil had called in his movements earlier that day when he'd left the clubhouse, causing King to send Hyde and me to watch him.

Hyde frowned. "You occupied, King?"

"Yeah." His voice was tight. Reserved. Before we could ask any more questions, he said, "Call me if you have anything. Otherwise I'm busy."

"What the fuck?" Hyde asked to no one in particular when King abruptly ended the call.

I shrugged. "We'll find out soon enough."

Hyde stared at me. "Where's your fucking head at these days, brother?"

I didn't like the accusation I heard. Hyde had been riding my ass for days, and I'd had enough. "Where the fuck do you think it is?"

"I'll tell you where it's not. It's not focused on your club, and that shit needs to stop today. We need you alert and ready at a moment's notice, and I'm not convinced you're any of those things."

My shoulders tightened and I clenched my fists. I'd fucking knock him out if he kept this shit up. "I'm here every-fucking-day, from almost sun up to way past sun-fucking-down, Hyde. I'm giving everything to this club and I'm ready for whatever Silver Hell bring at us. I don't know what the fuck's gotten into you this week, but I'm goddam tired of you breathing down my fucking neck for something I haven't done."

His glare didn't let up. "So that's why you forgot to tell us that Silver Hell had a meeting with Sutherland this week and why you were late for Church two days ago. Yeah, I'd say your commitment is solid, Nitro." He turned the keys in the ignition. "Sort your shit out and do it fast."

* * *

I sat back in the armchair, wrapped my hand around my dick, and watched as Tatum came towards me. I'd been thinking

182

about her all fucking day. Her sweet cunt was never far from my thoughts these days. Almost three weeks of fucking her daily, usually twice a day, and I had turned into a junkie. I craved being inside her in a way I'd never craved pussy. Hell, the fact I kept coming back for more even though I knew she'd never let me fuck her the way I wanted to, said a fuck of a lot.

"Been thinking about you today," she said as she stood in front of me, positioning her feet on the floor either side of my legs.

I ran my eyes over her naked body and pressed a hand to her thigh, curling my fingers around her leg. I continued to slide my other hand up and down my dick. "Tell me what you were thinking."

"I was wondering how it would feel if you fucked me bare."

I gripped her leg harder and pumped my cock a little faster. Her voice was like a stream of sex floating all around me. She intoxicated me with that fucking voice, almost as much as she did with her scent and her touch and her taste. "You wanna feel my dick, skin-to-skin, Vegas?"

She bent and her legs slid along mine as she sat on me. I wished like hell I was naked, too. One thrust and I'd be inside her. She linked her hands around my neck. "I bet you're thinking that if you didn't have those jeans on right now, you'd be inside me already."

Tatum's mind worked in ways I appreciated. Smart as hell and dirty as fuck, she was in sync with me when it came to sex. Except when it came to letting me take my blade to her. "How about you take them off so I can show you how good I feel?"

She pressed her body hard against mine and brought her lips close to my mouth. So damn close I could feel her breath. Could practically taste her. "How about I drag this out so that by the time you show me how good it feels, you're worked up as fuck and you bring your fury with you."

I scooped her hair into my hand and tugged it. "My fury?"

She rocked into me. "Yeah," she murmured, biting my bottom lip and sucking it into her mouth. "I like it when you slam that dick of yours into me like you're trying to push it all the way through me."

"Jesus," I hissed. "You're a dirty fucking girl, Vegas."

Her eyes held mine. "I'm an honest fucking girl, Nitro. I don't pussyfoot around when it comes to sex. I like cock and I fucking love yours. *And* I have no issues telling a guy how I like him to use his cock."

Her honesty was something that drew me to her. I liked her no-bullshit approach to life. Letting go of her hair, I ran my hands down her back and cupped her ass when I reached it. Holding her tight, I pushed up out of the chair, taking her with me. Her legs wrapped around my body and I walked us into her bedroom.

I deposited her on the bed and then undid my jeans. Her eyes tracked my movements and her breathing picked up as she watched my clothes fall to the ground.

Lowering myself to the bed, I moved over her. I slid my dick through her wetness and said, "Do you know what *I* have no issues with?"

"What?" she panted.

"With a woman who tells me like it is. And whose cunt is as greedy as yours is for me."

She folded her legs around me and clung tightly. "Well, I'm telling you right now, you need to get that dick inside me and you need to do it fast."

My eyes searched hers. "I don't have a condom on, Tatum."

She knew what I was asking and what I was saying. At her nod and, "I know," my restraint snapped and I thrust inside her exactly how she liked it. *With all the fury I'd been living that day.*

"Oh, God," Tatum moaned, squeezing me harder. "Yes!"

Fuck, being inside Tatum was where I needed to be. It was as if I broke away from the world the minute I entered her. All the complicated shit in my life was left behind, all the worry eased, all the baggage I carried dropped. When I was deep in her, all I chased was the hush, the calm, the fucking peace that being with her brought me.

Her fingernails clawed down my back as I pounded into her. She met every thrust, taking it hungrily and pushing me for more. In return, I drove my dick as far into her as I could, as hard as I fucking could, giving her the fury she wanted.

I fucked her like a savage.

Wild.

Clawing at each other.

Teeth biting.

Breathless.

I didn't hold anything back and neither did she. Our bodies collided in a violent rush of demand and desire. We both needed this. Almost as much as the air we breathed.

"Fuck… fuck… *fuck*," she panted as she squeezed me deep inside her and came. Her eyes closed and she slowed her movements as she drew every drop of pleasure from her orgasm.

I'd watched Tatum come every single time I'd fucked her. I made a point never to miss it because she was so fucking beautiful when she had my dick buried inside making her feel good. It was the only time I saw the real Tatum, the one who let herself feel and experience everything happening to her. The rest of the time she held me at arm's length, throwing wall after

185

wall up at me. Guarding that cracked heart of hers. Not that I wanted her heart, but I wanted a peek inside. I wanted to know what made her so damn fearless and so fucking fragile all at the same time.

My balls tightened and I rammed into her one last time before coming inside her. Every muscle in my body tensed as the orgasm tore through me, releasing a fuckload of pent-up pressure.

I collapsed onto the bed beside her. Spent. Completely done for. It was the first time I'd ever fucked a woman without a condom and it was fucking amazing. Turning, I found her watching me, a look of absolute bliss on her face.

Smiling, she said, "I could give up exercise at the moment."

"You want me to up my game, Vegas? I could work out those muscles of yours more often."

She rolled my way, curling her arms into her body. "Fuck, I don't think I could take it more than twice a day from you."

"You wanna test that theory?"

Another smile on her lips. "You don't give up easily, do you?"

"Never have, never will. What's the point of life if you crack at the first sign of hardship."

"Who taught you that? Your parents?"

I stared at her. We'd never talked much after sex. Usually we were both in a rush to get out the door in the morning or we passed out exhausted late at night. This was new and I wasn't sure if it was a road I wanted to travel with her.

When I didn't answer, she pushed me. "I'm actually not thinking it was your parents."

That was enough for me to bite. "You've got it all figured out, have you?" My words came out a little harshly. She had no fucking clue what my parents taught me.

186

Reaching across the bed, she trailed a finger along my lips. "And there's the Nitro I haven't seen in a few weeks."

Irritated, I sat up and threw my legs over the side of the bed. "Let's not do this, Tatum."

"Do what?"

Glancing back at her, I bit out, "Let's not turn this into something it's not."

"Oh, so just because we fuck, we can't talk?" Her voice rose, letting me know I'd pissed her off.

I stood and reached for my jeans. "You were never interested in talking before."

She sat up and glared at me. "Yeah, well maybe I wanna talk now." Moving off the bed, she came to me. "Maybe I'm interested to know stuff about the guy I'm screwing."

I kept moving, doing up my jeans. I then grabbed my shirt off the floor and threw it over my head. When I was dressed with my boots on, I eyed her. "Maybe it's time to call it quits. Neither of us wanted anything but sex, so let's not push it."

I exited her place without a backwards glance. I had to keep moving forward. Away. Getting myself involved with Tatum in any way other than just sleeping with her was a bad idea. I knew it in my gut. And I knew it in my fucking heart.

* * *

"What the hell crawled up your ass?" Renee demanded the next morning while we discussed the driving test she would be taking at some point. She wanted to do it soon, while I didn't.

I scowled at her as I settled against the kitchen counter and took a gulp of coffee. Ignoring her question, I said, "I'm just saying that you're gonna need a hell of a lot more practice before you go for your licence."

187

She placed her hand on her hip and threw me a glare. "I've almost clocked up my hours. I'm a good driver. When are you going to admit that instead of being an asshole to me about how I need to get more practice in?"

I raked my fingers through my hair. "I never said you weren't a good dri—"

"Yes, you did! Well, you insinuated it when you said I needed more hours up before you'd let me go for my test. And a head's up, I don't need your permission to sit my damn test. You're not my father."

Fucking hell. Renee knew how to fucking wound. Something she'd learnt from her mother. I gathered the shred of patience I had left for this conversation. If it had been anyone other than my niece, I would have lost my cool long ago. "I know I'm not your father," I grit out. "But I'm the only father figure you've known, so you'll listen when I've got something to say. You *are* a good driver, Renee, but the thousands of hours experience I have driving gives me a better perspective on this. I don't want you out there on the roads with all the dickheads who don't give a shit about you, your safety or your fucking life, until you've clocked up some more hours. And I don't give a fuck if the government says you only need a hundred and twenty hours, I say you need more. You're fucking precious to me and I'll guard your life with everything I have, so that means this argument is over. I win."

She stared at me in stunned silence.

I drank some more coffee and barked, "What?" Jesus, I swore if she kept pushing me, testing me, I really would lose my shit. It had been a rough night of little sleep after I'd left Tatum's and I didn't have the patience I usually did with her.

"That is maybe one of the nicest things you've ever said to me." Her voice cracked and it looked like tears were pooling in her eyes. "I'm sorry I said that thing about you not being my dad. You mightn't be my father but you practically raised me and I love you for it." She broke down at that point, confusing the hell out of me. Where had that come from? Renee wasn't one to cry easily.

I pulled her into my arms. "Fuck, kiddo, I know." I was fucking useless when it came to this shit. It was a good thing I had no kids of my own because I'd fail them when it came to dealing with emotions. When she moved out of my embrace, I said, "What's going on, Renee?"

She wiped the tears from her face. "Nothing. I'm just being stupid."

When she tried to walk away, I grabbed her arm. "Don't ever say that. You're not stupid and nothing you feel is stupid." I hated her reluctance to open up, but I hated more that Marilyn and I had taught her that. Because we had. Kids learnt from example. I knew that better than anyone, and the example we'd set was to shut down and avoid feelings.

Tears tracked down her cheeks again. Blinking through them and sniffling, she managed to get out, "It's everything. Mum, life, your club, Dustin… it's too much. I don't know how to deal with it anymore."

Fuck.

I scrubbed my hand over my face. Her words hit me in the gut. They rang true for me, too. Our fucked-up family and my club problems weighed me down like a tonne of bricks on my shoulders most days. The last few weeks had been a reprieve almost. The weight had felt bearable for some reason, but the heaviness had returned overnight. It caused my mood that morning and my lack of patience with Renee.

"I'm going to fix this, Renee."

She stared at me as if she didn't quite believe me. However, she nodded and said softly, "I hope so."

It was the quiet desperation I heard in her voice that made me swear to myself that I would make good on my promise. No fucking way would I chance Renee living in the same darkness her mother did.

Chapter Twenty-Six

Tatum

"Scars" by Papa Roach

I exited the car park and headed towards the front door of the club. The warmth of the late September day spread across my back as I walked and inhaled the spring scent I loved. It was my favourite time of year. Right before the heat of summer. It could have been worse, I guessed. I could have lived in Queensland.

"Tatum, wait up," Posey called out from behind.

I slowed and gave her a smile when she caught up. "Hey, girl, why are you here so early?" She wasn't due at work for a few more hours.

"I had a hair appointment nearby. Didn't want to make the drive home to then just come back."

I eyed her long dark hair. "Looking good." I took in her glow. "It's good to see you looking so happy."

She smiled. "Yeah, life is better and I have you to thank for that. Thank you for caring when so many wouldn't have." The genuine gratitude was clear in her voice.

"I'm glad." This kind of exchange was awkward for me. It wasn't often that anyone bothered to thank me for anything. Not even Billy half the time.

Thankfully, we were interrupted when Duvall joined us. Posey quickly excused herself, clearly nervous about being near him.

He watched her go. "She's not a bad kid. Just got mixed up with the wrong guy."

I laughed. "Kid? She's not much younger than us."

"Age doesn't mean shit when your maturity levels are out of whack, Tatum."

"That's true." I narrowed my eyes at him. "Why do you look so tired? They working you hard?"

He sighed. "When do they not?"

Duvall was a good-looking guy. Blond hair, a strong jaw, and blue eyes that saw more than anyone knew gave him a face that women never forgot. And when they got a look at his tall, well-built body they threw themselves at him. The thing I respected the hell out of was the fact he never used any of those things to work his way through a string of women. Duvall was one of the good guys. His kindness and honesty were just a couple of the reasons I forgave his attitude towards me since I'd left the law. I knew he was disappointed in the choices I'd made for my life and that his disappointment manifested as moodiness or anger.

I jerked my chin at the club. "What brings you out here?"

His eyes held mine. "You."

There was something in his tone that made me want to walk away from this conversation. But I didn't. My friend deserved more than that. "What's up?"

"How are you?"

Oh, God. I definitely did not want to have *this* conversation. Duvall liked to push me for more than I wanted to give. He came from a touchy-feely family who spewed their emotions all over the damn place. Great people, but I was out when it came to doing that. I gave him a smile, as if that would be enough. "I'm doing well."

"Yeah, see that's where I don't believe you." And out came the side of Duvall I didn't like—his arrogant side. This was the

192

Duvall who thought he knew better than me. He didn't drag his arrogance out often, but when he did, I hated it because it usually ended in us having a fight.

I cocked my head, my annoyance flaring. "Why?" I challenged him, my tone one step away from bitchy.

"Tatum, don't bullshit me. I see straight through it."

"I don't know what bullshit you think I'm feeding you, or why you think that, but I'm telling you that I'm okay and life is good."

He raked his fingers through his hair and muttered, "Fuck." He paused for a beat before throwing out, "I've seen the footage of you leaving the casino with that asshole biker, so I bloody know you are not okay."

Oh fuck. I thought only Silver Hell had seen that footage. My mouth formed an *oh*, but I quickly snapped it shut when he zeroed in on it. "It's not what you thin—"

Anger filled his features. "For fuck's sake, don't give me that line. I deserve more than that from you." He thumped his chest, his eyes wild. "*I* was the one who was there for you when Randall tossed you to the wolves. *I* was the one who picked up the pieces with you after he broke you. And *I'm* the one who has stuck by your side all this time. I deserve more than your lies."

I knew I should have avoided this conversation. It had gone from bad to epic proportions of fucked in less than a minute. I couldn't tell Duvall the truth, but I had to give him something because otherwise he would go after Nitro for something he didn't do. My mind raced with an answer, and for once, it failed. This was usually one of my strengths, stringing a line of bullshit together to get people out of shit, but not that day. Instead I stood in front of my oldest friend—the one who had stuck by me even though he never knew the truth of why I

193

committed the sins I did—and stared at him in silence while my heart cracked a little more, if that was even possible.

I was tired of the lies.

Exhausted by the thought of hiding parts of my life for a second longer.

I didn't want to live like this anymore. I wanted the life I should have had, not this one.

When I didn't say anything, Duvall grabbed my bicep. "He beat you, Tatum! Black and blue. How can you stand here and deny that when it was clear as day to see on that footage? Fuck, I can't even wrap my head around you dating him after that."

I didn't attempt to wriggle out of his hold. I just wanted this to all go away. But I couldn't figure out what excuse to give him to make him leave it be.

Neither of us heard men approaching. We were both so engrossed in our conversation. It wasn't until King's voice cut through the air that we turned to see him watching Duvall with a murderous gaze.

"Let her go or you'll have me to deal with." He didn't raise his voice but he spoke in a low, threatening tone that couldn't be mistaken. I had no doubt that King would hurt Duvall if he didn't do as ordered. The thing I couldn't work out, though, was why King was taking my back.

Duvall dropped my arm and stepped back. He opened his mouth to speak, but something caught his attention behind King and suddenly he stalked towards whatever it was.

And then he began issuing his own threats. "You fucking asshole! I'm going to make you pay for what you did to her!"

I turned just in time to see Duvall throw a punch and to see Nitro duck to avoid it before landing his fist on Duvall's face. He knocked Duvall backwards and raised his fist as if he was about to punch him again, but then thought better of it and dropped his arm.

King yanked Duvall away from Nitro and roared, "Enough!" as Duvall attempted to get another punch in.

Nitro's eyes locked onto mine and I felt the familiar pull to him. The need he stirred in me was too great to ignore. It had been two weeks since he'd walked out of my house and never came back. I hadn't seen him or heard from him in that time. And I hadn't gone looking for him because he'd made it clear what he wanted.

I couldn't deal with any of them at that moment. I turned and walked away, picking up my pace as I moved so as to avoid any of them stopping me. But Nitro was faster than me, and a moment later, his hand curled around my arm. "Tatum, stop," he commanded.

I closed my eyes and held my breath for a beat. On an exhale, I turned to face him. "What do you want, Nitro? I've gotta get to work."

It was a lie and he knew it. Ignoring what I said, he asked, "You good?"

Emotions I never knew existed exploded out of me in a violent burst. "I'm sick of you asking me that goddam question! Do you even *care* if I'm good?" I threw my words at him as if they were fire and would burn him. I had no clue where my anger had come from or why I was directing it at him, but I couldn't stop myself.

His nostrils flared and his eyes mirrored the anger I felt. He, however, managed to keep his in check. "I told you I don't play games and I don't do shit for any reason but how it appears, so when I ask you if you're good, I mean it."

I searched his eyes and knew right down to my bones that he meant every word he said. Nitro might have been many things but dishonest was not one of them. "I'm good."

His gaze dropped to my arm where Duvall had held me. "What's his game?"

"What do you mean?"

"Why did he come at me like that?"

"He's seen the surveillance of us leaving the casino."

His mind worked quickly, putting it together. "So he thinks I did that to you." And then he surprised me. "You seeing him now?"

"What? No. Why?" His question threw me, completely bewildering me.

"Vegas, a man doesn't get that worked up unless the woman means something to him. I've seen the way he looks at you and it's pretty fucking clear he wants you. I need to know what I'm dealing with here. So, are you seeing him?"

My mind was still trying to unscramble itself. "No, I'm not seeing him."

He nodded. "Okay." He took a step back as if he was going to leave, but then he stopped and ran his eyes over my body. Slowly. As if he was committing it to memory. "I'll look into this and let you know what I find. As far as I knew, that surveillance had been destroyed."

And then he headed into the club with King, leaving me standing there all kinds of confused. Seeing him, speaking to him, hell, just being in his presence, made me realise how much I'd missed him. I hadn't let a man into my life on a regular basis like I had with Nitro since my husband left me nearly two years ago. Sleeping together, spending nights together… we might not have shared anything from our lives with each other, but we'd shared our bodies in ways that meant something to me.

196

Shit.

I wanted him again.

My skin craved his touch.

My mind craved the escape his caress allowed.

And as much as I struggled admitting it, my soul craved the safety of his embrace.

Trouble was, he didn't seem interested in any of that. I'd only ever been someone he had to watch over for his club. And I was still that person now that Duvall had involved himself.

"Are you still dating him?"

I spun around to find Duvall staring at me, wild-eyed. "No. We're done." He didn't need to know that Nitro and I were never dating.

"Good."

He left me then. I didn't know where this would all end up. I should have cared. I should have chased after him to set him straight and convince him to drop it. But all I cared about was coping with the emptiness slaying me. The problem with that was I had no fucking clue how to make it go away and I knew that coping was a crock of shit. I could numb the pain and try to hide from it, but I could never fucking *cope* with it.

Chapter Twenty-Seven

Nitro

"It Ain't Easy" by Blake Shelton

I rested my arms on the counter of the bar, scanning the club patrons. Not looking for anyone or anything in particular, just absently people watching. Eyeing a leggy blonde, my mind immediately went to Tatum. Hell, my mind didn't need a shove to go there. It lived there.

It had been three days since I'd run into her outside Billy's club. Three days. Not that I was counting. Fuck, who the hell was I kidding? The days added to the tally my mind kept. The tally screaming at me that the reason my dick was hard with a desperate need that no other woman could fill was because it had been nearly three weeks since I'd been with Tatum.

"Where the fuck are you, man?" Devil asked, drawing my attention back to him. When I stared blankly at him, he added, "You might be sitting on that stool next to me but you aren't here. You haven't been for weeks."

I took a swig of my rum. I'd even started drinking the same fucking drink as she did. "I've got shit going on."

He threw back some of his beer, a look of "don't give me that shit" on his face. "Brother, I know the look of a man in the middle of a pussy affair and you're wearing that look right now. She something special or just a root you can't get out of your head?"

My jaw clenched. I didn't like him referring to Tatum as a root. Trouble was I had no fucking clue what she was to me anymore. "You ever had a woman fuck with your mind, Devil?"

He chuckled. "Dude, they all do that."

"Not like this."

His smile morphed into a serious expression. "Fuck, you've never gone there with a chick before?"

"Nope. Don't need another person to take care of in my life."

"So, what, you just fuck 'em and leave?"

I drank some more rum. "They always know the score." I shrugged. "Some of them stick around for a bit."

"So this one's turned into something more?"

I leant my head back before stretching my neck side-to-side. Fuck, my shoulders were tight. Exhaling hard, I said, "I don't know what the fuck she's turned into. All I know is that I can't get her out of my damn head. And that I'm sitting here in a fucking bar spilling my shit to you in ways I never thought I ever would." *Fuck.*

He slapped me on the back and grinned at me. "Hate to break it to you, Nitro, but she's turned into something more. Looks like you've found someone else to take care of in your life after all." He paused for a beat. "My advice to you, brother, is to accept your fate for what it is and then lay the fuck down and let that pussy whip you. No use fighting love."

As I sat processing his words, a voice I hadn't heard in years cut through the noise of the club, causing ice to slither down my spine. "Rhys."

My head snapped up to find Joseph standing next to us, watching me with eyes I'd hoped to fuck never to see again in my lifetime. I pushed up off the stool and stood, invading his personal space. Gripping his shirt, I snarled, "What the fuck are you doing in Sydney?"

He didn't flinch. "Came to see you, my boy."

I clenched the material of his shirt before letting it go, shoving him away at the same time. "Yeah, well there's nothing to see here, so I suggest you crawl back to where you came from."

He watched me for a moment before nodding and saying, "Good."

I glared at him. "*Good?*"

The smile that danced across his lips pissed me the hell off. "Yes, good. I can do a lot with that anger of yours."

Oh no, he didn't. *No, he fucking didn't.* "The days of you doing anything with me are long fucking over, Joseph." Fuck, he always did have a way of pushing my buttons.

"We can do this a few different ways, Rhys. One of them entails you choosing to come back to me. The other—"

Fury punched through me. That he'd ever think I'd go back to him. I shoved my face in his. "You had your shot at me and you more than fucked it up. I never want to see you again. And if I do, I promise you it will be the last fucking time." I pressed my hands to his chest and pushed him away from me. "Now get the *fuck* out of here."

He contemplated that and then did the smartest thing he'd ever done—he left.

"Fuck!" I yelled as I watched him go.

Fucking hell.

"Who was that?" Devil asked.

Memories ripped my heart right open, bleeding the darkest, angriest blood I'd oozed in years.

I gritted my teeth and clenched and unclenched my fists over and over as my body filled with rage. Meeting Devil's eyes, I said, "My uncle."

* * *

Four hours later, I was three sheets to the wind, walking the cement path to Tatum's front door. My head was a messed-up shit fight and I couldn't, no matter how much I tried, even begin to pick through my thoughts. I tried to numb the choking pain but failed. The memories of what Joseph had done to our family played in my mind like a fucking movie and no alcohol could rid me of those. I'd spent nineteen years trying to forget. I thought I'd worked them out of me. But five minutes in his goddam presence and I was right back there living it all over again.

Motherfucker.

I reached the door and came to an abrupt stop. What the fuck made me think this was a good idea? My mind was already fucked up with Tatum. I didn't need to add to that.

"Fuck," I muttered.

I stood there for another minute going back and forth with myself before I made the final decision that this really *was* a bad idea.

Exiting her property, I told myself Devil was wrong—Tatum hadn't become someone special to me. Good sex was just that. And I could find that anywhere.

Chapter Twenty-Eight

Tatum

"(Baby I've Got You) On My Mind" by Powderfinger

"Tell me how he makes you feel when you're together."

I looked at my therapist and contemplated her question. We'd been working together for weeks now and I'd finally brought Nitro up with her. I'd resisted doing that but after seeing him last week, I'd cracked. I was fairly sure I was spiralling into a chaotic mess of despair and defeat. Rock bottom would be one way to describe it. So, in my hopelessness, I decided to lay everything on the table with her. I decided to finally give her every piece of my soul and prayed that we could fix me.

"I hated him at first. Hated that he saved me when all I wanted was to be dead. Dead with Christopher. And he was so mean that I hated him even more. But then he saved me again and started showing me another side of him." I wrapped my arms around my body and stared at her, remembering the night I slept next to him the first time. "He makes me feel safe. Which sounds ludicrous even to me, but it's the truth."

"Tatum, we can't make ourselves feel something that's not there, just like we can't alter the way people make us feel. It's not ludicrous to say that he makes you feel safe. But what you have to do now is decide what you want to do with that feeling. Do you want to spend more time with him? Get to know him better?"

"I don't know."

She watched me closely. The way she saw me, *really saw me*, made me feel uncomfortable. I wanted to turn away from her gaze. I didn't want her to see me. But I knew I had to let her. If I had any hope of fixing myself, I had to allow her to help me.

"I think you do know," she said simply, guiding me. She never told me what to do. That didn't seem to be how she worked. I'd never spent time with a therapist before so I had no idea how they worked, but I'd expected more help making decisions.

I unwrapped my arms from around my body and curled my legs under me on the couch. God, why was this shit so hard? Blowing out a long breath, I said, "I want to sleep with him. But I don't know if I want more than that. And besides, he doesn't want more. Hell, he doesn't even want sex with me."

"Tell me, why do you have to know everything all at once? Do you think decisions through all the way from beginning to resolution for everything you do in your life?"

"Yes."

"Why?"

"It's the way I'm wired. I can't help it."

She leant forward. "You're a survivor, Tatum. You're strong and capable. You can help anything you want in your life."

Fuck, she was pissing me off today. "Maybe I don't want to fucking help it. I like the way I live my life."

"If you like the way you live your life, you wouldn't be here. I challenge you to think some more about that this week. Consider the possibilities of not thinking everything through and discarding ideas because you *think* you know how it will end."

I shoved my fingers through my hair, feeling all kinds of agitated. My body was a bundle of nervous, angry energy and I didn't even know why. In desperation, I blurted out the thought

I hadn't been able to let go of for weeks. "Why am I not getting better? I've been coming here for weeks and I feel worse than I did at the beginning. I just want to be fixed and it's not happening!"

She watched me for a moment. Again. Always silently watching. And then—"We've been digging deep. You've been dredging up memories, hurts, and deeply rooted pain, Tatum. We're challenging everything you've ever thought, and examining if your thought patterns are useful, whether they serve you or hurt you. This is a process and unfortunately you can't escape it. What you do need to do is trust it. Move through it rather than against it. And know that slowly it will lead you out of all this pain and uncertainty you're feeling. The other thing? Don't try to fight your feelings as they come up. After years of avoiding them, you have to learn to live with them."

I left the session just as confused as when I'd entered it. But for the first time, I considered the possibility that maybe it was okay to be confused. Maybe she was right and I didn't need all the answers right away.

* * *

"*You're* watching TV?" Monroe's shock vibrated through the phone that night when I told her I was going to watch *Game of Thrones*.

I laughed as I held the phone to my ear while making myself a Milo at the kitchen counter. "Yeah, and it starts in fifteen minutes so I have to get off the phone soon."

"You never watch television. What the hell has gotten into you?"

"I've decided to try new things."

204

She remained silent for a moment. When she spoke again, her voice had softened. "I love that, babe."

I inhaled deeply, letting the love I heard from her settle into my bones. "I love *you*, Monroe. I don't tell you that often enough."

"Oh, geez, you *really* are trying new things, aren't you?"

I smiled. "That was where you were supposed to tell me that you love me, too."

"Pffft, I tell you that all the time." She spoke the truth. Monroe's side of the family inherited the touchy-feely genes while mine didn't.

"Yeah, well you can tell me again. I won't hold it against you."

"Fuck me, Tatum, this shrink you're seeing is worth her weight in gold. And for the record, I love you, too."

I stirred my drink. "Okay, now that's out of the way, tell me how you're going with your search for a pierced cock."

"Ugh. Let's not go there."

Laughing, I said, "You know what we need?"

"What?"

"A girls' night out. You can look for Mr. Pierced and I can look for Mr. Not Closed Off."

She turned silent again.

When she didn't speak, I said, "You still there, Roe?"

"Yeah," she said softly, her voice cracking. "This is nice."

"What?"

"Us, talking girls' nights outs and men and dating. It's been too long since we've done this."

I knew what she was saying. *Since I shut down on her and retreated from life.* "Yeah, it's nice."

A knock on my front door interrupted us and I ended the call after promising that we would definitely have a night out soon.

The new lightness I felt was both strange and wonderful. I'd come home from the therapy session and cried for an hour and then slept for two. When I woke, it was as if the tears and the sleep were therapy in themselves. I woke with a desire to cook dinner and watch television. I couldn't remember the last time I looked forward to such simple things.

I reached the front door and checked in the peephole to see who it was. My belly fluttered at the sight of Nitro standing on the other side. And in that moment, I knew the therapist was right. *Again*. I *did* know whether I wanted to see him again. The proof was in the way my body responded to him, the way my heart sped up when he was near.

I opened the door and smiled as our eyes met. "Nitro."

Heat flared in his gaze. He couldn't even hide it and I wasn't sure he was trying to. The way he looked at me made me think he'd come here for something other than club business. "We need to talk."

I moved aside. "Okay."

He stepped inside and I followed him into the house. We'd almost made it to the kitchen when he suddenly turned to me, snaked his arm around my waist and pushed me up against the wall. Pressing his body hard to mine, his fingers worked their way into my hair and his mouth found mine.

Every inch of my skin burned with desire. I thought I'd seen passion from Nitro. I thought he'd given every piece of himself when he'd fucked me. I hadn't seen anything yet. Nitro gave new meaning to intensity with this kiss. With the way his whole body commanded my attention and demanded I give him what he wanted.

When he ended the kiss, eyes full of hunger lingered on my mouth for a beat. He then shifted his gaze to meet mine. His hands remained in my hair, his body against mine. "I can't go another night without you, Vegas."

His raspy voice, full of raw need, washed over me. God, how I'd missed this voice. Missed this man.

I slid my hands up his body to take hold of his face. Pulling it down to mine, I took his passion and I raised it. I kissed him for what felt like forever. When we finally pulled apart, we were both breathless, panting for more. "Thank fuck," I said as I practically crawled up his body.

He held me tightly and walked us into my bedroom while I wrapped everything I had around him.

Legs.

Arms.

Hands.

Feet.

Hope.

Chapter Twenty-Nine

Nitro

"It Goes Like This" by Thomas Rhett

I traced lazy circles over Tatum's hip while she slept. It was still dark outside, but I couldn't sleep. I'd woken up hard as hell for her and that need had only grown the more I watched and touched her.

I hadn't meant to, but I passed out after I fucked her last night. The sex had been intense. Fuelled by all the fucked-up emotions inside of me. She'd thrown her shit at me, too. I'd felt it in the way she clung and clawed and marked me with her teeth. It had been off the charts and had completely wiped me so that I slept for seven straight hours afterwards. Sleeping that long was something I never did.

She stirred and rolled over. Still half asleep, she swung a leg over my body. Next came her arm, which landed across my chest, her hand snaking under me. She rested her head in the space between my shoulder and face. I thought she would fall back asleep, but she surprised me when her mouth kissed my skin, a small moan escaping.

Placing my hand on her ass, I murmured, "Morning, Vegas."

She kissed her way from my chest, up my throat, to my mouth. Pulling my bottom lip between her teeth, she met my gaze and smiled. Her knee then dug into the mattress and she moved to sit on top of me.

My eyes dropped to her tits. I fucking loved her tits. Could spend hours with my mouth on them. That morning, though, she had other ideas.

Tilting my face back up, she demanded, "Tell me how this is going to go down between us."

I gripped her hips and rocked up against her. "Fuck, I like this bossy side of you. It's making me harder than I already was."

She didn't smile. "I need to know, Nitro."

"As in you want a play-by-play of the next ten years or you want to know if I've just come for a quick fuck?"

She sat back and ran her hands through her hair. Again, my eyes were drawn to her tits. Couldn't help myself. "Fuck," she muttered. "She's fucking right. *Shit.*"

I watched in fascination as Tatum lost her shit. I didn't know what she was rambling about, but it was sexy as hell seeing her do it. When a pained look crossed her face, I pressed a finger to her lips, silencing her. "You know how hot you look when you do that?"

She scowled as she smacked my hand away. "I'm here having a mental breakdown and all you're thinking about is fucking me?"

I grinned, loving this. "This ain't anything new. I'm *always* thinking about fucking you."

She seemed to like that because her expression softened. But she kept up the hard-ass routine. "Yeah, well maybe you could think about something other than pussy for a minute."

"I could think about tits instead, or ass. Or tits *and* ass. Hell, I could even get on board thinking about your mouth wrapped around my cock."

She rolled her eyes, but I saw the amusement there. "Who knew you could be so playful, Nitro?"

I smacked her ass lightly. "Okay, tell me who is right."

209

"Huh?"

"Before... you were muttering something about some woman being right. What did you mean?"

She sighed. "My therapist. She says these things to me that I don't agree with at the time, but then I'm always proven wrong. It drives me fucking crazy."

My respect for Tatum only grew in that moment. "What did she say that was right this time?"

"She told me that perhaps I didn't always need to be looking into the future trying to figure out how situations would turn out to decide whether to pursue them. I argued with her, but just now when you asked me about seeing ten years down the track, it made me think that maybe she was right. Maybe I don't need to think that far ahead with you."

I already liked her shrink. "In answer to your question, this wasn't just about getting laid last night."

She stilled. "Okay," she said softly.

I decided brutal honesty was the best way forward. "I can't give you a play-by-play, though, Vegas."

Watching me quietly, she thought about that for a minute. And then she shifted so she was lying on top of me instead of sitting. Her lips lingered on mine for a beat before she smiled. "I can work with that."

* * *

"Billy's raised his price," King said later that day. He'd called me, Hyde, Kick and Devil into the office to discuss our gun supplies. We still hadn't worked out what Dragon had planned, but we knew he had stocked his supplies high.

"Jesus, he's already overpriced," Kick said. His recovery was going well but I knew he was sick of being cooped up in the

210

clubhouse where King had been keeping him. They'd argued repeatedly over it, but King remained adamant. It didn't surprise me. Kick was King's golden boy, always coming through with whatever King needed. I'd seen the fear in King's eyes when we'd brought Kick in after being shot. He hadn't slept until he knew Kick would survive. And these days he was taking no chances. I figured Kick would be stuck in the clubhouse for weeks still.

"Well, you know my thoughts on Billy," I said.

"And you know that there aren't many other options," Hyde snapped.

"Maybe we need to look outside Sydney," I said, glaring at Hyde.

Devil cut in. "Well, whoever we get them from, we need to make sure they're not going to screw us over down the track and withhold supply like Sutherland has."

King nodded. "Agreed. And I want our stockpile doubled."

I whistled low. We already had a huge stockpile. It was a risk to double it. Heat from the cops had been circling us for weeks. They were busting their balls trying to clean up the city and had targeted Silver Hell and Black Deeds. Bronze had managed to keep us out of it but we were kidding ourselves if we thought that could last forever. Carrying a large supply of guns could come back to bite us in the ass if they raided us. "You sure about that, King?"

His jaw clenched. "Yes. Put the feelers out, Nitro. Find us a new supplier or get Billy to lower his price."

I nodded. King was notorious for not changing his mind once made up.

"How much longer are we going to hold out with this truce?" Hyde asked. He'd been pushing King to rethink the whole thing. Dangerous, I thought. If we broke it, we risked the heat shining our way from the cops and we also risked Dragon being steps ahead of us and coming out guns blazing. It was better to hold off and figure out his plan first.

"As long as it takes," King snapped. "We rush this, Hyde, and we could lose everything." King wasn't known for his patience, and I could tell the strain this waiting had put on him. Reaching for his phone, he said, "I'm heading out for a bit. Call me if you need me."

"Where the hell does he go every day?" Devil asked after King left the office.

I wondered the same thing. It had been going on for weeks. King kept shit close to his chest, though, so none of us knew.

"Got no idea," I said. "Who wants to come with me to find us some guns?"

Kick lifted a brow. "You got a lead on someone?"

I smirked at him. "Sit down, fucker. You're not going anywhere."

He blew out a long breath. "Fuck, King is fuckin' killing me here. Hell, even Evie isn't giving me hell about taking it easy anymore."

Devil slapped him on the back, grinning like a fool. "Remind me to never take a bullet for the club. Doesn't seem like you get much for it except King locking you up and your woman locking her pussy up."

Kick had been vocal in his pain over not getting fucked for weeks after he was shot. He groaned. "This shit with King needs to fuckin' end. I'll get you what you need, Nitro."

"Not a fucking chance in hell am I going against King," I said.

Hyde took charge. "I'm with Nitro today. Kick stays here and Devil is on Dragon." He looked at me. "We good to go?"

Hyde was the last person I wanted to spend the day with. Shit hadn't settled between us since he spoke his mind about me not being committed to the club. But I nodded and followed him out to our bikes. I just had to get through the day. work with Hyde to fix our supplier issue, and then get back to Tatum's sweet pussy.

Chapter Thirty

Tatum

"Unpack Your Heart" by Phillip Phillips

"A man that studieth revenge keeps his own wounds green. Why that?" Nitro asked as his finger glided over the tattoo on my thigh. He'd just fucked me for two hours, and I was sleepy, but he hadn't taken his hands off me since I'd returned from the bathroom ten minutes ago and his touch kept me awake.

I stared at the words from Francis Bacon that I'd chosen and swallowed hard. "It's a warning."

"For what?"

"That my desire for revenge isn't good for my mental health."

His eyes found mine. "Revenge for your brother's murder?"

"Yeah, for that..." *and for so much more.*

He shifted so he was lying on his side with one leg over mine, his body propped up on his arm, his head resting against his hand. Running a finger along my collarbone, he said, "What else is running around in that pretty head of yours, Vegas? What other revenge do you want?"

Sharing personal stuff with each other hadn't been part of our relationship before. He'd pretty much always shut down on me whenever I asked him something, and I hadn't volunteered much either. But we'd taken a step forward, and although I had no play-by-play guiding me as to what this relationship could be, I sensed the change in him. He was interested. Wanted to know more. And while I felt more fear over sharing my heart than I did over doing things grown men would shrink from, I decided to take a chance on him. "I've spent hours plotting my ex-husband's death. Almost every bad thing that's happened to me in the last couple of years is a direct result of the shit he put me through. It would be easy to kill him. And to get away with it."

I held my breath and diverted my eyes from his. I'd already said too much. Nitro would surely get up and walk out the door after that confession. I couldn't imagine anyone but Monroe choosing to stand by me once they knew the thoughts in my head and the things I'd done.

He tilted my chin so I looked back up at him. "What did he do to you?" There was no judgement in his tone, no repulsion in the way he looked at me.

Letting out the breath I held, I shook my head. "Let's not talk about this, Nitro. It's done and in the past and I'm trying to move on from it." My cheeks heated with the self-disgust I always felt when I thought about Randall. All the disgust I felt towards myself stemmed from him, because every shameful thing I'd done was for him.

He shifted on the bed again, this time to press harder against me and to drape his arm over my chest, almost as if he was trying to pin me down. "I have someone in my life who I want dead, too. The shit he did to my family and me… I want him deader than fucking dead. I want to do it slowly, make him hurt and beg for forgiveness. Forgiveness I'll never give."

His declaration came out harshly, his pain still sharp. I heard what he was telling me without saying it out loud. This was a safe place between the two of us.

"I met Randall when I was twenty, when I was a naïve uni student just trying to put myself through a law degree. He was seven years older than me and seemed so sophisticated with his own business, expensive car, flashy house. You name it, he had it. And he used all that shit to fool me. After growing up with nothing, I was determined to have things for myself, nice things. I wanted the big house, the cars, the holidays, everything. A year after we met, he proposed and I said yes. It wasn't until we'd been married for about five years that I opened my eyes to who I'd really married. But, God, us women are fucking dumb sometimes. I swore I could fix him, change him, make *us* better. If only *I* did better, he'd stop lying to me, stop treating me like a fool."

The pressure in my chest became hard to bear. It was like a heavy weight pressing down on me. I needed out from under Nitro's hold. Pushing his arm away, I forced myself to a sitting position and drew my legs up so my knees were against my chest. I wrapped my arms around my legs and dropped my head to my knees, allowing my tears to fall.

Sobs racked my body, and I let them. I didn't try to stop any of it. I just let myself move through the emotions as my therapist had suggested. Anger, hurt, shame—I let it all hit me. Most of all, though, I stopped hiding from my self-hatred. I let it bleed out of me.

Lifting my head, I eyed Nitro through my tears. He watched me silently, his hand placed reassuringly on my back. Wiping at my tears and getting myself together, I continued, "Randall had an importing business and he did well with it, but he always wanted more. More sales, more income, bigger and flashier everything. Was always looking for the next big thing in business to give him the wealth he craved. He managed to get himself into debt and that's when he turned nasty and mean towards me. We fought all the time. Nothing I did was ever good enough. So I decided I had to help him somehow." I paused for a moment, willing the tears to hold off until I got this out. "That

216

was when Billy came to me with an offer. I was working in the DPP, and he needed someone to help get him off some charges. I'd known him for about four years, and although I knew he was dirty, I liked him. He'd always been good to me. Before I started working with the DPP, I'd done some legal work for him so I knew what he was into. Anyway, he offered me good cash to help him. One case led to another, and it just spiralled out of control. I did whatever I needed to do to make his problems go away, including lying for him and forging signatures. I always told myself that once I had the money Randall needed to get himself out of shit our problems would go away and I could stop doing that work for Billy. Turned out that the day Randall had the ninety thousand he needed to clear all his debt was the day that *he* went away."

Nitro frowned. "He left you?"

I nodded. "Yeah," I said softly. "For his long-term mistress who I never knew about."

Nitro's jaw clenched and his shoulders tensed. "So that motherfucker took the cash you'd sold your fucking soul for and did the fucking dirty on you?"

I gulped back a sob. "Yes," I whispered. "And then it all went to shit after that. My whole life… fucked. I lost everything."

"The DPP found out what you'd done," Nitro said, putting it all together.

"Yes. I was disbarred. My friends, who were all lawyers, walked away from me. I lost my home, my car, everything. The only people I had left were Chris, Monroe, Duvall and Billy."

"That's when you started working for Billy?"

I nodded. Taking a deep breath in an effort to stop more tears, I said, "I did this to myself. Everything I don't have now is my own fault. I was stupid to fall for someone like Randall. Stupid to think he would give me the things I was desperate for.

217

And even dumber for wanting those things in the first place. I threw my career away for nothing."

"Fuck, Tatum," he started. "We do crazy shit for our family sometimes. Anything to make them happy. You weren't stupid to fall for someone. He's the asshole in all this."

More tears fell. I couldn't hold them in any longer. "He didn't even call when Chris died.... I don't know what I expected, but I thought no matter what had happened between us, he might care enough to check on me. I guess I know once and for all how much he actually cared about me."

"Why was Chris murdered?" he asked quietly.

"He was involved in some bad shit. Mostly car theft. He ran with a gang from the time he was fifteen and just got deeper and deeper into shit. I tried to get him out, but it was ingrained in him. He went off the rails when he was nineteen, mentally, and after that, he just never seemed to get his life together. Had delusions of being untouchable. He went into direct opposition with Silver Hell, selling stolen cars cheaply. They didn't like it because he was undercutting them. In the end, they solved their problem by killing him."

"Fuck," he muttered. "Are your parents still alive?"

I shook my head. "No. Dad passed away nine years ago, and Mum died from breast cancer last year. Just before Chris died."

His eyes filled with sorrow and he wiped my tears as they fell harder. His touch was so tender. Full of care. When my tears didn't subside, he pulled me into his arms and held me until I stopped crying. Nitro's embrace was everything I'd never had from a man in my life. My father had been so busy providing for our family that his time had been scarce. He'd also been preoccupied with desperately trying to figure out how to get my mother to love him as much as he did her, which meant his emotional capacity was stretched thin when it came to his kids.

And as far as my ex-husband was concerned, I couldn't recall a time he'd ever comforted me the way Nitro was. *My nightmare slayer.*

* * *

I stood in the doorway to my bedroom and leant against the doorjamb watching Nitro put on his boots. He'd woken me an hour earlier with a hard-on that needed taking care of, but we'd been interrupted when King had called asking him to meet in an hour. We'd taken care of that hard-on, but it had been faster than either of us had wanted because, with traffic, he'd be pushing it to meet King on time.

"Here," I said, pushing off from the doorjamb and shoving a thermos at him.

He stood and closed the distance between us. "Coffee?"

"Yeah, figured I didn't get time to cook you breakfast so I'd make coffee for your drive."

Taking the thermos, he said, "Since when do you cook me breakfast, woman?"

Woman.

That word and the way it rolled off his tongue hit every single nerve ending in my body. Before I knew it, my arms were looped around his neck and my body was pressed up against his. "There's a first time for everything. Maybe tomorrow if you're lucky."

A sexy smile made its way across his face and his hand curved over my ass. Slowly. The kind of slow that made my vagina roll over and beg for mercy. But there would be no mercy that morning. He had to get to work. "You a good cook, Vegas?"

219

I gripped the back of his neck. "You better believe it. You won't know whether you want me to open my legs or my cookbook."

Heat flared in his eyes and he moved his mouth to my ear. "Pussy always trumps food."

I unhooked my hands from around his neck and let him go. This was moving into dangerous territory. "You should leave before I try and stop you."

"Yeah," he said gruffly. Grabbing his keys, he made his way to the front door. As he reached for the handle, his phone rang. "What's up, Dustin?" he answered the call, pulling the door open.

I followed him outside to his ute, catching pieces of the conversation.

"No, I can't come home right now and help you. I've gotta get to work," he said. I picked up that Dustin was stressing over something and Nitro was attempting to calm him down.

I placed my hand on his forearm to draw his attention. When I had it, I said, "Is he okay? Can I help?"

Nitro stared at me for a beat, contemplating what I said before nodding. "Dustin, give me a sec." He moved the phone away from his mouth to say to me, "He's got a job interview this morning and is stressing. Have you got time to go and talk him down?"

I nodded. "Yes."

"Thanks." He ended his call with Dustin, promising I'd be there soon. Yanking the door to his ute open, he said, "Thanks for that. He's always a mess when he has an interview. Usually I'm there to calm him."

I loved how he was there for his family. Moving into him, my lips found his, lingering there not wanting to let him go. "I'll talk him through it."

He watched me for a moment, his arm resting on the top of the door. It seemed like he was mulling something over, but all he ended up saying was, "Appreciate it." And then he closed the door, kicked over the engine and reversed out of the driveway.

I kept my gaze on his ute until I couldn't see it anymore. Wrapping my arms around my body, I headed back inside. The fact he trusted me to help his brother didn't escape my attention. I wondered how many others he allowed into his life in that way?

* * *

"Right, tell me about this interview," I said to Dustin as I dumped my bag on Nitro's kitchen table a little while after he'd called for help.

He paced nervously and stared at me with a desperate look of fear. "What do you want to know?"

I smiled, trying to gain his trust. I'd never seen anyone so scared about a job interview before. "What's the job?"

"It's for a cleaning job at a school."

"And have you done that kind of work before?"

He twisted his hands together. "Yes."

"Great! So you've got experience. That will look good for you." I glanced at the table, looking for a resume. "Have you got a resume?"

His eyes widened. "Shit! Yes… no. Oh, fuck, Tatum…."

I moved to him and placed my hands on his shoulders. "Breathe, Dustin. Deep breath in, then out."

He nodded and did what I said, taking a deep breath. On an exhale, he said, "I don't know where it is."

"What time is the interview?"

"Eleven thirty."

221

It was only just after eight. "Okay, this is what we're gonna do. You're going to follow me to my work and we're going to type up a new resume for you. We'll print it there and then you can drive to your interview."

His breaths were coming faster, and I wasn't convinced he would get through this hiccup. But he nodded his agreement.

I brought out my stern voice. The one I often used on my girls when they were having a moment at work. "You've made it through the first hurdle, Dustin. Getting an interview is hard these days. So, pull up your panties and let's get this shit done, because you're going to kick ass at this interview. And I'm going to make sure you have the best resume to impress them with."

His eyes widened again, and I thought we might have a problem for sure, but he ended up grinning and moving into action.

As I followed him out of Nitro's house, I realised it was the second day in a row that I was going to work with a smile on my face.

Chapter Thirty-One

Nitro

"The Story" by Brandi Carlile

I stared at Joseph as he entered King's office. Bewildered, I turned to King. "You've gotta be fucking kidding! *He's* who you wanna buy fucking guns off?"

King had called me in early to meet with him, Hyde, and a potential new supplier. The last person I'd expected to see walk through that door was my fucking uncle.

"You two know each other?" King asked, looking between us.

"He's my fucking uncle, and I'll be fucked if I work with him," I thundered.

Joseph's mouth spread out into a thin line as he regarded me with irritation. "My nephew always was overdramatic."

I clenched my teeth, fists, and every fucking part of my body because it all strained to lash out and punch the motherfucker. Or choke the life out of him. His memories were clearly distorted. I'd never lived an overdramatic moment in my life. He made sure of that.

King's face wrinkled with confusion. His gaze swung to me. "I didn't know you had any other family."

I turned to Joseph and shot a hate-filled glare his way. "As far as I'm concerned, I don't."

Before anyone could speak again, Joseph cut in. "This has got nothing to do with family. This is purely business, gentlemen. I have the weapons you need and, as discussed, I'm happy to lower my price for the first six months' worth of shipments if we agree to a twelve-month term to begin with."

Hyde whistled as scepticism filled his expression. "That's a sweet deal. What do you get out of it?"

"I'm looking to do more business in Sydney. You'd be my first client."

Hyde crossed his arms over his chest. "Yeah, but what do you really get out of it, because us being your first client isn't much to gain in exchange for six months of cheap guns."

Joseph's vein ticked in his temple. No one in the room besides me understood that tick, though. Probably didn't even see it either. He was pissed, and I guessed it was because Hyde had hit the nail on the fucking head. "You can bet your ass he's got an ulterior motive," I threw out.

All eyes came to me.

Joseph's features darkened, but he held his shit together. He always had been good at doing that. Except when I pushed him too far and he showed me just what us Lockwood's were capable of. "I do have an ulterior motive. I own Melbourne when it comes to guns and have done so for fifteen years. New players are coming into the market, and while I'd prefer not to have the competition, I can't stop it. So, I've chosen to expand to keep my business running. And I see Storm as a potential ally. This deal is my way of fostering that relationship."

I watched in disbelief as King and Hyde seemed to buy that crock of shit. But I held my tongue. Better to wait for him to leave to have this out with them.

"Okay, Joseph, leave it with us. We'll discuss this and get back to you soon," King said.

As Joseph left, he handed me a business card. "My phone number, son, for when you come to your senses."

I took the card, but only because he thrust it upon me before I registered what he said. He was delusional if he thought I'd use it.

Once he left the office, I turned to King and Hyde. "We can't use him."

King settled against the desk and crossed his feet in front of him. "Why not?"

"That bullshit about expanding in Sydney to save his business is a lie. If a deal with him seems too good to be true, it is."

"I take it you're not close to him?" King said.

I shook my head. "Haven't been for nineteen years and don't intend to be ever again."

"What happened?" Hyde asked.

This was a story I never wanted to revisit. However, I had to give them something, a piece of it at least, to make them understand how evil Joseph was. "You know much about him and his business?"

"I know that he's built a fucking empire from nothing," King said. "And that he's known to be a ruthless motherfucker."

"Yeah, well, that empire he built from nothing? It came from building an army of soldiers willing to do his dirty work at his beck and call. And those soldiers? He finds them on the street and in the gutters, cleans them up and then brainwashes them into robots who have no fucking clue what they're doing. He uses them to pimp drugs, women, guns…. You name it, he sells it. And if someone gets in the way of all that? His soldiers are trained to take care of problems."

King pushed off from the desk. "Nitro, I just want guns and I want them cheap, and I want to buy them from someone who won't fuck us over. I don't really give a fuck what Joseph's business is. So long as he has what we need, that's all that matters."

225

My shoulders tensed. "So you'll consider this?"

"Yeah, I will."

My vision blurred with red rage. The urge to punch shit took over my body and I knew I had to get out of King's office before I did something I'd regret. Jabbing my finger at him, I said, "I'm telling you both now, if you do this, you'll live to regret it."

I turned and ripped the door open.

The thing that pissed me off the most wasn't that Joseph had wormed his way into Storm or that he was in Sydney. It was that I'd taken my eye off the ball with him. I'd kept track of his movements for fucking years, always making sure I knew what he was up to. I hadn't checked up on him for a couple of months and now there he fucking was.

Motherfucker.

* * *

I entered my house in a foul mood that night. All I wanted was a cold beer and to zone the fuck out in front of the television for a few hours. I wasn't even sure if I'd make it over to see Tatum after that. It was probably safer to stay away with the mood I was in. However, my plans were turned on their head when I walked into the kitchen to grab a beer out of the fridge.

"Nitro." Tatum sat at the island bench and smiled at me while Dustin stood on the other side cooking.

He glanced up. "I'm making Tatum's favourite dinner."

I lifted a brow, confused as fuck as to what was going on here. Dustin never cooked. I wasn't even sure if he knew how to. He usually existed on takeaway or two-minute noodles. Continuing to the fridge, I reached in for the beer. "Are we celebrating something?"

Dustin ignored my question. "Do you know what Tatum's favourite meal is?"

I leant against the pantry. "Can't say I do." Jesus, I needed to shake this shitty mood; otherwise, I'd piss everyone off.

Dustin smiled triumphantly, as if he had the secrets of the world locked away in his head. "It's nachos, steak, mashed potato and porridge."

I just about spat my beer out. Shooting my attention to Tatum, I found her trying to hold back a laugh. My lips twitched and my mood shifted. "You don't say?" I said, not letting her eyes go.

She hopped off the stool and walked to where I stood. Sliding her hands around my waist, she planted a kiss on my lips. "Did you have a bad day, grumpy?"

I hooked my arm around her and dropped my hand to her ass. "Nothing that your favourite dinner can't fix," I murmured.

Laughter escaped her lips. "Good."

Dustin eyed us as he wiped his hands on a tea towel. "I've just gotta go grab my phone. Can you guys watch the potatoes?"

I nodded. "Yeah, buddy."

After he had left us, Tatum whispered, "Dustin asked me what my favourite things to eat were. He didn't tell me what he was planning so I just rattled off the things I like the most. Now he thinks that I eat them all together for dinner."

I chuckled, feeling some of the tension in my shoulders easing. "He has a soft spot for you so I'd expect to be eating that dinner often. I've gotta say, I've never seen him cook before. Is there an occasion?"

"If you're asking me why I'm here for dinner, the answer is because Dustin wanted to thank me for helping him ace his interview today."

The moment sat between us. Things were shifting fast in our relationship, and I had feelings rushing at me that were so foreign I didn't know what to do with them. I decided at that moment just to give her my honesty. My truth. And she could do with it whatever she chose.

I took a swig of my beer. "I like that you're here for dinner."

Her arms tightened around me. "I like it, too," she said softly and fuck if that didn't hit me right in the gut.

"We're here!" Renee's voice filtered into the kitchen, and I jerked my head up to see her and Marilyn join us.

"The whole fucking family, huh?" I said.

Tatum laughed and moved out of my embrace. "Yeah, Dustin said he wanted to cook for everyone."

"Hi Tatum," Renee said, hitting her with a smile. "This is my mum, Marilyn."

I watched my sister. She and Renee had moved back home just over two weeks ago, against my wishes, but we'd been arguing about it for weeks so I'd given in. She'd been seeing her shrink and doing the work, but she'd retreated. She hadn't returned to work after time off while she'd been in hospital receiving treatment, and I was concerned that the longer she stayed away, the harder it would be to go back.

She smiled at Tatum. "Hi," she said hesitantly.

Tatum returned her smile, magnified. I knew she was trying hard here because she didn't usually smile that brightly. "Hi, Marilyn. It's lovely to meet you."

Dustin returned to the kitchen and resumed cooking. Renee and Tatum discussed an assignment Renee was having hell with—a legal studies essay, which was right up Tatum's alley. Marilyn's shyness kicked in, but she joined in every now and then. And I watched my family begin to get to know the woman

228

I'd let into my life. It was the oddest fucking night of my life and yet one of the best.

* * *

"Marilyn is so reserved," Tatum said later that night as she lay next to me, her fingers drawing patterns on my chest. "I couldn't work out whether she liked me or not."

I tightened my arm around her. "She liked you."

She pushed up so she was resting on her elbow. "Really? How could you tell?"

I took in Tatum's questions, her tone and the expression on her face. Smoothing her hair, I said, "You really want her to like you, don't you?"

She hesitated for a brief moment before nodding. "Yeah, I do."

"Why?"

Her eyes darted away from mine, and I saw the vulnerability in her that she didn't often show the world.

I tilted her chin so she looked at me again. "Don't hide from me, Vegas."

She watched me silently. Always thinking. Always trying to figure out if she could trust me with shit. I didn't blame her, though. Trust was one of the most sacred things you could give another person. "I like your family. Like, a lot. They're funny and kind, and they make me feel welcome. I always wanted a home filled with laughter and fun, but we never had that. Even when Chris and I were older, the two of us never had that. I was always running around after him, making sure he was still alive and okay. And he was looking out for me, too, but there wasn't a lot of fun times."

229

"What did you have growing up?" She'd not mentioned her parents much, so I wondered how bad it was.

She settled back against me, curled in close, arm draped over my chest. "My mum was an unhappy woman. She was bored and unfulfilled in her life and never really did fun stuff with us as kids. When she was nine, we came home from school one day and she was gone. No note, no nothing. She'd just packed a bag and disappeared. My father was devastated because she was the love of his life and he'd always gone above and beyond to try and make her happy. Nothing he did was ever good enough, though."

Jesus, even my early childhood had been better than hers. "But she came back?" I recalled that Tatum had mentioned her mother so I figured she'd been in her life later on.

"Yeah, a year after she left, she returned. It was one of the happiest days of my childhood, but I quickly realised happiness doesn't always last. Our home only grew quieter and sadder as we all tiptoed around trying to keep Mum happy so she never left us again."

"Your parents stayed together?"

"Yep, until the day Dad died. And Mum was just as unhappy without him, so I hope she figured out it was her all along who'd failed, not him." She sounded so harsh towards her mother, but I couldn't blame her.

"You two weren't close?"

"I tried, I really did. But when someone doesn't want to do anything to help their own happiness, it's hard to be around them. That dark place they're in will eventually crush your joy. I was already running low on that so I decided I had to stay away as much as I could. I probably saw more of her last year while she was dying than I did for years." She twisted her head to look up at me. "Guilt makes you do shit like that."

230

"It doesn't sound like you had much to feel guilty over."

"Guilt is a woman's cross to bear, Nitro. We're suckers when it comes to feeling guilty over every damn thing. Hell, we'll even take everyone else's shit and feel guilty for that, too."

She laid her head back on my chest and we fell silent. And then I remembered her earlier question about how I knew that Marilyn liked her. "I know Lynny liked you because she asked you how we met. She never asks people stuff if she doesn't like them. She can't be bothered to engage if she doesn't see a point to it. And when she was leaving, she made a point to say goodbye to you. Again, if she wasn't interested in getting to know you, my sister wouldn't say goodbye. She doesn't use manners like most people do."

"What happened to her, Nitro?"

"As in just recently or are you asking why she's so withdrawn in general?"

She moved so she sat cross-legged next to me. "Both."

I sat up with my back to the headboard of the bed. Talking about Marilyn wasn't something I did, except with Renee, Dustin, and Marilyn's doctor. And as much as we annoyed the fuck out of each other sometimes, I'd go to my grave to protect her. But I'd come to the realisation that Marilyn needed more people in her corner, in her life, and if Tatum wanted to get to know her better, she'd need help to do that because Marilyn wouldn't open up easily.

"Lynny was the kid who didn't make friends easily. She was withdrawn and sad a lot. Possibly depressed as a teen, but there was never a diagnosis, so I can't be sure. Our parents died in a car crash when I was twelve. Lynny was six and Dustin was nine. We went to live with our Uncle Joseph in Melbourne. He's not a good man and living with him was not good for her. Joseph didn't allow us to leave the house except to go to school.

231

He treated us like slaves around his house." I took a breath. Dragging this shit up was something I hated to do. Hated to remember what he put us through. "Joseph was involved deeply in organised crime and is now one of the top dogs in Australia. He deals in guns, drugs, and prostitutes. Back then, though, he was building his business up. The day I turned thirteen, he started teaching me how to shoot a gun. By the time I turned fifteen, I knew how to shoot any gun given to me, kill with a knife, and torture someone to get information. Dustin was slow developmentally so Joseph had no interest in him. And Lynny was a girl so she was only good for stuff around the house. Even when she was young, like seven, he put her to work. Most of the time, though, she spent in her bedroom by herself."

Tatum stared at me in shock. "Oh my God, Nitro, that's awful."

"Yeah, and it fucked us all up. Joseph trained me as a soldier. It was regimented and brutal. Some of the shit he put me through.... It's deeply ingrained in me, Tatum. I'm violent because of him and no matter how hard I might want to change that, I can't. You need to know this about me because sometimes I can't switch it off."

Fuck, she needed to take this in. I didn't want to hurt her, but fuck knew what was down the track. I couldn't predict the future and I sure as hell couldn't always predict my own behaviour. The wiring in my brain had been screwed with, and my reactions to situations and people weren't always what I thought they would be. Sometimes the rage blinded me and I was helpless to react in any way but with violence.

Tatum pushed up so she was kneeling and then she straddled me. Bringing her hands to my face, she cupped my cheeks and kissed me. It was unlike any of our other kisses. There was no wild energy to it, just an intimacy that was new. When she ended the kiss, she said, "I know you have that violence and darkness in you, Nitro, but I've seen so much more than that. You saved my life when you could have easily chosen a different path. Even when I begged you to end my life, you didn't. And yes, I've seen your inner struggle with your actions, but I feel safe with you. I know you get pissed off with me, but you always protect me. And that's more than I can say for most of the people who have been in my life."

I ran my hands over the bare skin of her back. "You don't know what you're saying, Vegas. You hardly know me."

"I've seen you when your club was at war. When you killed a man, when a bomb almost killed us, and when you came back from an ambush where you had to fight for your life and those of your fellow club members. War shows us who we are. It drags us to our deepest depths and reveals just what we would do to survive. Good and bad." She gripped my face harder. "You showed me that you're a fighter, and you're loyal and that you put others before yourself. I might not know all the little ins and outs that make you, you, like what your favourite colour is or what your dreams are in life or what your favourite dinner is, but I know your character, and that's something a lot of people don't ever truly find out about the people in their lives."

I stared at her. Fuck, she'd surprised me again. And shown me just how fucking deep and intelligent she was. Leaning forward, I held her close and moved us so she lay on the bed with me on top of her. Pressing my mouth to hers, I kissed her hard. Rough. I tore a moan from her lips. And when I finished, I rasped, "You're something fucking else, you know that?"

She smiled up at me, her lips swollen from our kiss. "Only because you told me."

That right there pissed me off. That no man had ever shown her how fucking amazing she was or made her believe in herself.

I would make that shit my mission. I'd show Tatum what I saw when I looked at her, and I'd make her understand the truth in it.

Chapter Thirty-Two

Tatum

"Arms" by Christina Perri

Nitro moved behind me as I brushed my teeth after our shower together the next morning. Well, if you could call using my finger to spread toothpaste over my teeth. It was the first time I'd stayed at his house after we started sleeping together and it hadn't been planned, so I had no clothes or toiletries. He'd offered me his toothbrush, but I was funny about germs. He'd then made fun of me for doing all sorts of things with my mouth, yet not wanting to share a toothbrush. I'd told him that if he wanted to keep making fun of me, I'd happily stop doing those things with my mouth, at which point he immediately stopped making fun of me.

Sliding his arm around me and slipping his hand inside the towel I wore to find skin, he said, "You want a clean shirt to wear home?" While he waited for my reply, he dropped his mouth to my shoulder and kissed me.

I watched him in the mirror, my belly fluttering with sensations that were unfamiliar to me. Everything in that moment sparked a surge of happiness in me. The way he held me, touched me, spoke to me, and the question he asked. Such a simple question, but one that showed me where his mind was at in our relationship. This feeling of closeness was something I didn't want to admit to needing, because my failed attempt at it in the past made me unwilling to try for it again.

His eyes met mine in the mirror, and I smiled. "I want that black one with the skull on it."

The skin around his eyes creased as a smile hit them. "Of course you do."

I frowned, not sure what he meant.

His hand inside my towel grazed my breast as it swept across my stomach. "You love your skulls. Most of your clothes have one on them."

The flutters in my belly whooshed deep in my core. *He paid attention to my clothes?* I turned to face him. "You're a damn contradiction, Nitro. I swear I am constantly surprised by the things you say and do."

"That makes two of us," he said, his voice all husky.

We held each other. No talking, no caressing, just taking the other in, thinking. And then Dustin broke the moment.

"Nitro, we need milk! I thought you usually had some long life stuff in the cupboard, but I can't find it," he called out from the kitchen.

Nitro's chest shook with a chuckle and he briefly dropped his forehead to mine. "Fucking hell." Looking back at me, he muttered, "That would be because your favourite dinner includes porridge and he used it all. Fucking porridge with steak and nachos and shit."

I smacked him lightly on the arm. "Don't knock porridge for dinner, dude."

His eyes twinkled with amusement and heat all at once. "Vegas, I have a new appreciation for porridge."

"Nitro! Did you hear me?" Dustin yelled out.

Nitro let me go. With regret clear in his eyes. "You want a coffee?"

I nodded and tracked his movements as he left the bathroom. This was a good morning. And not just because I'd had hot sex with him. No, it had more to do with a feeling swirling around everything in this house and the people in it. A feeling I knew I could no longer deny loving.

* * *

I put my knife and fork down and looked at Duvall. He sat across from me in the new café I'd chosen for our lunch. I'd decided we needed a fresh start, and new surroundings felt fitting.

"I've started seeing Nitro," I said, waiting for him to lose his shit at me.

He put his cutlery down, too. Leaning his elbows on the table, he said, "Okay."

I frowned. "That's it? No lecture?" I'd expected an argument over it. Especially since Nitro still hadn't worked out how Duvall had seen that footage, which meant I hadn't talked to him about it in order to clear up the fact it hadn't been Nitro who beat me up that night.

Sighing, he said, "Tatum, you've always been a woman who does what she wants. You're independent and don't like being told what others think of your choices. I've told you what I think. That's all I can do."

Duvall was one of my closest friends. Well, he used to be. But he didn't know me very well, and that was my fault. He'd tried to get to know me, but I'd always held pieces of myself back. The pieces I was ashamed of. I wasn't sure I wanted one of my closest friends to not know me anymore. "I never told you the full truth about why my marriage ended."

Surprise flared on his face and he leant back in his seat. "So it wasn't just because your dickhead ex cheated on you?"

237

"No." Sucking in a long breath, I laid my heart out for him. "Randall had a lot of debt and just kept clocking up more. And he fought with me all the time over that and everything else in our life. In my wisdom, I decided the way to fix our marriage would be to help him solve his debt problem."

"So you took bribes off Billy," he said slowly, piecing it together.

"Yes, that's why I took those bribes."

"Fuck, Tatum," he swore. "Why didn't you tell me?"

"You say that as if the reason why I did it makes it more understandable when it doesn't."

"It does."

I shook my head. "No," I said with force. "It doesn't. The fact is I gave up on everything I believed in to do what I did. I told myself at first that it would just be that once, but it quickly grew too easy to make good cash. As my marriage disintegrated, I became more desperate to fix it. Billy just had to look at me back then, and I was panting to help him."

He fell silent for a beat. "I understand it because he gave me what I needed, too. So don't think you're the only one who threw something away."

My heart cracked for what Duvall did for his family. The deal he signed with the devil was done from a much better place than the one I signed. "You did what you did for your sister, Duvall. You had no other choice." She had ALS and desperately needed money for care. I knew he'd gone to hell making the decision to allow Billy to pay for her medical bills, but I would have made the exact same choice.

He never talked about what he'd done, especially not since his sister died six months ago. He ignored what I said and asked, "So why did you take a damn job with him?"

238

I flattened my lips as I considered that question. "It would be easy to say the reason was because he was the only person offering me a job at the time. But it runs deeper than that, and I'm not sure even I fully understand my reasons."

"Try me."

"By the time I was disbarred, I'd changed. Everything that happened made me into a different person. It made me harder, but it also made me want to help people who stared at life from a place of no hope—"

"Fuck, you'd always wanted to help those people, Tatum."

I nodded. "Yeah," I murmured. "Billy originally asked me to help one of his strippers out of a legal mess caused by an abusive ex who played the system so well that he had the upper hand. Helping her led to him finding more work for me with the people who worked for him and here we are."

"Do you ever think of leaving and finding a job away from the filth?"

He didn't understand me, and I wasn't sure he ever would because we looked at life through different eyes. "Duvall, I don't judge the filth, as you call it. To me, it's just people trying to live their lives the best way they can at that moment. We all have parts of ourselves we wish were different, better maybe. The parts of us that have been fucked up by life and the people in it. Sure, some don't want to change their lives, and that's their choice, but I'm there for those who do. Sometimes along the way I have to do things I don't agree with or that I wouldn't choose to do, but I do them because in the end they help me achieve my goal. And these days, my motivation isn't greed." It was that greed, along with my blind trust in a man who had no respect for me that made me feel so ashamed. Back then, he'd made me feel like I wasn't enough and that was why he'd cheated on me. Not feeling like I was enough had proven to be a hard feeling to recover from.

He drummed his fingers lightly on the table, listening to me but seemingly miles away in his thoughts. "So the end justifies the means, then?"

I leant forward and met his gaze. "Yes," I said softly, "sometimes it does."

He listened and he processed, but in the end he said, "We're going to have to agree to disagree on that one."

I smiled. "That's the beauty of friendship, right?"

"I guess it is."

It always had been that way for our friendship. We'd often argued over cases and the rights and wrongs of the world. And we'd always been able to forget all that shit when it came to our friendship. "Thank you for being a good friend."

He lifted a brow. "You call me not giving you hell for dating a biker, a good friend?"

How would I ever convince him of the truth? "He doesn't beat me. I can't get into it all, but what you saw on that footage wasn't even close to what you think."

"I believe you." When I gave him a confused look, he elaborated. "I looked into it more and found out about the murder at the casino that night. I put shit together, Tatum, and figured he must have been involved in it. And for you to have anything to do with him after that, I figure that dead biker deserved everything he got. Still doesn't make me happy that you've chosen to get involved with Storm."

I was stunned by what he said. "You're turning a blind eye?"

He drank some of his water. "I'm not a cop. I don't have a case on my desk to prosecute and as far as I know, the DPP aren't looking into it either. There's nothing to turn a blind eye to as far as I'm concerned."

I reached across the table and placed my hand on his arm. "And you don't believe the end justifies the means," I murmured.

"I believe in your happiness, Tatum. I don't want to see you hurting anymore, and if this is what makes you happy, I'll put my shit aside." His eyes bored into mine. "Tell me you're happy and I'll not say another word about you choosing a biker."

I took a deep breath. "I'm happy."

He flinched a little at my answer, and I realised that while Duvall said he wanted me to be happy, he didn't necessarily want Nitro to be the one to give me that. However, he gave me a tight smile and said, "Good."

I loved him for that. If you couldn't allow your friends to be happy in the way they chose, you couldn't call yourself a friend.

* * *

On my way home from work that afternoon, Billy called in a pissed-off mood. "I swear I'm going to close this damn club down, Tatum. It's a never-fucking-ending headache of staff fucking up and quitting on me."

I laughed as I steered the car around a corner. "You threaten this on a daily basis, Billy. I think it's time for an intervention. Maybe some Xanax mixed with some vodka and we could throw in some other shit too if you need it."

He wasn't amused. He never was, but I put up with him regardless of the fact he had no sense of humour. "This isn't helping."

"Okay, tell me what you need. I'll make it happen."

"I need a fucking new cleaner. And I need them tonight." He said it like he doubted my ability to produce the goods.

I smiled. "Done."

241

He took a moment to reply. "Why do you sound so fucking joyful today?"

"Because I am. Now, hang up so I can go get your cleaner."

He grumbled some more shit before finally ending the call. I pulled the car over so I could access the files I stored in my Dropbox on my phone. Dustin's résumé was stored in there and it had his phone number in it. Once I'd located what I needed, I dialled him.

"Hello?" He didn't know my number and sounded hesitant.

"Dustin, it's Tatum. I have a job for you."

"Huh?"

"A cleaning job. Do you still need a job?"

"Oh… yes, I do!" Excitement filled my ears.

"Are you free tonight? Because they need you right away."

"Yes!" Dustin's easy nature had to be his best trait.

I gave him all the information and called the club to talk with the woman who he'd work with that night, organising with her to hold his hand a little. As I drove home with the intent to relax in the bath for hours, I thought about how happy and grateful Dustin was for the opportunity I'd just found him. That was what made my job worth doing.

Chapter Thirty-Three

Nitro

"One Night Girl" by Blake Shelton

I banged on Tatum's door, irritated as fuck at her. She took her sweet time answering me and it only gave that irritation time to grow.

Swinging the door open, she said, "Jesus, Nitro, why all the banging?"

I clenched my jaw. "You got Dustin a job with Billy?"

"Yes."

"Why the fuck would you do that?"

She gripped the door as if she was about to slam it in my face. "If you're going to come here and yell at me without giving me a chance to explain myself, you can leave right now and come back when you've calmed down."

Fuck.

I shoved my fingers through my hair. I needed to rein this anger in, but fuck if I could. Billy being in the mix made sure of that. Taking a step inside, I said, "I'm not leaving. We're discussing this." Before she had a chance to argue, I entered her house and made my way to her living room.

She closed the door, loudly. When she met me in the living room, she demanded, "Right, seems as though you've decided you're staying, tell me what you have against Billy."

Fuck, just his name caused my anger to spike. "Marilyn works for a bank and Billy was a customer there. Had been for a couple of years and over that time he slowly gained her trust and eventually asked her out on a date. She said no, repeatedly, until the day he finally broke her down and got the answer he wanted. They started dating and it made her happier than ever. She smiled and laughed more often and started living her life in a way I'd never seen. It lasted for six months until the night I received a call from Renee to tell me her mother had taken a bottle of pills and was unconscious on the bathroom floor."

I stopped to take a few short breaths. Remembering that time in our lives was difficult as fuck. I'd thought my sister was dead. It was why I'd been so angry the day I'd found her passed out on my couch recently. And why I'd pushed for her to be admitted to the hospital. I couldn't lose Lynny.

Tatum's battle stance softened as she listened to me. "What happened between them?"

"You ever see Billy date?"

She shook her head. "No, he keeps his women separate to work. Doesn't bring them to the clubs ever."

"Figures. Marilyn thought she was special to him, thought they were exclusive. Turned out Billy didn't do exclusive and was seeing another woman at the same time."

"Nitro, from what I know, Billy is up front about that when he dates. Women know where they stand with him."

My eyes widened. "Are you fucking defending that motherfucker?"

She reached for my arm, gripping it. "No," she said calmly. "I'm not saying what I think either way, but I would imagine that Marilyn would have been made aware of what their relationship really was."

I ripped my arm out of her grasp. "Fuck, Tatum, she tried to kill herself over him. She had a fucking breakdown after that.

You're a woman—how the hell can you stand there and defend a man who treats women that way?"

"So, you're telling me that you've never used women before? Never dated casually or simply screwed random women as you pleased?"

"Don't fucking turn this around on me! I'm not the one we're talking about right now."

"That is true, but can't you see that you're being a hypocrite about this?"

I grabbed the back of my neck and rubbed it. Glaring at her, I said, "I'm standing here telling you that he ruined her and all you can say is that I'm a fucking hypocrite? Every woman I've ever slept with knew what the score was. I don't lie about that shit."

She'd been calm up until that point, but she was beginning to lose her cool. "No, you're not listening to me. I'm sorry that his actions hurt her and that she harmed herself. You have every right to feel hurt and angry for her too. But Billy didn't do anything wrong. You can't hold him responsible for her overdosing. That choice was completely hers." She moved close to me and placed her hand on my arm again. "Nitro, I get it. I totally get it. I wanted to blame everyone for all the bad shit that happened to me, but in the end, I chose how I reacted to what people did to me. Randall treated me so badly, but it was me who chose to ruin my life over him. He never made me do any of it. Just like Billy never made Marilyn take those pills and swallow them. At some point, we have to take ownership of our choices in life."

I stared at her in silence. I believed in owning your actions, but I'd never looked at Marilyn like that. I'd always felt the need to protect her. Something had fucked her up at a young age, I was sure of it. She always fobbed me off whenever I asked her. Told me I was wrong. But I wasn't convinced. As a result, I had

245

always held others accountable when Marilyn was hurt. Looking at it from Tatum's point of view, it made me consider a different side to the argument.

Scrubbing a hand over my face, I said, "You're right, we do have to take ownership of our choices, but fuck, Tatum, I find it hard to force that kind of responsibility on Lynny."

She nodded. "I know," she said softly.

"That Silver Hell biker? You wanna know what he did to her?"

She closed her eyes and held her breath for a beat. I felt her pain right along with her. That fucking biker stole something from both of us. When she opened her eyes, she nodded. "Yes, but we need to sit for this."

When we were both sitting on her couch, I said, "Back at the beginning of the year, King took revenge on one of their bikers for shit he did to King's sister. Killed the asshole. When the club found out, they started a war against our club. We didn't realise for a while, though, because it wasn't in-your-face shit that they did to begin with. They eventually escalated it, hurting our families and killing club members."

"What did they do?"

"They started off with things we didn't realise came from them. Break-ins, assault, theft, shit like that. They targeted Dustin, causing him to lose his job and the place where he lived. He'd been in share accommodation for ages and they got to the woman he rented the room from. Bribed her to report false rape charges to the police against Dustin. That all got sorted out by a cop friend, but he was left homeless and still hasn't found a permanent place to live."

"That's why he lives with you now," she said as she worked it out.

246

"Yeah. It was a low fucking act what they did to him, but what they did to Marilyn was worse."

Her lips flattened. "I hate them, and you haven't even told me what it was yet."

"Four of them held up the bank where she works. That in itself was bad enough, because her nerves are shot and that would have been a lot for her to cope with on its own. But while three of them robbed the bank, one of them dragged her out the back and raped her. He then randomly showed up every now and then when she did her groceries, taunting her and threatening to rape her again. After he did it three times, she stopped going out in public. She'd already stopped going to work, but after that, she completely shut down and stopped living her life."

Tears tracked Tatum's cheeks and her hand covered her mouth. And then the heaving sobs came. I pulled her into my arms and we held each other for a long time.

When she let me go, I said, "So you see why I protect the fuck out of her? Why I have trouble letting people like Billy off the hook for their careless actions?"

She nodded as she took hold of my face. "I do. And I'm so sorry for everything you've both been through."

"Yeah. Marilyn's had more shit happen to her than any person deserves in their lifetime."

"I'm sorry I organised that job for Dustin without running it by you first."

I wrapped my hand around her forearm. "No, I was a prick about that. I shouldn't have come over here throwing my weight around. There was nothing for you to run by me. I appreciate you looking out for him."

She pulled a pained face. "Yeah, but now he's working for the guy you hate."

"And I'll just have to suck that up. If Dustin wants that job, it's his decision."

A smile tugged at her lips. "Is this Nitro backing down?" Her playful tone cut through the tension and was a welcome break from the conversation we'd been having.

I pulled her onto my lap and held her tightly. "You fucking cause me to back down all over the damn place, Vegas."

She brushed a kiss across my lips. "I like that. I've never had that before."

"Trust me, it's a first for me, too," I growled, feeling every bit of the heat between us. How she managed to calm the anger out of me, I wasn't sure. All that lingered was the kind of passion that made me want to fuck her all night long.

I ran my hands down her back, to the bottom of her T-shirt so I could slip my hands under it and feel skin. I gripped her waist as her hands moved to my neck and our mouths found each other. The sexual energy between us had spiked from the anger that sat between us when I first arrived, and I growled deeply as she kissed me with a wild urgency. We might have still had moments of confusion with each other, but there was never any confusion as far as sex was concerned—we both desperately wanted each other.

She clawed at my hair as she crushed her body to mine and moaned. Tearing her mouth away as she ended the kiss, she begged, "Fuck, Nitro, I need you inside me right fucking now." Fumbling madly at the button on my jeans, she showed me just how desperate for me she was.

Hell, she was hot.

I let her fiddle with my pants; I needed that mouth of hers again. Catching her in another kiss, I forced my tongue inside as I moved my hands to the back of her head so I could hold her in place. I didn't want to be interrupted from what I was doing.

248

Kissing Tatum turned me on so damn much. Foreplay should always begin with her mouth as far as I was concerned. For a long fucking time.

She struggled against my hold, trying to end the kiss.

I chuckled as I let her go. Moving my hands to her back, I said, "You want my cock in that beautiful pussy of yours, Vegas? I don't think I've ever seen you so eager."

She had her hands in my pants and my cock sprung free. Biting her lip, she wrapped her hand around it and gave me a tug. I lifted my hips and thrust into her hand, suddenly on board with what she wanted.

Meeting my eyes, she said, "Now who's eager?"

Leaning forward so I could get close to her mouth again, I said, "I'm always eager. Fuck, I could live inside you and never leave again."

Her breathing hitched. "You wanna start that now?"

"As soon as I do this," I said before finally pressing my lips to hers again.

She didn't fight me on that kiss, and when I was done, I lifted her shirt over her head. Dropping it on the floor, I then flicked her bra undone and removed it. She slid off my lap and made fast work of taking her shorts and panties off, and I sucked in a breath at her naked body.

Tatum was fucking stunning. She was perfect with her soft curves that I loved sliding my hands over, and her strength that was an excellent match to my power when I fucked her. The thing I loved the most, though, was that when she stood naked in front of me, there was nothing in our way. Slowly, she was allowing me to strip back the invisible layers that guarded her soul at all other times. Sometimes she tried to run from me, but those times were becoming less and less. One day, she'd give it all to me.

I stood and yanked my jeans and briefs off before sitting back down, taking her with me. She straddled my lap and took hold of my face with both hands as she caught my mouth in another searing kiss. Ending it, breathless, she begged, "Can I please have this cock now?"

Jesus, I felt her demand deep in my gut. My hands went straight to her hips and I lifted her to position her over my dick. When I had her where I wanted her, I thrust up and inside her.

"Fuck," I rasped. Nothing was better than being inside my woman. *Fucking nothing.*

Her hands gripped my shoulders.

Fingers digging in.

Head back.

Neck exposed.

A sexy-as-fuck sound coming from her mouth.

I licked her throat as we fucked, inspiring her to claw at my skin, scratching me. Growling deeply, I sunk my teeth into her, marking her as mine.

"I love your fucking teeth," she cried out, her pussy squeezing around my dick. She fucked me madly, her body bouncing, her tits all over the place, hair everywhere.

"Jesus, I'm going to come," I said, pretty fucking sure I couldn't hold it back much longer.

"Me too," she panted, and on a roar, with one last hard slam into her, I came.

She orgasmed a moment later, right before she collapsed against me. When I caught my breath, I moved her hair off her face so I could find her eyes. "Did I wear you out, Vegas?"

Cracking one eye open, she said, "Nope. I'm ready to go again. You?"

Placing my arms around her, I chuckled. "You are so full of shit, but my dick will be ready for you to suck soon if you want."

She swatted me playfully. "You need to run me a bath and pour me a wine. Then we can discuss what I'm going to do with your cock."

Later that night, when she slept next to me, I traced circles over her hip and thought about how far we'd come. We still didn't have a play-by-play for this relationship, but I was slowly seeing a future I'd never imagined before. A future with Tatum by my side.

* * *

The next day, I decided to get to the bottom of why my uncle was in Sydney and why he wanted to sell discounted guns to Storm. No way did I buy any of the shit he'd fed King.

I called ahead and organised to meet at his hotel. He requested I come up to his room and against my better judgement, I did.

"Take a seat," he said when I entered his room. He gestured at one of the lounges in the large suite he had.

"I'll stand. This won't take long."

He watched me with the cold gaze I knew well. "As you will, then." Pouring a drink, he said, "It's good to see you've come to your senses, son."

I had to restrain myself from punching him. His reference to me as his fucking son was one I despised. "I haven't. And don't fucking call me that. I'm only here to find out the truth behind you showing up on Storm's doorstep peddling guns."

Looking at me over the rim of the glass as he drank the water he'd poured, he said, "I want you to run my Sydney operation. I

251

trained you for that and I want what I put my time and money into all those years ago."

The way he said it sounded like he fully expected to get what he came for. There was a cold and calculated tone to what he said that iced my veins. I clenched my fists, remembering I'd been strong enough to escape him once before and that I would remain strong against him again. He didn't own me anymore. "There is nothing you can say or do that would ever make me say yes to that."

He regarded that statement and slowly placed his glass on the coffee table next to him. Looking back up at me, he said, "Oh, I will find a way, Rhys. I'm surprised at your lack of memory."

"What memory?" Fuck, I knew he was leading me down a path I didn't want to go, but the question fell out before I could stop it.

"Don't you remember how I always found ways to bend you? To force you to do what I wanted. That brain of yours is wired to respond to me after all the time I put into your training. Don't think for a minute that I won't get what I want again. I've been patient all these years you've been gone. I've been building the empire I always said I would and now we are ready for your return."

Bile rose in my throat, burning. I swallowed it down hard and clenched my fists again. The desire to knock him out was overwhelming, but I refused to give Joseph the satisfaction of knowing he'd affected me. "You're as psycho as I remember, believing your own bullshit."

As I took a step towards the door to leave, he said, "I'm a patient man, Rhys, but even I have my limits. If you don't come around soon, I will find a way to change your mind."

With one last glance at him, I exited the room. Stalking down the corridor to the lift, I focused on getting my breathing under control and my thoughts back on track. Joseph had messed with them to the point they weren't straight. Memories from the past flashed in and out, bringing up images of my training that made me want to vomit. By the time I hit the elevator, sweat had beaded on my forehead, and my breathing was as far from being under control as it fucking could be.

I stepped into the elevator. Dizziness took over as the tiny space closed in on me, and I thought for sure I would pass out. My phone rang, but it sounded far away. Fumbling, I pulled it out of my pocket. "Yeah?"

Tatum's voice came through the line. "Nitro, are you okay? You sound off."

"Keep talking." I needed something to take my mind off what was happening.

"Huh?"

"Tell me anything, Vegas. I need the distraction." I focused my gaze on the numbers counting down the floors.

She paused for only a moment more. And then—"Something I detest doing more than almost anything else is grocery shopping. It's boring as fuck and a waste of time. Online shopping is where it's at these days. But, when you run out of things in the pantry that you love, when you thought you had a good supply... I detest that, too—"

The elevator reached the ground floor and I stepped out of it. Tatum's voice filtered in and out of my mind as I walked the distance to the hotel exit.

"—Milo. That is the absolute worst. I really don't wanna go shopping on my way home from work. I don't suppose you have any in your pantry?"

I walked through the exit and breathed in the fresh air. My lungs expanded, taking much-needed oxygen in. The feeling that I was going to faint passed and I relaxed a little.

"Nitro? Are you still there?"

I gripped the phone harder as I made my way to my bike. "Yeah. Sorry about that. What were you saying about me having some shit in my pantry?"

"Milo. Do you have any?"

"How the hell did you get onto the topic of Milo?"

"Well, you did tell me to talk about *anything*, and that was the thing I was thinking about at that moment," she grumbled. And then softly, "Are you okay now?"

"Yeah," I said gruffly. I hadn't been prepared for that reaction at all. I needed to be better prepared mentally the next time I saw Joseph.

"Good," she said, and I waited for her to ask me what happened, but she didn't. Tatum knew how to push my buttons, but she also knew when to let shit be. And that was something I really fucking liked about her.

* * *

"Where are we at with the guns?" I asked King late that afternoon while we sat drinking together in the clubhouse bar.

He eyed me over his beer. "I want a decision by the end of this week. We'll take a vote at Church."

"Which way are you leaning?"

"With Joseph."

Not the answer I wanted to hear, but the one I figured I'd get. "I saw him this morning. He's a fucking psychopath, King. You don't want anything to do with him."

"What did he do to you to make you hate him so much?"

Showing weakness was something Joseph had taught me never to do. Sharing what he'd done to me with Tatum had been one thing, but blurting that shit out to my club president was a whole other matter. "He fucked my family up, King. In every

254

way you can imagine. I'm loyal to this club, and have been for fifteen years, but that will be tested if we get into bed with Joseph."

His jaw clenched. "What are you telling me, Nitro? That you'd want out of the club?"

"I don't know. Storm is in my blood. It's my family now, and I would do anything to protect my family. The thing is, though, that when you invite outsiders into your home, you have to have a level of trust there that they won't fuck you over. Otherwise you've got nothing. I'm telling you that I will never trust Joseph, so if he's invited to work with our family, shit's gonna get fucked up for me."

King listened and then nodded. "I hear you, brother, and I will take that into consideration. But you've gotta understand that our family has been threatened, and I will do anything I need to do to make sure we don't go down. If it turns out that Joseph is the best decision for us, I won't hesitate to make it."

A commotion in the hallway drew our attention, and I turned to find Devil and Hyde entering the bar with the Silver Hell president in front of them. Dragon's gaze met King's and he made his way over to where we sat.

King shoved his chair back, furious. "What the fuck?" he demanded.

Dragon raised his hands at the same time that Hyde said, "He wants to talk to you about the shit that's been going down."

King's cold eyes met Dragon's. "Haven't we done all the talking we need to?"

"I've got new information that you're going to want to know," Dragon said, his body as tense as King's.

"You came alone?" King asked.

Dragon nodded and Hyde confirmed it for King.

Dragon had some fucking balls to come on his own. It made me wonder what the hell he was about to tell King. I figured it had to be something that guaranteed his safety.

King nodded at the table. "All right then, let's hear it."

Dragon pulled up a seat and started talking. "I recently learnt that we have a common enemy. Angelo Gambarro." He paused, waiting for King's reaction. King scowled and nodded for him to continue. "He's been out for your blood since you killed his uncle. As for us, he wants in on our territory. When he discovered that our clubs had issues, he started playing us against each other."

"As in he's responsible for some of the shit that's been happening?"

Dragon nodded. "Yeah. As in, he's responsible for that car bomb as well as some other stuff you think we did."

"Motherfucker," King swore.

"I don't know about you, but I fucking want him dead. And I think we have a better chance of bringing him down if we do it together."

King stared at Dragon as if that was the last thing he expected to come out of his mouth. "After everything we've been through, you really think that's a fucking possibility?"

"If there's one thing I hate the most, it's being played, King. You and me, our clubs, we're upfront about the shit that goes down between us, but this cunt fucking cheated his way to get what he wants. I'll be fucking damned if I let him achieve his goal."

Honour among thieves.

Before King could respond, Hyde threw out, "Fuck it, King, he's right."

"I agree," Devil said.

King turned to the room. "Anyone against this idea?"

256

Mass agreement filled the room. King eyed me. "Nitro?"

I nodded. "I'm with Dragon. I say bury him."

The shifting loyalties of the underbelly were well known. How long we'd align ourselves with Silver Hell was to be seen, but for now I'd happily pursue our common goal of seeing Gambarro go down.

King walked Dragon out and spent about ten minutes talking with him. When he returned, he shared some of the shit they'd discussed. He looked at me as he said, "Dragon's going to talk with Sutherland to organise for him to supply us with guns again."

I exhaled a long breath.

Thank fuck.

Chapter Thirty-Four

Tatum

"Breathe" by Faith Hill

I smiled at Monroe as I fumbled in my bag for my phone. "Fuck, where is it?" I muttered. I could hardly feel my fingers, which made it really fucking hard to find the phone.

"Hurry up, girl. I've got cock waiting for me."

Our eyes met and we laughed in unison, both drunk from way too much alcohol. Our girls' night out had started at my place and quickly moved to this club where we'd spent the night drinking and searching for a man for Monroe.

"Got it!" I yelled loudly when I located the phone.

Monroe motioned with her hands for me to hurry up. That was a struggle because my brain was so fuzzy I couldn't remember the damn pattern lock on my phone.

"Ugh," Monroe grumbled. "This is why you should get a bloody iPhone, babe."

I playfully smacked her. It was an old argument of ours. I preferred Samsung, and she harassed me to swap across. "Shut up," I muttered, continuing to swipe all over the place.

"Fuck, how many attempts do you get before it locks you out? I can*not* miss out on this dick!"

"I know! You'll never let me forget it if you do."

She placed her hand over mine and stopped me from swiping. "Wait! Give me his number and we can call it from my phone."

I grimaced. "I don't know his number."

I traced patterns again and almost screamed my relief when I finally unlocked the phone.

Her eyes lit up. "You got it?"

"Yes, now let me just find his number," I said, scrolling for Nitro's number.

A few moments later, he answered, concern in his voice. "Vegas. You okay?"

"Yeah."

"You still out with Monroe?"

I laughed as she started flapping her hands at me to speed shit along. Fuck, we were wasted. I could hardly hold myself up let alone get my brain to work faster.

"Tatum?" Nitro's voice sounded in my ear again, dragging my attention from Monroe.

"Shit, sorry." I couldn't stop laughing because Monroe was hilarious in her agony over missing out on cock. "What are you doing right now?"

"Watching TV. Why?"

"Well, Monroe's finally found herself a pierced dick and so she's going home with him. They're not going my way, so I have to either catch a cab or... I thought you could come pick me up. I could then show you my appreciation in ways you'd like."

"Really? What ways exactly are we talking here?"

I smiled, loving his playful tone. "Don't go getting too excited there, dude. I'm not talking knives here." That idea still freaked me out. Thankfully he hadn't brought it up again.

He chuckled. "You kill me, Vegas. I've got my hand on my dick and you turn it soft in one sentence."

"Do you not think I can get you hard again? Have I failed you yet?"

259

"There's a first time for everything. What you got for me if it's not knives?"

Monroe widened her eyes and mouthed something about hurrying the hell up. I nodded and said to Nitro, "Okay, dude, we need to hurry this along. Monroe's getting the shits with me. How about I blow you first and then I sit on your face and come all over it? After that, it's your choice. I'll do anything you want."

"Fuck, I think I might have to wash that filthy mouth of yours out."

"That'd be no fun. You'd hate it if I didn't talk dirty to you."

"True. Okay, I'll be there in about fifteen minutes. Make Monroe wait with you until I get there. I don't want you outside by yourself."

I hung up and Monroe narrowed her eyes at me. Waving her hand at my face, she said, "What's that look?"

"What look?"

She pointed at my face. "The dreamy look."

I shoved my phone back in my bag and hit her with a smile. "He likes me."

She stared at me in surprise before bursting into laughter. "Of course he fucking likes you, Tatum! I mean, he only saved your life twice and spends every spare minute he has with you."

I thought about that. She was right. He did. "Damn."

She shook her head as if she was frustrated with me. "I swear, you're hard work sometimes. I know Randall screwed up your self-esteem, but have you taken a look in the mirror lately? You're fucking hot. And that heart of yours? It's so giving and caring, any guy would be dumb not to want it."

"He told me to make you wait with me because he didn't want me waiting on my own." My heart felt like it might burst at the knowledge he worried over me.

She grinned. "The biker came good." Monroe was still hesitant about me seeing Nitro, but I could see her softening towards him.

"Yeah," I murmured, my mind already thinking ahead to seeing him. Although he'd slept over my place the night before and I'd woken up with him that morning, it wasn't enough. I couldn't get enough of the man.

* * *

"Oh God…. Fuck!" I yelled as I came, throwing my head back.

Nitro held my ass while I rode his face. He gripped me harder when I screamed out, his tongue still working its magic on my pussy. When I tried to move off him, he didn't let me go. A growl came from him and I shuddered as another ripple of pleasure worked its way through me.

Placing my hand on his head, I said, "I can't take much more, Nitro. Your tongue is going to make my pussy explode from too much of a good thing."

His hold on me loosened and he finally allowed me to move. Settling myself on the bed next to him, I lay flat on my back and flung my arms out. The alcohol and the orgasm were working together to make me sleepy and I closed my eyes.

He rolled onto his side and cupped my breast. "I'm sure there was talk of sex after you sucked me off and sat on my face."

I cracked an eye open and looked at him. "Yeah, well you're just too good at what you do and now I'm exhausted."

He dropped a kiss on my breast before leaving the bed. I didn't have the energy to see what he was doing, but I figured

261

he'd headed into the bathroom. When he returned five or so minutes later, I was almost asleep.

The bed dipped and he spooned me. It woke me up a little and I decided to use the bathroom before I passed out. Stumbling, I made my way there and did what I had to before walking back to the bedroom. On the way, my dress caught my eye. It was on the floor and I bent to pick it up, almost falling headfirst.

"Shit," I said, reaching out for the bed to stop my fall.

Nitro moved off the bed to help me. "You okay?"

"Yeah, I just wanted to pick up my dress so it doesn't get wrinkled," I said, draping the dress over the chair in his room. "Seems as though I have to wear it home tomorrow. You know, it'd be good if you had space for me to leave some clothes here for times like this. I'm going to have to go home in the morning and get ready for brunch with the girls. If I had shit here, I could have just gotten ready here." God, I was rambling in my drunken state. I stopped when I noticed Nitro staring at me, frozen to the spot. "What's wrong?" I asked.

He didn't reply at first, but then he said, "Nothing. Get your ass back in bed so I can fuck you again."

I stared at him, confused as hell, but that could have been the alcohol. He'd gone from concerned to bossy and demanding in under a minute, though, so I couldn't be sure it was just the alcohol. "Did I say something wrong?"

He scooped me up and dumped me on the bed. "We're done with talking." He positioned himself over me, his mouth on mine in a kiss that swept all thoughts from my mind. "And you're done with even contemplating sleep."

I might have been ready for sleep before, but Nitro soon had me panting for his cock. Who was I kidding? He always did.

* * *

"Call me when you're ready. I'll swing back and pick you up," Nitro said as he pulled up to the kerb.

I undid my seatbelt and turned to face him, ignoring the headache I had. I'd been expecting the mother of all hangovers, but the universe was looking after me and all I had was a sore head. My God, the man was gorgeous. He sat watching me with his hand resting on the steering wheel, his heavily tatted arm muscles on full display in a fitted black tee. His brown eyes watched me with heat, as if the last thing he wanted to do was let me leave the ute. As if *all* he wanted to do was throw me down onto the back seat and sink himself deep inside me.

"Thanks for driving me today," I said, right before I captured his lips in a long kiss. One that told him I wanted him to throw me onto that back seat too.

"Fuck, Tatum," he muttered when I let his mouth go. "You wanna kiss me like that, you just might not make it to brunch."

My heart beat rapidly as I let his desire soak in. It had been a long time since a man had wanted me as much as Nitro did. It felt so damn good. Reaching for the door handle, I said, "I'll cook you dinner tonight." A Saturday night in with Nitro was exactly what I needed.

I swung my legs out of his ute and as I closed the door behind me, the sound of his door closing caught my attention. Glancing up, I watched as he made his way around to my side of the car. His stride was determined, and butterflies whooshed in my stomach as our eyes met.

His hand went straight to my waist when he reached me, and he backed me up against the car. His grip was firm, his touch electric. Bending his face to mine, he bruised my lips with a kiss.

263

A kiss that went on and on. By the time he let me go, I was breathless. Dazed.

"I can't wait until tonight," he rasped. "As soon as you're done here, you're mine."

With that, he left me to walk back around to the driver side, leaving me standing there in such a turned-on state I wasn't sure I would make it through brunch.

By the time I sat down across from Monroe and Posey, I had recovered enough to string a sentence together. Staring at both of them, I said, "Have you ever been so into a guy that you can't even think about anything except getting back to him?"

Monroe's lips curled up into a smile. "You've got it bad for Nitro, haven't you?"

I took a deep breath and then exhaled hard. "Yeah. I'm finding it hard to concentrate on work. My house is a mess because when I'm home, I'm either in bed with him or wasting time thinking about him.... God, I've even let my exercise go. This feels so overwhelming some days, like it's completely out of control. Tell me you've experienced this."

Monroe frowned. "You didn't have that with Randall?"

"No. I thought I did, but comparing it, I didn't. Not even in the beginning when it was all new and lacking the baggage we accumulated along the way."

"Why did you marry him, babe?" Monroe asked softly.

"God, I think I was just young and naïve. Dad had just passed away and Randall caught me in a vulnerable moment when I felt alone and lost. Chris was there for me, but he was busy with his shit, and I had started to feel like I didn't know where home was anymore. Marrying Randall felt like a new start and a new chance at happiness."

Posey watched me with a look that said she knew exactly what I meant. "He offered the easy path to what you thought you

264

wanted," she murmured. "Except it turned out that nothing good in life ever comes easy and you should have known that."

I nodded. "Exactly."

"So this thing with Nitro, what is it?" Monroe asked.

"It's not just sex, but we haven't labelled it."

"What do you want it to be?" Monroe asked.

As I contemplated her question, I let my fears in, but I didn't let them control me. It scared the shit out of me to think about letting Nitro into my life more than I already had, but at the same time I felt it deep in my soul that I wanted to take that step. "I want him. He's moody and can be an ass, but he looks out for me. He's honest and considers all the little details in life in such a way that shows me how deeply he's able to care for someone. I want a man who is all about the details."

"What exactly does that mean?"

I reached for the water on the table and poured myself a glass. "He listens and watches and pays attention to the things I say and do. And to the shit I've been through. And he takes it all into consideration and it shows in the way he treats me. He does the same with his family. His actions aren't always all about him. I'm not saying he gets it right all the time, but the fact he tries means something to me."

"It's hard to find a man like that," Posey said.

"Is your ex still being an ass?" Monroe asked her.

"No, he's leaving me alone. Whatever Billy's guy said to him worked."

"You should come out with us on our next girls' night," Monroe said. "The hangover is totally worth it."

"That's because she found pierced cock," I threw in. "And because Monroe hardly ever gets hangovers. Personally, I think that's her superpower."

Posey laughed and sat forward. "Tell me more!"

Monroe's eyes lit up. She loved talking about sex and dicks more than any woman I knew. "Well, I was *really* drunk so I might be wrong, but I'm not convinced that dude knows how to use what he's got to its full potential. The piercing felt good, but I don't remember fireworks. And damn it, I want fireworks."

"Okay tell me, what is fireworks to you?" Posey asked.

"I want to come out of my skin because the need the guy has for me is too much. I want to feel him everywhere, in my toes, my fingertips, in my mind, and deep in my belly. His touch, his breathing, his sounds, what he says, the way he moves... it should all consume me until every thought of mine is focused solely on him. And I want him to give me an orgasm I'm still feeling the next morning."

Posey and I sat staring at Monroe as she described everything she wanted. Posey, wide-eyed, me with a smile.

"What?" Monroe asked.

"That was the perfect description," I said.

"Jesus, you have that with Nitro, don't you, you lucky bitch?"

I laughed. "Let's order lunch before you start crying."

"Ugh. I hate you," she muttered. "I find a pierced cock and I *still* don't get fireworks. I bet you got fireworks last night."

"All night long, Roe."

She dropped her head to the table and banged it a couple of times in the kind of dramatic performance she was well known for. When she lifted her head, she said, "Right, girls' night is on every Friday night until I find fireworks." Looking at me, she added, "And I don't give two fucks if you're having a Milo Friday, you're still coming out to help me find my man."

Posey cut in. "What's Milo Friday?"

Monroe turned to her. "Oh, honey, you don't want to know." She then proceeded to fill Posey in on my love for Milo, omitting the full details of what had happened recently, but giving her enough information to understand why she didn't love Milo Fridays.

We ordered meals after that and spent the next two hours laughing and sharing stories from our week. Monroe had been right when she'd said we should invite Posey to brunch. I'd been hesitant because I never mixed my work life with my personal life, but this was fun. And fun was something I hadn't let into my life for far too long. It was exactly what I needed. *Friends.*

Chapter Thirty-Five

Nitro

"Love's Poster Child" by Keith Urban

I slid my arm around Tatum's waist and pulled her close while we made the short walk from my bike to the clubhouse entrance. Loud music filled the night air, along with laughter and lots of talking. The party was in full swing.

I'd picked Tatum up from brunch the day before and we'd spent the time since then either in her bed, her kitchen or on her couch. The invitation to come with me to the club get together had slipped out of my mouth before I realised it was happening. But there was no doubt in my mind, I wanted her there.

As we entered the clubhouse, she looked up at me. "Looks like things are going well with the club. Compared to the last time I was here." We hardly ever discussed Storm when we were together. She never asked and it wasn't in my nature to bring club business up with anyone who wasn't a member.

"Yeah, things have improved." A hell of a fucking lot, now that Joseph's guns were out of the picture.

"Nitro!" Devil called out when he spotted us. He sat on one of the couches with a chick on his lap, a smile a mile wide on his face.

As I took a step in his direction, Tatum held back. "You go," she said, "I'm going to say hi to Kree."

I followed her gaze to see Kree approaching. Smacking her ass, I let her go and headed over to see Devil.

He jerked his chin at Tatum. "She the one who's been fucking with your head?"

Glancing at Tatum, I nodded. "Yeah," I said, distracted by the smile on her face. She was fucking beautiful when she smiled.

Devil motioned for the chick to move off his lap. She pouted and grumbled some shit I couldn't hear.

"Babe, I told you I'd be busy until later," he said to her as he stood.

"You're always busy," she snapped, snatching her bag up off the table.

Devil watched as she took a step away from him. "Where you going? I thought we were on for later?"

"I'm going to find someone who doesn't ignore me," she said, leaving.

Devil shook his head as he stared after her. "Fuck. Women."

"You gonna go after her, brother? What's that thing you told me about laying down and letting pussy whip you?"

He turned to me with a huge grin and slapped me on the back. "Nah, Nitro, I'm a lover, not a fighter. That one's got a temper on her. She's too fucking much for me to handle. I'd rather get a drink."

A few minutes later, we had beer and I sucked some back while I watched Tatum with Kree. Her gaze caught mine and I jerked my chin at her to get over here. She lifted a finger to indicate she'd be a minute. When her attention shifted back to Kree, I dropped my eyes to check out her ass. She'd worn those skintight jeans of hers I loved, and I struggled to drag my gaze from them.

"Nitro." King's voice sliced through the air and I looked around to find him standing next to Devil. "I see you brought the blonde with you."

I held his gaze. I knew what he was asking. King never missed a beat and always liked to know what members were up to in their private lives. The crazy fucker was the most paranoid person I knew and was always concerned that outsiders would come in with an agenda.

Nodding, I said, "Yeah. That a problem?"

He drank some of his whisky while silently contemplating that. Finally, he said, "If you don't think it will be, I trust that."

The noise in the room picked up and we all turned to see Kick and Evie enter, a huge smile on Kick's face as he held his wife close.

"That fucker ever stop smiling?" Devil asked.

"You'd be smiling like that too if King had finally let you back out into the real world," I said.

Devil grinned. "True."

King changed the subject. "Anyone know Kree's story?"

I drank some beer before answering him. "Nope. All I know is she's from Brisbane. Nash recommended her when Kick asked and to be honest, she was a good recommendation. Always on time, works hard and keeps to herself."

King watched her as she laughed with Tatum. "Yeah, but I wanna know everything there is to know about anyone working here. Find out and get back to me."

Tatum said goodbye to Kree and walked to where we stood as Kree exited the room. She met King's gaze and pushed her shoulders back, standing tall. She never backed down and I fucking loved that about her.

"Tatum Lee, I see you've decided to hang out with us again," King said, his voice dangerously low. I felt my protective streak kick in and knew that if he pushed this with her, I wouldn't be able to stop myself from stepping in for her. And I wasn't sure how that would go down with King.

270

Before she could answer him, Devil's eyes were drawn to the other side of the room and he whistled low. "Fuck me... I'm out of here." With that, he strode towards a brunette I'd never seen before.

Tatum held King's gaze. "This time it's completely my choice to be here, King."

"We're not gonna have a conflict of interests, are we?"

She frowned. "To do with what?"

"Your boss."

"Whatever happens between your club and Billy has nothing to do with me, so no, no conflict of interests."

He drank the rest of his whisky and reached across to place the empty glass on the counter. When he looked at her again, he said, "Good."

"Why did you take my back when my lawyer friend, Duvall, was giving me a hard time outside Billy's club?"

His nostrils flared as he remembered that encounter. "Tatum, if a person looks out for me or someone I care about, I look out for them. You were there for Evie when she needed someone. I won't forget that."

"King!" Kick motioned for King to come over. It looked like he and some of the guys were revved up about something and King left us to check it out.

Tatum's arms circled me as she moved close. Her mouth pressed to my throat and she kissed me there before lifting her face to me. Smiling, she said, "I'm glad you brought me. I needed to come back here and change the feelings I associate with this place."

Placing my hand on her ass, I said, "Is that working?"

"It will."

I held her gaze for a long few moments as unsaid words passed between us. "A lot's changed since then."

271

"Yeah, it has."

I dropped my face and placed my mouth close to her ear so she could hear what I said. So she couldn't mistake a word of it. "I want a lot more to change still, Vegas."

Her arms tightened around me. "Me too."

* * *

Five hours later, the party was in full swing, but I was ready to take Tatum home. Hell, I'd been ready to leave for four and a half fucking hours. But the club needed the time together to let our hair down after months of being tightly wound, so I stayed. The only member who seemed unable to relax was Hyde. He sat in the corner drinking all night, mostly alone, and mostly with a scowl on his face. That wasn't unusual behaviour for him, though. Jekyll and fucking Hyde. He was either up or down, happy or grumpy as fuck. There was no in-between for him.

Tatum had made an effort to meet all the boys and find something to talk with them all about. She and King had even had a drink together. Surprised the fuck out of me. I watched her as she laughed with Evie. Sucking back my beer, I realised how much I wanted to make her happy. The only people I'd truly cared about in that way were Marilyn, Dustin, and Renee. I'd do anything to ease their burdens and make them smile. And I'd do the same for Tatum.

I left my beer on the counter and strode over to where she stood. Sliding my arm around her waist, I said, "You good to go, Vegas?"

Evie smiled. "She's all yours, Nitro."

Tatum's eyes sparkled with the sexy glint she often gave me. "You got something good planned?"

Fuck if that didn't hit me fair in the dick. I gripped her harder. "Careful what you ask, because you might not like what it's in my head," I growled.

Her eyes widened in question. She knew what I referred to. I hadn't brought up my desire for knife play again after the first time I asked her, but every day we spent together was a day closer to me doing that. My need for it with her had only grown since we started sleeping together.

She turned to me and placed her hand on my chest, spreading heat there. "I'm good to go," she said, a little breathless and a whole lot turned on.

We said our goodbyes and I guided her outside, through the maze of bodies still partying hard. They'd last all night, some into tomorrow. I didn't miss those days. Not when I had Tatum to go home with.

The minute I had her alone outside, I dragged her up against a wall, my hands either side of her. "You know what I've been thinking about all night?" I asked as my lips grazed hers, my teeth nipping at them.

Her hands made their way into my hair. "What?"

I traced her lips with my finger, my erection straining against my jeans. "This lipstick staining my dick."

She pulled my hair and my breathing grew ragged. I fucking loved it when she was rough with me. Pulling my face down to hers, she bit my bottom lip and kissed me hard as fuck. It was as if she was laying claim to my mouth. When she came up for air, she said, "You wanna know what *I've* been thinking about?"

Fuck, I wanted to know every damn thought that ever crossed her mind. "Tell me," I demanded.

Rubbing my cock through my jeans, she said, "This. I can't get enough of it." Moving her face closer so our lips almost touched again, she added, "Of you. I can't get enough of you."

Just as I was about to lift her over my shoulder and carry her to my bike, a voice broke through the night, shattering the moment into pieces.

"Rhys."

I spun around to come face-to-face with Joseph. My body tensed. Soldier mode triggered like a fucking dog responding to his master. "What the hell are you doing here?"

His gaze shifted to Tatum and a smile snaked across his face. "You're being rude, son. Introduce me to your girl."

I moved in an attempt to block her from his sight. "Not fucking likely."

The smile on his lips morphed into displeasure. "I've warned you, Rhys, either you give me what I want or I'll find a way to make you."

His threat was loud and clear, and it fuelled anger in me I didn't recognise. Taking the step needed to get in his face, I grabbed his shirt and yanked on it. "I hear you, Joseph, but what you fail to understand is that I'm not the boy who used to cower in front of you. I'm not the boy who you beat until he passed out. And I'm sure as fuck not a man who doesn't protect what's his. You wanna come at me? You fucking come, but be prepared to die trying."

With that, I shoved him away from me, took hold of Tatum and dragged her as far away from that piece of filth and evil as fast as I could.

No fucking way would he win against me. Not anymore.

Chapter Thirty-Six

Tatum

"Home" by Phillip Phillips

I rifled through Nitro's drawers looking for a T-shirt. Anxiety riddled me because I was running late for work. He'd woken me just after five to have sex and then we'd both fallen back asleep. When I'd woken up again, it was nearly eight. It was not a good day to be late for work. Billy had me scheduled in for a meeting with his lawyer to go over the game plan for a case coming up, and I had less than an hour to get home, get dressed and get to that meeting.

"Nitro!" I called out. "Where are all your damn shirts?"

"In my drawer," he yelled from the bathroom, his tone irritated.

I slammed the drawer shut. "Don't you take that tone with me," I snapped, bending over to snatch up my panties that lay on the floor. If only I'd insisted on him taking me home last night instead of giving in to his demand for me to stay at his house. He'd been on edge after the run-in with his uncle, and I'd sensed his need to protect, so I agreed to stay over.

As I stood, he appeared in the doorway, a shitty look on his face. Jerking his chin at the wardrobe, he said, "Did you check in there?" *Still with the tone.*

Taking a deep breath, I said, "I know you're angry about your uncle and all, but don't bring that mood to me. All I asked was where your shirts were."

He scrubbed his hand over his face and blew out a long breath. Without saying another word, he walked to the wardrobe, rummaged around in it and found me a shirt. Passing it to me, he said, "Here." And then—"You almost ready?"

I decided it really would be best if I just ignored him that day. At least until he got his head together. Throwing the shirt on, I nodded and grabbed my stuff off the bed. "Yeah."

We were almost out the front door when Renee ran in, breathless. "Sorry, I'm late!"

Nitro halted and I almost ran into him. "What for?" he asked.

She gave him a confused look. "Ah, for my driving lesson. The one you promised to give me before school this morning."

"Fuck," he muttered. "I can't do it this morning. I'm sorry, I forgot."

"Shit," I apologised, joining their conversation. "Sorry, Renee, it's my fault. I need him to drive me home so I can get to work on time."

She waved me off, but her disappointment with Nitro remained. "Can you do it after school, then?"

"I wish I could, but I've got club stuff on all day." I could hear, clear as day, his regret, but Renee wasn't taking it in.

"How am I supposed to clock up the hours you want me to if no one will take me driving? Mum can't do it and she can't afford to pay for lessons, so you're pretty much it," she said, staring at him with a hard expression.

"I can take you," I offered. "I can finish work early today."

Nitro moved so he could look at both of us. "No. I'll figure something out." His voice was firm, leaving no room for me to misunderstand that he didn't want me driving with his niece.

His words were like a slap in the face. "You don't trust me to take Renee driving?"

He grimaced. "Fuck, Tatum, it's not that—"

276

"Well, what is it?"

"It's—" he started, but Renee cut him off.

"He doesn't trust anyone else on the road, Tatum. It's not you. But I would like to say that at some point, you're gonna have to let me out there, Nitro, so it may as well be with someone you *do* trust."

Trust.

As we stood watching each other, my breathing slowed. If anyone understood how hard it was to give trust to someone, it was me. And yet, I desperately wanted Nitro to give me his. I wouldn't hold it against him if he wasn't ready yet, but I realised how much I wanted it.

He rubbed the back of his neck as time ticked on. It felt like minutes had passed when in reality it was only moments. Finally, he said, "Okay, you take her today." His words came out haltingly, but he did give me his consent, and that meant everything.

* * *

"So, you and Nitro, where's that heading?" Renee asked later that day as we sat in traffic. We'd been driving for almost half an hour and she'd avoided all talk of my relationship with her uncle in that time. I'd been waiting for it, though.

"I honestly don't know," I admitted.

She glanced at me quickly before turning her eyes back to the road. "Really? You don't know what you want?"

I loved her bluntness. "If you'd asked me at first what I wanted, I would have told you I didn't want a relationship. Now, I want that, but what I don't know is what Nitro wants. So who knows where it will all end up."

277

She grinned. "I can tell you that I've never seen him date a woman. You coming for dinner and meeting us all was huge." She waved her hand in the air. "Well, I know we'd already met, but it was different at dinner. And he smiled a lot that night. He never smiles."

"So what you're telling me is that I've got half a shot."

Her grin turned into a laugh and she looked at me again. "You really have no idea, do you? I think you've probably got *less* than half a shot of getting *rid* of him."

Her words settled in deep. They felt good. *This* felt good. I liked Renee and I liked spending time with Nitro's family. "What was it like growing up with him for an uncle?" I imagined Nitro to have been completely overprotective and overbearing, but I wondered what it felt like for her.

She was silent for a beat, thinking. "Nitro was the best dad I ever had," she said simply, but those words told me everything.

I smiled. "Have you ever met your biological father?"

"No. Mum was so young when she fell pregnant. They were both kids. Nitro took on that role from the beginning. I mean, he practically raised Mum, too."

I frowned. "I thought they lived with their uncle?"

"They did until Nitro got them out. Mum was only thirteen then. Nitro was almost eighteen. He got them a place to live and put food on the table. He also made sure Mum and Dustin finished school."

I fell silent, lost in my thoughts. Nitro was the kind of man you thought you knew when you met him. He gave the impression of being unemotional and very cold. But truth be told, he wasn't that person at all. Underneath the layers of moody and bossy and distant, was a man who cared very much.

"You know, Mum would be dead by now if it weren't for Nitro. And I wouldn't care about living as much as I do unless he'd taught me that. He always said that it didn't matter how much I wanted to give up, I couldn't. That even if I felt like no one cared whether I existed, there was always someone out there who needed me. He made me believe I was born for a reason." She paused for a beat, and took a deep breath before adding, "I had a lot of shitty thoughts about my birth, that I was a mistake and probably not even wanted, but Nitro took the time to help me see otherwise." Her voice cracked a little, and I saw a vulnerable side to her I hadn't seen before.

I touched her arm gently. It felt weird to do it, because the only person I was touchy feely with was Monroe. But I couldn't deny the urge. "He's right."

She smiled and nodded. However, the moment was broken when the car behind rear-ended us.

"Oh my, God, Nitro is going to kill me!" Renee yelled in a panic. She was driving his ute and although he hadn't said anything to either of us, I knew she was focused on returning it to him with no scratches. She wanted to prove to him that she could be trusted on the roads and with his car.

"Pull over to the kerb and I'll get out and speak to them," I said, craning my neck to see who had hit us. The car behind, however, had heavily tinted windows so I couldn't get a look at them.

After she pulled over, I exited the car and made my way to the back to inspect the damage. Before I had the chance, though, a deep voice called out my name. Looking towards the car behind us, I saw Nitro's uncle leave it and head my way.

What the fuck?

I stared in confusion.

Why is he here?

All the things Nitro had told me about this man rushed at me. And when he stood in front of me, I felt the evil rolling off him. He oozed it. In the way he watched me, in the twisted smile he gave and in the way he held himself, towering over me as if he could crush me. But I stood straight and didn't show my feelings. Something I was good at.

"Joseph," I greeted him.

"I see that Rhys has told you about me."

I ignored what he said and cut straight to the chase. "What do you want? Because I'm taking it that you hitting us was no accident."

He pulled a business card from his shirt pocket. Handing it to me, he said, "Give that to Nitro. I'll have his car fixed."

The last thing I wanted was to take that card, but I figured this would go a lot faster and smoother if I did. "Was there a particular reason you wanted us to pull over and talk to you?" No way was I pretending this was anything but what it clearly was.

His face darkened. "Just pass that card along to Nitro." He turned to leave me but glanced back for a moment. "I see what he sees in you and I have to say that you'd make an excellent addition to my organisation, too. Tell him that also."

I stared after him for a long while, and it wasn't until I could no longer see his car that I realised I was shaking. I had no doubt that Joseph really was pure evil. It bled from him like blood. And it scared the absolute fuck out of me.

Chapter Thirty-Seven

Nitro

"My Own Prison" by Creed

Rage burned in my gut and blinded my vision. Joseph approaching Tatum and Renee pushed me over the edge, to the point where I could no longer control my impulse to lash out. I wanted to kill him. However, he'd trained me so well that I could control that urge. Killing took careful preparation and planning, but I'd settle for hurting him. His death would come later.

I banged on his hotel room door and waited for him to answer it. I'd called ahead, so he knew I was coming. The bastard never saw my fist coming, though. He thought he'd indoctrinated me enough that I would never turn on him. He should have been smarter.

My punch knocked him onto his ass. I stepped inside the room, the door closing behind me, and reached down to grab hold of his shirt. Pulling him up, I punched him hard again. He didn't fall, just stumbled back a few feet.

We stared at each other. My breaths came hard and fast. His were calm. As if he'd expected the confrontation. Fuck, had he planned my reaction and I hadn't seen that coming?

"This is the Rhys I've been waiting for," he said, fucking with my mind again.

Jesus.

I needed to figure out his game or else he was going to win.

"Leave Tatum out of this!" I roared. "If you go near her again, I will fucking kill you." When he didn't say anything, but just stood there with a smile on his face, I added, "I will fucking rip your heart out of your chest if you fuck with her."

He looked down and straightened his shirt, smoothing it as if that was all he cared about. Lifting his face back up slowly, he met my gaze. The smile had been replaced with the cold glare I knew so well. "Now I know for sure where your loyalties lie. I clearly taught you nothing," he spat harshly.

I knew going to him would reveal as much, but I couldn't stop myself. And I would deal with the consequences of that. I'd make sure Tatum and my family were safe at all times. I would never allow him to get close to them again.

"You taught me more than I care to understand, Joseph. But I'm a good soldier thanks to you, and I will have your blood on my hands one day."

He lifted a brow casually, as if he didn't believe a word I said. "Is that a threat, son?"

I took three determined strides in his direction and punched him again. "No, it's a fucking promise."

He stumbled backwards, raising his hand to cover his face where I'd punched him. The motherfucker *still* didn't retaliate.

As I was trying to process the fact he was taking everything I gave him, the door opened and clicked shut as someone entered. Joseph's eyes sparked with pleasure as he looked beyond me. Turning, I was confronted with a face I knew well. A face that caused a strong physical reaction in me. The kind of reaction that years of conditioning produced.

Terror sliced through my gut and bile forced its way up. Doubling over, I struggled for breath.

"Rhys, it's been a long time."

His voice was like acid washing over me.

282

It burnt.

The heat was too much.

I squeezed my eyes shut.

Panting.

He can't touch me again.

They can't hurt us anymore.

I pushed some short, sharp breaths out, trying desperately to get my shit under control.

My skin was on fucking fire.

I covered my ears, trying to dull the roar there and dropped to my knees, unable to hold myself up any longer.

And then the first kick came.

My uncle's right-hand man, William, kicked me repeatedly, like he had done so many times. My whole body blazed with pain as his boot connected with my gut, my legs, my arms and my head.

When he decided I'd had enough of his boot, he yanked me up and punched me. The force of his punch landed me on my ass, and I took a blow to my head when the back of it hit the edge of the coffee table. Something in that punch woke my fighter side, though. I'd never stood up to William when I was younger, but fuck if I wouldn't now.

Shutting down my conditioned response to him, I pushed my way up off the floor. Raising my fists and roaring out my anger, I lunged at him. He blocked my punch, but I didn't give up. I would never give up again.

I fought like the soldier they'd trained me to be. I landed punch after punch on him, but he also got some in. My body didn't feel the pain, though. I was running on pure adrenalin and rage. There was no time for feeling anything.

I didn't stop until he lay sprawled on the carpet in front of me. Unconscious. Staring up at Joseph, I fought for my breaths, but I managed to spit out, "Fuck you."

He stepped over William and came to me, our faces close. "That will be the last time you speak to me that way."

His declaration was like an ominous message. One that meant nothing to me because I'd already made the decision to kill him. However, as I raised my hands to choke the life out of him, a loud knock on the door sounded.

"Ah, that will be my guests," he said and moved around me to let them in.

My mind failed in its efforts to keep up, and I missed my chance to end his life when five men entered the room. I could take on Joseph, but I couldn't take on that many at once.

I met Joseph's gaze. "This isn't done," I said and then exited the room before he could reply.

I managed to make it out of the hotel. My bloody appearance drew a lot of attention, but no one bothered me. The only thing that bothered me were my memories of William and Joseph and what they'd put me through all those years ago.

William may have hurt my body and drew blood, but those fucking memories hacked at me, ripping open old wounds I thought had healed. Wounds I was beginning to think may never heal.

Chapter Thirty-Eight

Tatum

"Dust to Dust" by The Civil Wars

I'd just put silverside on to cook when Nitro turned up at my place, bloody and beaten. I'd seen him like that before, but I flinched as he stood on my doorstep looking at me through eyes full of pain. It wasn't the wounds or the blood that caused my reaction; it was the torment radiating from him.

Pulling the door wide open, I let him in and watched as he walked to the kitchen. While he held himself like the warrior I knew him to be, there was something completely off about him.

Facing me, he said, "Are you good?"

It was such a simple question, but those three words were all Nitro ever wanted to know. He always wanted to make sure I was okay. They may have been plain words, but they held depth. And I knew they were words he reserved only for those he cared about.

I nodded, cupping his face. He was asking if Joseph had shaken me up. When I'd called to tell him what had happened, he'd been furious. But he'd also been concerned about Joseph scaring Renee and me. "Yeah, but you're not. Let me clean you up." Memories of the last time I cleaned him up surfaced. It wasn't that long ago, but everything had changed since then.

After I'd gathered what I needed, I sat him down at my kitchen table and stood in between his legs while I gently began the task of carefully cleaning blood from his face. Darkness had fallen outside and the only sound I could hear in the quiet of the night was Nitro's laboured breathing. I didn't initiate conversation, figuring he'd talk if he wanted. But I also figured he probably wouldn't.

He surprised me when he did speak. His words came out so quietly that I almost didn't hear them. "Ever had anyone in your life who scared the absolute fuck out of you, Vegas?" His hand gripped the back of my thigh. I not only heard his agony, but I also felt it in the way his hand clung to me.

"Yes." It was almost a whisper. I didn't want to remember this. But I knew that for Nitro, I would if he needed me to.

His fingers dug in to my leg harder. "Who?"

My eyes closed for a moment and I swallowed hard as my heart threatened to crash through my chest. "We used to have these neighbours when I was thirteen who had a son a couple of years older than me. He liked me, but I wasn't interested in him. For two years, he tried to get me to go out with him. At first he was harmless, but then he turned nasty. He started stalking me, always turning up where I was and letting me know he was watching. My parents were too distracted with their marriage that they didn't notice what was going on. And I didn't want to burden them by telling them."

"Even back then you didn't like asking for help," he murmured.

I held his chin and tipped his face up to me so I could wash the blood off his neck. "Yes, even back then," I said as our eyes locked. "So when I had just turned fifteen, he upped his game. He started confronting me more and touching me when he did. He'd whisper shit in my ear and tell me the things he wanted to do to me. The guy was seventeen then, and I'm pretty sure he already had psychopathic tendencies. The shit he wanted to do to me was violent. I told my parents who spoke to his parents.

Of course, they didn't believe it. Dad took it to the police, but there wasn't anything they could do without proof."

"What happened?" Nitro asked through gritted teeth.

I stared at him, not wanting to go on. He moved his hands to my waist and held me there, his touch reassuring. Protective. It said, "I've got you."

Taking a deep breath, I shared one of my greatest regrets. "The threats went on for weeks, until the point where I was scared out of my wits. I wasn't eating, hardly slept, and spent my days too frightened to leave the house. This was during the school holidays and Chris was away during those weeks. When he came home and found out what had been happening, he beat the guy up and tried to protect me. A few weeks passed and I didn't see him anywhere. We thought he'd backed off. And then there was a party at the end of the summer holidays. I went with my friends and told Chris I'd be fine because it was a party and the guy usually only approached me when I was alone. We all drank a fair bit that night and my friends all got trashed. And that's when the guy took his shot."

"He attacked you?" It was like Nitro was holding his breath while he waited for my reply.

I shook my head as a single tear slid down my face. "No. I was walking down the road to go home when he pulled up in his car. He trailed me for ages, not saying much, just staring at me like a crazy guy. I called Chris to come and get me, and in that time, the guy tried to actually run me down with his car. I ran into the bush to get away from him and he came after me. But that was when Christ arrived, so he didn't get to me before Chris started punching him. They fought for ages, until Chris had beaten him so badly that he didn't walk for over a week."

287

I'd stopped washing Nitro's face as I told him the story. He stood and pulled me into his arms when I finished. I hesitated to embrace him, though, because I didn't want to hurt him.

Pulling back a little, he found my eyes. "Put your arms around me, Tatum," he said gruffly.

"I don't want to hurt you."

He gave me a look that told me just to do it, so I did, and he held me tighter. We stayed like that for a long time until finally he let me go and said, "What happened to the guy after that?"

"His parents agreed with mine to keep quiet and not go to the police with what happened. They didn't want Chris to be charged with assault. Their family ended up moving away after that, and we never saw or heard from that guy again." I dropped my eyes as I thought about what that assault did to Chris. When I found his gaze again, I said, "The thing was, though, that one of the local gangs took notice of Chris after that. They saw him as a fighter and wanted him on their crew because of his fighting ability. And from then on, he was always tied up with crime and violence and drugs."

"Fuck," Nitro swore, his hands cradling my head. "You can't blame yourself for that shit. He made his choices, and you couldn't control them."

"I should have called the police that night, instead of Chris. If it wasn't for that, he would never have caught the eye of that gang and his whole life would have been different." I was lost in my memories and thoughts. I'd lived with this regret for years and it had been stirred when Chris was murdered. It almost suffocated me some days. I was convinced it would never let me out of its grip.

Nitro's jaw clenched. "Regret is a bitch, Vegas. A motherfucking bitch." He spat his words out as if he couldn't get

288

rid of them fast enough. Like they twisted in his gut and he needed them out to ease that pain.

"Who scares you?" I whispered, my heart beating wildly again. Nitro wasn't a man who I thought would scare easily, if at all. When he'd thrown that question out there, I knew it was because someone did.

His chest rose and fell hard and fast. "My uncle had this man who did most of his training for him. Joseph would find the soldiers and then William would beat them into submission. He was ex-army and specialised in torture. He programmed us to respond to him with fear." He stared at me while he talked, almost vacantly, and I could see how much his memories consumed him. How much they still owned him.

And then it hit me.

"Did you see William today?"

His heavy breaths filled the silence. He nodded. "I thought I was done with all that. Thought they had no control over me anymore. Turns out I was wrong about all of it."

He let me go and I quickly reached for him, managing to hook my hand around his neck, stopping him from moving away from me. "But you fought back today?" His wounds told me that much.

"Yeah, but that doesn't count for fucking much if simply being in William's presence causes me to lose my shit." His face contorted. "I couldn't breathe, couldn't think straight. I almost fucking threw up." His voice was ragged, and I read all the things he wasn't saying in between what he was saying. My strong man cracked that day and he couldn't make sense of it.

I knew there was nothing I could say that would make this any better. No words would ease his torment. So I simply held my hand out to him and when he took it, I led him to my bedroom.

289

Lifting his shirt over his head, I pressed my mouth to his chest. He'd taken punches all over his body from what I could see, so my kisses were a whisper across his skin in an effort not to hurt him further. Though there was no wild abandon, my passion simmered deep.

Moving down his body, I undid the button on his jeans and lowered the zip. He hissed as I removed his pants. A moment later, he pulled me back up so our faces were close.

Running his finger down between my breasts, he said, "This looks good on you."

I glanced down at his shirt I wore. "Yeah, it does. I'm keeping it."

"Yeah, you should." He took it off and threw it on the floor. "But you shouldn't wear it often," he added while he flicked my bra undone and removed it, too. His mouth closed over my breast and he sucked my nipple between his lips.

I loved the sight of Nitro's head bent so he could suck and lick my breasts. Running my fingers through his hair, I moaned as he worked his way across to my other nipple. His tender touch was in stark contrast to his fury that I craved. But this other side of him was a side I could love just as much.

He growled deeply as his arms circled my body and he lifted me.

"Wait," I said, concerned. "I don't want you to hurt yourself any more than you already are."

"Wrap your legs around me, because I'm going to fuck you, even if it kills me."

I did what he said because one look at his determined expression told me he meant every word. Once my legs were around him, he walked me to the bed and placed me on it. He then slid his hands up my legs, hooked his fingers into my panties and pulled them off.

"Fuck, you're beautiful," he rasped as he straddled me. His attention was completely on my body, and his gaze lingered on every inch of me. His hands and mouth moved over my skin slowly, as if he was making art on me. He seemed spellbound and in turn, I was too, because this wasn't the Nitro I knew. And it stunned me that he could be like this, especially after the violent beating he'd taken.

Fucking Nitro was usually like diving into a raging ocean. The beautiful frenzy of it both exhausted and calmed me. I'd never experienced anything like it in my life. Sex had become more than just a physical act with him. Even though it could be furious and brutal, I knew we both used it as a way of dealing with our darkness. It soothed us. If only for that time we were joined as one, we breathed a little easier.

But the way he caressed me was a whole other thing. I'd never been touched like I was priceless and precious before, and that was how Nitro was touching me. It soothed me in a way I'd never imagined possible.

He surrounded me with care.

He wrapped me in devotion.

He breathed life into me.

When Nitro finally entered me, he'd found his fury again, and he fucked me with that rough energy I hungered for. We were a storm and serenity all rolled into one. But it was the storm we both needed the most.

Chapter Thirty-Nine

Nitro

"The Pretender" by The Foo Fighters

I watched King as he entered the room. He'd called Church unexpectedly, and that always meant he had something to tell us. Something was going down, and I was on edge.

His eyes met mine before he spoke. I didn't like what I saw there.

Apprehension.

Regret.

Determination.

Tearing his gaze from mine, he looked around the room. His body was rigid as fuck and when he finally announced his news, I understood why.

"We're not buying guns off Sutherland. We'll be proceeding with the deal Joseph Lockwood brought to us."

It was a fucking kick in the gut. The tension I'd been carrying for months finally threatened to snap and I shoved my chair back and stood.

"Why?" I thundered, unable to hold my anger back.

King turned to me. There was no anger there, no glare, nothing. Just a shitload of unspoken apologies. "I don't trust Dragon. We might be in bed with him over this Gambarro shit, but I don't want to rely on Sutherland if Dragon's in his ear. Fuck knows what could happen down the track after we're finished with Gambarro. Better to build a relationship with another supplier now."

I pointed my finger at the bruises on my face and body. "Jesus Christ, King, you've seen what he's capable of. I'd rather get in bed with Billy if our only other option is Joseph."

He ran his hand over his face as he shook his head. "With the amount of guns and ammo we need, that option is off the table. Billy would bleed us dry with what he charges." He didn't acknowledge the beating I'd taken, but then our world was full of violence, so I shouldn't have been surprised. Still, it cut that he didn't care.

"Fuck!" I spun around and punched the wall, letting my anger flow out of me.

Hyde spoke up. "I'm on board with using Joseph."

Of course he fucking was. And so, it turned out, was everyone else. The mighty dollar guaranteed that. With the tens of thousands of dollars we'd save buying from Joseph, they all jumped in quickly with their support for the decision.

Then King twisted the knife in further. "The deal is going down today. And Nitro?"

I stared at him. "What?"

"Joseph had one stipulation for this deal to go ahead."

"What?" Tension punched through every part of my body in anticipation of what his requirement could be. Joseph would surely use this as some way to drag me back to him.

King held my gaze in the way he did when he wanted no argument. "He wants you there."

My mind raced with what his reasoning for this was. There had to be a trap. There always was with Joseph.

"Nitro?"

My head snapped up. There were so many questions that King was asking me. Was I on board? Would I do what he asked? *Were my loyalties with the club?* I nodded. "Yes."

He returned my nod. "We leave in an hour."

* * *

Joseph's car pulled into the warehouse and parked next to the truck that had already arrived. He exited the black SUV and walked our way, his gaze not leaving mine.

King stepped forward, meeting him. They exchanged words, but I couldn't hear what was said. My ears roared as my demons circled so even if I'd been closer, I probably wouldn't have made out what they were saying. I'd spent the last hour going over and over what Joseph's goal could be with having me there. I'd come up fucking short, and that only meant my vigilance was extreme.

King raised his arm and motioned for me to join them. I closed the distance without hesitation. If Joseph wanted me there, he wouldn't see any of my uneasiness. However, just as I almost reached them, William circled around from the back of the truck and came my way.

Fuck.

Sweat broke out on my forehead and my throat turned dry. The nightmares of my childhood screamed to life when I realised he wore the exact outfit he'd worn years ago while drilling obedience into me. Black cargo pants, black tee and black combat boots. The fucking bastard knew it would be a trigger for me, but I was getting better at fighting those goddam triggers. My physical reactions weren't so controlled, but I worked overtime trying to shut them down.

"William," I greeted him, holding my body up straight.

Disappointment flashed across his face for a second before he scrubbed it away and gave me a tight smile. "Rhys, we meet again."

"We do." Our faces were a mess of violent bruising and swelling, and if his body felt anything like mine, it was in some pain. But there we were, years after I thought I'd never see him again.

"Can we get this done?" King asked with a scowl. He'd pulled me aside after Church and told me he'd do his best to push the delivery through fast so I didn't have to be around Joseph for long.

I'd seen King's reluctance to take this deal and in between the words of what he said to me, I'd understood his reasons. I didn't like them, or necessarily agree with them, but I got why he took this path.

Joseph motioned for William to take care of business with King while he walked my way. Eyeing my bruises, he said, "Your father would be proud of you, Rhys. He never did see eye-to-eye with me about your potential."

He made no sense to me. "What the fuck does that mean?"

His lips curled into an evil smile. "My brother had such noble dreams for your future. He wanted you to have what he never did. Told me once that you were smart enough to be a doctor or a lawyer or even a scientist. You did love science after all. I was the one who saw you for who you really were. Smart as a whip and able to make decisions on your feet. I knew that with the right training you could lead an army. The fact you're still fighting me on your destiny, he'd be proud of that." He paused for a moment and his evil fucking smile grew. "It's a good thing I didn't allow him to be around to help you fight me."

My breathing slowed. "You what?"

He watched me closely with a look of triumph. "Did you think that car crash was an accident all those years ago, son?"

The car crash when I was twelve.

The one that killed both my parents.

The deaths that forced us to live with Joseph.

Motherfucker.

Every emotion I'd ever buried roared in my head. In my body. Through every fucking part of me. He'd taken my parents from me and he'd taken my life, too. Every good thing I ever had died that day. Joseph had extinguished all the light in my life and filled it with darkness instead.

I will kill him.

My loyalty to King and the club shattered. Once we left this warehouse, I would make a fucking plan and I would rip the life from Joseph's body.

King blurred into focus as Joseph shifted away. Coming to me, he said, "We're done, Nitro. Time to go."

I blinked.

Forcing out a harsh breath, I snapped back to attention. Turning, I stalked to the van we'd come in. I didn't give Joseph another glance, didn't want to look at him more than I had to. The next time I saw him would be the last.

* * *

I glanced at my phone, looking for a text from Tatum. I'd sent her one twenty minutes earlier and hadn't heard back. Unusual for her. She never took more than ten minutes to reply.

"You gonna finish that beer or just stare at your phone all afternoon?" Devil asked.

My hand squeezed around the phone and I looked up at him. After I drank what was left in my bottle, I said, "Just waiting on a message."

He chuckled. "Well, that's fucking obvious. You whipped bastard."

I stared at the empty bottle in my hand. If whipped was feeling anxious when you didn't hear from the woman you shared your bed with each night, then yeah, I was fucking whipped. If it was worrying about her when she wasn't with you, and thinking about her all the fucking time, then I was absolutely, 100 percent whipped. Something I never thought I'd be. And something that scared the shit out of me. Not because I didn't want to feel that way about her, but because being with me could be dangerous for her. To hold that responsibility in my hands was more than I thought I could handle at times.

I took a deep breath and met Devil's gaze again. "Yeah, you could be on to something there, brother."

He grew serious. "I like Tatum. Not that it matters what I think, but a chick like that, who doesn't take your shit and who stands by you regardless, that's a chick worth having in your life."

"You ever had that before?"

"Yeah, but I always fuck it up. One day I might get that shit right." He jerked his chin at the bar. "You want another beer?"

I nodded, and he left me alone while he headed to the bar. Staring at my phone again, I decided to call Tatum, but as I swiped to dial her number, the phone rang. It wasn't a number I knew.

When I answered it, a man's voice sounded. "Is that Rhys Lockwood?"

My gut tightened. No one called me that anymore. Except for Joseph, but this wasn't my uncle on the line and sounded too formal to be anyone he would associate with. "Speaking."

"Rhys, it's Matt Logan here, Marilyn's psychologist."

I dropped my head into my hand as fear filled me. "Is she okay?" He never phoned me. This couldn't be good.

"To be honest, I'm not convinced she is. I just had a phone call from her and she was in such a state that I called an ambulance to her house. This phone call to you is highly unusual, I never do this, but I feel it's crucial I pass some information on to you." He took a breath before continuing, "Marilyn saw the man who raped her today."

The man who raped her? I fucking killed that man. There was no way she could have seen him.

"Doc, that's not possible. That guy is dead."

"I'm not referring to the recent rape. I'm referring to the ones from when she was a child."

The room spun.

I gripped the phone so tightly it should have shattered into pieces.

My mind ran in a million different directions.

This couldn't be happening.

"You're telling me that my sister was raped when she was a child?"

Silence.

And then——"I thought you knew."

I was on my feet before I realised it and walking out of the clubhouse. I could hardly process what he was telling me. My need for violence was extreme. I wanted to punch and kick and thrash and scream this injustice out of me.

Not my Lynny.

It was where her darkness came from, and I'd never known. She'd kept this shit wrapped up tight and it had almost killed her. I should have been there for her. More. I should have done more.

"Rhys, are you still on the line?"

"Yeah, I'm here." The words came out a strangled mess. "Who did this to her?"

Deep in my gut I knew. I fucking knew.

"It was your uncle," he said quietly, his words full of regret. "I'm sorry you're hearing this from me. I honestly thought she'd told you."

I clenched my fists as I made my way to my bike. "What happened today? Did he hurt her?" I would fucking drag his death out for this. I would make him hurt so fucking much for every ounce of pain he'd caused Marilyn.

"No, he didn't approach her. She saw him outside her house. Apparently, he was sitting in a car looking at the house for a while and then drove off. I thought it appropriate you know this information so you could take steps to avoid him coming near her again."

I'd fucking take steps. Joseph would *never* set foot near Marilyn again.

I needed to get off the phone and deal with this. "Thanks, Doc. I've got this covered."

I ended the call and started my bike. Screaming out of the parking lot, I almost collided with Kick who was entering. Narrowly missing him, I sped towards Marilyn's house. The ambulance might get there before me, but in case not, I wanted to check on her.

The ride home passed in a blur and as I pulled around the corner of her street, I watched an ambulance drive away.

299

My phone had vibrated with a call on the way there so I took a moment to stop and check who it had been. I was still waiting to hear back from Tatum.

There was one missed call from Devil. No message. I'd call him later. All I wanted to do was head to Joseph and deal with him. I didn't want to involve Devil or any Storm members in that. I needed to put the past to rest by myself. And I also didn't want to waste time waiting for help.

My phone rang before I pulled back out into the traffic. I placed it to my ear without checking caller ID. "Yeah?"

"Rhys."

I froze.

Joseph.

A dark cloud circled over me as my gut twisted.

When I didn't speak, he said, "I have something of yours."

My world crashed down around me.

I dry-heaved.

Every good thing I had in my life, he ruined.

Tatum.

"Do not lay a finger on her, Joseph."

"Oh, my boy, I've already laid every finger I have on her."

I clutched my stomach and dry-heaved again as the ticking of a time bomb blasted in my head.

Joseph continued, "You can have her back, Rhys, so long as you give me what I want. It's a fair exchange. But the longer you take to come to me, the more I'm tempted to sample her and find out what it is she has that you've traded everything for."

I didn't think he could wreck me more than he already had. I was wrong. The thought of him touching Tatum delivered me into a new state of madness. Complete and utter madness.

"Text me where you are. I'll be there."

300

I jabbed at the phone to end the call and slammed my hand down on my bike. "Fuck!" I roared, letting it all out.

This was unbearable.

It was every fear I'd ever had come to life.

To be the reason her life was in danger was a living hell.

And to even think about losing her spiralled me into a dark abyss full of violence and brutality.

He would pay dearly for this. And for everything else he'd ever done to my family and me.

Chapter Forty

Tatum

"Russian Roulette" by Rihanna

Pain radiated down my cheek where Joseph gripped it, his fingers digging into my skin. Hard. If there was one thing this asshole knew, it was how to inflict agony.

"He says he's on his way, but we shall see," he said, his crazy eyes boring into me. "We shall find out if he really cares for you or not."

I wanted to spit in his face and claw out his motherfucking eyes. I also wanted to cut his balls off and shove them down his throat to shut him the hell up. This man never stopped talking. He loved the sound of his own voice.

I didn't doubt Nitro.

I knew he'd come.

It was just a matter of time, and I was good at getting through shit, so I could handle myself until he arrived. I refused to allow Joseph to scare me. Nitro would come and he would kill him. Just like he'd done to that goddam biker months ago.

He won't fail me.

"I've done my research on you, Tatum. You were a lawyer and a good one from what I can work out. How the fuck did you end up with a biker?"

Go to hell, asshole.

I'm not telling you a thing.

He squeezed my face. "Tell me!"

I struggled under his hold, trying to shake my face from his grip. It worked, but only for a moment. He didn't squeeze me again, but he did slap me so hard that the force of it knocked me over. Me and the chair I was tied to.

My head hit the cement with a thud and I saw stars. My ears rang and more pain tore through my body. It especially hurt in my shoulder, which had slammed into the concrete.

Joseph's men moved me back into a sitting position. He had five men in the room with us and I'd heard more outside. I wasn't sure where he'd brought me. All I knew was that the room I was in was fairly large and seemed like an industrial warehouse with a cement floor and high roof. It was warm, too. No air conditioning.

Joseph crouched in front of me and placed his hands on my legs. They were tied together, as were my hands. I wanted to shove his hands off me, but I couldn't, so instead I took a deep breath and reminded myself that Nitro was on the way.

"You and Rhys are a perfect match. Both as stubborn as the other. I'm only going to ask you this once more, Tatum, and if you don't answer me, we're going to have a problem. How did you meet him?"

I didn't conceal the hate I had for him. "Why the fuck do you care?"

He jerked up and nodded at someone behind me. Hands landed on my shoulders, pulling me back against the chair. A second later, Joseph's fist slammed into my face. He punched me so hard I struggled for breath. It was like I was drowning and couldn't work my way back up for air, all while excruciating pain consumed me.

I counted to twenty before I finally managed to draw a long breath of air into my lungs. It had been short bursts of air up until that point, which hardly felt like life-sustaining oxygen.

303

As I wheezed and fought for air, the door opened and two men entered. I tried to focus on them to see who they were, but everyone had blurred and I couldn't make out a damn thing.

And then I heard his voice.

"Vegas."

His boots thudded on the cement and I knew he was coming my way, but then they stopped.

"Fucking let me go!" His voice ricocheted around the room, and I finally zeroed in on him to see that two of Joseph's men had restrained him, holding him back from me.

"All in good time, son," Joseph said. His back was to me and he'd moved towards Nitro.

"I told you not to fucking hurt her," Nitro snarled.

"When will you ever learn that I don't listen to you? It's you who needs to listen to me," Joseph said. I hated hearing him talk to Nitro like that. Hated knowing the power he still held over him.

My sight returned to full capacity and I stared at Nitro, taking in his eyes. They were dead. Oh, there was life there, but the way he looked at Joseph was as if he wasn't even looking at another human being. I was certain he'd come to kill and that he'd switched off the human side of himself to do it.

He struggled and fought to escape the men holding him back. When that didn't work, he kicked out at Joseph, landing a hard kick to his groin.

Joseph grunted loudly and boomed, "You wanna fight, Rhys? Let's see what happens when you do that."

He spun around, stalked back to me and grabbed my neck. Yanking me to a standing position, with the chair hanging off me, he snarled, "This face won't be recognisable if you keep that shit up."

304

My breaths turned choppy as I stared at him up close. I believed every word he said. Joseph didn't seem to make empty threats.

"Stop!" Nitro yelled.

Joseph didn't loosen his grip on me, but he turned to face Nitro. "Are you coming to your senses?"

Nitro nodded but didn't say anything.

Joseph let me go and pushed me back to a sitting position. He then strode back to Nitro and punched him hard in the gut. I cringed as Nitro bent forward, winded.

And then the punches kept coming.

Joseph was savage. It was as if he was on auto-pilot. Nitro was his punching bag, and he worked out his anger on him.

I couldn't watch. It was brutal and bloodthirsty. I couldn't even imagine doing what he was doing to my worst enemy. As much as I might want to hurt someone, I wouldn't have the stomach for it.

It lasted longer than I cared to think about. It felt like an eternity.

Joseph was breathless when he finally ordered, "Take him away."

I didn't know what he planned, but the two guys holding Nitro up took him out of the room. Joseph faced me and for the first time since I'd arrived in that shithole a few hours prior, fear filled me. I believed Nitro would get us out of there, but I didn't want to think about what we'd have to go through first.

He came to me and ran his finger slowly down my face. "I'll be back," he said.

They were his last words before he left me alone in the room. As the door clicked shut behind him, I exhaled. I attempted to give myself a pep talk, but no matter how hard I tried, it didn't work. Because this wasn't just about me. I could pep talk the fuck out of shit if it only involved me. But Nitro's life was at stake, too, and that drove more fear into me than I knew what to do with.

I couldn't lose him.

* * *

Joseph left me alone for hours. It was dark by the time he came back. There was one tiny window in the room and night had fallen a long time before he returned.

"Dinner," he said as he dumped a tray of food on the floor in front of me. I didn't look at it, but rather kept my eyes on him. "You need to use the toilet?"

I couldn't figure out why he cared. But I took the opportunity he presented and nodded. "Yes," I croaked. My face was in a world of pain and I found it hard to talk.

He placed a hand on the back of my chair and motioned with his other hand for me to stand. My hands were tied behind my back and as I stood, he held the chair in place so my hands could slide up.

He then said, "Come."

I soon realised he meant for me to shuffle my way to the toilet because he didn't undo the rope he'd tied around my ankles.

The toilet wasn't far from the room, but it took me ages to get there. Joseph became frustrated with me and curled one hand around my throat and the other around my waist so he could pull me along. My bare feet dragged along the cement most of the way after that, and they were a bloody mess of cuts and scratches at the end of the journey.

He kicked open the toilet door and pushed me inside. I stared at him, wondering how the fuck I was supposed to use the toilet if I couldn't undo my pants. He met my gaze and his eyes glinted with an evil smile. Before I knew what was happening, he flicked the button on my pants and slid the zip down. He then gripped my pants and yanked them down.

He hissed as his eyes landed on my lacy panties. "Rhys is a lucky man. I bet he spends most of his spare time inside this cunt," he said as he slid a finger inside my panties.

I froze.

Oh, God, no.

This could not be happening.

I squeezed my legs together. "Don't fucking touch me." My heart beat so damn fast I thought it might explode, but I was proud as fuck that my voice held no trace of my fear.

"You're a feisty one," he murmured, but he let his hand linger near my vagina.

The sound of shoes on the cement in the hallway signalled someone approaching. "Joseph! We need you."

His eyes met mine. "It's your lucky day." With that, he pulled my panties down so I could use the toilet. "Be there in a minute," he yelled back, not taking his eyes off me.

I hated every fucking minute of this. But I never stopped telling myself that Nitro would get us out of here.

I had to believe that.

I finished using the toilet, and he pulled my pants back up and returned me to the room that sadly was mine. He undid the rope around my wrists and I ate the dinner of chicken and salad that he'd given me while one of his men watched. When I finished, my hands were secured together again. The guy left the room and I sat staring at the door, willing it to open. Willing Nitro to burst through and tell me everyone was dead and we could leave.

That never happened.

* * *

I didn't see Joseph for another day and a half. His men delivered one meal to me in that time and took me to the toilet twice. Other than that, I saw nothing and heard nothing. I had no idea what was going on outside of the room I was in. If I thought I'd lived through hell before, that had nothing on this. This kind of hell could send a person mad. The not knowing was the worst, but equally as bad was the silence and time alone. It did crazy shit to my mind.

My relief when Joseph finally showed his face again, was short-lived. He entered the room and then Nitro was shoved in after him. I almost vomited when I saw Nitro. He'd been so badly beaten that his face was swollen and he could hardly open his eyes. Dried blood coated his face and where there was no blood, there were bruises and cuts. His body was in so much pain that he walked with a hunch and grunted with each step he took. The pain in my face from being punched felt like nothing compared to the hurt blaring from him.

Joseph eyed me. "Rhys is more stubborn than I thought. He still refuses to join my army, so I figured I'd give him some reasons."

Moving behind me, he wrapped his hand around my throat and squeezed hard until I couldn't draw breath. I couldn't move my legs and I couldn't move my hands because they were still tied together. All I could do was sit there and struggle for air. I gasped and frantically tried to suck air in through my nose, but he realised that and blocked that passage, too.

Nitro screamed for him to stop, but soon I couldn't even hear that. All I could hear was the blood roaring in my ears as death beckoned. My head and body thrashed as I fought and finally Joseph let me go, sending me to the floor in an almighty crash. I fell headfirst, smashing my face into the concrete. Pain splintered through my head and radiated to every part of my body.

"Let her go!" Nitro roared, his voice making its way to me as I lay gasping for air.

"Not until you agree to my terms, son," Joseph said right before he kicked me in the stomach.

He then ordered two of his men to haul me up and he beat me in the same manner that he'd beaten Nitro the last time I saw him.

Time stood still.

I heard Nitro yelling that he would do whatever Joseph wanted, but I couldn't push my way through the haze of pain circling me.

Bone crunching.

Blood spilling.

My soul breaking.

I wasn't sure I would survive this.

I wasn't sure I wanted to.

The pain was too great and death seemed easier.

Eventually the punches stopped coming.

I lay curled up in a ball on the cement.

Boots sounded next to me, until they were a distant noise I could hardly hear. The door clicked shut.

And then came silence.

Beautiful silence.

I was alone.

Floating.

Drifting.

Dreaming of heaven.

Arms embraced me.

309

Pulled me into a lap.

Warm breath whispered across my skin.

A hand gently smoothed my hair.

"I'm so sorry, Vegas." Nitro's grief-stricken voice broke through the haze, and I blinked my eyes open.

He stared down at me. His eyes were filled with tears. And pain. So much pain. I didn't want there to be any more of that for either of us. We'd had enough. Done our time. Paid the price for our sins.

He rocked me for what felt like hours. It could have been. Or it may have only been minutes. It didn't matter how long it was. The only thing that mattered was that those final moments together were filled with so much care. The kind of care a person searches their whole life for. In those moments, Nitro loved me.

Chapter Forty-One

Nitro

"State Of My Head" by Shinedown

"Send her home."

Joseph narrowed his eyes at me. "And then?"

"And then I will do what you want."

He watched me closely for a few moments. "You will give up Storm."

I winced as I shifted my weight onto one foot. My leg screamed with pain and I needed to take most of the load off it, but it only brought more pain to the other one. Joseph's beatings over the last two days had been severe. Worse than any I'd ever received. I could barely see him through swollen eyes, and bruises covered every inch of me.

My chest squeezed at the thought of what Joseph had done to Tatum earlier. He'd beaten her so badly that I thought he would go too far and kill her. It surprised me that he'd left me alone with her when he was finished. In hindsight, though, I realised he used it as another way to break me.

If watching her go down hadn't been enough, sitting with her had shattered me. Holding Tatum in my arms and knowing that everything I saw and heard was because she'd chosen to be with me had torn a chunk out of my heart. I'd realised just how much she meant to me and that I would do anything to keep her safe. Agreeing to return to Joseph had been a small price to pay in return for her life.

"I will give up Storm," I agreed.

"Very well," he said and took the few steps to the door of the room where he kept me locked up.

"Joseph," I called after him. When he faced me, I said, "If you ever lay your hand on her again or hurt her in any way emotionally or physically, I will leave you and I will never come back. I will fight you to my death if I have to, but I won't allow Tatum to be hurt again."

He smiled that evil fucking smile of his that I wanted to wipe off his face. "It seems we have found your reason, Rhys."

"My reason?"

"Your reason to stay with me. I won't touch her unless you leave, and you won't leave unless I touch her."

I allowed him to believe that because it guaranteed Tatum's safety. "Come and get me once she's gone. We have shit to discuss."

He raised a brow. "Now this is more like the soldier I raised, son."

"Don't fucking call me that."

"And there's the man you've become. We just need to find a way to merge the two sides of you."

He slipped out the door, and I doubled over in agony. Clutching my stomach, I pushed out a few sharp breaths. My entire body was alive with this pain. I was aware, though, that it wasn't just physical pain. My soul was bleeding. It was oozing the blackest shit it had ever known. Joseph would not get away with any of this. I would die to ensure it.

* * *

Joseph returned sooner than I thought he would. "William has taken her home," he announced as he entered the room.

"Was she in a state fit enough to call someone for help?" She needed a doctor to check her out.

"Yes."

Thank fuck.

"Right, so you need to bring me up to speed on your business." *And get me out of this fucking room.* It was bare except for one chair. I'd spent my time in there pacing and plotting revenge. The few hours of sleep I'd managed had been on the cold cement floor, which had been agonising as hell.

He closed the distance between us in two determined strides, his face clouding over with annoyance. "You don't tell me what to do. That's the first thing you must relearn."

I stared into his dark eyes. "So tell me then, how is this going to go down? Because I thought you wanted me back to run your new Sydney operations."

"You're testing my patience, son."

I clenched my jaw. He called me that to push me and I refused to show him what it did to me. I needed to lock my emotions down again.

When I didn't say anything, he spoke again. "We've got a meeting with a new client tonight. Eric Bones. I want you there with William and me so you can begin building a relationship with him."

I already knew Eric Bones. He was a Storm ally and if I was in that meeting, news would travel fast.

"Joseph, I have to leave the club first. If they hear word of this before I tell King, there will be hell to pay."

"You think I give a fuck about a motorcycle club, Rhys? I could crush them in the blink of an eye."

"No, you couldn't." He had no fucking idea.

He grabbed my shirt and yanked me to him so our faces were close. "You forget what resources I have. With the knowledge you have of Storm's business and King's way of thinking, we can bring that club down together." He let go and shoved me backwards. "We start work on that tonight."

I stared at him while he walked to the door. My next question was one I didn't want to know the answer to. "What do you have planned?"

He looked back at me, his eyes glinting with menace. "Eric Bones is desperate for cash. I've agreed to sell guns to him cheaply in exchange for his loyalty. He's also going to flood the market with cheap coke from me, undercutting the club. And you're going to help by giving him details of Storm's trade so he can use that information against them. Tonight."

He exited the room without another word, and I stood in shock at what he wanted me to do. Joseph was a smart motherfucker. Forcing me to disregard my club loyalty achieved two things for him. One, it showed I was serious about returning to him. And two, it ensured my ties to Storm were cut. Because no way would the club take me back if I betrayed them like this.

* * *

Eric Bones inspected me. Every bruise and cut on my face were noted, as was the way I grimaced each time I moved. Finally, he met my eyes. "You've left Storm?"

Joseph and William sat either side of me, their bodies rigid while they waited for my answer. William had spent the drive to the meeting point trying to drill his special brand of fear into me. I'd anticipated that, though, so I had done my best to prepare my mind for it. And I'd succeeded. So far.

"Yes."

His eyes widened and he whistled. "Fuck. Never thought I'd see the day, Nitro." Jerking his chin at my face, he said, "They do that to you?"

My mouth flattened into a hard line. I needed to get this shit over with as fast as possible. Sitting there discussing my club was not fucking helpful.

Before I could reply, Joseph stepped in. "No, I did that to him." Leaning his arms on the table, he added, "This is what happens when I'm not happy."

Eric's brows lifted and I took in his nervousness. I hoped to hell he was reconsidering his involvement with Joseph. With a shaky laugh, he said, "Remind me never to piss you off."

"You will do well to remember this," Joseph said. "Now, can we get down to business?"

Eric tapped his fingers on the table, jittery. "Umm, yeah, about that…."

"Yes?" Joseph's voice was low. Dangerous.

William leant forward. "You haven't changed your mind, have you, Eric? That wouldn't make Joseph very happy." There was no mistaking his threat. William had a presence that shrieked danger.

Eric stared at him. The fear rolled off him as he assessed William who had been silent up until that point. Swallowing hard, he said, "I just need a little more time to get some shit worked out."

"This happens today or not at all," Joseph said.

Eric's indecision was blatantly obvious in the way he said he wanted in on the deal while his body language said the complete opposite.

Raking his fingers through his hair, he said, "Man, honestly, I just need a few more days and then we're sweet. I don't have the cash for the guns yet."

Joseph fumed next to me. I watched as he splayed his hand out on the table in the way he did when his urge was actually to punch someone. It was one of his control mechanisms.

Silence filled the air for a minute while Joseph considered what Eric had said. Finally, he stood. "Three days, Eric. If you're not ready then, you're dead."

As William and I stood to leave with Joseph, I took in Eric's expression. He looked like he was about to shit his pants.

Greed was a dirty fucking thing. It made you do shit you thought you'd never do. I'd watched countless men fall after a relationship with it. I hoped that Eric gave up on this deal, but something told me that the threat of death wasn't something a man like him would be willing to risk. Men like him would rather sleep with the devil than give everything up for some peace.

I wasn't like Eric Bones.

I'd choose death over the devil every time.

* * *

I slept on the cement floor again that night. Not that I got many hours of actual sleep in. Probably two at the most. My body hurt too damn much on the floor. On top of that, I couldn't shut my mind off. I spent most of the night worrying about Tatum. I wasn't a praying man, but I prayed like fuck that she'd received the medical attention she needed. I also prayed that Marilyn was okay and that Renee and Dustin were dealing with it all.

When the sun rose, I paced the room while I waited for Joseph to arrive. He hadn't said anything to me when we'd returned from the meeting with Eric Bones. He'd been furious with Bones, and because I knew Joseph's evil mind well, I knew

316

some of that fury stemmed from the fact my hand hadn't been forced to declare my loyalty to him over Storm. I'd been given a reprieve, and all I could hope was that three days was enough time to show Joseph where my true loyalty lay.

He didn't show his face that morning, but William did. He turned up wearing his cargo pants, black tee, and combat boots, which told me what kind of day it was going to be.

Throwing clean clothes at me, he fired his orders. "You've got five minutes for a shower and then I want you waiting outside dressed in these. You and me are gonna spend the day together getting reacquainted."

I followed him to the shower and did what he'd said. The day was going to be tough enough as it was, I didn't need to start arguing with him early on.

When I was done, he led me to a Jeep that was parked in the large open area of the warehouse and indicated for me to get in the back. He joined me there while another man slid into the driver seat. We were then driven about an hour away to what I guessed was Joseph's base camp for soldier training. William blindfolded me at the beginning of the journey so I had no sense of where they'd taken me. When the blindfold was removed, we were parked in the middle of the bush.

"Out," William barked.

He then proceeded to put me through my paces. Their land was dense with trees, but they'd cleared a section that held the shit I knew was designed to break a man. Trenches of muddy water, pits of mud, steel cages over deep troughs of water that could drown a man, dangling wires designed to shock, and a bath of ice were some of William's favourite things. He could spend hours doing this part of his training. Brutalisation was designed to start the process of ripping a man's sense of self-worth from him. It was just one aspect of what William did. And he did it well.

I spent the next five hours following his orders. I ran his fucking obstacle course and didn't back down from any of it, even though my body was in excruciating pain the whole time. Hell, it had already been in a world full of hurt before I started. William's goal was clearly to kick that up a notch, and he succeeded.

At the end of the five hours, he came to me and grabbed me around the throat. "You think you can beat me, soldier?" I knew from the way he spat his words out that he was pissed at me.

I held his gaze triumphantly. What he didn't realise was that the day was exactly what I'd needed. My conditioned response to him was still there, but my mind was in a whole new place. They didn't understand that by hurting Tatum they'd splintered my mind and screwed with the wiring they'd put in place years ago. So while I still felt that stirring of fear when I looked at William, I was able to mentally withstand it. The five hours spent with him doing his training, and surviving those hours mentally strong as fuck at the end, only solidified my ability to ignore the fear he tried to draw out.

"I know I fucking can. I might have agreed to work with Joseph again, but it'll be a cold fucking day in hell before I fall at your feet," I gritted out. "Your power over me is dead."

His lips curled up into a snarl. "We'll see about that."

He dragged me to the ice bath and forced me into it. I wanted to fight him off and force *him* into it, but I knew I had to be smart. If I had any chance at saving myself and my family, I needed to wait for the perfect moment to kill both him and Joseph together.

I immediately began hyperventilating, drawing in very fast and deep breaths as the cold water surrounded me. William watched with smug satisfaction as I fought for air. My body was going into shock. I knew the process because he'd subjected me to it many times. I just had to get through these first few minutes, get my breathing under control and then last until he pulled me out of the water.

Easier said than fucking done.

"You think this is going to be a walk in the fucking park, Rhys?"

My teeth chattered as I stared up at him, still struggling for breath. I couldn't reply, but then, he wasn't looking for a reply. He was simply trying to strike fear.

Crouching, he said, "It's been a good nineteen years since I've had the pleasure of training you. My program has evolved and this is just the beginning, soldier."

I sucked air in as deep as I could. And I went to battle with my mind. He would never break me again. *Never.* As my muscles grew weak the longer he left me in there, and the pain in my body increased, I attempted to focus on Tatum. I imagined her smile, her eyes, her laugh, her fight. God, how I loved her fight. I'd never met a woman with the spirit she had. My thoughts drifted to the future. I wanted one with her. I knew that. When I escaped this hell, I would make it happen. I'd give her everything she'd never had before. Starting off with space in my fucking wardrobe.

"Almost five minutes, Rhys. You ready to fall at my feet again?"

I blinked slowly as I processed his words. Five minutes was a long time to be in icy water. Almost too long. I knew that. Hypothermia could kill me if I didn't get out soon. And yet I refused to give in to William.

I waited it out. And eventually he was the one to crack. But not before my muscles became so weak I couldn't walk when he dragged me from the bath. My coordination took a hit, too. After he had pulled me out, he left me on the ground and organised for the Jeep to be brought over. He and the driver managed to get me into the back seat. William yanked my clothes off and wrapped me in a light blanket he had stashed in the back as the driver sped all the way back to the warehouse.

I drifted in and out of consciousness.

So cold.

So fucking cold.

Chapter Forty-Two

Tatum

"XO" by Beyonce

I lay on my hospital bed, drugged up on heavy-duty painkillers the doctor had me taking for all the injuries Joseph had inflicted on me and watched as Monroe walked into the room.

Meeting my eyes with a small smile, she said, "She's safe."

I closed my eyes and exhaled, ignoring the pain in my face as I did that. Opening them again, I asked, "Dustin?"

She nodded. "He's safe, too. And Renee assured me her mother is okay in the hospital. Renee has moved into Nitro's house to be with Dustin until Nitro comes home."

I stared at her in silence while tears filled my eyes and fear clogged my throat. "What if he doesn't come home?" I whispered. My throat was scratchy and sore, which made it difficult to talk.

I'd been in hospital for two days after being treated for multiple injuries including fractured ribs and a collapsed lung. Monroe hadn't left my side until today when I'd been conscious enough to ask her to check on Nitro's family. I was relieved to know they were safe.

Monroe took hold of my hand. Gently, because it hurt, too. Every inch of me did. "Your guy is tough, babe. He's going to get through whatever he has to and then he's going to come home. King was here yesterday, and the club is looking for him. They'll find him. You can't keep much hidden from bikers."

She was right. But a lot could have happened in two days. The longer he was gone, the more concerned I grew. I just prayed that when they did find him, he was alive. My heart hurt worse than my entire body when I thought about him not making it out of that hellhole.

My phone rang and Monroe released my hand so she could answer it. After working out it was Billy, she held it up to my ear.

"Hey," I croaked.

"Fuck, Tatum," he said, pausing for a moment. I was fairly sure I heard devastation in his voice. "Thank fuck you're awake." His voice broke then. "When I saw you lying in that hospital bed last night with all those tubes in you and those fucking bruises and all that swelling...." He cleared his throat. "This shit has to stop. I swear to fucking God if anyone touches you again I will personally kill them."

A torrent of emotions flooded me, his agony my undoing. Tears streamed down my cheeks, which was a bloody nightmare because it fucking hurt to wipe them from my face. So I let them fall and just waited for them to dry. "I'm done with being beaten up, too, Billy." A little humour always helped. Especially with men who didn't know what to do with their emotions.

"Yeah," he said gruffly and then he added quietly, "Any news on Nitro?"

"No," I whispered, unable to speak any louder. I knew if I did, the tears would flow harder than they already were.

"Okay," he said. "You rest. I've been in touch with King and will help them find the motherfucking cunt who did this to you."

"Thanks, Billy." I jerked my head at Monroe to let her know I was done. Thank God Billy didn't have it in him to talk about shit, because I couldn't have handled any more. It hurt both my body and my soul to discuss this entire situation.

Monroe placed my phone down and picked up hers. Swiping it, she brought the Internet up as she settled into the seat next to the bed. Giving me a cheeky grin, she said, "Right, because you're going to be in here for days according to the doctor, and we need things to keep us occupied, we're going to surf this new singles site I found that has a lot of pierced cock on it." Her eyes lit up. "And when I say a lot, I mean a fuckload."

If I could have smiled without it hurting, I would have. Monroe knew me so well. She understood that I just didn't have it in me to acknowledge my feelings. She knew when to push me and when to distract me. And it seemed her preferred way for the next few days was going to be with pierced cock.

"Okay, hit me. Show me what they've got," I whispered.

She grinned. "I knew I could count on you to help a sister out."

We'd been scrolling for a good fifteen minutes when King entered my room. I met his gaze and was taken aback at what I saw there. So much anguish. Something I never imagined King feeling.

"Tatum," he greeted me, coming towards the bed.

"Have you found him?" Monroe said as she shot out of the chair.

He shook his head. "No, not yet. But I've got half of fucking Sydney on it so it's just a matter of time."

Disappointment filled me. I'd hoped he had come with good news.

He moved closer to me. "I just wanted to see how you were doing," he said, surprising me even more. His gaze travelled over me and he hissed at what he saw. "I should have listened to him," he murmured.

"What about?" I said.

He let out a long breath as regret settled into every line on his face. "Nitro warned me about getting into bed with Joseph. I was so screwed up in the head over this fucking war we're in that I thought I knew best." Scrubbing his face, he added, "It's just another example of when I didn't know best. And now we all have to deal with the consequences."

This was a whole new side to King that I never imagined existed. The regret and anguish he expressed were real, and he seemed to feel it deeply.

Ignoring the pain it caused, I reached my hand out for his and when he gave it to me, I gently squeezed it. "We all fuck up in life, King. It's what we do after that counts."

He regarded me for a few moments, holding my hand in silence. When he placed it gently back on the bed, he said, "It's a bitter pill to swallow, though. It's a mistake I won't make again."

Monroe asked him a few questions, but I couldn't keep up with them. Tiredness took over and as much as I tried to keep my eyes open, I couldn't. The last thing I heard King say was, "As soon as we find him, Tatum will know."

Sleep claimed me then, and I drifted into a web of nightmares where I never saw Nitro again.

Chapter Forty-Three

Nitro

"The Unforgiven" by Metallica

It had been three days since I'd seen Tatum. I'd dreamt of her during the fitful bouts of sleep I'd had in those days. Mostly I had nightmares about her not surviving Joseph's torture. In reality, I knew she would most likely have been okay once she'd sought medical treatment. But my mind liked to fuck with me and make me deal with my darkest fears. Never seeing her again was a nightmare that wouldn't let up.

Joseph still had me locked away in the tiny room where I'd been for days. The four walls closed in on me a little more each day, but still I managed to keep my shit together, even when I'd ended up with hypothermia the day before. Joseph had been furious with William over that. He'd abandoned his harsh treatment of me for the day and given me excellent medical care, which meant I was okay. Exhausted, but at least I was still alive.

The day passed slowly. William didn't show his face, but Joseph spent some time with me. He'd surprised me by talking about his plans for the Sydney arm of his operation. Sitting with him for those hours, listening to everything he'd said and pretending to be interested in it made me feel sick. But I'd got through it by telling myself that my chance to end all this would come soon enough. I just had to be patient.

He'd left me alone for hours in the afternoon. Stir crazy and me spent that time together. I was close to climbing the walls by the time he returned later that night.

Jerking his chin towards the door, he said, "Come. We have that meeting with Eric Bones and I want you there again."

I followed him down the long hallway and out into the open-plan area of the warehouse. There were fewer men there than I'd assumed. William was nowhere to be seen, and I wondered where he was. In total, there were only six men. They were unloading a semi-trailer full of large wooden boxes, stacking them onto pallets.

We cut through the area and exited the building into the dark night. The outside wasn't lit up and it took my eyes a moment to adjust, but when they did, I could see we were alone.

Joseph headed towards the Jeep parked at the end of the building. He insisted I walk ahead of him. Again, I wondered where William was.

"William not coming with us?" I asked.

"No." His reply was short and begged no more discussion, so I left it alone. I was intrigued as hell, though. Those two seemed as united as they had nineteen years ago, but maybe appearances were misleading.

We reached the Jeep, and as Joseph unlocked it, the sound of someone running our way drew our attention.

"Joseph, wait up!" William called out, and I heard the hiss of disapproval that left Joseph's mouth.

"I told you that Rhys and I would do this alone," he snapped.

William came to a halt when he reached us. Ignoring me, he said, "You need me."

"Not tonight I don't."

I watched as William exploded in front of me. For a man whose emotions were always so contained, this told me there was something very wrong between them.

"I have been with you from the very beginning, Joseph. Loyal to a fucking fault. No way am I going to sit back and watch while your asshole nephew worms his way into my spot. *No fucking way*!"

Rage contorted Joseph's face and he made the mistake I'd been waiting days for. He turned his back on me to roar something at William. I didn't take in what he said because I was too focused on the gun holstered at his waist. His shirt covered it, but I made out the shape.

There was no time for thinking; I had to react. Reaching out, I pulled his gun from the holster at the same time as I hooked my arm around his neck and squeezed him hard. His fingers curled around my arm, trying to pry it away, but I tightened my grip, determined not to let go, even if every movement hurt my aching body.

My intent had been to shoot William first, before he could react, but the fucker's reflexes were faster than I thought they would be. I pointed the gun at him while he aimed his at me.

"Put the fucking gun down, Rhys, or I *will* shoot you!" he bellowed.

Adrenaline surged through me. It blocked out enough of the pain I was in so I could focus on what I had to do. "You let me kill him and his business is yours, William." It was a lie. I would never allow William to walk away from this alive.

Joseph tried to fight me off, his body jerking in my hold. "He's lying, William!" he yelled.

"Am I? Tell me, William, what have you received in return for your decades of loyalty to this man? Besides him fucking your

327

wife, that is." I had no idea if that was true, but I didn't doubt it could be.

When William froze, I knew I'd hit gold.

"Lies!" Joseph roared. "It's a goddam lie and you know it."

I watched William closely, waiting for his attention to be distracted enough for me to shoot him. However, his army training was too ingrained and he didn't take his eyes off me for one second.

"I'm not sure I believe you, Joseph," he said. "I know for a fact that you've slept with——"

A shot rang out in the night air and a bullet cut William off. He stopped talking and fell to the ground at the same time as a voice yelled out, "Nitro, we've got you covered, brother."

King.

Joseph continued to struggle in my hold, and since I didn't have William to contend with, I turned and shoved Joseph up against the car. Our eyes locked and in his I saw his huge ego. He didn't believe it was the end for him.

Pointing my gun at his head, I said, "You think your men are going to come out here and save your ass, don't you?"

"Of course they are, Rhys. I don't know why you thought you would get away with this."

The sound of heavy footsteps filled my ears and then King spoke. "You underestimated my club, Joseph."

Multiple gunshots sounded from inside the warehouse, and I knew Joseph's men wouldn't be an issue. His eyes widened at the realisation.

"That's what happens when you believe in your own importance a little too much," I said.

He managed to catch me by surprise when he shoved hard against me. I stumbled backwards, my heart hammering in my chest.

The moment had come.

The one that should have happened nineteen years ago.

My regret over not putting him in the ground then would never ease. Not since I knew the full extent of what he'd done to my family.

As I stumbled backwards, time slowed, and a movie reel of memories played in my mind. All the evil he'd perpetrated. My eyes met his and I screamed my hatred at him silently. Pointing the gun at his temple as he came at me, I shot him.

The reel of memories stopped.

My breathing slowed.

My body stilled.

King's hand on my arm snapped me back to attention. He didn't speak. He just nodded at me. Then he said, "I'll give you a few minutes, but we need to get out of here soon."

I looked down at Joseph and breathed through my rushing emotions. So many fucking emotions. They flooded my entire body and I didn't know what to do with them. After two decades of shutting them down, it was like a sucker punch.

"Fuck," I roared as my body jerked in agony. "You fucking asshole! You screwed us up and I never fucking knew just how much."

I bent at the waist and placed my hands on my knees. Sucking air down in long gasps, I attempted to gather my thoughts. My head was a clusterfuck and I had no idea how long it would take me to sort through it. All I knew was that everything had changed. Every-fucking-thing.

Straightening, I lifted the gun again and pumped more bullets into Joseph's head.

I then took one last deep breath.

Joseph was the past.

My future stretched ahead of me and never again would I allow anyone to hurt those I loved.

Chapter Forty-Four

Tatum

"Halo" by Beyonce

"Mum!"

Where was she?

I ran to her bedroom to find her.

She wasn't there.

I searched the whole house.

She was nowhere.

Tears fell down my cheeks as my body crumpled against the wall.

My heart raced in my chest.

She was always home. She never left us alone after school.

Chris entered the room and I knew from his face and the way his shoulders hunched over a little that he didn't have anything good to tell me.

"Mum's gone," he said, waving a piece of paper in the air, his eyes sad. "And she's never coming back."

"Vegas, I've got you." Nitro's voice cut into my nightmare, and I blinked my eyes open.

My heart beat faster as I stared up at him. I wasn't sure if he was really there or part of my dream. The sunlight filtered through the curtain, though, slanting rays of sunshine across his bruised face.

It was him.

He really was standing in front of me.

My nightmare slayer.

He stopped me when I tried to sit up. Shaking his head, he said, "Don't move, it'll hurt too much."

My mind raced with a million questions and my body felt like it would burst from the happiness rushing through it. "How? When did you get here? Is he dea—"

He placed a finger to my lips, silencing me. "It's early still. Go back to sleep. We'll talk later."

Like fuck.

I'd been waiting for him to come home for days. There was no way I could sleep even if I wanted to.

"I'm not sleeping, so you should just start talking now." Thank goodness my throat wasn't as sore anymore. It'd be easier to argue with him if necessary.

His lips twitched. "There's my girl," he rumbled quietly. Sitting on the chair that had been Monroe's for days, he said, "He's dead." It was as if the words had been ripped from the darkest part of his soul. I felt every sliver of his torment.

Overwhelming relief hit me like a tonne of bricks. My tears fell uncontrollably, and Nitro reached out to wipe them away. I stopped him and said, "It hurts to touch my face."

He moved his hand away, and I caught the clench of his fist as he did. His eyes travelled the length of my body before he looked back at my face. "I'm so sorry, Tatum."

The raw agony I heard in his voice and the devastation I saw in his eyes only made me cry harder. I reached for him, grasping for any contact. It hurt so much to do, but I didn't care. I needed his skin. His touch. When I found his hand, I linked my fingers through his. The instant calm I felt was what I'd been searching for. "You have nothing to be sorry for. If it wasn't for you, I might not be here now."

"If it wasn't for me, you would never have ended up like this."

332

I stared at him, letting my gaze trace his face. This man had been to hell and back for me and his family, and yet he had no care for himself. All he worried about was us.

"We're going to have to agree to disagree on this one, champ. These bruises and all this shit you see… it will disappear and heal. But my life? You gave me that, in ways you might never understand, and for that, I will be eternally grateful."

His gaze dropped to my lips and lingered there for a long time. "I want to kiss you," he murmured, deep in thought. He found my eyes again. "I won't, but I need you to know how fucking much I want to right now."

My tears that had almost dried up began flowing again. I was beginning to think they might never stop. Usually I hated crying in front of others, but with Nitro, I let them fall and didn't think twice. He was my safe place.

Moving closer to the bed, he gave my hand a gentle squeeze. The way he looked at me made me think he was about to say something that would make me cry more, but in the end, he said, "Did you just call me champ?"

It was such an out-of-the-blue question that I couldn't help but laugh. "Yeah, I did."

His lips curled into a smile, but he didn't say anything.

"Is that okay?" I asked.

"You can call me anything you fucking want, Vegas. Gotta say, though, I'm not sure about you using it when I make you come."

I grinned. "Let's test it out. See what you think."

He chuckled. And then he did something that made my cold, dark heart melt. He stood and gently placed a kiss on my forehead. A lingering kiss. It was as if he'd wrapped every tender emotion he could find in that kiss and given them to me.

333

"I never want to lose you." His eyes met mine and there was a fierce determination there that hadn't been there a moment ago. "You're mine, Tatum."

I pulled his face down to my level. Our lips didn't meet, but our souls did. "You're mine, too."

* * *

I fell asleep, waking again at lunchtime. Monroe sat next to me instead of Nitro and I frantically searched the room for him. I needed him to be there.

Monroe touched my hand. "He's stepped out for a minute, babe. He'll be back soon."

I took a deep breath. "Fuck, Roe, for a minute there I thought I'd dreamt him being here this morning. My heart can't take much more of this."

"Vegas."

My gaze immediately flicked to the door to find Nitro standing there watching me. He'd clearly heard what I said and seemed affected by it. I regretted that, but it was the truth—my heart really couldn't take too much more. I'd gone from keeping everyone out to cracking myself wide open for him. And it hurt so damn much to think of him not being there.

"I'm just waiting for a call from King. You good until then?"

I nodded. "Yeah."

He shifted his gaze to Monroe, and they had a moment before he turned and left.

She turned to face me, her eyes wide. "Jesus, sister, that man has gone all territorial over you. I've never seen anything like it in my life."

I frowned. "What do you mean?"

"He turned up late last night, and I mean *late*. Like, it was really fucking clear he wasn't waiting for this morning to come and see you. The nurse tried to send him away, but he refused to leave. He made a song and dance about it and they eventually gave in. I was almost asleep when he woke me up and told me to go home. Told me he had this now, which I'm guessing means he has *you* now. I argued with him for a while, but honestly, I don't know how you do it, he just doesn't fucking give in."

I smiled. "You feel my pain. He's a bossy fucker sometimes." I couldn't deny it, though; I loved the fact he wanted to be here that badly.

"*Sometimes?*"

Laughing, I conceded, "Okay, maybe more than sometimes."

She leant back in her seat and crossed her legs while angling her body towards me. "I got here just after nine this morning, and he did leave for just over an hour to go home and shower. Other than that, he's been here the whole time watching over you like a hawk." She dropped her voice. "I've gotta tell you, it's kinda hot. I think I might add bossy to my list of required things for my man."

"So you want a bossy guy who knows when to back off and when to take charge, who picks up after himself and has a pierced dick?"

She shook her head at me like I was clueless. "Babe, when you get out of here, you and I need to sit down so I can show you my list. There are a *lot* more things on it that just that."

I shifted and cried out as a shot of pain hit. It caused me to suck in a breath and close my eyes while I panted through it. When I opened my eyes again, Nitro stood in front of me, concern all over his face.

"The nurse is on her way," he said. "What else do you need?"

"Nothing, I'm good."

335

He pursed his lips. "You're in a hospital, in a shitload of pain. There's gotta be something I can get for you to help take your mind off it."

I lifted a brow. "You're in a shitload of pain, too, Nitro. How about you sit your ass down and just be with me? That would help me take my mind off it."

He gave me the look that told me I'd amused him. "We're not talking about me. We're discussing you. Give me something here, Vegas."

"Oh dear Lord," Monroe said. "You two are too much for me. I might head into work and see what I've missed over the last few days if you're cool with that, babe."

I nodded. "Yes, you should go. But bring me more Milo tonight, okay?"

"Fuck," Nitro muttered. "I ask you what you want and you give me nothing. I can get you fucking Milo." He stared at me with frustration, and I had to contain my laughter.

Monroe grinned. "She has a way of annoying the fuck out us, right? Never wants to be a burden, blah, blah, blah. Good luck, you're gonna need it. But I'm telling you now, big fella, you bring her Milo, and I'll make you hurt. The Milo is our thing."

With that, she grabbed her bag and exited the room while I laughed and Nitro stared after her with an expression I couldn't quite read.

When he turned back to me, he jerked his head in the direction she'd left. "You two definitely have the same genes."

"Does that mean you like her?" Randall had hated Monroe. He couldn't stand her "tell it like it is" manner and it had been awful trying to bring them together.

"I don't think we're gonna have a problem, but she's dreaming if she thinks I'm not getting you Milo."

"You didn't really answer my question," I said softly, realising how important it was to me that he got on with her. They were my two people; I needed them to like each other.

"Vegas, anyone who's important to you is important to me. But in answer to your question, yes, I like her. I imagine she'll frustrate the hell out of me the same as you do, but I respect a woman who doesn't take shit, and Monroe strikes me as that kind of woman."

He had me at "anyone who's important to you is important to me." That was what family did for each other. And it was exactly what I needed to hear. Family was everything.

Chapter Forty-Five

Nitro

"Broken" by Seether

The sound of my boots on the hospital lino was the only noise to be heard as I made the long trek to Marilyn's room. I'd spent the day with Tatum and only left once I knew she was safe with Monroe. I'd ignored the filthy glare Monroe gave me when she spied the Milo tin in the room. And I made no apologies to her. No fucking way was I not getting Tatum what she wanted. I almost laughed, though, when she placed a Milo tin next to mine. I liked the fact she stood her ground.

I rounded a corner and a few moments later entered Marilyn's room. She sat in the chair in the corner with her eyes closed, but they fluttered open when she heard me.

She shot out of the chair and came to me, flinging her arms around me. "Oh my God! I thought I'd never see you again!" She sobbed into my chest as I ignored the bolt of pain her hug inspired and wrapped my arms around her.

Smoothing her hair, I waited for her to let me go. I'd hold her for as long as she needed, though.

When she stopped sobbing and moved out of my embrace, she looked up at me with a questioning expression. I knew what she was asking, and I nodded. "He can't hurt you ever again, Lynny. I made sure of it."

Her hand flew to her face and she burst into tears again. I pulled her back to me, and we held each other for an eternity.

We'd been through so much shit together. We were always there for each other to the best of our abilities and always would be.

With my arms tight around her and my hand cradling her head, I said, "You should have told me what he did to you."

Stiffening, she tried to pull away.

"No," I said as I held her tighter. "Don't do that. You have nothing to be ashamed about or to hide from. *He* did that shit to you. You did nothing wrong. *You* don't hide away. Ever."

Her hands gripped my shirt and she buried her head in my chest while she cried.

"You hear me, Lynny? This isn't on you. I'll do everything in my power to help you believe that." I took a step back and forced her to look up at me. Her tear-stained face shattered me all over again. "Promise me you'll let me help."

She nodded. "I promise."

I stayed with her for a good couple of hours, watching television together and talking a little about her sessions with her psychologist. It was the first time she'd ever confided any of that type of stuff with me, and I felt like it was a whole new start for us and for our family. If we could find a way to move out of the darkness that had always consumed us, it really would be a new beginning.

* * *

King met me in the corridor outside Tatum's room when I arrived back there after visiting Marilyn. We hadn't spoken a great deal since the night before. He'd driven me to the hospital in almost complete silence and dropped me off, telling me he'd be back when he could. I'd gotten the impression he was overwhelmed by the whole situation, which was odd for King.

His eyes held an apology as he looked at me. Stepping closer, he jerked his chin towards Tatum. "She seems to be doing better."

"Yeah. She told me you've been checking in on her. I appreciate that."

He scrubbed his face. "Fuck, it's the least I can fucking do, Nitro. This shit is on me. He used our delivery time as his opportunity to kidnap Tatum. She'd be okay if I hadn't agreed to that deal."

"No, this shit is on Joseph. It wouldn't have changed the course of any of this if Storm hadn't taken that deal. He's been coming for me for years. I just didn't realise it." I recalled Tatum telling me that we can't hold people responsible for our choices in life. I wouldn't hold King responsible for Joseph's actions.

"Thank fuck for Eric Bones. He was the one who helped me find you. Said something about a deal he was supposed to make with Joseph and that he'd changed his mind about getting into bed with him."

I frowned. "How did Eric know where the warehouse was?"

"Turns out he's more switched on than we ever gave him credit for. He had some of his guys follow Joseph after he met with him a few days ago. Told me you were leaving Storm and thought it was strange, which was another trigger for him to think twice about the deal. He came to check that with me, thank fuck."

Monroe stepped out of the room, taking in King before looking at me. "Tatum's asleep so I'm going to head home. Are you staying?"

"Yeah. I'm not leaving this hospital until she does, except for when you're here."

"I've decided that even though you pissed me off with the Milo thing, I like you. You're exactly what Tatum needs in her life."

King interrupted. "The Milo thing?"

She turned to him. "Oh, you have no idea, dude." Pointing her thumb at me, she said, "This guy's trying to go all hero and shit on my girl, which is fine and all, but I draw the line at him taking over my responsibilities. Maybe you could help a girl out and have a quiet word with him. Tell him to back the fuck off with the Milo."

With that, she slung her handbag over her shoulder, gave me one last pointed look and left us.

King watched her go until he couldn't see her anymore. "Fuck, she's enough to get a man's dick to stand up and beg for more."

"You got a thing for redheads, brother?"

His eyes lit up. "That, and a mouth that tells it like it is." He whistled. "And those curves are something fucking else."

"You got a pierced dick, King? From what I've heard, that's what she's looking for."

His mouth stretched across his face in a smile that told me more about King than I ever needed to know. Lifting his chin at me, he said, "You get back to your woman. I'm heading to the clubhouse for a bit. I'll swing by again in the morning."

"Where are we at with Gambarro?"

"We're working with Dragon keeping tabs on what Gambarro's up to. I'm not sure about shit where Silver Hell's concerned. We might be working with them, but no way in hell do I trust those motherfuckers. We'll see what happens, but I've told the boys to stay alert and be ready for anything. Who knows when they could turn on us?"

"I agree."

341

He was quiet for a moment. "I should have listened to you, Nitro. Should have trusted you when you warned me about Joseph. I won't make that mistake again," he said solemnly.

I nodded and watched him leave. Joseph took a lot from me, but we all learned some lessons in the process. I'd always respected King and been loyal to him, but his loyalty to me was more than I'd ever had from anyone outside of my family. And it only strengthened mine in return.

* * *

Tatum eyed my house as I pulled the ute into the driveway. "Does this mean you're *not* taking me home?"

I smiled at her while she watched me with eyes that twinkled her happiness. The doctor had allowed her to finally leave the hospital that morning, and I'd told her I would take her home. "You got a problem with staying here, Vegas?"

She shrugged casually. "No problem, except you've got no furniture and no room for any of my clothes."

I leant over and caught her lips in a kiss. Thank fuck I could do that again since her pain wasn't as bad. I needed those lips like I fucking needed air. "You should get your ass out of this car and see for yourself. I bought some damn furniture."

Her eyes widened. "You did? When?"

I shook my head at her. "Fuck, always with the twenty questions."

"You're lucky you've got bruises and shit on you or else I'd smack you right now."

"My bruises are nothing, Tatum."

She cupped my cheek, looking at the marks on my face. "You keep saying that, but I know he would have hurt you worse than me. Why do you keep shutting down on me when I bring it up?"

"Because I won't give that motherfucker any more opportunities to hurt us. Yeah, he hurt me, but it was nothing compared to the pain of watching him hurt you. I won't talk about him with you again. That part of our lives together is done."

"Our lives together... I like the sound of that," she said softly, almost as if she wasn't sure what it meant or didn't fully believe it.

"Make no mistake, I intend to spend the rest of my life with you, Vegas."

Her hand moved to curl around my neck. "Look at you all bossy and shit. Do I even get a say in that?"

I'd heard of men thinking they owned women and I'd never bought into that bullshit, but sitting there, with my woman in front of me asking if she got a say in me spending my life with her caused some part of my brain to fire weirdly. As far as I was concerned, she was mine. No other man would ever touch her again; I'd make fucking sure of it. Jesus, if I could have laid her out on the back seat and shown her who she belonged to, I fucking would have. Instead, I showed her with my mouth, and when I was finished, I growled, "You always get a say, but if you think I'm ever going to listen to anything but a yes, you're kidding yourself. I'll fucking follow you to the ends of the earth if I have to. You were made for me and I was made for you."

She beamed at me. Fucking beamed. And then she made my whole fucking life when she said, "I was. Now shut up and show me where I can put my clothes. And it better not be just a drawer. I'm gonna be needing a wardrobe for the shit I'm moving in."

Chapter Forty-Six

Tatum

"Gone, Gone, Gone" by Phillip Phillips

Six weeks later

"Oh God!" Posey exclaimed as she doubled over with laughter. "I can't believe you said that to him, Monroe."

Monroe lifted her mimosa to her lips and drank some before saying, "It was true, though. Look, if a guy's gonna get his wang out after boasting about how big it is, it better be big. His wasn't. So I told him."

"I have to agree with Roe," I said. "Don't brag about shit you have no right bragging about."

Posey wiped her tears from her eyes and drank some of her wine. "You know, Friday afternoon drinks is the highlight of my week. Thank you for letting me join in."

Monroe lifted a brow. "Even if it's Milo Friday?"

I smacked her arm. "Shut the fuck up. I told you why it had to be Milo Friday this week."

"I just hope that Nitro doesn't think it's gonna be Milo Friday every damn week."

"This has nothing to do with h—"

"I don't know anything about Milo Friday," Nitro said, joining us at his kitchen table. His eyes met mine and although he wasn't smiling, they held affection.

"Really?" Monroe asked, perking up as if there was some juicy gossip to be had.

I sighed. "Okay so maybe I left some details out," I admitted, not wanting to be having this conversation in front of Nitro. Damn Monroe and her bullshit detector.

"Spill, sister," she demanded.

Nitro settled in with his arms folded across his chest. He knew I reserved every Friday night for the girls and had been surprised when I said it wasn't on this week and that he should keep the night free to hang out with me.

"Can we discuss this later?" I begged, widening my eyes at her so she'd get the idea that I *really* didn't want to talk about it.

She ignored me and shook her head. "Nope."

"Yeah, start talking, Vegas. I'm interested, too."

I looked at him again. God, I loved it when he called me Vegas. It had irritated the hell out of me when we'd first met, but not anymore. Nitro didn't do nicknames with anyone and he certainly didn't do terms of endearment unless you counted *kiddo*, which he called Renee. I'd come to realise how special Vegas was, and my cold heart treasured it. Not that my heart could be classified as cold anymore. It was warm as fuck these days, thanks to him.

"Okay, but you have to promise me you'll pretend like you didn't know," I said to him.

He frowned. "About what?"

I hopped off my stool and walked to him. Sliding my arms around his waist, I said, "Dustin's cooking you dinner tonight as a surprise thank you for helping him find his own place and moving him in. He didn't want you to know about it, so I promised him I would get you there without telling you why. That's why I couldn't do drinks tonight. It's the only night off he has this week."

345

His hand landed on my ass. When he spoke, his voice was all gravelly. "You amaze me."

"Why?"

"The way you love my family. It means a lot to me."

"Family's everything," I said softly.

"Yeah, they are." He dropped his mouth to mine and kissed me. "I'm gonna make it worth your while later to have missed Friday drinks."

I loved it when Nitro made me dirty promises like that. He never failed to deliver. "What are you gonna do?"

Monroe cleared her voice behind us. "Okay, you two, round that shit up. No one needs to hear about sex when they aren't getting any."

Nitro smacked my ass and grinned. Placing his mouth to my ear, he murmured, "Pussy on my tongue is a good way to start, I think."

Pushing him away, I said, "Stop teasing me. Go and have a shower and calm yourself down. And get ready to go out."

He kept grinning as he backed away holding his hands up in defence. "I don't wanna get started without you."

Monroe groaned. "Stop talking, Nitro, and keep fucking walking."

The sound of him laughing as he walked down the hallway filled the house. He'd started doing that a lot more often lately. It had to be one of my favourite sounds ever.

"Posey, you wanna come get a drink with me? I can't handle Milo Friday any longer," Monroe said as I turned back to join them. She may have been grumbling, but the smile she gave me was full of love.

I blew her a kiss. "I love you, too, Roe."

"Yeah, I know, sister. I love you, too. But you need to get your ass in that shower with your man. I'm not the kind of woman to ever get in the way of that." And by *that*, I knew she meant so much more than sex. Monroe might have referred almost everything she said back to sex, but she was as deep as they came when it had to do with relationships. She loved love. And she loved me being with Nitro.

I said my goodbyes, walking them out to Monroe's car and then made my way inside to the bathroom. The shower was already running and steam greeted me when I opened the door. Nitro liked his showers as hot as possible, and I had trouble seeing. But I could hear him.

The sound of him jerking off shot heat straight to my core. When he finally came into view, the first thing I saw was his back muscle flexing. He rested one forearm against the shower wall and his head hung forward while he pumped his cock with his hand.

I stood watching silently, turned-on as hell. My eyes greedily lapped up every inch of his powerful naked body. His tight ass that I loved to grip onto while he fucked me; those muscular arms that I loved around me; his strong legs that often held us up while he slammed into me against the wall. I could watch Nitro getting himself off for hours.

"Vegas…," he growled. "Get your lips around my dick."

My clothes were already half off and once I was naked, I stepped into the shower with him. I slid an arm around his waist as I moved to position myself between him and the wall.

His eyes met mine.

His hand continued to work his cock.

My whole body sang with desire.

"Fuck." He groaned as water streamed over us. "I've been thinking about you all fucking day."

Catching him around the neck, I pulled his face down to mine so I could kiss him. "Are you close to coming?"

347

He nodded, and I could tell by the way his body tensed that he was. "Yeah," he forced out, his breathing ragged.

"Well, champ, I'm not wrapping my lips around you. If your dick's that hard, I want it inside me."

Amusement flashed in his eyes and he pressed his mouth to mine again, demanding another kiss. When he was done, he muttered, "Champ...."

I grinned as I looped my arms around his neck. He let his dick go so he could take hold of my ass and lift me. Wrapping my legs around him, I closed my eyes as he thrust inside me. "Fuck," I cried and held on tight while he gave me what we both craved.

His fury.

And when we were done, he reminded me why I loved him. He pulled out and took hold of my face with both his hands. After he kissed me for a long time, he said, "I love you."

He gave me his unconditional love.

Loving Nitro was easy because there was nothing required in return. When he loved, he simply loved.

Chapter Forty-Seven

Nitro

"I'm In" by Keith Urban

"I got my licence!" Renee squealed as she flashed it at us. Her whole face lit up with happiness, and it hit me fair in the gut. It was about damn time our family had as much happiness as we'd had recently. It'd been almost two months since Joseph's death and instead of waking each day wondering what bad shit would happen, I woke only thinking of the good in my life.

Tatum grinned from where she sat on the couch next to me. We'd both finished work early and had spent the afternoon in bed and then in front of the television. She'd brought some work home and was finishing it off when Renee came barging through the front door.

"Fantastic!" Tatum said. "First go, too. Must be all those hours you did with me that helped you."

After I insisted she clock up more than the required 120 hours, Renee had worked her ass off and finished up with more than 150 hours, a lot of which had been done with Tatum.

I stood and moved to her. Pulling her into a hug, I said, "I'm proud of you, kiddo. Gotta say, though, there was no doubt in my mind that you'd pass."

Tears misted her eyes and she swallowed hard. "Thank you," she whispered.

"What for? Showing you how to drive? That wasn't hard. You've got nothing to thank me for."

She shook her head. "No, for being my dad. I know that sounds weird because my mum's your sister and all, but as far as I'm concerned, you're my dad. You did all the hours, lost all the sleep, cared for me when I was sick, gave up your house for us, paid for a lot of shit. You did all the things a dad does, so you're mine."

I took all that in and let it settle deep in my bones. I'd never wanted to be a dad. Never. It wasn't in my life plan, and Tatum had told me it wasn't in hers either, so there would be no kids for me. But this... this was everything. I pressed a kiss to her forehead and then pulled back to meet her gaze again. "I got the better end of the deal. I got you."

Tears slid down her face, but she smiled up at me and gave me her trademark wit. "True. Your life would have no meaning without me."

I grinned at her. "What time's your mum coming over? I need to get Tatum's ass moving and in that kitchen if it's gonna be soon."

"I thought you were cooking tonight," Tatum called out.

I turned my grin towards her. "You wore me out this afternoon, Vegas. A man needs to recuperate before he can spend hours cooking."

She rolled her eyes. "If Dustin can manage to make every single thing I love to eat for one meal, you can surely manage to cook a damn roast."

I placed my hand over my heart. "You wound me, woman."

A knock on the door interrupted us and I headed down the hallway to answer it. I was surprised to find Billy fucking Jones on the other side.

"Billy," I greeted him. We'd kept a civil distance to each other since Tatum had moved in, and while I'd come around a little in my opinion of him, we were far from friends.

He seemed as uncomfortable to be there as I was to have him there. Holding a folder out to me, he said, "These are for Tatum. They're documents she needs for the case she's working on."

I took the folder from him. "I'll pass them on."

"Thanks."

Silence descended on us. It was awkward as fuck while I waited for him to leave. I considered calling out to Tatum to let her know he was there, but I was a greedy asshole and didn't want to share the time I had with her.

He turned to leave, but stopped and glanced back at me. "She's a lot happier now."

I nodded, not really wanting to have this conversation with him.

"Because of you, I mean. She was never happy before you." He paused. "Don't fuck that up."

I clenched my jaw. I didn't need Billy Jones coming to my house and telling me not to fuck something up that I never would. I gripped the door, ready to close it. The only thing stopping me from slamming it in his face was Tatum.

He didn't wait for my response before leaving. Not that there would have been a response. At this point, the best I could manage was to simply keep the peace and not punch the fuck out of him. I knew Tatum hoped for more, but she never pushed me, and I appreciated the hell out of that. Who knew what the future held. I doubted Billy and me would ever be friendly, but Tatum had a way of getting me to do shit I never thought I would.

"Nitro!" Renee called out. I closed the door and headed back inside. "Mum's on her way now, so you should start cooking."

I passed Billy's folder to Tatum. "Billy dropped this off."

She smiled as she took it. "Thanks." She didn't appear surprised that he'd come or that I hadn't called her out to see him.

I narrowed my eyes at her. "Did you know he was coming over?"

She shrugged. "I figured he might."

"Fuck," I muttered under my breath. "You'll be the death of me, Vegas."

She waved me away with a laugh. "Go cook. I'm hungry."

Fifteen minutes later I slid a roast into the oven and thought about how my life had changed. Only for her would I be in a kitchen cooking a damn roast when I'd rather be on the couch with her tits pressed against me. She'd fast become the woman I spent my time trying to make happy; the woman I worried incessantly over; the one I planned my future around and the woman I wanted by my side until the day I died.

* * *

"You've been holding out on me, Nitro," Tatum said over dinner that night. "Who knew you could cook so well? Roast is one of my favourites so I think you're gonna be cooking it a lot more from now on."

Dustin frowned. "I never knew roast was one of your favourites. I'll make it next time I cook for you."

Tatum gave him a smile, but it wasn't the kind of smile I saw women give him all the time. The type of smile that said they felt sorry for him or that they thought it was a shame that a good-looking guy like him didn't have the intelligence they were looking for. Tatum's smile was genuine and it said she appreciated his thoughtfulness and that she loved him for it.

I loved *her* for that smile.

352

"Thank you, Dustin. But honestly, roast can be so expensive. I don't expect you to cook it for me."

His face lit up as he thought that over. "I could substitute the steak for roast every now and then. That would work."

I grinned at him. "Great idea, man."

He had the family over for dinner once a week since he'd moved out. Every Thursday night was Dustin's night. Unless he had to work, but generally he had Thursdays and Fridays off. He didn't cook Tatum's favourites every week, but rather he alternated between everyone's favourites. I had to hand it to Billy—he'd given Dustin a stable job that seemed to be doing wonders for his confidence.

"Roast is one of my favourites, too," Marilyn said. "But I prefer pork over lamb."

Dustin's eyes widened. "I never knew that!"

That was because Marilyn had kept so much about herself locked away inside for years. We hadn't known the real Marilyn. She'd been attending her psychologist appointments religiously and working hard at turning her life around. She'd even finally gone back to work five weeks prior and managed to find a way to get through her days there regardless of the anxiety she experienced. I was so fucking proud of her.

"Pork crackling!" Tatum said, smiling at Marilyn. Turning to Dustin, she asked, "Tell me you know how to make good crackling. I will love you forever if you do."

"I can google that," he said, and I had to chuckle at his enthusiasm. But then, that was Dustin. Always trying to make others happy. I guessed he took that upon himself when everyone in his family had been so damn unhappy.

I stretched one arm across the back of Tatum's chair and reached for my beer with the other arm. Whispering in her ear

353

while everyone else was talking and laughing, I said, "Marry me."

Her head snapped around and she looked at me with shock. "What?"

I grinned. "I said, marry me."

She stared in silence for a beat. And then my woman let loose on my ass. "That's a shitty proposal, Nitro. If you want me to commit to you, you're going to have to do about a hundred times better than that for a proposal."

My grin grew, and I kissed her before she could push me away. "I was just testing the waters, Vegas."

She narrowed her eyes at me. "You are so full of shit it isn't funny."

"And that right there is why I'm gonna marry your ass one day. Your fight gets me so fucking hard." I said it loud enough so that only she could hear.

"God, you are so romantic sometimes," she grumbled.

I kissed her again. "You wouldn't know what to do with romance."

"Maybe you should try it one day and we'll see just how much further it gets you with me."

"You're telling me it'll get me laid faster or more often?"

She smacked me, but I saw the laughter in her eyes. "I'm telling you that it might just blow your mind. Men have no fucking clue what the smallest romantic gesture is capable of achieving."

I kept my gaze on her while I sucked back some beer. If she wanted romance, I'd fucking give it to her. But not because I wanted to get laid or because I wanted my ring on her finger. I'd give it to her because it would make her happy and that was all I cared about. A smile on Tatum's face was like the sun shining on you when all you'd had was rain for weeks. And when she laughed... that shit was everything I lived for these days.

* * *

Tatum handed Devil a glass of Coke and said, "You wanna stay for dinner?"

Devil and I had been out in my shed for hours working on my bike. We were almost finished when Tatum arrived home from a day out shopping with Monroe.

"What you cooking, gorgeous?"

"I'm not cooking tonight. Nitro is."

He grinned at me. "I like your style, brother. Keeping your woman happy by cooking. Smart move."

Tatum knew that Devil and I always gave each other shit and clearly she decided she wanted in on that when she leant across and said to him, "It's not his cooking that keeps me happy. It's all in the way he uses that tongue of his when he l—"

Devil held up his hand and cut her off. "Nope, don't need to know any more. But fuck, Tatum, you sure you don't have a sister? I need a chick with a dirty mouth like yours."

She laughed, but before she could reply, King entered my backyard and came our way. He had a woman with him. I squinted to get a better look at her and stood there stunned when I realised who it was.

"Is that Jen?" Devil asked just as I worked it out.

"Yeah, brother, that's Jen."

"Fuck, I never saw that coming."

King had his arm around her as if they were together, which surprised me because they'd been apart for six years. The year after he'd become president had been turbulent for them, and

355

she'd walked away to be with another man. It had shattered him.

"King," I greeted him and then glanced at Jen and lifted my chin at her. "Jen."

"Hey, Nitro," she said, her voice shaky. She clung to King like she never wanted to let go.

Tension rolled off King's body while he eyed Tatum. "Can you do me a favour, Tatum?"

"Sure." She clearly sensed the tension too.

He let go of Jen and said, "Can you take Jen inside and make her some tea. Peppermint if you've got it by any chance. I need a minute with the boys."

Tatum gave Jen a smile. "I'm not sure if we've got peppermint, but I'll check."

"Thank you," Jen said softly. Something was very wrong with her. Jen wasn't a soft woman. Hell, I recalled screaming matches between her and King that had lasted days.

Once they'd left us, King scrubbed his face and swore. "You got a beer, Nitro?"

"Yeah." I grabbed one out of the fridge in the shed and came back to him. "What the fuck is going on, King? Because from what I can see, something bad is going down here."

He drank over half the bottle in one go and then took a deep breath. "Only Kick knows this, but the guy Jen left me for used to beat her. Pretty badly. She finally left him and we found her a safe house in Broken Hill. Through Brian. Something got her spooked there so she left and moved in with a friend in Goulburn. The bastard tracked her down a few months ago, and she called me at midnight one night, scared out of her mind. I've been spending time with her the last couple of months trying to make sure she was safe. She refused to move back to Sydney, which pissed me off, but I couldn't force her to come back.

Then last night I got a call that he's threatened her again, so I put my fucking foot down. She's moving in with me until I can find this motherfucker and fix the problem."

"So you want us to help with that?" Devil said.

"Yeah, but as well as that, Dragon just gave word that he's ready to start the attacks on Gambarro."

The last couple of months had been quiet on the Gambarro front. He'd been dealing with a police investigation into shit that involved his businesses and it had kept him busy, which worked out for Silver Hell and us. It had given us the time we needed to prepare ourselves to take him and his organisation down.

"We're ready for this, King," I said.

"Yeah, but not when I need to give my attention to Jen. I told Dragon I wanted to wait, but he's not listening. He wants this shit to start on Monday."

Two days.

"So what's the plan?" I asked. "And what did Hyde say?"

"I can't get hold of Hyde. That's another problem we have."

In my opinion, that was the worst news out of all this. Hyde had been off the radar a lot lately. Devil and I had been covering for him.

When neither Devil nor I said anything, King narrowed his eyes at us. "What the fuck is going on with Hyde and why the fuck don't I know about it?"

"I honestly don't know, brother," I said. "There have been a few times where we've needed him and haven't been able to reach him. Nothing major, though, so we didn't want to bother you with it."

"Fuck, Nitro, I'm your fucking president. How the hell am I supposed to run a fucking club if I don't know everything?"

I raised my hand in a defensive gesture. "It won't happen again."

King shoved his fingers through his hair while he scowled at us. Finally, he blew out a harsh breath. "Okay, I'm gonna take Jen home and get her sorted. Then I'm calling Church for tomorrow. And Nitro?" His eyes bored into mine. "Get ready to step up if I can't find Hyde."

* * *

King's words played on my mind all afternoon and night. Tatum had picked up on my uneasiness and asked me a couple of times about it. I'd changed the subject each time and managed to divert her attention with sex. She was smart enough, though, to know something was going on. After she showered that night she came to me again.

"I don't expect you to give up club business, but can you at least tell me if everything's okay? Because it feels like it isn't and I need to be prepared for shit, Nitro. I mean, I can suit up with the best of them. Maybe I can help you. Who knows? But I refuse to be the woman who scurries away to the corner and remains oblivious to problems."

I sat on the couch and took in the sight of my woman standing before me offering to go to battle with me. *And* with the family I'd chosen for myself—my club. It was the most beautiful fucking sight I'd ever seen. Tatum was love and loyalty and family all rolled into one.

Standing, I went to her. "It fucking terrifies me, Vegas," I murmured as I curled my hand around her neck.

She placed her hand on mine around her neck. "What terrifies you?"

"Losing you."

"You're not going to lose me."

358

She had no idea of what was to come. She'd only witnessed the war we'd had with Silver Hell. The one we had planned for Gambarro would likely guarantee more death and destruction. It was the gamble we took when we joined Storm. We agreed to lay down our lives for our brothers if needed. And I would if I had to.

The thing I struggled with was inviting death into my home, into my blood family.

"Storm is about to go to war with Angelo Gambarro."

Her eyes widened, but only for a moment. She tried to hide her emotions, but I saw them. And she was right to be scared. But still, my woman stayed strong for me. "When?"

"In two days. We've been planning it for months. It's a huge operation and one that could put your life at risk."

She took a moment and then she said, "Right, so you tell me what I have to do, and I'll do it. Whatever you need. Even if that's just being there for you at night to massage your tired muscles and love you enough to get you through the next day, I'm your girl. But if you need me to do more, you tell me that too."

Fuck me, she was something else. I pulled her to me and kissed her as if it was our last kiss ever. We needed to take what we could from each other in case the unthinkable happened. When I ended the kiss, I said, "I love you, Tatum. You're the woman I never thought existed. And you're the woman I'm going to marry one day even if it takes me all my life to get that proposal right."

She ran her hand gently down my face. "I love you more. And I'm pretty sure if you'd tacked a 'will you marry me?' onto the end of that, I would have said yes. Screw romance. All I need is your arms around me, and your heart beating next to mine and I'm a happy girl."

"Will you marry me?" My breathing slowed while I waited for her answer. One word and she'd make me the happiest man alive.

She smiled up at me and ran her hand down from my face to my chest. Placing it over my heart, she said, "This is mine and always will be." Standing on her toes, she kissed me and then she whispered the only word I wanted to hear. "Yes."

It didn't matter what life threw at me any more. With Tatum by my side, and my family in a happy place, I had everything I ever needed. She was wrong about romance, though. I was determined as fuck to crack that sucker and make her the happiest woman on earth.

Epilogue

Tatum

"If I Could Fly" by One Direction

I poured myself a rum and Coke and downed half of it straight away. Placing the glass on the kitchen counter, I took a deep breath.

I can do this.

I want to do this.

I trust him.

The front door opened and closed, and then Nitro's boots thudded on the wood floor as he made his way to the kitchen where I waited for him.

He'd been at the clubhouse all day where I presumed they discussed their plan for the next day. I took in his body as he watched me. He was so tense. I didn't blame him. The club had a lot to deal with.

His eyes dropped to the bottle of rum on the counter.

"You want me to make you a drink?" I asked.

He nodded. "Thanks. I'm just gonna take a shower."

When I was alone again, I thought about everything we'd discussed the night before. I'd meant every word I said about being there for him however he needed. It was what you did for family. I'd been doing it for those I loved all my life, but this, with Nitro, felt different. He was the man I'd waited all my life to find, and I would lay my life down for him if he needed me to. I'd go to hell and back for him.

I took our drinks into the living room and curled up on the couch with my feet tucked under me. Sipping my rum slowly, I waited for Nitro to return.

"You good?"

I turned to find him standing next to the couch, freshly showered and dressed only in a pair of grey sweatpants. Water dripped from his messy, just-washed hair. His beard, which I loved, needed a trim, but as far as I was concerned, it was still hot as hell.

I nodded and patted the couch next to me. "Yeah. Come, sit."

When he sat next to me, he ran his finger down my face and said, "You seem off, Vegas. What's happening in this pretty mind?"

Before I could answer, something behind me caught his attention. And then he noticed everything I'd done to the house. "Fuck," he murmured. "Did a rainbow explode in here?"

I wiggled so I could move closer to him. Crawling into his lap, I said, "Do you like it? Or do we need to get rid of some of it?"

His hands gripped my waist as he continued to look around the room. When he'd finished, he said, "I like it."

I'd spent the day decorating the house. Nitro had added some furniture when I'd been in hospital, but we still needed more. And we needed some colour in the place. I'd brought rugs, candles, pillows, artwork and a few other decorations. I'd also printed some photos of our families and us and hung them on the walls.

I smiled and the tension that had worked its way into my shoulders eased. Reaching up, I detangled his hair with my fingers. "I worked something out about us today."

His arms moved around my body and he hugged me. "Yeah? What's that?"

After I'd finished combing his hair, I threaded my fingers into the back of it and left them there. "Well, I got to thinking about the fact that neither of us has had a home for a long time. We've had houses, but a house isn't a home. I mean, you didn't even have much furniture, let alone anything else. And when I asked you once about it, you told me you gave all your furniture to Marilyn when she moved out."

He smiled and it reached his eyes. I loved that I made him feel that. "You've got a good memory."

"I do. I'm a lawyer. Remember? You can't get anything by me, champ."

His chuckle rippled through my soul and it felt so damn good. "Duly noted."

"A home is love, Nitro, and I think you must have felt alone after Marilyn and Renee left. Is that why you didn't replace your furniture? Were you waiting for them to come back?" I held my breath a little while I waited for his answer. I wondered if he'd dig deep for me or brush it off.

"No," he said, and I thought that might be all I'd get out of him, but he surprised me when he kept going. "I wasn't waiting for them to come back. I didn't want that for them. I wanted Marilyn to stand on her own two feet. But I had no reason to fill my place with shit once they left."

My heart broke for him and what he'd been through in his life. I could only hope that my love would help bandage his soul back together and bring him the happiness he deserved.

"You have a reason now."

"Yeah, I do."

I traced patterns on the skin at the nape of his neck. "Everyone needs a home, and you're mine. It's not this house. It's not a building. It's wherever you are. That's my home."

His arms tightened around me and our bodies pressed together. "I fucking love you, woman. Especially when you get all deep on me. I'm so damn hard for you right now. And for the record, my home is wherever you are. With or without furniture. I don't give a shit if we sleep on the dirt, so long as I've got you with me."

"For the record, there will be no sleeping on dirt. Well, *you* could sleep on the dirt and I will just lie on top of you, but this body ain't touching dirt."

He pushed up off the couch, taking me with him, and walked me into the bedroom. It seemed to be one of his favourite things to do—always carrying me to the bedroom. Not that I complained. Depositing me on the floor, he reached for my T-shirt. "Now that we've got that sorted, can I please fuck my woman?"

I let him remove my shirt and then I placed my hand on his arm to stop him. Stepping close, I said, "So long as you use your knife on me."

His breathing slowed, right along with his movements. His eyes met mine, searching. "You sure about that, Vegas? I didn't think you were into the knife."

My heart beat faster in my chest and I took a breath. "I realised something else about you today." At his questioning look, I continued. "The knife is all about trust, right?"

He nodded slowly. "Yeah."

"And you're not going to cut me, are you?"

"Not unless you want me to."

I bit my lip. "Well, I think it could be hot for you to cut my clothes off."

A growl came from deep in his chest. "Fuck," he swore, his face a mask of desire.

"I trust you, Nitro."

He moved to his bedside table and removed his knife. A moment later, he stood in front of me. "Don't move. I need you to not make any sudden movements. If you need to, let me know first."

I nodded, more turned on than I'd been, maybe ever.

He placed the tip of the knife against the skin between my breasts. The cold metal and the fear I felt sent a shiver through me. I wasn't scared of Nitro. I trusted him completely. But there was still an erotic element of fear to all of this.

I wore skimpy denim shorts, and he flicked the button open and pulled the zip down. While he held the knife to my chest, he slid his other hand into my panties. He ran the blade down my body at the same time that he ran his fingers through my pussy.

I was so damn wet for him that he easily pushed two fingers inside me. He fingered me for a few moments, his eyes never leaving mine. "You want me to keep this up or do you want my tongue now?"

"I want all of the above."

He kissed me while his fingers reached deeper inside. Ending the kiss, he dragged my bottom lip between his teeth before saying, "So fucking greedy."

A second later, my shorts were thrown across the room. He traced over my panties with his knife, transfixed by what he was doing. Every single nerve ending of mine blazed with lust. I was way past ready for him to slice them off.

Turning me so my back faced him, he then ran the knife over my ass. When he was done, he pulled the knife away and hooked an arm around me across my chest, holding me against him. His erection ground into me and his teeth sunk into my neck. He bit me and I moaned.

"I want you to lie on the bed," he said against my ear.

I crawled onto the bed, making sure to treat him to an eyeful of my ass along the way. I'd barely positioned myself on my back when he straddled me. The knife drew my attention as he glided the tip of it over my stomach. I couldn't help it, I sucked my tummy in. It was a combination of nerves and excitement. I wanted him to use the knife on me, but it scared me all at the same time.

His eyes met mine. "I can put the knife away, Tatum." The care I heard caused my heart to flutter. How Nitro had changed from when I met him. But even back then, if I'd known him better I would have realised that, in his own way, he'd been caring for me from that very first moment.

"No, I want this. I want *us* to have this."

He took his time thinking about that and then he brought the knife to my bra. Taking hold of the fabric with his left hand, he sliced through the centre. "We'll start slow. I'll work you up to more as we go."

My core clenched at what *more* might be. As I watched him cut the straps of my bra, I suddenly had visions of rough, angry sex with that knife. Oh God, Nitro's fury combined with his knife would be hot. I needed that in my life.

His mouth dropped to my breasts and after spending some time with each one, he kissed his way slowly down to my pussy. I loved it when he did that because I was blessed with the vision of his strong shoulders, his muscular arms and his powerful back. *Him concentrating on giving me pleasure.* There would never be a better sight in the world than my man focused completely on me.

He slowly sliced my panties into pieces, his attention dividing between watching what he was doing and watching my face. It was as if in between each cut he checked to make sure I was still okay. But that was Nitro all over—always making sure I was good.

When he had me completely naked, he ran his blade over me one last time, starting at my throat and going down to my thighs. He then placed the knife on the bedside table and moved over me, caging me in with his arms either side of my body on the mattress.

I smiled up at him as I placed my hands against his chest. "Thank you," I whispered.

A frown flickered across his face. "What for?"

"For going so slow. I know it takes a lot for you to slow this down. I promise I'll be up for fast and rough soon."

"Fuck, Vegas, I'll take sex with you any way I can get it. You don't understand, do you?"

"Understand what?"

His eyes searched my face. "That as much as I can't get enough of your pussy, that's not the reason I'm here in this bed with you." He kissed me then. His tongue demanded I open up to him and kiss him with everything I had. It was the longest kiss we'd ever shared, and I was breathless by the time he ended it. "I'm here with you now, and every other time, because of what's in here," he said, placing his hand over my heart. "And if what's in here needs me to be slow or rough or whatever, that's what I'll be. Because *you* give *me* everything I need, and I'll always give that back to you."

I hadn't thought I could love him more. Turned out I was wrong. I loved Nitro in ways I'd never imagined. My soul breathed when I was with him and I smiled like I hadn't before. He was my love. He was my home.

Acknowledgements

This book was a labour of absolute love. When I first plotted it out, I assumed it would be a certain length, however it went way over that length and became a longer story that took me months longer to write than I thought it would. In between all that, I had family things going on that honestly almost made me put this book on hold until I could get my mind back on task. And throw a three week overseas signing trip into the mix, and I am fairly sure I almost lost the plot over the last month.

I've shared all of that because it leads me in to thank two very special people in my life who this book would not have made it to publication without.

Jodie O'Brien - Seriously, I know each book is a mad rush of stress for me (and for you just by being associated with me lol) in the last few weeks before release, but this one takes the cake, dude. There were moments there this time where I didn't know if it would all come together. I'm fairly sure that the only reason it did was due to you and Becky. I can't thank you enough for all the support and encouragement you give me on a daily basis. And for the amazing friendship you've blessed me with. We need a #FatTuesdays very soon!!

Becky Johnson - My beautiful editor. I love working with you. End of. No, wait, I have more. Thank you, thank you, thank you for working with me on this book in the way that you did. I always get super stressed about letting you down by missing deadlines and you just magically took that stress away. I don't think you'll ever know how much that helped me this time. I'm sorry I made you cry. No, not really ;) But let's see if I can do it again in Devil's book.

Letitia Hasser - my amazing cover designer. I don't know how you put up with me, Letitia! Seriously, you must dread seeing my name pop up in your emails. Thank you so much for all your time spent getting this cover exactly how I wanted it. It is absolutely perfect for Nitro! xx

My readers - Thank you so much for being so patient for this book. I'm excited now to be writing the rest of the series back-to-back and getting them out to you soon. Eeeekkk, I hope you loved Nitro & Tatum. And their people (man I adore Monroe and Dustin!!). If you're on Facebook, you should join my reader group and chat with me about books and shit :) I LOVE chatting books! I'm on a rockstar roll at the moment (have you read Stoned by Mandi Beck yet?? You should check that book out!!).

My Stormchasers - I love you girls!! Thank you for hanging out with me and for loving my characters and stories like I do .

My bloggers - Yes, I'm claiming you as mine!! Thank you so much for sharing my books, reading them and reviewing them. And for all the long hours you do blogging. I am so very thankful for your support.

My author friends - Thank you to these amazing friends for checking in on me while I was writing this book and dealing with family stuff. Your words of support mean the world to me - Chelle Bliss, Natalie Gayle, Jani Kay, Amo Jones, Fiona Archer,

Rachel Brookes, Margaret McHeyzer, DM Earl. Thank you to all my other author friends also. I'd be here all day if I listed everyone, but if we chat online, you know who you are. Love you all xx

About The Author

Dreamer.
Coffee Lover.
Gypsy at heart.
Bad boy addict.

USA Today Bestselling Aussie author who writes about alpha men & the women they love.

When I'm not creating with words you will find me either creating with paper, paint & ink, exploring the world or curled up with a good book and chocolate.

I love Keith Urban, Maroon 5, Pink, Florida Georgia Line, Bon Jovi, Matchbox 20, Lady Antebellum and pretty much any singer/band that is country or rock.

I'm addicted to Scandal, Suits, Nashville, The Good Wife & wish that they would create a never-ending season of Sons of Anarchy.

I'm thankful to have found amazing readers who share my alpha addiction and love my story writing style. I'm also thankful that many of these readers have become friends. The best thing in the world is finding your tribe.

www.ninalevinebooks.com